THE
CITY
BEAUTIFUL

ADEN POLYDOROS

PRESS

Recycling programs for this product may not exist in your area.

ISBN-13: 978-1-335-45274-0

The City Beautiful

First published in 2021. This edition published in 2022.

For questions and comments about the quality of this book, please contact us at CustomerService@Harlequin.com.

Inkyard Press
22 Adelaide St. West, 41st Floor
Toronto, Ontario M5H 4E3, Canada
www.InkyardPress.com

Printed in U.S.A.

Praise for *The City Beautiful*

"Like a darkly compelling dream; I dare readers to try to put down this queer triumph of a book where myth, mystery, and death lurk around every corner of the Windy City."
—Sarah Glenn Marsh, author of the Reign of the Fallen series

"One-part historical fantasy, one-part gothic thriller, this genre-blending story has something for everyone."
—Kalyn Josephson, author of the Storm Crow duology

"With a keen eye for historical details, Polydoros deftly weaves together a gruesome murder mystery, a beautiful romance, and a rich depiction of Jewish life in the 19th century."
—Allison Saft, author of *Down Comes the Night*

"Polydoros is not afraid to tear aside the façade of beauty and civility to confront the darkest aspects of human nature, no holds barred."
—Sophie Gonzales, author of *Only Mostly Devastated*

"Details rich with specificity and research, and its joys tinged with sorrow...make it all the more moving."
—NPR

★ "Polydoros seamlessly blends a murder mystery with Jewish folklore in this haunting historical fantasy."   —*Publishers Weekly*, starred review

★ "A gorgeous, disturbing, visceral, and mystical experience."
—*BookPage*, starred review

★ "A wild ride of a queer gothic fantasy that's a must-have for YA fantasy collections."   —*School Library Journal*, starred review

★ "A triumph, showcasing queer love, illuminating historical events, and guiding readers to an enthralling ending."   —*Booklist*, starred review

CONTENTS

**This book contains content and themes
that may be difficult for some readers.
For a list of content warnings, please visit adenpolydoros.com.**

To the readers who will see themselves in these pages.

1

ANGUISHED SOBS ECHOED down the winding stairwell, bouncing off the walls like the cries of strange birds. Here on Maxwell Street, weeping was as common as bawling babies, quarreling, and laughter. Along with housing a kingdom of rats and roaches, the walls between tenements were paper-thin, so I was constantly involved in the personal lives of my neighbors, whether I wanted to be or not.

As the sobbing continued unabated, I wheeled my bicycle into the third-floor corridor. My next-door neighbor Mrs. Brenner stood in the hall with a red-haired woman I didn't recognize. Mrs. Brenner was a shadchante, a professional marriage broker. She took her job so seriously, she would try to wed off anything with a pulse. Apparently, this time it hadn't gone over very well.

"Moishe's a good boy," the stranger said in a quaking voice. Tears streaked her cheeks, her face red and blotchy. "He minds his own business. He goes to night school. He isn't a trouble-maker like that Aaron Holtz; he wouldn't just run off without saying anything."

The woman wiped her eyes and looked at me.

"Oy, he looks like Moishe!" she exclaimed, pressing her palms to her face. "For a moment, I thought—"

A sob tore through her body. I reached for my handkerchief, but by the time I pulled it from my pocket, she was already hurrying down the hall.

"I'm sorry," I told Mrs. Brenner as the woman disappeared into the stairwell. "I hope I didn't intrude."

She blotted her forehead with a lace-fringed hanky. "It's fine, Alter. She was just leaving."

Even with the gaslights dimmed and the hallway windows cranked open, a swampish heat encased us like mud. I couldn't wait to get out on the fire escape and enjoy the sliced melon left in the icebox.

"That was Mrs. Walden," Mrs. Brenner said as I stuffed my handkerchief back into my pocket. "It seems her son never came home from work three days ago."

I tried envisioning Moishe Walden. I thought he might be the slender ginger-haired boy who always had a bisl of mandelbrot or rugelach to share during learning. Shy and soft-spoken, he had never struck me as the kind of person to run off. He was a year or two younger than me and at least four centimeters shorter. Although I had green eyes instead of hazel ones, and my hair was chestnut brown and wavy, I supposed to his mother there must've been some resemblance.

"Did she go to the police?" I asked, resting my bicycle against the wall. I didn't have much confidence in law and order, but it seemed like something a mother might do.

"You know how it is." Sighing, Mrs. Brenner tucked back a curl that had escaped from her tichel. With her yellow dress and dark silk headscarf, she matched the black-eyed Susans sprouting in her apartment's window box. "Just another immigrant boy wowed by the big city. The third one these last two months apparently." Her voice dripped with sarcasm. "They told her that if he doesn't turn up in a few weeks, they'll look into it. Feh! You wonder what they're paid for."

"The third one?" I frowned. "I heard about Aaron Holtz, but who was the other?"

"Another of my clients. Josef Loew."

I sensed a pattern here. "Was Moishe also your client?"

"Yes, and we even had a date picked out. Tonight, Fourth of July. His mother's been looking everywhere for him, the poor dear. She was hoping he might show up, but as you can see..." With another laborious sigh, she gestured around her. "He's nowhere to be found."

I wasn't too worried. Boys ran away all the time, and even fathers left without a word to escape having to care for their families back in the old country. Besides, as far as I was concerned, being one of Mrs. Brenner's clients was more than enough to make a person skip town.

Ever since I had turned seventeen, she had brought it upon herself to take my case free of charge. With my mother and little sisters across the Atlantic and my father somewhere beneath it, Mrs. Brenner had declared her intervention a mitzvah, a commandment of God. More like a conspiracy of the Evil One.

The results had so far been disastrous. Just last week, she had tried setting me up with Raizel Ackermann on the first floor, in a dinner that had exploded into a heated argument over anarchism. Raizel believed that society as a whole was corrupt, and that true freedom and liberty would only be achieved once the power structure was dismantled completely and capitalism abolished. I thought it was a pipe dream, and told her as much. The debate had ended with me getting a cup of lukewarm tea dumped in my lap while Raizel's parents watched on in utter horror.

Mrs. Brenner gave me a keen look. "You know, she's still in there."

"Who?" Hopefully not Raizel, otherwise Mrs. Brenner might end up with another of her eligible bachelors vanishing into the night.

"Elkie Strauss. She's from a good family, not like that Ackermann girl downstairs. Elkie is as peaceful as a dove and as lovely as a lily of the valley." Mrs. Brenner leaned forward, her eyes gleaming in determination. "You won't find another like her in all of Chicago, my dear."

Right, a dove and a lily of the valley. If Mrs. Brenner thought plagiarizing the Song of Songs would convince me to ruin my Fourth of July, she was sadly mistaken. I volunteered at our shul's burial society, and every month, I found myself reciting the Song of Songs over a fresh corpse. Not exactly what I'd call romantic.

"It's really not a good time," I said, backing away before she could drag me into her apartment by force.

"Oh, *Alter*," Mrs. Brenner cried, aghast. "I thought you were a *kind* boy. You wouldn't be so *cruel* as to leave a girl and her parents waiting *alone*, would you? You'll break her mother's heart!"

I hesitated. Well, when she worded it like that...

"Besides, I made my special kishka. I know how much you love it."

Her special—oh God. I cringed at the thought. Her beef-liver kishka was as heavy as cement and came out looking the same way it went in, which was never a good sign. No wonder Moishe hadn't shown up. Before I could come up with a convincing excuse to avoid death by indigestion, a hand fell on my lower back.

"I'm afraid Alter already has a commitment tonight," a teasing voice said from behind us.

The hand slipped away, and my roommate Yakov stepped around me to face Mrs. Brenner head-on. He was eight centimeters taller than me, but he could move so silently sometimes, like he wasn't walking on the same cheap, groaning floorboards as the rest of us.

At the sight of him, Mrs. Brenner's eyes narrowed, and her mouth pursed tightly. She had been cold to him since the day he arrived. She would ignore him outright when they passed in the halls, and kept a wide berth, as though if she strayed into his path, their proximity alone might scald her. I wondered, what had he said to make her so curt? What had he done?

"Ah. I see." Mrs. Brenner wrinkled her nose, probably offended by the scent of coal smoke Yakov had carried with him from the trainyard. She looked like she wanted to argue, decided against it, and stepped inside her apartment.

"A commitment, eh?" I said, once the door had shut behind her. I couldn't stop thinking about the patch of warmth Yakov's hand had left on my back, the heat and weight of his touch.

"Something a bit more enjoyable than a matchmaking meeting." He turned, favoring me with a smile that made me weak in the knees. "We can't have her marry you off too soon. She thinks you're a real catch, you know that?"

"More like a real paycheck, and she isn't even right about that. No money, dead father. Nobody's going to want to marry a charity case."

He cocked his head. "You don't sound too disappointed."

The way he said it made my face itch. Every so often, Yakov would look at me or say something in a certain way, and I'd have the suspicion that he could see my desire. I wished I could tell him the truth. Instead I forced a smile. "One family's more than enough to worry about."

Every extra penny from my job at the newspaper went

to my mother and sisters back in Romania. We had over a hundred dollars saved away. Enough to pay for ship tickets, a wagon to Iași, and the train ride from there to Bucharest and the port city of Constanța. They wouldn't have to walk to the sea like my father and I had done. I had made sure of that. All I needed to do was raise another forty dollars and I'd be able to get them here.

"Did you see the woman sitting on the stairs?" Yakov asked as he unlocked our garret room door. The key was stubborn, and he wiggled it back and forth. "The one who was crying?"

"Did she have red hair?"

"Like a carrot."

"That's Mrs. Walden from shul. Her son, Moishe, went missing."

He stopped turning the key. "What?"

"He probably just ran away to keep Mrs. Brenner from wedding him off." I waited for Yakov to laugh, but he never did.

His gas-flame-blue eyes chilled over, and his jawline firmed. "I see."

"Don't look so worried," I said. "Boys run away."

I would know. The boy who I once considered to be my closest friend had only ended up in Chicago because he'd stowed away on a train from Grand Central Depot. He hadn't even bothered checking the destination.

"Then again, Moishe's not the only one who's disappeared lately," I added, when Yakov didn't answer. "Aaron Holtz went missing, too, and so did Josef Loew."

"Right. I'm sure it's nothing to worry about." Yakov said the words slowly, carefully, like handling shattered glass. "People leave here all the time."

The inside of our apartment was a riot of voices and bumped elbows. There was barely enough space for four people, much less the jumble of mattresses, boxes, and clothing filling the cramped room.

A night on the town meant a nice waistcoat and jacket, polished shoes, and bowler hats. When Yakov and I entered, our two other roommates, Dovid and Haskel, were already dressed and on their way out.

"Good thing we caught you two in time," Haskel said, his brown eyes bright and cheerful beneath a thatch of curls. "We're going to a dance hall down in the Levee. You should come, too."

As I got a good look at him, I tried not to laugh. He was trying desperately to cultivate a mustache on his upper lip and had filled in the empty areas with what looked like brown shoe polish.

Yakov was a bit more unforgiving: "Haskel, I think you have a bit of shmutz on your face. Right here."

A burning flush crept all the way to Haskel's collar. He took out his handkerchief and blotted furiously at his upper lip, his freckles standing out like specks of dirt against his reddening complexion.

Beside him, Dovid snickered. "I told you it wasn't convincing."

Haskel glowered at him. "Not everyone is as hairy as an ape."

"You sound jealous," Dovid said, tweaking his own mustache. Not only did he seem to be able to grow facial hair overnight, but a generous layer of black hair covered his arms and legs. "You should be. I had a better mustache when I was thirteen."

"So then, it's true that when you were born, your mother took one look at you and said, 'vey iz mir, it's a dog?'" Haskel shot back, before turning to us. "Really, you two should come.

Please. Don't leave me alone with him, Yasha. He'll scare away all the girls. They'll think he's a bear."

"I'm afraid we already have plans," Yakov said, then looked at me. "Alter and I are going to the street fair down by the market. Unless he prefers to go dancing."

"I'd rather not break a leg," I said. Besides, I knew how a visit to the dance hall would end—standing alone in the corner, wishing I had stayed home. Maybe a girl would approach, and I'd have to mutter an excuse, drift away, and wait in dread for the long walk back, when Haskel and Dovid would tease me mercilessly.

"So frum." Dovid rolled his eyes, heading for the door. "So pious, he can't even look at a woman. A true tzaddik, that Alter Rosen."

"You're one to talk, Dovid," Yakov said. "When was the last time you danced with a girl?"

"Just the other night."

"Nu? Who was she—your left hand or your right?"

Haskel laughed as Dovid's cheeks reddened. I began to chuckle, then caught myself as Dovid shot me a sour look.

As the door banged shut behind the two of them, Yakov turned to me. "Dovid has drek for brains. Don't let him drag you down."

"He doesn't."

Yakov didn't look convinced.

"You don't have to defend me, you know," I added.

"But I like to."

Yakov had always been this way, ever since he had arrived on Maxwell Street back in April. Collected and steadfast, always sure what to say in the moment. He was predictable when it came to his gestures of kindness, putting down Dovid's bullying in an instant or bringing home extra meals if he knew

I hadn't eaten. If he saw me standing alone at the dance hall, he would come join me.

I enjoyed that about him. I had known boys who were unpredictable and short-tempered, who roared through life like a whirlwind and never once looked back. Yakov was different. He lived his life quietly, calmly, and that made me feel safe and secure, as though he were the breakwall that held back Maxwell Street's noise and chaos. He made this place truly feel like home.

Yakov exchanged his broadcloth jacket for a pin-striped waistcoat and tied his cravat with deft hands. A trained elegance shone through even his briefest gestures and steady posture.

Like everyone on Maxwell Street, Yakov had a story to tell, a place he left behind. He had grown up in a small town near Kiev in the Russian Empire. But when he told me of his past, he made it sound as though he had been born in his thirteenth year—vivid narrations of years spent in the cities of Varshe and Lemberg, along with lengthy visits to Italy, France, and Germany in the company of his uncle, some scholar of European history at the Imperial University.

In his low smoky baritone, Yakov would regale me with descriptions of the River Spree at sunset, spangled with purple and gold; or overgrown ruins along the Mediterranean, fragrant with the scent of honeysuckle and dappled in indigo shadows; Paris in midwinter, a white city spired with icicles and sparkling hoarfrost.

He did not speak of his childhood. He did not speak of his mother or father, except to tell me once how they had been taken from this world.

I wanted so badly to reciprocate, but what could I tell him that would ever compare to such adventures? My childhood was an endless blur of narrow streets of dirt and cobblestone, my squabbling baby sisters, and the rural silence. After two years in Chicago, it all felt terribly boring and rustic.

"I'm ready to go if you are," Yakov said, once he secured his watch chain in place.

"I'm ready," I said, and he took me by the shoulder and drew me from the room.

Chicago was just beginning to settle in for the night. Horse-drawn carts and carriages lumbered past us. The creak of their wheels joined the calls of the pushcart vendors clustered along the curb. Each breath I took was soured by the scorched, sickly sweet odor of the glue processing plants, while the canal, polluted with animal carcasses from the slaughterhouses, reeked of ghastly carnage.

The city was constantly changing—day by day, old buildings were being knocked down to make room for newer ones and a labyrinth of streetcar rails was being laid. With the city ever-expanding, it would only be a matter of time before the marshland at its outskirts was filled in and built upon.

As we walked, Yakov fished his cigarette case from his pocket. He was left-handed, and it always fascinated me to see the way he handled things, like a street magician's parlor tricks. He offered me a cigarette, but I shook my head. In the corner of my eye, I watched him draw a match from his brass vesta case and light it with an unassuming flick of his fingers.

Another bouquet of flames bloomed across the night sky. In the fireworks' diminishing glow, the tenement houses across the street seemed precarious, as though they would collapse into ruin and rubble at any moment.

Back in Romania, there was no celebration like this, not even on the day commemorating when Wallachia and Moldavia had united to form the kingdom. If there had been one, my family would have stayed inside anyway. Celebrating meant drinking, which meant that once it got dark, some men might decide to take a little tour through the Jewish quarter.

It was different here. We didn't have to hide behind bolted shutters and locked doors. We were a part of the community, not severed from it.

"I've been waiting for this night for a long time," Yakov said, taking a drag of his cigarette.

"Oh, right, this is your first Fourth of July here. It's really something, isn't it?"

"It is."

"Aren't the fireworks amazing?"

"Beautiful." He looked at me as he said it. Smoke curled from his proud lips, as though the same crackling sparks that lent his blue eyes their intensity now stoked a blaze beneath his skin. "I'm glad we could do this. I want to savor it."

"As do I," I said softly, and we continued on our way.

As we neared the market, the warm glow of firelight beckoned us closer. The ground was littered with rotten fruit and corn silk, their fermented scent lacing the more pleasant aromas of sizzling sausages and beer. Music wafted through the dusk—the trill and wail of a klezmer's violin rivaled by a woman fiddling a lively Irish jig.

In front of the dusty storefronts where the peddlers would spread their secondhand wares on Sunday mornings, the threadbare awnings had been unrolled to shade carts and tables overladen with food and drinks. For a penny apiece, an elderly Italian man scraped up careful balls of lemon ice into miniature glasses.

Yakov stopped me when I held out a coin, closing my fingers around the copper. "Allow me. You have your family."

"It's only a penny."

"I received a raise at work, so let me treat you tonight."

"Thank you," I said as he handed me one of the glasses.

There was only enough for a couple mouthfuls, but I savored each lick.

Yakov's lips quirked in a smile. "Alter, you missed a drop."

Oh no. Before I could swipe it away, he brushed his finger across my cheek, close enough to my mouth that I felt a shiver of longing pass through me. "Right here."

As we continued down the street, I wiped my face with the back of my hand. I prayed the darkness would hide the blush burning my cheeks.

"Food next," Yakov declared, his gaze roving up and down the rows. "Ah, over here."

We ate hot beef sausages served on split buns and slathered with whole-grain mustard, followed by deep-fried knishes stuffed with mashed potatoes and caramelized onions. We washed it all down with root beer and pithy lemonade.

Then it was the shell game, and craps, and three-card monte. Yakov won the first two games, but when it came time to find the Lady at three-card monte, he uncovered a worthless heart. He squatted in front of the apple crate the dealer had set up as a makeshift table and flipped down another nickel. "Again."

The dealer laid out another three cards, each one heavily creased. Yakov considered the arrangement, his gaze flicking back and forth, before pointing toward the middlemost card.

The dealer flipped it over with an alligator's smile. Nine of spades.

The man pocketed the coin. "Better luck next time, kid."

Yakov bit his lower lip, staring down at the spread of cards.

"It's a trick," I whispered, resting on my haunches beside him. "No one wins this game, Yakov."

"I know, but..." His gaze returned to the cards. "I wanted to win all three games."

"You won the other two. That's an accomplishment enough. It's better to stop while you're ahead."

He said nothing. Down the street, a firecracker sprayed crimson sparks across the sky. Even after the flames died down, I thought I could still see their glow reflected in his blue eyes, the memory of fire.

A commotion drew my attention across the lot. At the other end of the street, a small crowd had gathered.

"Let's take a look." Cramming the last bit of knish in my mouth, I took Yakov by the wrist and pulled him closer.

It was a monkey and an organ grinder. The monkey scampered up to the people who had gathered to listen, cupping its hands for coins. When it came to us, Yakov gave it the dime left over from his winnings, as though he could only leave here with less than what he had brought.

I chuckled, a bit taken aback. "That monkey's going to eat well tonight. I think it gets paid better than I do."

He glanced over. "Speaking of which, have you shown your boss that article yet? The one about growing up in Romania?"

"I need to work on it some more," I said.

"Alter, you've been working on it for weeks now. Have some confidence or you'll end up running the printing presses forever."

"It's just...it's not ready." I looked down at the monkey. "Mr. Stieglitz has said before, he isn't interested in stories about the old country. And it isn't an article, not really. It's just memories."

"Sometimes those are the most important thing."

As the organ grinder reached the end of his song, the crowd applauded, and the monkey danced. Their clapping was joined by the sudden rustling of wings overhead. I searched the indigo sky for the noise's source. Night jays, no doubt.

When I looked back down, Yakov's smile had faded. He

had his pocket watch in one hand, held to the glow of a lantern. He snapped its case shut and slipped it into his pocket.

He averted his gaze. "I'm sorry. I need to go."

"It's not even eight yet."

"I'm going to a show at the Fair, and if I wait any longer, I'll be late." He hesitated. "I'd invite you to come along, but I'm meeting someone from back home. Besides, I suspect it's not your kind of show."

My face felt paralyzed. I understood it now. This had only been an appetizer for him, an interlude before the main event. He hadn't gotten dressed up so nicely to attend a street fair with me, it had been to go to the real fair, the World's Fair, with someone more special to him. Of course. It shouldn't have upset me. It shouldn't have felt like a punch to the gut.

"I—I see." Taking a deep breath, I forced a smile. "It's all right. I'm actually rather tired. I think I'll just head home."

He placed his hand on my arm. "Let me walk with you."

I brushed his hand away and took a step back, hating the sting of his words, hating my own pettiness even more. Why was I so upset? He had always been kind to me. It wasn't as though he would change his plans just to suit me.

"No, it's all right," I repeated. "You go to your show."

Not your kind of show. Long after I had returned to our room and retreated to the fire escape, Yakov's words echoed in my head. *Not your kind of show.*

Sighing, I stretched out on the mattress I had left to air out on the platform and stared at the night sky, exposed in bits and pieces through the fluttering clotheslines. All the fireworks had died down, and there was only darkness now.

Not your kind of show.

The statement was harmless, but the memory of it made my cheeks burn. It felt like an insult. How did he see me? Did he think that I was too cold? Too prudish?

I cringed. Too frum?

I liked to think we were close. We had shared in our griefs. I had told him about my father's sickness, and he had told me about the accident. Yet there was still so much I didn't know, so many things I wanted to ask him. Such as: *Why do you cry out at night, Yakov? Were you having a nightmare? It's okay, you can tell me. I won't tell anyone.*

I'll never tell.

Everything about Yakov intrigued me. I yearned to uncover all his history, like parting the petals of a closed bud. But there was danger in getting close to a person, any person. The only way to ensure that nobody found out how rotten I was inside, was if I kept my distance. Over and over, I reminded myself: be careful and give him nothing he could use against you. Don't trust him, don't get too close to him, and don't feel. Never feel.

DOVID AND HASKEL returned when it was still dark, reeking of booze and sweat, and passed out the moment they crashed into their separate cots. When I rose at six o'clock to prepare for work, Yakov's bed was still empty, the blanket smoothed and folded. I stared at it as I went through my morning routine—washing my hands, putting on tallis and tefillin and davening.

I had said Shacharis so many times, I didn't even need to concentrate on the prayers' words. Instead, numbers raced through my head. Ninety dollars for three steerage tickets. Sixty cents per day for food. No, make that seventy just to be safe. But what if my mother or sisters needed a doctor? And once they arrived here, what about train and ferry tickets?

When I had first started raising money for my family's passage, it had felt impossible. I had been so afraid I'd never be able to save enough money to get them here. Now that I was so close, it terrified me to actually think of their arrival. I couldn't stop imagining the three of them being hustled down the gangway of Ellis Island, my mother gripping the twins' hands tightly, the Statue of Liberty turned toward the shore, as though having forsaken them. The Hebrew Immigrant Aid Society would be able to point my mother in the right direction, even help her get tickets at the train station. But there would also be a myriad of predators stalking the streets of Manhattan, waiting for new arrivals.

I couldn't stand the thought of Rivka and Gittel being carried off by America's false glitz. By the whoremongers and sweatshop bosses. By the cruelness.

After saying the Pesukei DeZimra, I asked God for protection, strength, and endurance. Nobody answered, and the silence grew heavier. The strip of leather that bound my arm became as hefty and cumbersome as a chain. Slowly, I unwrapped the tefillin from around my arm and lowered its twin from my brow. As I put them away in their velvet bag, Dovid stirred and groaned.

He cracked open one eye and regarded me blearily. "What time is it?"

I glanced at the clock. "Six twenty."

He laid his arm over his eyes. "Oh, kill me."

"Whatever you drank looks well on its way to."

He laughed, then groaned.

"Yakov isn't home yet," I said.

"Nu? He probably found a girl."

"Maybe," I agreed reluctantly, but I didn't think that was the case.

As Dovid rolled back under the covers, I poked through my grocery box's contents. Ugh. The loaf of bread was already as hard as a rock, no good for anything but boiled dumplings. As for the half bushel of potatoes, they had begun to sprout in their sack.

"Lovely." Sighing, I scrounged my finances journal out

from under my pillow and tried to figure out what I could afford at the market.

For a city whose economy was built on slaughter, kosher meat remained an unobtainable luxury. How could I spend thirty cents on a kilo of beef roast, when I could get twice as many potatoes for a fifth of that price? That extra quarter-dollar would mean two more meals for my sisters, a fraction of a train ticket, or part of a bribe to pay off corrupt officials.

"I guess it's more potatoes," I muttered, glancing at the sack. My stomach turned at the thought of boiled potatoes, or mashed potatoes, or potato latkes fried in schmaltz. No, if I had to eat another potato today, I'd turn into one. Maybe I could grab something small before work.

I was in the process of buttoning my shoes when someone knocked on the door. Three hard knocks, insistent, impatient.

Yakov.

"I'm coming, just hold on." Setting down my buttonhook, I rose to my feet. I was forced to walk lopsidedly across the room with one shoe on and one foot bare, weaving through the mess of furniture and junk.

Two more knocks, then a light rapping of the knuckles, like a message in Morse code. A cry for help.

"I said I'm coming." Annoyed, I twisted the lock and threw open the door. "Yakov, did you lose your..."

I trailed off.

A man in a dark blue uniform stood at the threshold. Underneath the leather brim of his cap, his pale eyes looked me up and down. He opened his mouth and shot out words in a fast staccato I could hardly make sense of.

"Can you repeat that?" I asked in English. "Slower, please."

"Police." He stretched out the word: *Puuh-leece*. "Is this the residence of Yakov Kogan?"

"The what?"

"The residence. The home. The abode." He sighed impatiently. "Does Yakov Kogan live here?"

"Yes." I stepped out into the hall. "Er, what's this about? What did he do?"

Out of the four of us, Yakov was the last one I expected to get arrested. Must've been some show.

"He didn't do anything." The officer looked at me with flat pity in his eyes. "He's dead."

"You can start by telling me your name," the officer said, tapping his fountain pen against the desk. He had introduced himself as Johnathon Rariden, a mouthful of syllables I struggled to wrap my tongue around.

"Alter Rosen." The precinct's Yiddish-speaking detective was absent, so I spoke in halting English, question after question flung at me like pummeling fists. My eyes ached in the harsh sunlight spearing through the office's wooden blinds.

Officer Rariden lifted his eyebrows. "Can you spell that out?"

"A-l-t-e-r R-o—"

"That will do. Alter. An unusual name, that."

I supposed that to Officer Rariden, it sounded rather silly. As a Christian, he wouldn't know that my first name was a talisman. I had spent the first week of my life at the threshold between two worlds, too sick to suckle, too weak to wail. My parents had been so afraid the Angel of Death would take me, they'd given me the name Alter to confuse him into thinking I was an old man. Undesirable.

Over the years, I had come to realize that my name was as much a mirror as a talisman—by hiding me, it diverted the Angel of Death's vulgar gaze to the people around me. Childhood friends were ravished by illness and violence. An adder bit my cousin in the forest deep, its venom rotting her from the inside out. And the infant who I should have called brother had been strangled to death with the noose of his own umbilical.

And then, of course, there was my father.

"How long have you known Yakov?" Officer Rariden asked after jotting down my name.

"A few months." I shifted in my chair, the cane seat hard and uncomfortable. "He showed up at the tenement back in early April."

"Did he have any living relatives?"

"He told me his parents died in an accident."

"An accident?"

"A cow knocked over a lantern."

"This wouldn't happen to have been in 1871, would it?" He cocked a brow. "The Great Chicago Fire?"

"Uh, no? He was born in 1874, I think."

"All right then." Officer Rariden sighed, rubbing his face. I could tell that he was annoyed, and I had a sinking feeling that my English was to blame. "What was he doing at the Columbian Exposition last night?"

"The what?"

"The White City." When I didn't answer, he groaned in exasperation. "The Fair. The World's Fair. Jesus Christ. If you're going to live here, you should at least know the names of the Fair."

I did, just not in English.

"He was with a landsman—er, friend, I think? I'm sorry. I don't know." I tapped my fingertips nervously against the cup of coffee the officer had given me. "He said something about a show."

Officer Rariden grunted and jotted something else into his book. When he shifted to dip his pen in the inkwell, the sunlight caught the gold buttons on his uniform jacket and made them glint like blades. I stared down at my coffee, afraid that if I made eye contact, he would read it as insolence.

Officer Rariden glanced up at me. "Have you visited the World's Fair before?"

I laughed. Somehow, it struck me as hilarious that this man assumed I could afford the Fair's entry fee, when I was living crammed in an apartment with three other boys and every spare penny went to my family overseas. Then I realized that now there would be only two other boys sharing the garret room, and a lump built in my throat.

"What's so funny?" Officer Rariden asked bluntly.

A shameful heat crept over my cheeks. I didn't have the words to answer, so I shrugged and took a sloppy gulp of coffee to avoid saying more.

Officer Rariden cleared his throat and continued on. My hunger had honed itself into a tight, throbbing knot, but I felt too nauseated to eat the hard mandelbrot-like cookies he offered me with my drink. I didn't think I'd be able to eat again.

I took out my father's pocket watch to check the time, running my thumb over the smooth glass window. Its familiar weight soothed me.

Sometimes, I imagined that if I wound it backward instead of forward, or perhaps just pressed it to my ear and listened for long enough, I might hear my father's voice coming from somewhere deep within the chirring cogs. Except it wouldn't be his warm laughter, but how he had sounded in his final days, after the typhus had gnawed him to the bone. His wheezing, and his indistinct whispers, and the groans of pain and misery.

Officer Rariden lifted his eyebrows as I slipped the watch back into my pocket. "Do you need to be somewhere?"

"No. I just…the time."

"There's a clock up there." He gestured to the wall.

I didn't know what to say, so I smiled in discomfort until he continued the interview.

"How did he die?" I asked, several questions later.

"Drowning."

My breath caught in my throat.

"We found him in the lagoon, caught in a gondola's mooring rope." Officer Rariden sighed, rubbing the bridge of his nose. "His wallet and house keys were in the dirt by the bank. He might have been searching for them in the dark or trying to undo his belt buckle. Then he slipped or struck his head on a low-hanging branch and fell into the water."

As Officer Rariden kept talking, my eyes burned. His words floated down to me, hollow and echoing. If what he said was true, Yakov had only been in the water a short while before a patrolman had spotted him. The wall of the lagoon formed a shallow slope, and where he'd fallen in, it had been no more than waist-deep. Shallow enough for him to be revealed in lantern light, but deep enough for him to drown.

I swallowed hard, telling myself not to cry, *don't you dare cry*. It wasn't like what happened to my father.

"I imagine he was drunk like most of Chicago," Officer Rariden continued in a low, bored drawl. "So drunk he didn't even know where he was."

"No. That wouldn't be like him."

It made no sense. How could Yakov be alive one moment, then gone the next? We were practically the same age.

"Either way, it was an accident," Officer Rariden said, picking a bit of dirt out from under his nail. "The paperwork has already been filed, and the death certificate has been signed. Since he doesn't have any living relatives, you'll have to arrange for someone to pick up the body or it will be taken to the potter's field at Dunning."

"Yakov." His name lodged in my throat like a stone. "He

must have someone stay with him until his funeral, and he needs to be buried as soon as possible."

His gaze flicked up. "Do you know of someone who can arrange that?"

"Yes." I took a deep breath. "I can."

For the last year, I had volunteered at my shul's chevra kadisha, the society responsible for preparing the dead in accordance with our laws and customs. It comforted me to give others the same burial that my father had been deprived. Until now, I had never personally known those who had passed. I wanted desperately to step back into that role, the role of a stranger. It would have made things so much easier for what I must do next.

As Officer Rariden led me from his office, a sudden commotion drew my attention to the ground floor. I stopped at the balcony to get a better look.

"Two months!" a voice exclaimed from below. "Two months, Aaron's been gone. No telegrams, no postcards. Now another boy is, too, and all you can tell me is, 'boys, they run off'?"

The voice was familiar, but it took me a moment to pair it to a name, because the only time I had heard Raizel speak was in Yiddish or German. In comparison, her English was as sharp as a blade, each syllable honed into a serrated edge.

She leaned over the counter, palms flat against the wood, glowering at the young deputy who had allowed me to use the station's phone to call work. With his shiny pink cheeks and rail-thin figure, the man didn't look much older than me or Raizel. He took in her words with a befuddled expression, his cup of coffee forgotten in his hand.

"Miss," he began, "you're going to have to—"

"So, Moishe Walden then. Did he just run off, too? Nu?" Transitioning seamlessly into Yiddish, she added savagely, "Do you have gefilte fish for brains?"

The deputy gaped at her as though she'd slapped him across the face. His cheeks reddened. Whether he knew the language or not, the insult was clear in her voice. He cleared his throat and began again, more firmly this time, "Please, miss, uh—"

"Ackermann, as I told you this Monday and the week before. How many times do I have to come here before you start—"

He lifted his hand to placate her. "Please calm yourself."

"Calm? I'll show you…" Raizel trailed off when I came down the stairs. As soon as our gazes met, her mouth puckered as if she had swallowed a spoonful of horseradish. Likely, she was remembering the tea incident last week at Mrs. Brenner's place.

From the way Raizel looked at me, one never would've guessed that we both worked at newspapers. She had devoted herself to the *Arbeiter-Zeitung*, a German-language worker's paper infamous for its role in the Haymarket Bombing. I worked the printing presses at the *Idisher Kuryer*, which rarely delved into politics and spent its page space kvetching about community controversies.

"Is this a police station or a circus?" Officer Rariden snapped, leaning over the second-floor balcony. "If you cannot control yourself, leave. As you well know, we don't have the resources to hunt down runaway teens. Perhaps your people ought to get in the habit of looking over their own."

"Feh!" She shook her head in disgust. "You just don't care. None of you."

I passed her, but she caught up to me at the door and blew upward to stir an errant strand of hair out of her sepia-brown eyes. A union button was pinned to the collar of her simple green dress.

"Can you believe that schmo? He says that Aaron ran off, maybe freight-hopped to St. Louis or Cincinnati." Raizel raked a hand through her hair. "As far as they're concerned, good riddance, one less disobedient worker to worry about. Must be something in the water here, because news on Maxwell Street is that Mrs. Walden's son is gone, too."

"I know." I exhaled slowly. "Listen, I can't talk now, Raizel."

She narrowed her eyes. "Wait a minute, what are you doing here, Alter? Don't tell me you were arrested?" She chuckled in disbelief. "You? What did you do?"

"No. There's…" My voice broke abruptly, as though I was thirteen again. I tried a second time. "There's been an accident. Yakov is dead."

Her eyes widened. "What did you say?"

"They found him at the fairgrounds. He fell into one of the lagoons and drowned."

"Oh, I—" It took Raizel a moment to find her voice again. "I'm so sorry. I know you two were close."

"He was my closest friend here. One of my only ones." Just saying those words was like clawing open a wound. I curled my fingers into a fist and dug my nails into my palm. Somehow, pain felt proper; it steadied my voice and soothed my shaky breath. "I need to go. They'll be taking Yakov to the tahara house, and I want to wait with him."

I didn't know how long Yakov had been lying on the ground after the Columbian Guards had dragged him from the water. But I knew they wouldn't have recited psalms. They might have smoked in front of him, or sipped from their canteens, or eaten bread and let the crumbs drop carelessly on his body. Even talking about the dead in front of the dead was a violation.

I didn't want Yakov to be alone again in the police wagon. He had been left alone long enough.

3

AS THE SUN climbed the eastern sky, I gathered with the others in the tahara house's washing room. There were four of us—Lev, Gavril, Sender, and me. Five if you counted Yakov, who waited for us on a table, under a sheet.

"Are you sure that you want to do this, Alter?" Lev asked quietly from his place at right of the table. He was the Rosh, the leader and guide. With his neatly groomed white beard and distinguished features, he had the bearing of a holy tzaddik.

"I need to." I forced myself to look at the table. "It's the last thing I can do for him."

I couldn't make out Yakov's features through the white linen, only the shape of his form. The gaslights cast flickering shadows over the shroud, as though something was moving under there.

Steeling my nerves, I retrieved the sponge from the porcelain basin at my side. "I'm staying."

Lev nodded toward Gavril, who stood at the head of the table. Grizzled and stoic, Gavril drew the shroud from over Yakov's head.

Tears prickled my eyes at the sight of Yakov's familiar features, and my knees weakened beneath me. Just twelve hours ago, he had still been alive. His hand had been warm when he touched me. I bit my inner cheek until I tasted my own blood, knowing that any show of grief would exile me.

In the last eleven months of volunteering at the chevra kadisha, I had washed old men who perished on the streets, workers killed in factory accidents, and children taken by illness. Yet even the grievous injuries of a man gored by a steer at the Yards hadn't shaken me like this. They had been a way for me to heal from my father's untimely death, while this simply ripped apart the scar tissue.

Taking a deep breath, I dipped the sponge into warm water.

As we cleaned Yakov's head, Lev recited from the Song of Songs:

"His head is as the finest gold; his locks are curled, black as a raven. His eyes are like doves beside rivulets of water, bathing in milk, fitly set."

Yakov's skin held an ashy pallor, his dark hair a stiff bramble. A cloudy film blanketed the brilliant blue of his eyes. There was dirt on his lips, dirt in his hair. A livid bruise necklaced his throat.

I washed the grime from his cheeks and under his jawline. A scatter of droplets beaded on the bruise, trickling down to gather in the hollow of his neck. The sight of it sickened me.

They'd found him caught in a mooring rope, Officer Rariden had said, but could a mooring rope really have caused something like this? He must have been heavily entangled, and maybe when the Columbian Guards had tried to tug it off him, the rope had only tightened further.

"His jaws are like a bed of spice, growths of aromatic plants; his lips are roses, dripping with flowing myrrh."

Lev's deep timbre echoed through the room, his voice as

soulful and resonant as when he led prayers as the chazzan in shul. In all my months volunteering here, I had only seen him weep once, when we had prepared a child who he later told us reminded him of his own grandson.

The face. The neck. The chest.

"His hands are wheels of gold, set with chrysolite; his abdomen is a block of ivory, overlaid with sapphires."

I had always found this verse, which was a metaphor for the glory of God, to be deeply moving. It reminded me that even the dead possessed HaShem's sanctity and divine beauty and that no manner of defilement could take that away. But with each word that left Lev's mouth, my grip on the sponge grew tighter.

I submerged the sponge in the basin to hide my trembling, dismayed by the depths of my rage. My teeth clenched so tightly that pain radiated through my jaw. I wanted to turn to Lev, seize him by the shirt and shake him violently, and scream that this was all wrong. There was no glory or sanctity here.

Once Yakov's right side was clean, we covered it with the sheet once more. Next was his left side, the port-wine birthmark that dripped like blood down his muscular forearm, the slim fingers I had once imagined curling around me.

Using a blunt sterling blade, I scraped away the soot engrained under his cuticles, relics of his job tending to train boilers. Each time, the sheet was lifted only high enough to expose the area we were washing, making it feel as though there wasn't a whole person beneath the linen, just a puzzle of disembodied parts.

"His legs are pillars of marble, founded upon sockets of fine gold, his appearance is like the Lebanon, chosen as the cedars."

After washing Yakov's front, we turned him onto his side. The air hissed from between my teeth as the pitiless gaslight shone upon his back. His torso was disfigured by an old burn scar that stretched across his spine and midsection, coiling like a shed snakeskin around his left hip.

Yakov had always changed into his boilersuit at work, claiming that he didn't want to soil his street clothes. He wore a long shirt to sleep even on stifling midsummer nights. In the three months he rented our room, I'd never seen his bare back.

Something happened to me, the scar seemed to say. *Something terrible.*

He had told me about the barn fire, but he had never told me that he, too, had been caught in it.

I immersed the sponge and turned my focus back to the task, trying to pretend the scar wasn't there. Right. It was no different than the puckering smallpox marks or old surgical scars I found on other bodies.

Death was ugly, I had learned, but life could be even uglier and unfathomably cruel.

"His palate is sweet, and he is altogether desirable; this is my beloved, and this is my friend, O daughters of Jerusalem."

Upon hearing the final verse, the urge to weep pierced me like a knife in the gut. It fully dawned on me, I would never see Yakov again after this. He'd never smile again. I'd never look into these blue eyes again. We wouldn't be interring him in the Atlantic, but a pauper's grave was just as permanent.

Glancing my way, Gavril furrowed his brows. We couldn't speak while tending to the dead, but his gaze conveyed his worry well enough. I shivered. What did he see in my face?

As soiled water sluiced down the table legs, we transferred Yakov to a slotted board attached to the pulley system overhead. Some burial societies poured buckets of water over the dead to ritually purify them, but ours had a mikveh built specifically for that purpose.

Gavril and Sender handled the ropes while Lev and I guided the board to the shallow bath at the other end of the room.

I removed the shroud and folded it over my arm as Yakov's body was lowered into the water.

The creak of the pulley and the low, strained groan of the rope tore at my nerves. Even the sound of the water sloshing against the bath's tiled sides became inexplicably abrasive. To maintain Yakov's dignity, Gavril and Sender turned their faces away, and Lev kept his gaze planted on the ceiling. I began to look away, too, only to find my gaze drawn helplessly to the mikveh once more.

Centimeter by centimeter, the water claimed Yakov. It crept up his bare skin, his chest, his head. His hair drifted around his face in an inky halo.

Taking a shallow breath, I drew in the scent of brine, though we were hundreds of kilometers from any ocean and the purification bath was filled with clean rainwater. I couldn't look away, frozen as still as a pillar of salt.

"And I will pour upon you pure water," Lev recited from Ezekiel, "and you will be purified of all your defilements."

The glow from the oil lamps failed to reach the bottom of the mikveh. The water grew bluer, darker. Bubbles burst from Yakov's mouth and raced to the surface. His chest rose. His fingers twitched.

"—and from all your abominations I will purify—"

He *looked* at me.

"Wait," I cried, dropping the shroud. "Wait, he's still alive!"

I reached for the rope without thinking, trying to seize it from Sender's hands so that I could haul Yakov up and keep him from drowning. We grappled with the rope, grunting for control. In spite of having the sunless complexion and slight build of a yeshiva student, Sender clung onto the cord as tenaciously as a terrier, even going so far as to bare his teeth. I wanted to throttle him.

"What's wrong with you?" Sender demanded, sweat dewing on his brow. "Let go, Alter!"

"Pull him up, pull him up." The words flew from my mouth in a savage, breathless chant that I barely recognized as my own. "There's still time to save him. Damnit, listen to me, there's still time!"

As I wrestled for control of the rope, a second pair of hands dug into my shoulders, trying to drag me back. The pulley swayed violently overhead. Raw, distorted sounds echoed in my ears—indistinct shouts, the groan of the ungreased pulley, a heavy thud as the board crashed against the porcelain tiles lining the bath, and the stomach-churning splash of a body tumbling into the water.

I glanced down at the tub—*oh, God, where did he go? Where did he go?*—and then Sender gave a hard yank on the rope that tore it from my hands. Palms stinging, I reeled back, the alarmed voices merging into a dull liquid roar. My foot landed in a puddle, and without knowing how I fell, I found myself underwater.

Bubbles streamed from my lips as I sank deeper into the water. I reached out to touch the mikveh's walls, but there were only even greater depths and the bitter taste of salt flooding my mouth.

I thrashed around, heavily disoriented. In a split second, my surroundings had changed. The clean, orderly room of the tahara house was gone, replaced by an endless abyss. Water all around me, water high above me. The dark, churning depths seemed to stretch on for an eternity, while the mikveh should have been no more than waist deep.

I looked into the chasm below. Something. Some *thing* was down there in the shadows, the same thing that had taken my father, and it would destroy me. I knew it would.

No sooner had I perceived the presence swimming far

below than I sensed another one right beside me. I lifted my head and looked into Yakov's bright blue eyes. He drifted within hand's reach.

"I couldn't do it. I tried, but I couldn't do it. My whole body froze." No bubbles rushed from his lips, because he didn't need to breathe anymore. "Please, you have to help me. You have to."

If I spoke, I'd drown. So I took Yakov by the shoulders to save him.

Whimpering through a mouth filled with water, he grasped hold of my waist with trembling hands. His fingers dug into my side, reaching in. His nails scraped against my rib cage; he seized my spine as though it were a pillar, void of pain but with unbearable pressure.

Terrified, I tried to shove him away, but our skin had fused. I could hear his voice now in the crook of my neck, reverberating through my bones and the pounding pulse of my blood. Speaking words I couldn't understand, Russian or the like, incoherent and fraught with panic.

In the back of my mind lingered an awareness of the hideous irrationality of this situation, but at the forefront, there was only blind terror. If we stayed down here, we would drown together.

I kicked my feet, trying to drag us up and away from the presence lurking below. Yakov's arms were grafted to me, his legs hopelessly entangled in mine; our muscles twitched uncontrollably, trying to reconcile ourselves. Two hearts hammered against my breastbone. I couldn't scream, for we shared a mouth now.

"Alter?" a voice called from far away as the water lifted up around us, as if displaced by a massive form that swam unseen through the black depths below. "Alter, can you hear me?"

Fingers closed around my shoulder. Wincing, I opened my

eyes, blinking droplets from them. Seawater? No, just tepid rainwater from the mikveh.

A pale face hovered over me. I scrambled back, thinking it was Yakov. As my vision cleared, I recognized Gavril's gray eyes and squarish features.

A humorless smile bent his lips. "Ah, so you've finally decided to rejoin the world of the living?"

I coughed, my mouth still pickled with the taste of salt water. My entire body ached, my muscles in knots and my limbs as stiff as boards. Through bleary eyes, I took in the sight of the tahara room's tile floor and the oil lamps casting their sullen glow.

Yakov's body had been returned to the table and was covered by a clean sheet. From where I sat, the lump didn't even look like the shape of a person. It could have been anything under there, or nothing at all.

"What were you thinking, Alter?" Lev hissed, suddenly towering over me. His face was dead-white and contorted in fury. I had never seen him show anger. I wouldn't even have thought he was capable of it.

"I... I thought..." I trailed off. My heart throbbed so fiercely that I could almost believe there were two separate beats. "I saw him move."

"You fainted," Gavril said, but Lev was unforgiving.

"Never in my life have I..." Lev shook his head in disgust. "Get out."

"What?"

"You can't be here." He pointed toward the door. "Just leave."

"No, you don't understand. Just let me explain." I picked up my yarmulke from where it had fallen. It was wrong to talk in front of Yakov like this, but I couldn't stop. I felt a desperate need to tell the others what I had seen. "Yakov opened his eyes. I know he did. He was still breathing. And when I fell into the water, he—"

"Come," Gavril said, his hand closing around my shoulder. "I'll walk you home."

"I'm not a child," I said, sharper than I'd intended, and tore free of his grip. "I can do it myself."

"Meshugener," Sender muttered under his breath as I passed him on my way out. His clothes were soaked almost as badly as my own.

I threw open the door, resisting the impulse to look back to see if the men were watching me. In the hall, I stopped to collect myself. Breathing heavily, I pressed my hands over my face. Where I had imagined Yakov reaching through me, my skin itched and burned.

I was certain I had seen Yakov move. Could I have only imagined it?

Just air in the lungs, you fool, I thought, swallowing down the miserable laugh that welled in my throat. *Just air in the lungs, and now everyone's going to think you're a damn meshugener. You might as well check yourself into Dunning Asylum before they can do it for you.*

Yet the mikveh. The water. The dream. It had felt so real.

I shook my head, trying to shove the whole matter aside. *It was only a dream, just leave it at that and go.*

I changed into my street clothes in the adjacent dressing room, but I had to stop because my fingers were trembling so violently that I couldn't button my shirt. My legs struggled to hold my weight. I sank against the wall, slid to the floor.

Panting and bowed over, I ground my palms against my eyes. Even then I couldn't escape from the memory of Yakov under a sheet, or Yakov in the mikveh, Yakov with a scarred back and bruises around his neck, and oh God—he really was gone, wasn't he?

Why did it feel like something had been ripped from me the moment Gavril had pulled back the shroud? Why couldn't I stop thinking of how I'd spoken to Yakov just hours before, a smile teasing his lips?

There would be no funeral, because he had come to America alone. No family members sitting shiva, no yahrzeit candle to commemorate his death. It would be as though he'd never existed at all.

That was what you really became when you died. Not a body under a sheet, not even dust, but an absence. A person-size gap. I would know.

My throat tightened into a pinhole, and an involuntary choking sound escaped my clenched teeth. The volunteers would be dressing Yakov now in pristine white garments. They would be putting him in a coffin. They would be placing broken pottery over his eyes and mouth. I couldn't let them hear me. I pressed my wrist against my mouth, bit down as hard as I could, and began to sob.

4

EVERYWHERE I TURNED were walls of flames, and the sky was an obsidian sea. I fled down alleyways as dark and stifling as the gullets of dragons, through sizzling sparks and palls of smoke, under clotheslines fluttering with singed sheets. Whips of fire crackled through the clouds. I reached the river, salvation! Except the water was black with soot, and shroud-swaddled bodies bobbed in the shallows. Overhead, something skirted through the smoke. I could not see it, but I heard the steady wick of its wings, like the flapping of oilcloth.

As the beast's shadow descended over me, I awoke with my heart slamming against my rib cage and my mouth as dry as ashes. A shrill clamor filled my ears as my room swam into focus.

Lurching onto my side, I groped for my brass alarm clock. I stilled the ringing bells with a clammy palm. Kicking away the sweaty sheets, I drew in deep breaths, waiting for my heartbeat to return to normal.

The sun was already high in the sky, a filmy white disc that winked at me through my window. It must have rained, for the glass was beaded with moisture, and water licked the brim of the leak bucket in the corner.

Exhausted, I sank against the mattress and promised myself another minute to fully wake up. My back ached as though someone had sat on me while I slept, and my throat was sore. Staring at the brown water stain on the ceiling, I counted the droplets plunking from the saturated plaster.

Strange with the dream. Ever since my father's death, I had been plagued by nightmares of water and sickness. Never fire.

"Hey, Alter," Haskel said, and I turned my head. He lay on his back, maybe looking at the same water stain. Either way, he wouldn't meet my eye.

"What is it?" I asked.

"Is it quick, do you think?"

"Is what quick?"

"To drown."

My tongue felt glued to the roof of my mouth. I swallowed, tried to speak. Couldn't.

"Or is it slow? Does it hurt?"

"I don't know." My voice came out very small.

"What a way to go." Rolling over onto his side, he turned his back to me. Across the room, Dovid didn't even stir, though my alarm had surely woken him.

Yesterday, after I had pulled myself together well enough to leave the tahara house without breaking down sobbing, I had gone home. I spent the rest of the day in bed, racked by chills and cramping muscles, and choked down the leftover potato kugel and beef kishka that Mrs. Brenner kindly brought over for dinner. The muscle cramps had returned with a vengeance. Had I torn something during my struggle over the rope?

Aching body or not, Head Editor Stieglitz and Press Supervisor Weiss would be expecting me at the *Idisher Kuryer*'s office at eight o'clock sharp. I forced myself to climb out of bed. As I went through my morning routine, the pain slowly faded, while the sense of disquiet lingered like a bad stench. Yakov's death had thrown the world out of orbit, sent it hurtling. Anything might happen today.

The remnants of Mrs. Brenner's kugel had become stiff and brown, with an oily bottom. I forced it down just the same. It was nothing like my mother's cooking, but it was either that or stale bread. Besides, if I didn't eat now, I'd have to wait until my lunch break.

"Alter," Dovid said as I opened the door.

I looked back at him. He had finally crawled out from under the covers.

"If you keep stooping over like that, people are going to think you really *are* an old man," he said, turning my name into a pun.

"Funny." I rubbed my back. "I think I hurt a muscle yesterday when I..."

As I trailed off, Dovid's weak smile faded. Without a word, he drew back into his cocoon of blankets. I wheeled my bike into the hallway, feeling stained.

On my way out, I knocked on Mrs. Brenner's door. When she opened it, I held the empty kugel pan out to her.

She flinched at the sight of me.

"A-Alter." She drew in an unsteady breath and offered me a smile. "You startled me. I thought you were someone else."

"Sorry."

"No, dear." She took the kugel pan, holding the edge with the tips of her fingers, as though it was hot to the touch or profoundly unclean. "No. It's nothing to apologize for."

"Thank you for the dinner last night." I forced a smile of my own. "It was delicious."

"I'm glad to see you ate it all." Mrs. Brenner stepped toward me, then hesitated. "Alter, I know you've been skipping meals. I can see it in your face. You know, if you ever need something, you'll come to me, won't you? Won't you?"

My throat clogged with gratitude. I felt my smile quiver on my lips, in danger of falling away entirely. "It's fine. Thank you, but I am quite all right."

She looked unconvinced. I didn't want to rely on her kindness, especially not now, when death felt treacherously close. Nothing good had ever come from getting close to others. One way or another, it always ended in blood.

Raizel was waiting in the lobby when I came downstairs, flipping through a newspaper. She tucked it under her arm as I approached. Peeking out from under her straw hat, wisps of mahogany hair garlanded her ears like a laurel wreath.

"How are you faring?" she asked.

"I'm fine, thank you. Just tired."

"I can tell." She paused. "Listen, Alter, don't you think it's a little strange that so many boys have run off recently? And now with your roommate—"

"Yakov drowned, Raizel. It was an accident. The police said so."

"And Aaron ran off to Cincinnati," she said flatly.

Her words disturbed me. I didn't want to talk about this. I didn't even want to think about it.

"I'm sorry, but I need to get to work," I said, turning away.

She dropped her paper in my bicycle basket as I passed. When I looked back, she favored me with a brief smile. "Mrs. Brenner told me you were tutored in German. To cheer you up, here's something a bit more interesting than the Talmud."

Once the front door banged shut behind me, I retrieved the paper from my basket and sighed at the title.

The *Arbeiter-Zeitung*. Of course. As if I wanted any more of the drek Raizel had tried peddling me at Mrs. Brenner's dinner table. The tea hadn't even finished steeping before Raizel had asked me if I heard how Governor Altgeld had pardoned the surviving anarchists responsible for the Haymarket bombing back in '86. Once I told her I had, she immediately leaped into a passionate speech about the merits of the labor movement, the brutality of the Pinkerton Agency, and the need for sudden, even violent change.

I wasn't ready to get behind a class war, and told her so. Not that it would have done much good if I'd agreed with her. After Raizel stormed out in a fury, I learned that Mrs. Brenner had spent the fifteen minutes before my arrival regaling her parents about my family's success in the textiles industry, as if that could make up for a dead father and absent mother. Conveniently, Mrs. Brenner had omitted that by the time I was twelve, we were left destitute.

I dropped the paper in the rubbish bin on my way down the street. The last thing I needed was to be swept up in someone else's revolution, when I was battling my own war trying to get my family here.

5

THE CHAOS OF Chicago was even worse than the disarray of wagons, horses, and dray carts on Piatra Neamt's market days. Pedaling down Maxwell Street, I took care to stay away from the hansom cabs and wagons that rushed through the road as though they were racing to see who could mow down the most pedestrians.

Two years here, and I still hadn't quite adjusted to the city's loudness and bustle. I was afraid I'd never feel at home, that I'd always find myself flinching away from train whistles or the metallic uproar of streetcars.

No matter. I just had to remind myself this city wouldn't ruin me. Soon, I'd get my mother and sisters here. And if I worked hard, eventually we could move to one of those idyllic little villages nestled up alongside Lake Michigan, unsullied by the coal smoke. Except not Lake Forest. They didn't allow Jews there.

Outside of raising the funds to bring my family over, I had a hard time envisioning my future. I'd have liked to go to school, but it cost too much, and I didn't have the time.

Besides, with my English skills, I'd be lucky to test into the kindergarten.

In those months of anticipation before we had left Romania, my mind had brimmed with dreams of the future. My father called America a goldene medina where even poor Jews could make a name for themselves, where anything was possible. He saw men like Levi Strauss and Jacob Davis as icons, proof of the success waiting for us here. For a man who had built his fortune from the ground up and seen it demolished overnight, he had been so hopeful. He had fooled himself, and like a child listening to a bubbe-meise, I had believed every single word of it.

We would start a family business in Chicago's garment district. We would persevere and make a name for ourselves, and I would go to school, an English school where Jews were able to learn right beside gentiles. It had all seemed like a wonderful dream, and with my father's death, it had dissolved like one, too.

I didn't know what I wanted to do with my life anymore. I used to dream about exploring the world, but now each time I closed my eyes, I was haunted by numbers. Ninety dollars for steamship tickets. Seventy cents a day for food. Ten dollars for railway tickets, and another ten for lodgings. Fifteen for miscellaneous expenses and fees.

My mother and little sisters weren't to blame for how things had turned out, but a part of me resented them for having to put my life on hold.

Three blocks from my tenement, I reached the tahara house. I turned down the street after it, weaving my way through the familiar sprawl of tenements and small businesses. When I crossed the river's northern bend, I avoided glancing at the brownish water churning below, noxious with runoff from the slaughterhouses.

I loathed to admit it, but my dream had put me on edge. If I looked down, I was afraid the water might be black with soot. There might be corpses.

Soon enough, I reached that area of the riverfront known as Smokey Hollow, an industrial labyrinth of factories and workshops. The smoke was so thick that it billowed through the roads in drifts as wide as glaciers, dimming the sunlight until it became impossible to tell whether it was morning or midday.

I turned down a side street of narrow limestone offices, stopped at the third building, and wheeled my bicycle through its wrought-iron gates.

The second floor of the *Idisher Kuryer* was all office space, while the ground level was devoted to the printing presses and the supplies associated with the trade. I hung my coat on the rack and stowed my bicycle in a back room, amid ink pots and reams of blank paper. Before taking my place at the Linotype machine in the far corner, I double-checked that the tassels of my tzitzis, the tunic-like garment I wore under my shirt and waistcoat, were still tucked into my pants. I had no desire to acquaint myself with the machine's crushing gears and movements.

The Linotype machine resembled a medieval torture device with its hulking metal form and the wisps of steam curling from the cauldron of molten lead in its core. I sat down at the keyboard and leafed through the stack of typewritten articles on the nearby tray.

More of the usual. News of the shul being built across from the chevra kadisha, due to be complete by the end of summer. An interest piece about pushcart vendors at the Sunday market. A report about a fourteen-year-old worker's accidental death at one of the Union Stockyards' kosher slaughterhouses, accompanied by a brief statement by the factory boss, Mr. Katz. I scoffed as I scanned over an opinion piece calling for the assimilation of Eastern European immigrants into Chicago's well-established German reform community. The author made it sound as though we were only an inconvenience until we cut our hair and hung up our tzitzis. I hated the idea that to be considered a worthy American, I had to hack away parts of myself, become a more acceptable Jew, an invisible one. And I hated that in spite of my resentment, a part of me deeply wanted to anyway.

I set the article aside to finish last. It would take me all morning to copy the text into the machine, which would cast typeset blocks from each line. It was tedious work and sometimes the fumes gave me headaches that lingered all day, but I knew it wasn't permanent. It couldn't be. There had to be more than this.

I positioned an article on the tray in front of me and began typing, falling into a steady rhythm. The steady clatter of the machine numbed my nerves. Each time I turned out a new line of text it felt like magic, words forming from slugs of molten lead. By the end of the first article, the machine had created dozens of slender metal blocks, some scarcely wider than the edge of a silver dollar, arranged into squares. I carefully secured them in the metal frame that would be used to print a single newspaper page.

As I worked, my thoughts strayed to Yakov and how he had been on the evening he died. How he had come into the hall so silently, the way he always had, as though he were already becoming a ghost. His low purr, the stroke of his fingertips upon my lower back. I shivered. I could almost feel it now.

I pinched my wrist to banish the thoughts and turned my attention back to the task at hand. Words must be typed and driven into place, parts must be oiled. Yet as I worked, I couldn't get Raizel's words out of my head. The police had done nothing to search for Aaron, and likely they had treated Yakov's death with the same indifference.

What were the chances that three Jewish immigrants would disappear in just two months, and then a fourth would end up dead? If the water hadn't rejected Yakov, he would have merely been another disappearance.

The police had called it an accident, but of course they would have. There was too much invested in the World's Fair to risk poor publicity. An accident was bad enough, but a murder? The newspapers wouldn't let a story like that go buried.

A stir of voices broke me from my daze. I looked across the room as the head editor, Mr. Stieglitz, entered, accompanied by his entourage of journalists. All smartly dressed men in three-piece suits and silk ascots, their hair slicked back and watch chains glinting.

If the police wouldn't care about several missing boys and a single drowned one, maybe the public would. I eased to my feet, swallowed down the unease playing havoc on my guts, and approached them.

Mr. Stieglitz was a tall man, with a penchant for corduroy suits and ornate silver-tipped canes. Just as I kept my sidelocks trimmed short and tucked behind my ears, he favored the narrow beard and generous mustache of the Stockyard bosses. We had both made concessions for this new American life; it was inevitable. Indeed, sometimes I felt a buried anger for my yarmulke and tasseled tzitzis, which I feared would always exclude me from becoming truly, visibly American.

Mr. Stieglitz turned to me as I neared. "Good morning, Mister...er...?"

"Rosen. Alter Rosen."

"Of course. How may I help you?" Although we had only spoken a handful of times, he used informal pronouns to refer to me, as one would use with a friend or small child. It made me feel hopelessly small.

"I think I have a story for you, sir. Something big."

"Is that so?" He lifted his eyebrows. "Well, what is it, then?"

I clammed up, my confidence deflating at the edge of derision in his voice. Maybe it was a coincidence after all. What would I know? I set type. I worked the printers. I had grown up in a small town. These men had been born and raised in Chicago, and though they still spoke the old tongue, their accents were Americanized. We were nothing at all alike.

"It's about my roommate, sir. Yakov Kogan. He was found dead at the fairgrounds yesterday. The police called it a drowning—"

"Yes, you have my sympathies. May his memory be a blessing." Mr. Stieglitz turned to the other newsmen, who were watching us with amused half smiles.

"Sir."

He looked back, his brows twitching. Already, the first hint of annoyance had surfaced. "Yes?"

"I don't think it was a drowning, Mr. Stieglitz. I think the police just said that because they don't care, or because they didn't want to cause bad publicity. Three other boys on Maxwell Street have disappeared recently, too, and the police have done nothing to investigate. They've just been dismissed as runaways." I could see his eyes glazing over. I began speaking more quickly, trying to get the words in before he shut me out for good. "I think you should have one of the journalists write about this. This is clearly something that the public should know about."

"Mr. Rosen, I have no intention of sending my journalists out on a wild-goose chase."

"I can look into it, sir. I can even write it."

"You? Write an article?" He exchanged a look with the

other journalists, who were struggling to contain their smirks. "You're an apprentice typesetter, Mr. Rosen."

"But I've read plenty of articles."

"That does not mean you have the talent necessary to write them." He took a deep breath, as though I was straining his patience. "More important, do you know what kind of paper this is?"

I tried to speak, but my lips began to tremble, and I closed them right away.

"We do not publish gossip. We do not publish drivel. We certainly do not begin accusing the police of shirking their duties. Do I make myself clear?"

"Yes, sir," I whispered.

"Good. Now, return to your station. Those presses won't work themselves."

He continued on his way. One of the journalists, a broad-faced man who had watched the exchange with curiosity, stopped beside me. His mustache drooped like the whiskers of a catfish. I recognized him as Mr. Lewin, who had joined the newspaper several months ago. More than once, I had heard him rave about the *Chicago Daily Journal* and the *Chicago Times*, English-language papers where he saw the future.

"He gave you quite the chewing-out, didn't he?" he said, once Stieglitz and the others were out of earshot. "I wouldn't mind hearing more about what you had to say."

As I told Mr. Lewin about the disappearances, he nodded sagely, his mouth cocked in a thoughtful smile.

"That's certainly unusual. As for your friend, you have my sympathies. May his memory be a blessing."

"May HaShem avenge his blood." The words left my mouth before I even realized it, the Hebrew sharp on the tongue, like splinters. HaShem yikkom damo.

"You're truly certain of it, aren't you?" Mr. Lewin studied me carefully. "That your friend was killed."

"I don't know how to explain it. I just..." I hesitated. "If you had seen Yakov, you would understand. I've volunteered at the burial society for nearly a year now, and I've prepared more people than I can count. This was different."

It wasn't just the bruise around his throat. It wasn't falling into the mikveh—that was grief and exhaustion. No. I couldn't explain it, but somehow I knew that something *terrible* had happened to him.

Mr. Lewin gave it some consideration. "These other boys who have disappeared, you say you know them?"

"Not personally, but I'd see them around Maxwell Street."

"Hmm. I see." He nodded. "Once you're done arranging the typeset, let Mr. Weiss take over the rest of the printing. I have a task for you."

A jolt of shock rippled through me. I couldn't believe he actually *believed* me. "So, you think I should write the article?"

"Maybe, but I need you to look into this more." Mr. Lewin thrust a finger at me. "Establish a groundwork. You say your friend died at the World's Fair?"

"Yes. The police thought he slipped into the water and drowned, but there was a bruise on his neck."

As I said it, I traced my fingers over my throat. I had lifted my hand without even realizing it. The skin under my jaw felt swollen and tender.

"Do you speak English?"

Shaken, I lowered my hand to my side. "A little. I can understand and read it well enough, but—"

"Go to the fairgrounds. Talk to people. See what you can learn." He gave me a hearty slap on the back, his gaze sparking with excitement. "This could prove to be a very interesting article indeed."

I hesitated. "Sir..."

"What is it? What's the matter?"

I looked at my feet, my cheeks heating up. "I can't afford the admission."

"Do I look like a charity to you? You want this article to be written, you need to pay your dues."

I returned to my station to find my supervisor, Mr. Weiss, examining the newest tray I had prepared. He was a printing veteran whose hands bore the scars of the clunky outdated presses, several fingers misshapen from old fractures and curled inward like claws.

I went to his side. "Sir, after I finish typesetting the pages, Mr. Lewin wants me to go to the fairgrounds to research an article."

Mr. Weiss didn't answer. As he examined the die-blocks, his gaze darkened.

"Sir?" I asked tentatively.

"Is this some kind of joke?" Mr. Weiss's voice came from deep in his throat, as low and foreboding as the grumbling of a bear. And like a bear, he looked ready to take a bite out of me.

"I don't..." I trailed off. "I don't know what you..."

"Well, boy?" he demanded, stepping aside so that I could get a better look at the tray. "Tell me, what is this supposed to mean?"

The lines of metal text swarmed before my eyes. I blinked, wiping away the sweat forming on my neck. It took me a moment to realize what I was looking at, since the letterpress blocks were arranged as mirror images of the true text. Instead of the final article, it was a single sentence, copied over and over again in cold lead.

זאָלסט אים דערהרגענען

Zolst im derhargenen.

You must kill him.

The corners of my vision darkened as if saturated with ink. As I took a step back, the floor rolled beneath me, and the air grew denser, stifling. Mr. Weiss's mouth continued to move, but his words were lost beneath a deep, liquid roar.

Terror filled me. I wasn't in control of my body. This was something else.

"I didn't do it." My voice echoed hollowly in my ears. "I don't know how that got there, but I didn't do it."

Even as the words left my mouth, I knew how absurd they sounded. I had spent the last several hours at the Linotype machine. No one else could have done this.

With a grunt of disgust, Mr. Weiss scooped the lead blocks from their scaffold and threw them into the melting pot.

"I'm sorry," I whispered as he sat down at the machine to examine the other tray I had completed. "I'll retype it. I'll—"

"Go," he snapped, waving his gnarled hand at me. "You said you had to go? Then just go."

6

OUTSIDE, COAL SMOKE billowed like dragon's breath from the chimneys of the workshops. Unlike the fog in my hometown, the smoke wouldn't burn away with the rising sun. It would only grow thicker as the day dragged on, until it blanketed everything.

At the nearby train station, people crowded elbow-to-elbow, the air filled with a multitude of voices. I purchased a ticket from the kiosk man. On the platform, I found a spot to stand away from the crowds.

My face felt hot and swollen, and the ache in my back had returned with a vengeance. Rubbing my eyes, I stepped away from the brink of the platform as the train raced by. I was always a little afraid that if I stood close enough to the edge, a strange urge might come over me. All it would take was one step or two. I didn't have to *want* to do it. I just would.

Once the train stopped, I entered the third car and took an empty seat at the back. To distract myself, I glanced at the newspaper the man next to me was poring over. Emblazoned

across the page were the words SECOND HUMAN FOOT
FOUND ON LAKE MICHIGAN BEACH.

Foot? That couldn't be right. What had happened to the
rest of the person?

The man got off at the next stop, leaving his newspaper behind. I picked it up and read the article. It was buried on the
ninth page like an afterthought. Some words were a mystery
to me, but I got the gist of the story after scanning it over
twice more. Over the last several months, body parts had been
discovered in the lake or on its shore, and it wasn't only feet
like the headline suggested. A fisherman had caught a human
torso in his net, and three weeks after that, a little girl for-
aging for crayfish had found a skull picked clean by the fish.
Unidentifiable.

Nauseated, I set the paper aside as the train arrived at the
South Park Avenue station, the second-to-last stop. The platform was teeming with people dressed for the World's Fair, a
riot of bright colors at odds with the surrounding cityscape.

The train car rapidly filled with bodies. An older man
nearly elbowed me in the face as he was trying to find room
to sit. Deciding it would be better to stand the rest of the way
than risk bloodying my nose, I rose to my feet and offered
him my seat. A young gentleman shouldered past me in the
process, not even bothering to glance my way before continuing to the back of the car.

The train jolted forward once more. As I grasped onto the
leather hoop hanging from the rods overhead, my skin prickled
with the disquieting sense of being watched. A quick glance
around the car failed to reveal anything amiss.

A few minutes later, the World's Fair appeared past the
window. To my right was a pillared building whose four cupolas dominated the skyline. Other structures loomed in the

distance, and beyond it all lingered Lake Michigan's vast liquid darkness.

As the train rumbled to a halt, I followed the other passengers onto the platform. A clamoring tide of people filled the concourse. Just going down the long staircase was as strenuous as fighting against a current. Finally, I reached the ticket counter.

"Excuse me," I said in English to the woman on the other side of the kiosk's window. "I heard that a boy drowned here last night. Do you know anything about that?"

She looked up in disinterest. "Fifty cents, please."

Three hours' wage was a high price to pay for answers, but I reached into my overcoat pocket for my billfold. My hand came back empty. No. No. In a panic, I patted down my other pocket and then my pants and waistcoat as well.

"I think you dropped this," a low, melodic voice said in Yiddish from behind me. I turned.

It was the young dandy who had brushed past me on the train, now standing so close I nearly brushed shoulders with him. His mussed brown curls and full lips gave him an air of innocence, but his hazel eyes were as hard and wary as those of a meadow viper, his handsome face all sharp edges.

His *face*.

Life continued around us, but it felt as though time itself had come to a standstill. My feet were riveted to the pavestones.

It couldn't be.

"This is yours, isn't it?" He held my billfold out to me, a smirk teasing his lips. "You can tell by how worn and creased it is."

I didn't move. Certainly, to any observers, I must have looked deranged.

"Well?"

I reached out to retrieve it from him, knowing by then that I hadn't dropped it. He'd reached into my pocket and taken it.

As my fingers closed around the leather edge, he took my wrist with his other hand and leaned in closer. "Hello, Alex."

I swallowed hard. "Frankie…"

I had arrived in Chicago two years ago, but I had only lived in my apartment for the last ten months. Before that, I had been with Frankie, and I hadn't been doing anything as kosher as working the Linotype or fetching coffee.

His smile remained, but his eyes grew even colder still. "It's been a while, boychik."

Before I could answer, the woman at the ticket counter cleared her throat.

"Excuse me," she said loudly, as though shouting at me would suddenly make me more fluent in English. "There are others waiting in line. That will be fifty cents."

Cheeks burning, I pushed two quarters through the gap under the window. The woman tore a ticket from a long reel of them and passed it through. Frankie tried to follow me as I hurried off, but people chastised him to wait his turn.

Passing through the station's doors, I was confronted by the stunning sight of the Fair's forecourt. Towering white buildings rose all around me, each of them a wealth of pillars, cupolas, and statuary. American flags sailed proudly from every rooftop, rippling in the summer breeze.

Frankie had taken me to the World's Fair during its construction, when the buildings had been half-formed. For a small sum, we had been allowed to watch from afar as hundreds of workers crawled ant-like over the lumber skeletons. Back then, I had only been able to imagine the White City's splendor. To see it in person was just as shocking on my system as a whiff of smelling salts.

The sun shone off the golden dome of the building ahead,

making a beacon of it. Eager to put some distance between Frankie and me, I circled around the building and arrived at a path overlooking a long basin. A woman sold popcorn and candied nuts on my left, and a band played under the rotunda to my right. A man strode by in a pristine white coat and high fur cap, like a hero from a Slavic fairy tale.

I stepped up to the edge of the basin and gaped. At the other end of the pool, a massive statue stood thirty meters tall, a globe held aloft in her left hand and a staff in her right. Her arms and face were plaster made to resemble marble, her gown gilded in gold leaf that, upon catching the burnished sun, transformed her garment into a mantle of fire.

She was as noble a figure as the Statue of Liberty that had greeted me when I arrived at Castle Garden two years before. But in her resolute pose and raised arms, there existed an undeniable hostility, as if she were preparing to march into battle. A goddess of war.

"Alex, wait," Frankie called after me as I continued down the path.

I ignored him, although I knew that would do little good. He caught up within moments.

"We all thought you were dead, you know." Frankie kept pace with me. "Dead or worse, but look at you. With those tzitzis, you look like a regular mensch."

To emphasize his point, he tugged at one of the tassels hanging from the garment's four corners. I slapped his hand away and kept on walking, refusing to acknowledge him.

"Oh, come now, where are you going?"

"Leave me alone, Frankie."

Desperate to escape him, I entered the next building I came across—the Krupp Pavilion, a fortresslike structure whose tower was adorned with decorative eagles and the red, white and black flag of the German Empire.

Once I passed through the double doors, the temperature plummeted. Cold air radiated from a towering indoor fountain that sprayed water over coiled copper tubing, trickling down by some new science to form blocks of ice at its base.

Frankie clung to my trail, following me past riveted metal machines, past imposing cannons and naval guns, past armored plates and display cases of mortars and bullets. Someday, these weapons might be used in war, but now they only served as the backdrop for a waking nightmare.

He cornered me behind a massive steel ship propeller, leaning close enough that the heat of his breath fanned across my cheeks.

"One night you're there, the next you're gone. No goodbye. Not even a word. And you've been here this entire time, hiding." In the dusky shadows, Frankie's eyes were as luminously gold as the constellations of dust motes floating above our heads. "Look how shabby your clothes are, you good mensch. Look at your shoes... You think no one sees the candlewax stoppering their holes? You're looking thin. You're looking unwell. You've fallen on hard times, haven't you, bubbeleh?"

"Go jump in the lake," I growled, and pushed past him, heading for the exit.

"Just last week, they found Victor in the Chicago River," Frankie called after me as I threw open the doors and stumbled into the deliriously bright sunlight. "Or what was left of him anyway. Some bastard gutted him like a fish."

I froze in the entrance of the Krupp Pavilion, chilled to the bone although the sun beat hot on my face. One hand still on the door, the knob cold against my palm. As Frankie's words echoed in my head, I turned and looked back into the chamber. He stood beneath the naval gun, his form in darkness.

"Victor is dead," Frankie repeated. "Victor. The kid with the chipped tooth. Velvel. You remember him. I know you do."

His blunt statement had a gravitational pull, drawing me back into the room. The door swished shut, blanketing us in the cool dim.

"He's dead?" I whispered so softly that only I could hear, because saying it aloud would make it real.

"I knew that would get your attention," Frankie said, his voice as tight as a garrote. "He looked up to you, Alex, do you realize that? I still remember how he followed after you like a baby duck. When you left, he visited the hospitals and morgues, searching for you. He *cared*."

I waited for Frankie to tell me that it was a lie, just a cruel way to take me by the scruff and yank me around and force me to confront the past I had spent the last year trying to forget. He stared at me, anger buried shallowly in his gaze, his mouth a tight line. And I knew he had told the truth.

Somehow, obscenely, Victor's death felt like justice. Like punishment. For what—who knew? For fear and weakness. For surviving when my father hadn't.

"I don't go by Alex anymore," I said at last. I had tried using that name for a while, just another way to leave behind the shtetl. Maybe, deep down, I had felt that if I took another name, an Americanized one, I'd finally break free of this darkness that followed me everywhere. I should have known there was no escaping it.

"Alter then." He studied me with those magnetizing tawny eyes of his, eyes that had haunted my daydreams since the day I met him. "Say we get out of this heat and talk more over cold drinks? You must be burning up under all those layers."

We walked along the canal. We made an odd pair, I supposed, me as I was and Frankie in his fine clothes, his golden watch chain glinting. His thick accent betrayed him as a member of the tribe, but that was the only proof—he kept his head uncovered and his sideburns shaved. Nobody would suspect he had grown up in a household even more religious than my own.

I stared at my feet as I walked, avoiding looking into the sun-spangled water. Each time we crossed over a bridge, I thought, *Is this it? Is this where Yakov fell in?*

"You look different." Frankie's gaze lingered on me. "Do you know what 'alter' means in English?"

"To change."

"To *be* changed."

"It's been a year," I said.

"That's not what I mean." But he didn't tell me what he meant, and I didn't ask. I felt trapped, bound tight by his familiar glances. He looked at me as though he could see under all my layers. His hand rested on my shoulder, hovering light as a hummingbird, and it was all I could think about.

"You look different, too," I mumbled, my eye drawn by the glimmer of the double Albert watch chain draped across his slim waist. An attractive bloodstone fob hung from the center chain, directing the gaze from silver button to silver button, then downward still. "Who'd you steal your clothes from?"

"For a good mensch, you're still damn rude. Someone ought to teach you some manners."

I flushed at the heat in his low purr, annoyed by him and his knowing smirk and by the betrayal of my body. I hated how nervous he made me, like I was balancing on the edge of a rooftop. He'd always had that effect on me, filling me with dizzying exhilaration one moment, then sending me into a nervous, stuttering panic the next.

"Have you been here before?" I asked, once we had continued farther down the boulevard. He seemed to know where he was going.

"Oh, all the time." His gaze flicked down to my clothes,

and his smirk only grew. "Some of us aren't living hand-to-mouth. Some of us have risen in the world."

Risen or not, it soon became clear to me that Frankie hadn't climbed above his old habits. As he brushed his hair out of his eyes, the sun shone upon the fresh scabs marring his knuckles. I had a feeling the heavy silver rings he wore on his fingers weren't just a way to flaunt his newfound fortune, but a handsomer alternative to the brass knuckle-dusters he once carried tucked in his pocket. Even now, I wouldn't doubt he had something a bit more dangerous than a watch hidden on his person.

Yet I followed.

7

TWO YEARS HAD passed since the day I met Frankie, but our first encounter was engraved in my memory like a knife wound. It was only days after my father had died. The medical examinations I had endured at Castle Garden had sapped my last reserves of strength. After an exhausting journey from Manhattan, I had turned up at the Chicago address my father had made me memorize.

It was supposed to be the home of a landsman, a good man who would help us find work. Instead, I arrived at a scorched plot. The tenement had been destroyed in a fire two months before, and our friend from Piatra Neamț had been taken with it.

I walked aimlessly, dragging my trunk behind me. It was early January, and the winter chill sucked the air as dry as a bone. I had bundled myself in three layers of clothes and tugged on my warmest fur hat, but even that wasn't enough to keep out the wind.

As I wandered up and down the streets, I turned bitter and

angry. I never should have come here. My ancestors hadn't lived and died on this land, hadn't bled into its soil.

I wanted to curse at my father, scream and shout. It served him right to die like that, feverish and so weak at the end that he was croaking nonsense. He should have known; he should have *known*! This was what happened when you went places you didn't belong.

I stopped to rest my aching legs and sat down on my trunk along the roadside. If I cried, the tears would freeze on my cheeks, so I yanked at my hair instead, trying to tear out fistfuls. Maybe if I bled, I'd feel something more than this wrenching grief.

"Look at that hair," a boy said in Yiddish. "He's so fresh off the boat, I'll bet he still smells like fish."

My heartbeat quickened as I looked up to find myself surrounded by a group of teens. They were dressed like gentiles, and most wore no hats, as though to spite the nasty weather and spit in the face of tradition.

"When did you land?" The boy stepped to the front of the crowd. His dialect was of the east, Lithuania or the like. In spite of his unkempt hair and uncovered head, his musical cadence suggested he had been educated in a yeshiva. The Talmud had no punctuation marks. When reciting its texts, one raised and lowered one's voice to replicate the natural pauses provided by commas and periods, stopping for emphasis or to take on a questioning tone. It was singular to yeshiva students.

His contradicting qualities made me wary. I rose to my feet and wrestled my trunk onto its wooden wheels.

"Can you understand me?" the boy asked, stepping in my way. The others crowded around me, boxing me in. "Hey? Don't you know Yiddish? What about Russian? *Vy ponimayete menya?*"

"Leave me alone," I said, and tried to step around the pack

leader. He grabbed my coattail, bringing me to a halt with ease. I reached down to pry off his hand, but my fingers wouldn't move properly.

"Easy there. Oy, you're practically frozen. What happened to your gloves?" Then, almost absently, he took my hand between both of his and rubbed it firmly to restore the circulation. His palms were warm and rough, a startling contrast to his long, agile fingers, the fingers of a scribe or ketubah painter. As he moved onto my other hand, either not caring what the other boys might think or just entirely oblivious to it, he continued talking to me in that mesmerizing lilt of his. "The name's Frankie, and this is my crew. You look like you could use some help. Are you all alone here?"

Maybe it was the way he massaged the feeling back into my hands, or his yeshivish cadence, or those magnetizing bourbon-colored eyes, but something told me I could confide in him.

"I am." The words were like spitting out stones, heavy and choking. "My name's Alter."

"You don't look like an old man," he teased, turning my name into a pun. "Hey, Victor, give him your gloves before his fingers fall off."

The short kid with the chipped tooth passed over his gloves, which were more holes than leather. Mumbling thanks, I slid the gloves on.

"Do you know of a boardinghouse around here?" I asked. "One where they speak Yiddish?"

"Why would you want that when we could get you a bed for next to free?"

Narrowing my eyes, I waited for Frankie to laugh. When I realized he was serious, I licked my lips, my mouth drier than I cared to admit. He thought he was so smooth, but I could see his sharp edges.

"Who're you working for?" I demanded.

Frankie lifted his eyebrows, scowling as though I had offended him. "I'm no one's grunt. I work for myself. It's something the Americans called entrepreneurship. There's an attic down in the Levee, all made up with beds from a boarding-house that got shuttered."

"Actually, it was a brothel," Victor added helpfully, earning a reproachful look from Frankie.

"Shut up, Victor. Nobody wants to know that." Frankie turned back to me. "I rent the place. Split between us, it'll only cost you thirty cents a week. Best part is, I can get you a job, too."

I wasn't sure if I could catch something just by sleeping on used mattresses, and I wasn't ready to find out.

"Thank you, but I'd rather not get syphilis. I can find my own work, and my own bed, too." I stripped off the gloves and tried to hand them back to Frankie, but he refused to take them.

"You'll find work down in the sweatshops, will you now?" His voice was barbed with hidden knowledge. He looked me over, his gaze burning through my clothes. "That's a handsome coat. Shabby but a good cut. You're a tailor's son, aren't you?"

It stunned me how close he came to the truth. Before my father opened his own workshop, he had been a cloak-maker. When our entire fortune was lost to the surging waters of the Bistrița—a shipload of fabric and ready-made clothes gone in an instant—he returned to his former career. The coat was a gift made by his own hands, its elegant cut proof of his fine craftsmanship.

"That's what I thought," Frankie said, as though he could read it all in my face. He leaned forward, his breath wafting from his lips in cold vapors. "You'll do lovely in the textile mills, bubbeleh. Working sixteen hours a day, fourteen if you're lucky. The dye baths will burn the skin off your hands, and you'll come home stinking of piss and chemicals. It's so dark in those places, your eyes will go bad, too, if your body doesn't give out first."

Later, I would find out that before running off to Chicago, Frankie had worked with his father at a garment factory in Manhattan. He described it so vividly, a shiver passed through my body.

"What's in it for you?" I eyed Frankie's shabby clothes. His trouser hems were fraying to bits, but he had nice leather boots that hardly looked broken in.

"Nothing. I just know a lamb to slaughter when I see one."

Frankie's blunt words shocked me almost as much as his description of the sweatshops. I sputtered for a response. "I— I'm not a—"

"Trust me, you are." A smile surfaced on his lips, but it never reached his eyes. Something in his voice made my stomach clench. The way he said it, he seemed to know from experience. As though he had seen it before, over and over again, what happened to boys with nowhere else to go. "You just don't know it, and you won't until someone licks their chops clean of you. But don't worry, boychik, I won't let that happen. Stay with us, and we'll make a wolf out of you yet."

Slowly, I relented. I didn't know English, and I wouldn't last long in this weather. I could hear him out at least.

"What exactly do you do?" I asked.

Frankie's smile warmed. "We take from those who have more than enough to give."

FRANKIE AND I drank sweet iced cocoa at a teahouse in the Java Village, with a view of Ireland across the midway. The air was cooler in the shadow of the black-roofed huts, a pleasant breeze rolling off Lake Michigan.

The Java Village's novelty thrilled me at first, but the entire setup began to feel shallow the longer we sat there. The Javanese men and women looked downtrodden under the stares of other tourists. I was used to being stared at, too, but somehow this was different.

"Is there a Russia exhibit?" I asked Frankie once we were seated, wondering if Yakov might have gone there. "Or somewhere Jewish?"

"Somewhere Jewish? You mean like a shtetl?" He burst into laughter.

"What's so funny?"

"A shtetl. Oh, I can see it now. Students studying in some dim yeshiva. A Torah dedication, so the tourists can watch us kiss a scroll and parade it down the midway. So they can tell we're Jewish, everyone will be wearing prayer shawls and yarmulkes, or perhaps a Judenhut, if you want to add that delicious medieval undertone." He cocked his head. "I suppose maybe they'll even add a bit of scandalous excitement with a blood libel accusation, or bring in some Cossacks so we can re-create the Khmelnytsky Uprising. Now, *that* would be an attraction."

"You can attempt to contain your sarcasm," I said dully, but I caught the gist of what he was saying. In other words, the only time we were interesting was when we were accused of atrocities or being slaughtered in prodigious numbers.

One hundred thousand killed by Khmelnytsky's Cossack army, thousands more raped and tortured. The massacres had happened over two hundred years ago, but the wound they'd made in our cultural history was left raw and festering, like a fault line that may begin trembling again at any moment.

"Me? Contain my sarcasm?" Frankie quirked an eyebrow. "That's asking too much of me."

"Frankie, why did you come here?" I asked, after he had stilled his laughter. A horrible idea occurred to me. "Don't tell me you're working this place over?"

"That'd be a bit hard with all the Columbian Guards crawling around, wouldn't you agree?" Smirking, he nodded to a blue-uniformed man strolling down the midway. "Look at them. With how they strut about, you'd think they're the *Okhrana*, the secret police back in Russia. I wouldn't dare try anything with them around."

I remained unconvinced.

After a moment, he chuckled. "Oh, Alter, you should see your face. All right, I confess. I was on the train for work, not pleasure. This whole place is infested with cops, but not the platforms. I have the crew working them over. I'm simply there to collect." He glanced at his pocket watch. "I can't stay long. They'll be worrying where I am, and that's when mistakes get made."

I set my glass down. Just listening to him made me lose my appetite. I knew the kind of mistakes that could get made when feelings were involved. If one weren't careful, it could end in blood.

"You're shameless," I said, without much vigor. It was hard to justify judging him when I was guilty of his same crimes. True, I had tried to do teshuvah for my mistakes, but nothing would simply erase the pain I had caused.

"Shame is a word people use to try to control you." Frankie tapped his fingers against his cocoa glass. "But enough about me. Something tells me you aren't here to enjoy yourself. Unless, in your old age, this look of constipation has become your natural expression. Honestly, I can't tell."

I didn't take the bait.

"This is where you're supposed to laugh," Frankie said. "A snicker at the very least."

"It's not funny."

"Not funny?" He scoffed in disbelief. "You're just about the only Jew in Chicago without a sense of humor."

"Says the only Jew in Chicago incapable of telling a good joke." I rolled my eyes. "Now, you said Victor was found in the river?"

"Minus a few parts of him."

I choked on my cocoa. "You don't mean…?"

"No. Just that the wound was deep and messy, and he'd been in the water for a while. He'd started to float. That's how they found him. That's what happens to dead bodies, I suppose." His drumming fingers stilled, and his gaze wandered to the waterway running along the teahouse promenade. "It was over by Maxwell Street. Victor was living at a settlement house there. Before he died, he went back to the old ways, yarmulke and all."

"In other words, a good mensch," I said dryly.

"Right." Frankie smiled a little, only to sober up. "Not that being pious or a good person has ever protected anyone."

Seeing that I had finished my iced cocoa, he passed me his own glass with the unspoken expectation that I should drink the rest. I tried to push it back, but he wouldn't have it, so I took it upon myself to finish his leftovers.

As I lowered my glass, a distant blast echoed through the midway, followed by two more bangs in rapid succession. I flinched and looked around for the source of the noise. "Were those gunshots?"

"Probably from Buffalo Bill's across the street. You know how cowboys are."

No, I didn't know. But I wasn't about to admit that.

Frankie picked up the menu and gave it a cursory glance. "You should know, Victor isn't the only one who's gone missing. Just the only one who's been found."

I paused in the middle of drinking. "Wait. Have they all been Jews?"

"At least the ones I know of." He shrugged, fanning himself with the menu. "Not anyone in the crew, just friends of friends."

A ball of ice formed in the pit of my stomach. Frankie clearly saw no common pattern, but I did.

"Why're you giving me that look?" He narrowed his eyes. "What—you think someone's killing Jews now?"

"My roommate Yakov was found dead here yesterday. The police thought it was an accident, but I don't believe it. I saw his body, and he had a bruise around his throat as though he'd been strangled. That's why I came here, to investigate it. And three others have disappeared in the last couple months."

"Alter, this isn't Russia. There aren't pogroms here."

"I'm not talking about that, not anything state-sponsored."

"What then?"

"I don't know. Someone acting alone. Someone who hates us."

"This heat has gone to your head. You're talking like a meshugener."

Annoyed, I rose to my feet. "Thank you for the cocoa, but I have better things to do than sit around and let you insult me."

"Alter, wait." Frankie set aside the menu he had been fanning himself with. As I pushed back in my chair, he got up from his.

I didn't want to be here anymore. I didn't know how to explain to him that since Yakov's death, the world had turned upside down, everything going topsy-turvy like a tumble down a rabbit hole. The mikveh, the writing, and now this. This feeling in my gut, that there was something more at work here than just the two of us. Not divine providence, but...something.

"Alter." His voice softened as he touched my shoulder. "You're trembling."

I wanted so badly to lean into Frankie, lose myself in the heat and mooring strength of his body. But I brushed his hand away. All these old feelings, why did they have to come back now? Why couldn't the past just stay dead?

"I need to go back to work." I struggled to keep my voice steady.

"Your hands are freezing cold," he murmured. "Why are you so cold?"

I flinched away, chilled to the bone, as if I had one foot back in that wintry afternoon when I'd first met him. It was suffocating being here, surrounded by this noise, the surging crowds, and blinding splendor. If I stayed even a minute longer, I'd drown.

"Alter, wait," Frankie called. "I can help you."

"No, you can't." I turned and walked away, not looking back when Frankie said my name. I couldn't let him get close to me again, not after Yakov. I felt like a tornado, indiscriminately uprooting things and yanking them into my path. Nothing would ever harm me; I was the one that ruined everything around me. My father's death had proved that fact, and Yakov's had only reinforced it.

I was poison.

9

"YOU'RE GOING TO school?" Haskel asked when he saw me put my coat on the next evening. If the dark circles under his eyes were any clue, the last forty-eight hours had taken their toll on him as well. Instead of going to a saloon or dance hall with Dovid, he sat on his cot, playing game after game of solitaire. He stared at the cards as if they'd give him a glimpse into his fate.

"If I don't show up, someone else will take my seat." I buttoned my coat, averting my gaze.

I couldn't stop thinking about yesterday afternoon. After leaving Frankie, I had spent thirty minutes ducking around the Fair's outskirts, asking the workers if they'd seen Yakov on the Fourth of July. It was a complete waste of time. Nobody knew anything, and as I grew more agitated, my attempts at English dissolved into incoherence.

Even worse, Mr. Weiss gave me a scathing lecture when I showed up for work this morning, and put me to work cleaning and oiling all the presses. My palms were still stained with a dark crud of ink I'd scrubbed from the machines' crevices.

"I thought you'd be staying at home. You know, since you used to go to class with Yakov, and with him being..." Haskel trailed off, laying down another card.

Just the sound of Yakov's name made me tug my coat tighter around myself. I had been fighting with a chill ever since Yakov's death, and now my body grew even colder still, as though sleet flowed through my veins.

"I'm not sitting shiva for him," I said curtly, and stepped out the door.

The English night class was held several times a week in coordination with one of Maxwell Street's many Jewish aid organizations. It met in a classroom at the nearby high school, and it was so popular that although I arrived ten minutes early, a new student had already taken my place. When I saw the girl's face, I felt a jolt of surprise.

"That's my seat," I said as Raizel uncapped her travel inkwell.

"Is that so?" She lifted her eyebrows but made no effort to move. "Your name's not on it."

"What are you doing in a midlevel class? Don't you already know English?"

"I believe in self-improvement." She arranged her writing supplies on the desktop and opened her leather-bound journal to a blank page.

Apparently, Raizel wasn't entirely pitiless, because she scooted her chair in so I could reach the seat next to her.

"Look at us," I said, sitting down. "Mrs. Brenner would be pleased."

"Because I haven't thrown hot tea on you yet?"

"To be fair, it was only lukewarm."

"Oh, how forgiving of you." The corner of her mouth curled in a smile. "You should know, I have no intention of being anyone's angel in the house."

"I suspect your future husband will be dodging a great many teacups then."

It soothed me to banter with her. It made things feel a bit more normal.

"Perhaps I don't want a husband." She gave me a pointed look. "Perhaps I plan to keep cats as children."

I chuckled. "You'll break Mrs. Brenner's heart. I think she's intent on collecting a broker's commission from the both of us."

Raizel cocked her head, her gaze inquisitive. "And what do you want, Alter?"

Her direct question took me aback. We had reached a crossroads. This conversation could go two ways now. Two different directions, two different futures.

I knew what she expected to hear, but I couldn't bring myself to say it.

"I'd rather we just be friends," I muttered, preparing for the worst. I was shocked when a bright smile spread across her face, an almost *knowing* smile, as though we were linked by a shared solidarity.

"Ah, I had a feeling," she said. "So much for being able to read the future."

"What?"

Raizel cocked her head. "You don't know? Mrs. Brenner does palm and forehead readings on the side."

"You can't be serious."

"Haven't you wondered about why she gets so many visitors during odd hours?"

"I thought they were her matchmaking clients."

"She's very serious about it. Next time you visit, ask to see her copy of the *Khokhmes Hayad*." Raizel smirked. "She claims it's some medieval palm-reading guide, but I think it's just something she bought from a traveling kabbalist back in the old country."

Class progressed as usual. The teacher, Mrs. Spektor, had a name befitting her appearance. Tall and bony, with hair the same chilly gray as her eyes, she hovered over the class like a vengeful spirit. She would speak only English, gesturing or miming to give us hints, if she was feeling generous.

Mrs. Spektor wrote the new vocabulary words over the faded sketches of algebra lessons. The lines of numbers made me envious. I would have liked to come here during the daytime hours when the classes were in session, surrounded by boys my age, American boys with their open smiles and boisterous voices. I'd never have that opportunity, but it came as a bittersweet relief to know that my sisters would.

I wrote down the new words and tried my hand at translation when Mrs. Spektor called on me, but I couldn't focus. My hand was cramping badly, and my fountain pen kept swerving off course.

"Do you have a spare pen?" I asked Raizel.

"Why?"

"There's something wrong with mine." I wiped the nib on a cloth and tried again, but it was no better. The letters were coming out strange and blockish, neither English cursive nor the German-style *Kurrent* script I had been taught years ago by my tutor.

"Can I see?" she asked.

I handed the pen to her.

She tried it on her paper, examined the nib, and then shook her head. "Looks fine to me."

"No, the letters are all wrong." But I tried again once she handed the pen back to me, and this time the cursive flowed out the way I had been taught. "Huh. Maybe there was a blockage."

"Maybe you shouldn't try writing with your left hand," Raizel said blandly.

"I wasn't."

She gave me a strange look. Oh. She hadn't meant to be taken seriously. I sighed and turned my attention back to the chalkboard. Frankie would be glad to know he wasn't the only Jew in Chicago incapable of telling a good joke.

"So, what are you doing here really?" I asked, when Raizel answered the third question in a row, drawing envious glances from the other students. I spoke softly, to avoid earning another acidic look from Mrs. Spektor. "You can't be hoping to learn anything today."

She had been tapping her pen end against her cheek and stopped. "The advanced class meets at the other end of the building. It was canceled unexpectedly, so I came here."

"Canceled? Was your teacher sick?" Maybe I wasn't the only one feeling unwell lately.

"No, it had something to do with Mrs. Strauss's husband. He delivers ice down at the Stockyards. I suppose with the unrest that's going on, a striker accidentally caused his horse to spook."

"The unrest?"

"There's always unrest, of course, but the strikes have become particularly bad. I've heard that there's going to be walkouts any day now. There's even been talk that the Pinkerton Agency is going to be called in like they were in Pittsburgh last year."

She meant the Homestead Strike, which had ended in a shootout that left over a dozen men dead. I remembered how tense everyone had been after the news broke. For me, it had been just another sign that America was not the goldene medina my father had envisioned.

"I'm glad you're here," I said, turning in my seat to face her.

"There's actually something I'd like to ask you about. I know you've written articles for the *Arbeiter-Zeitung*."

"Under a pen name, but yes. I even got an opinion piece published in the *Freiheit* last September." Her voice swelled with pride. Based in New York, the *Freiheit* was even more notorious than the *Arbeiter-Zeitung* in its calls for revolution.

"I was wondering if—"

At the front of the room, Mrs. Spektor whacked her pointer against the desk.

"Mr. Rosen." Her voice was as wooden as the pointer she wielded. "If you must insist on talking in class, may I suggest you continue your conversation outside?"

With a meaningful look in my direction, Raizel gathered her things, rose to her feet, and left the room. I sat there for a moment longer, petrified in embarrassment, before following after her with my head ducked down.

Raizel waited for me outside, twisting her chin-length hair between her fingers. After the disastrous matchmaking attempt, Mrs. Brenner had gossiped to me that Raizel's parents had cut her hair short at a physician's advice, due to a touch of brain fever. But I had a feeling that brain fever might've just been another way of saying uncooperative, or outspoken, or brilliant. I had a suspicion she might have even cut it herself, considering the raggedy edges.

"Took your sweet time, didn't you?" she said. "I thought you'd stay in there forever."

"I was tempted to," I assured her, earning a hint of a smile.

Just by talking without a chaperone present, we were committing a social taboo. Still, something about this felt right. Felt proper. As a child, I had many friends who were girls, but somewhere along the way, new expectations had been enforced and I had been taught to keep my distance. It had always struck me as wrong, for a reason I couldn't articulate. Maybe this had been the right way all along.

"So, what were you going to say before Mrs. Spektor banished us from the classroom?" Raizel asked.

"The police don't care about the disappearances, but if we can stir up some public outrage, maybe that will inspire them to look into it."

"Good luck doing that."

"I mean it. I want to write an article about Yakov's death and the disappearances that have been happening on Maxwell Street. Like you said, it's too much of a coincidence that three boys from our tenement disappeared within the last two months. And it's not just them. Another boy I knew was found dead a few weeks ago. Stabbed. And then with Yakov..."

"You volunteer at the chevra kadisha, right? Did you see something that might suggest Yakov's death wasn't an accident?"

"He had bruises on his body." My hand lifted to my collar as though drawn by muscle memory. I loosened my ribbon tie to hide the gesture. "And a mark upon his throat, as though he had been strangled."

Raizel mulled it over. "Aaron was active with me in labor. For a while now, he'd been talking about getting a story published at the *Arbeiter-Zeitung*. He thought that if he could write just one article, it would open doors for him at the Socialist Labor Party or International Working People's Association. He thought he'd become famous and go on tours around the country. That he'd be like Daniel De Leon, the party's National Lecturer."

"For someone so famous, I've never heard of this De Leon person."

She gave me a withering look. "That's because you'd rather read about challah recipes and Torah dedications than pull your head out of the dirt. Mr. De Leon edits *The People* in New York—"

"Never heard of that one either."

"—but he's also been a lecturer at Columbia College and an attorney."

"You sound like you really admire him. Don't tell me you're aiming to be the next National Lecturer?"

"Very funny." She huffed. "My point is that even if Aaron had managed to get an article published, it isn't as though it'd earn him points with the SLP. I tried to tell him this, but he wouldn't listen. Anyway, a few days before Aaron disappeared, he kept telling me that he was following a story. Something that would really earn the editors' respect."

"What kind of story?"

"Nothing involving the labor movement, so it would never be published. It seemed so foolish when he first told me about it. It had something to do with the body parts they've found washed ashore Lake Michigan these last few months. You've heard about it, haven't you?"

"I saw an article in an English newspaper, but I couldn't understand all of it." I adjusted the brim of my cap, my lingering anxiety giving way to a slight discomfort at being out here in the open where anyone could see us. "I haven't really been paying attention to the news lately. With work and everything…"

I expected Raizel to make a quip about capitalism, but instead, she said, "Alter, are you familiar with Jack the Ripper?"

Her question took me aback. "I've heard of him, of course. Who hasn't?"

When my father and I had passed through Bucharest on our way to America, the Ripper had been the talk of the capital. A serial killer in London, preying on women. Dismemberment. Mutilations. Organs missing. Most of his known victims had been butchered outdoors, but I also remembered reading about torsos and limbs washing ashore the Thames. The killings had ended in 1891, nearly two years ago, but the killer had never been found.

"Aaron thought that someone was re-creating the Jack the Ripper killings," she said. "I tried telling him how foolish it was. I mean, most likely those body parts are just from bad business down in the Levee. The Valley Gang or the like. But he wouldn't let it go. He was fixated on it. He had heard of a place down in the Levee, somewhere called the Whitechapel Club. Whitechapel was the part of London where the Ripper's victims were found."

"The Whitechapel Club," I echoed. The name taunted me. I could have sworn I had heard about it before, during my time in Frankie's circle. My memories of that year were a revolving world of dark alleyways and breezy rooftops, dingy taverns and dance halls. But there were some places even Frankie refused to go.

"Personally, I thought it was just another journalist's legend. But if the Whitechapel Club really does exist, it would be one of the last places Aaron visited before his disappearance." She scowled at the wall. "I just wish there was someone who knew where to find it."

I took a deep breath. "I think I know someone who does."

10

THERE WAS ONLY one place Frankie would be on a night like this, and that was the Levee District cradling the city's southern edge, a labyrinth of saloons, dance halls, and brothels. It was where it had all started for me, and where I had ended things.

Though dusk hadn't yet unfurled into night, clusters of people gathered under eaves and in doorways, their faces lost to the gloom and weak gaslight. There was something solemn and reverent about the way they huddled within those shadowed niches, their voices soft enough to be indistinct, as though they were praying in tabernacles.

As I passed a boisterous group of workers released from their assembly lines, I yanked down the brim of my newsboy cap, afraid someone would recognize me.

I had spent the last year trying so hard to re-create myself, just being seen by an old pal would feel like bridging a dangerous gap between my current self and who I'd once been. Same for running across a member of my shul, although I doubted any of them planned to spend their evening in Chicago's decadent underbelly.

I broke away from the crowd. Down streets, through alleys, my palm pressed over my nose to block out the nauseating odors rising from trash heaps. At the end of an alley, when my route was cut off by a heap of crates and half-rotten lumber, I climbed a ladder to the roof.

Like any warren, the Levee had passageways known only to its inhabitants. The buildings were placed so closely together, it was easy to leap from rooftop to rooftop or race across rickety planks stretched over alleyways. During my first year in Chicago, I had become well-acquainted with this skyward route.

Finding solid ground on the level above, I wasn't surprised when I spotted a lit lantern several rooftops down. I studied the buildings around me, refamiliarizing myself. Some roofs were fitted with new chimneys or water towers, while other structures had fallen into further ruin. Still, even in the mounting darkness, I was able to pinpoint where I was and where I needed to go.

Squatting around their lantern, a young boy and girl startled when I landed beside them at the brink of the rooftop. A small treasure trove was scattered at their feet—pocket watches, coins, jewelry. As the girl scooped up her finds, the boy rose to his feet. I seized his wrist before he could bolt.

"Wait," I said in English as he tried to pull away. "Calm down, I'm no cop."

Once the kid stopped moving, I let go of him. He backed up, rubbing his arm warily. His friend shoveled their spoils into a burlap sack.

"Do you speak English?" I asked. "German? Yiddish?"

The girl and boy exchanged looks. They couldn't be older than thirteen.

"What do you want?" the girl in the mariner's cap asked in Yiddish. Her accent was tauntingly familiar.

"You're from Romania," I said.

She narrowed her eyes. "What's it to you?"

"Are you from Piatra Neamţ?"

"No. Fălticeni."

Fălticeni. The town was less than eighty kilometers from Piatra Neamţ. My family had traveled there twice for the annual trade fair, perched in a creaking wagon amid bolts of cotton and crepe. It was like a punch to the gut, knowing that a girl born there could end up a common pickpocket in the slums of the Levee. It made me feel as though my encounter with Frankie's crew hadn't been some freak accident, but predestined. That it had been written in the soil of Romania long before I was born.

"What's your name?" I asked.

"Bailey," she said, which probably meant that it had once been something like Baila or Bine.

"Are you with Frankie?"

The attic his pickpocketing crew rented could be accessed through the roof of this building. In the past, I had regularly gathered here with the others.

Looking back at those days, I was both appalled and impressed by how bold I had been, how risky, intoxicated by life on the edge. Frankie didn't know it, but he had given me more than just a means of surviving my first year in this city. He had been an anesthetic, a way to numb the pain of my father's death as well as any laudanum. And whenever I had stolen something, it was as though I had been transferring a bit of that grief to others, until the only time I felt alive was when I had stolen coins spilling from my hands.

All things had to end, and my time with Frankie's crew had been no different. The night I left him, he inadvertently showed me the truth about what it meant to survive in his world. It wasn't just running, excitement, or numbing myself with the thrill of the hunt. Sometimes, it meant staining one's hands with another man's blood.

"How do you know Frankie?" Bailey asked.

"We're friends. Can you tell me where he is?"

"He doesn't sleep here anymore. He says he needs to maintain appearances."

Considering the amount of money Frankie had invested in his new wardrobe, that didn't surprise me. For him, it had always been an upward climb. "You know where I can find him?"

"What's it worth to you?"

"Do I look like I have any money?"

Bailey glanced down at my clothes and sighed. "I'll bet all you have in your pockets are mothballs."

I winced inwardly. That wasn't too far from the truth. "Nu? You going to tell me where I can find him?"

"Oh, fine. He's probably at a place over on South Dearborn, called the Masthead."

"Is that a gentlemen's club?"

"There's nothing very gentlemanly about it," she said cryptically. "It's a big brownstone building with an old figurehead over the door. You can't miss it."

As the two thieves descended the fire escape, I called down to them, "If you want to find honest work, go to Hull House on Halsted Street. They'll be able to help you."

Neither one answered, or if they did, the howling wind drowned out their responses. I picked up their lantern and smothered the flame.

Against the ink-black expanse of Lake Michigan, lightning bolts rippled through the clouds like strange currents. This world was so much larger than I had once thought. I felt swallowed by its vastness. As the lightning faded into darkness, I descended the fire escape and continued on my way.

11

NEARLY AN HOUR later, I found myself at the doorstep of a stately two-story brownstone. True to Bailey's word, the lintel above the door was adorned with a figurehead carved as a mermaid, flakes of green peeling from her tail.

"Excuse me, but is this the Masthead?" I asked the man smoking a pipe on the front steps.

As the man turned to me, the gaslight fell upon his face. I winced involuntarily. He had a shaved head that looked like it had been used as a stickball one too many times.

"What's it to you?" The light glinted off his war-scape of a mouth; half his teeth were missing, the rest broken or capped in silver. "You know the word? Huh?"

"What word?"

"Bug off." He made a swatting motion with his hand.

I refused to budge. "I'm looking for Frankie Portnoy."

"I told you to bug off, before I do you a hard one."

I didn't know what a hard one was, and I wasn't very eager to find out.

"Fine, fine." I lifted my hands, backing away. "I'm leaving."

As I trudged off, I felt his gaze boring into me. I continued down the street, waiting until I was out of his sight before turning the corner and approaching the building from the other side.

I entered the alley that stretched alongside the Masthead. Empty bottles, bins of rubbish, crates. There was a locked door and a window cracked open, wisps of fragrant steam curling from the gap. I stopped by the window, breathing in the scents of stale beer and roasted meat. Low voices, the clatter of porcelain and metal. A kitchen.

Stepping away from the door, I studied the rest of the wall. About three meters up, there was a window.

I dragged one of the crates over and upturned it on its side, spilling out mounds of sodden wood shavings. As I clambered onto the crate, it shook and groaned beneath my weight. I pressed my palms against the wall, steadying myself, before testing the window above.

The pane creaked open when I pushed on it. I crawled through the opening and landed in a heap on the floor two meters below. I stumbled to my feet, rubbing my sore butt. No shouts of alarm or running guards. The noises from the kitchen must have drowned out the sound of my entry.

The corridor's walls were a deep forest green adorned with maple wainscoting. Amber-glass shades softened the gaslights. The hall opened up into a large room, where gentlemen sat smoking at lounges and seats. I stood afar, conscious of my worn clothes. What in the world was this place?

A bell rang.

"Ten minutes until showtime," a man with a white mustache announced from his seat by the hearth. He gave two more prim rings of his handbell. "Are all your bets placed, gentlemen? Hmm? Any last-minute wagers?"

More money exchanged hands. The mustached man was

collecting cash and writing down names. I didn't have to count the bills myself to realize that they were betting the equivalent of my monthly paycheck.

Gentlemen were rising now, drifting in a cloud of cigar smoke toward the same threshold where I stood. I backed away as they entered. The men paid no more mind to me than if I had been a ghost, and when I followed them down the corridor, no one asked me what I was doing in this place.

Maybe it was my clothing that offered me this rare invisibility. With the tassels of my tzitzis tucked into my pants and my newsboy cap pulled low, I was indistinguishable from any Christian. These men passed a thousand like me every day—the nameless doormen, the scrawny bootblacks, the chimney sweeps, and newsboys, and lamplighters—and they were so used to us, that we had become a part of the scenery.

At the rear of the building, a door led into the cellar below. The stairs creaked beneath my feet. A medley of unpleasant odors hung in the stuffy air—rotten teeth, sweat, stale beer, cigar smoke, animal piss. Gaslights illuminated a large brick chamber centered around a sunken stage of the sort used for rat-baiting and cockfighting. Except, instead of roosters or rats, the entertainment of the night appeared to be human.

Two young men faced each other in the ring, both barefoot and shirtless. I froze at the edge of the crowd, stunned.

The gaslight burned harsh on Frankie's face, stoking a fire in his tawny eyes and carving his features into cruel angles. Our gazes met only for a moment, but long enough for his opponent to lunge forward.

The other boy took a swing at Frankie, clipping his shoulder and sending him staggering back.

Frankie regained his balance and began circling the boy once more. His motions were smooth and effortless, refined, as though he were dancing a waltz. The boy made another lunge for him, but Frankie dodged the blow and delivered a punch of his own.

A coarse gurgling breath pushed from the boy's mouth. Reeling back, he spat out a bloody froth and a broken tooth onto the sawdust-strewn floor.

The other boy had several centimeters on Frankie, but Frankie had the lithe, compact build and ruthlessness of a Carpathian lynx. I quickly realized he relied on swiftness and ferocity to even the playing field. Before the boy could recover from the first strike, Frankie had already hit him a second time, then a third, pummeling his face.

I flinched with each blow, recalling the night I left him and the burglary job that had gone terribly wrong. It had been a different man Frankie had beaten, first with the butt of a revolver and then with his fists, but the sounds had been the same. The steady thud of knuckles striking flesh, the groans and ragged gasps, the scuffle of feet on the floor. I shivered.

On the fourth blow, his opponent crashed to the floor of the pit, adding to the dried bloodstains of his predecessors.

Frankie stepped back, his chiseled chest rising and falling in steady breaths. Blood flecked his knuckles, but it was not his own. As the dim, humid space filled with booing and shouts of triumph, Frankie met my gaze again and challenged me with a smirk.

I didn't smile back. I wished I'd never sought him out at all.

As he climbed out of the pit, I stepped to the corner of the room. He appeared to be in no hurry to join me, and instead spent the next five minutes mingling with the patrons, basking in the glow of his victory. He spoke to men. He shook hands. Several gave him calling cards, which he slipped into his pants pocket. Just when I thought he intended to ignore me entirely, he strolled over.

"Come with me," Frankie said quietly. We walked up the

stairs, back into the dim corridor, and up a second narrow stairway to the floor above. He pushed me through the first door we came across, which led into an empty billiard room.

"I have an hour until my next match." After lighting the gas lamps, Frankie walked over to the counter, where a decanter sat on a silver tray. He splashed some liquor into two tumblers, returned to my side, and handed me one.

"L'chaim," he toasted. To life.

"L'chaim," I echoed reluctantly, and tapped my glass against his.

He took a sip. "Try it. It's Kentucky bourbon."

I sampled the liquor. Just a nip was enough to sting my throat. When I set the glass on the counter, he lifted his brows.

"Too much for you?" he asked, polishing off his tumbler.

"I don't like it."

"You have no taste at all. I bet all you drink is kiddush wine." Frankie poured some more bourbon into his tumbler, took a sip, reconsidered. The cut crystal chimed as he set it down. He had smeared bloody fingerprints across the glass. "So, what are you doing here? With the way you ran off yesterday, I thought you wanted nothing to do with me."

"You've got blood on you."

"Well, don't just stare." He wiped his hands on the seat of his pants. "Speak up. How did you find me?"

"I went back to our old place. You're recruiting girls now?" It shouldn't have made a difference, but all I could think of was my own sisters. I never wanted them to live the life that I had.

"That's correct," Frankie said smoothly, with not an ounce of shame. "Oh, don't give me that look. You know, when I found Bailey, she was working in a brothel. They had taken her clothes so that she wouldn't leave. Can you imagine the horror of that, Alter? The humiliation? The despair?"

His stark questions caught me in a stranglehold. My cheeks burned. I felt like a foolish child.

"No, of course you can't." He answered his own question with a charming smile. "Ah…forgive me. This conversation is too uncouth for someone like you. You come from a good family, a good upbringing. You weren't born into this life; you fell down into it, your family's fortune gone in an instant, like something out of a bubbe-meise. Isn't that right?"

He maintained his calm demeanor, but his voice held a hint of venom. I felt myself shrink under his hooded gaze, all my words evaporating in an instant. I wished I could be like him, that I could wield my voice as brutally as a weapon. But I was so taken aback, I couldn't even respond.

"That's what I thought," Frankie said curtly, like a killing blow. "I never ask them to give anything away. Only take. And I have a code of honor. You have no right to judge me for what I do."

He was right. How could I judge him? Over and over, I had seen the truth on the washing table—this goldene medina demanded you to sacrifice your body. You must bleed to live here; you must give your sweat and tears. Then once Chicago had gorged itself on your suffering and sucked you down to the marrow, it would leave you for dead.

"I'm not here to judge you, Frankie," I said shakily, finding my voice.

"Then to what do I owe this pleasure?" Frankie asked, crossing his arms over his bare chest. The gaslights caught the gleam of sweat on his skin, accentuating the composed lines of his muscles, the steady rise and fall of his breast. "I don't suppose you're here to gamble?"

"No, I came here to ask for help. I've heard that there's a place somewhere in the Levee. Something called the Whitechapel Club. Have you ever heard of it?"

His eyes narrowed in recognition. "Whitechapel Club, you say?"

A spark of excitement rose inside me. "You know it?"

"I've been there," he purred, a dangerous light entering his eyes. He leaned forward, his breath tickling the side of my neck. "It's not this kind of club, to put it lightly. I have no desire to go back there."

"Can you tell me where I can find it?"

"I don't know, you sure you want to go? A good mensch like yourself ought to stick to something a bit more, dare I say, kosher."

"Frankie, I'm serious."

"If you want to know more, you're going to have to earn it, boychik."

"How—"

He placed his hand on my chest and pushed me back. It wasn't hard enough to make me fall, only stagger. With a wicked grin, he pivoted on his heel and rushed through the open door, calling over his shoulder, "You're going to have to catch me."

He hadn't changed at all. But I supposed that I hadn't changed much either, because I took off after him, yanking down the brim of my cap to keep it from flying off in the chase. By the time I entered the corridor, he had already reached its end. I followed him through a second door and up another stairway, bursting through the rooftop hatch.

Frankie stood on the roof ledge. He tsked at the sight of me. "You're going to have to do better than that."

"I thought you said you had another match in an hour," I panted. "Come on, Frankie. Get down from there. Just tell me what you know."

Instead, he leaped. I ran to the ledge. Wood groaned in protest as he raced across a narrow board bridging this rooftop to the next. No surprise. With an illegal gambling den in the basement, even gentlemen needed to be able to make a quick getaway.

As I reached the board, I found it old and weathered. It shifted beneath my feet as I tested it. I grimaced, stumbling back onto solid ground. The street below was a ten-meter drop.

"Don't tell me you're scared," Frankie teased from the other rooftop.

"Haha, go jump in the lake."

"Rude as ever, I see. So much for being a good mensch."

Slowly, I lowered myself onto the board. I eased across, spreading my arms to keep my balance. To think, just a year ago I would have followed him fearlessly, exhilarated and breathless each time the board groaned beneath me.

Back then, each time I had put my life on the line, it had felt like an exchange. I was putting myself in danger so that my sisters remained safe. I bled and bruised myself so that they didn't have to. All shtuss, of course. Now, I realized that deep down it was just another way to run from my total powerlessness in the face of death.

By the time I reached the other building, my legs were quivering so violently, I had to grasp hold of the ledge to steady myself. Once both my feet were on solid ground, I took an unsteady breath. The summer breeze riffled my clothes, chilling the sweat that beaded on the nape of my neck.

"Coming?" Frankie called, leaning against the chimney.

I followed.

At the next building, there was no plank at all, only a treacherous crevice that plunged into the alley below. The roof was built with an overhang, so that a narrow gap separated the two buildings. Less than two meters. I could manage that.

Following Frankie's example, I took a running leap. One

foot caught on the edge, while the other landed in empty air. I began to tip back. Blind with panic, I spread my arms, started to fall, would have fallen if Frankie hadn't seized a fistful of my shirt and yanked me forward. He hauled me over the edge, taking the brunt of my weight. We crashed against the rooftop in a tangle of limbs.

Kneeling over me, he smiled. His palm rested flat against my chest, hot like a brand. "Careful, boychik. You've lost your touch."

My shock gave way to anger. How could I be so stupid to follow him? How could he be so damn stupid to make me do this?

I gave him a violent shove with both hands, sending him onto his ass. As I stood, I smacked dust off the seat of my pants.

He rose to his feet with a stupid grin. "No gratitude, huh?"

"Gratitude?" My lips were numb and trembling. I could hardly speak. "You nearly got us both killed!"

"I didn't make you follow." He pushed his hair out of his face, his smile fading. "Look, I wasn't thinking. I just thought you'd enjoy it, pretending like things were the way they once were."

His admission pierced at something inside me. The anger drained from me in an instant, replaced by a deep sadness. "We can never go back to that, Frankie."

"I know." He wouldn't meet my eye.

"So, where is it?" I asked. "Where can I find the Whitechapel Club?"

"I'm not going to tell you, Alter. I'm going to take you there."

His words caught me off guard. My cheeks grew hot, my mind dizzy, like I was still toeing the ledge.

"It's not as though I *want* to go," he said, as though it had been my idea all along. "I have better things to do than escort you around the Levee. But now that you've gone clean, I'd hate for you to ruin your good sensibilities."

"Frankie, don't tell me you're worried about me?" I said, as payback. "That you want to protect me?"

Even the darkness couldn't hide the blush that colored his cheeks. He averted his gaze.

"Someone needs to. Besides, we won't be able to get in there without an invitation, and I know just who to ask." He took out his pocket watch and lit a match to read the dial. "Let's go back. I need to prepare for my next fight."

"I can't believe you make a living from beating people all day." I gave it some thought. "Actually, no, on second thought, I can."

He rolled his eyes. "It's not all day. It's several nights a week, and besides, it's only a stepping-stone. A side gig, as the Americans would say."

"Don't tell me you're stealing from the betting pool?"

Frankie looked unamused.

"I don't shit where I eat. What I do is take names and cards. I shake people's hands. I gamble and bet on other matches, and on the weekends, I go with my manager or the high rollers down to the races. I'm building a network, Alter. But it's…it's this damn accent." He shook his head in disgust. "I've tried so hard to get rid of it, but whenever I speak English, it comes through. Most don't know what it is—they don't acquaint themselves with the people down on Maxwell Street—so I tell them I'm Russian, and they don't question it. But they still know I'm not one of them. And that means they don't trust me. More important, they don't see me as an equal."

I knew that feeling all too well. Even at the office of the *Idisher Kuryer*, there was a power imbalance, and it wasn't just between press boys and editors. Most of the high-rank-ing editors and journalists had come to America many years ago. Some were even born here. I often heard them talk with disdain about the flood of immigrants from the east. They thought we were stuck in the old ways and unwilling to assimilate, when really, it was just a question of how much we were willing to give up to become American, and how fast.

I had never thought coming here would require me to sacrifice parts of myself. I wished my father had given me warning. I wanted to ask him what he would have done.

"If they don't trust you, then why do you take their cards?" I narrowed my eyes. "What exactly do you do for them?"

"Sometimes a lack of trust is a good thing. It means you don't have to get close to a person. See, it's not what I'm doing now, it's what I plan to do in the future. There are more ways to make money in the Levee than petty thievery, and people like them—" he jerked his chin in the direction of the Masthead "—the makhers, the bigwigs, they have the dirtiest consciences of them all. But they don't like to soil their hands, understand?"

I decided it would be better not to ask him what he meant by that, although I had a good idea. Provided his code of honor hadn't changed in the last ten months, blackmailing, corporate sabotage, and racketeering would still be fair game. Then again, considering how we had ended things after he'd beaten an innocent homeowner bloody, I wouldn't be surprised if he'd progressed to breaking kneecaps for profit.

I hated that I'd come back here. This would be the last time. I swore that to myself. One more night with Frankie, and after that, I'd cut him out of my life, and I'd never step foot in the Levee again.

Instead of risking another plunge, Frankie picked up a board leaning against the roof's low wall and positioned it over the gap. He gave the wood a slap for good measure, deemed it solid, and crossed over. Once he reached the other side, he held the board steady for me, with no teasing this time. It had begun to drizzle.

As I reached the Masthead's rooftop, Frankie gave a cursory glance down at my clothes. When he had seized my shirt to save me from falling, the front two tassels of my tzitzis had slipped from my pants.

"If you're going to wear tzitzis when we go to the Whitechapel Club, tuck the tassels in," he said.

"I planned to."

"And wear something nice." He lifted an eyebrow. "Do you have something nice?"

"Since when did you become such a dandy?" I asked sourly.

"Since I became tired of being looked at like trash." He smiled, but it was merely a muscle contraction. There was no humor in his eyes. "I realized something after you left, Alter. Appearances mean everything. In fact, they're the only important thing. They always have been. If it's wearing a nice suit and a golden watch, even a monster could walk among us."

12

BACK WHEN I had first come to Chicago, Frankie had made it his mission to acquaint me with the city. He had dragged me on foot from the ice-encrusted sprawl of Lake Michigan to the slaughterhouse district, which bustled with life even in the dead of winter. But it was Prairie Avenue and the Gold Coast that enthralled him the most, wealthy neighborhoods we were chased from with slurs and snobby looks.

At first, I had been thrilled by the city's vastness. But over time, I had come to miss the familiarity and sense of security I had known back in Piatra Neamţ. At least here on Maxwell Street, there was something akin to it.

The chevra kadisha was dark at this hour. Two doors down, I reached the new shul scheduled to open by summer's end, a two-story structure of wood with a pitched roof, skeletal as though burnt. The windows were like gouged eyes. I shivered as I passed, drawing my coat tighter around myself to keep out the rain and the cold.

Over the roar of the storm, I thought I heard footsteps and glanced over my shoulder. Darkness behind me, darkness ahead, the gas lamps sputtering in their glass cradles. Angry at myself for allowing the night to unsettle me like a child, I wiped the water from my face and continued walking.

"You're just imagining things," I muttered under my breath.

The quiet clatter of boot heels against cobblestones. I swiveled around and stared down the blackened street, searching the night for a silhouetted figure. It wasn't my imagination. Those *had* been footsteps.

"Who's there?" I called, my heart beating faster than I cared to admit. "I know you're out there. Show yourself!"

Back the way I had come, a shadow freed itself from the surrounding gloom. Slowly, it materialized into broad shoulders, a face shadowed by a tugged-down cap. It was too dark to make out the man's face, but he was heading straight toward me.

I rooted my feet to the ground, waiting for him to pass. Twenty meters became eighteen meters became fifteen. The rain and darkness conspired to hide his features. It could have been anyone under there.

Ten meters.

Sudden dread welled inside me, and my mouth went dry. My blood turned ice-cold. If I stayed here, something terrible was going to happen to me. If I even got a *look* at him, it would destroy me.

Eight meters.

Someone was standing behind me. I didn't see the person, but I could feel their presence, the way the air parted around their body. Warm breath prickled the damp skin on my neck.

"Run," Yakov whispered in my ear. I swiveled around, but he wasn't there. Of course he wasn't.

The footsteps were louder now, harder. The man was running.

I didn't look back. I broke into a dead sprint.

Through the rain, through the night. My lungs ached from exertion after the first two hundred meters, but I forced myself to push on. I took the alleys and side streets, falling back on my old habits. The dimness of these narrow places would hide me.

After ten months living on Maxwell Street, I knew my way around. But it was different at night. The neighborhood became darker, a labyrinth of clotheslines, rusty fire escapes, and brick walls. In the peripherals of my vision, the Hebrew letters on signs seemed to change, distorting into an alphabet I had never learned. Мясник over a grimy storefront, Аптека over another. When I looked back to make sure I was in the right neighborhood, the illusion was broken.

After I was certain I had lost the man, I stopped running and traced my way back to my tenement. When I passed a half-finished wall, I picked a brick from the scatter and carried it at my side, reassured by the block's weight and heft.

The gaslight had been kept burning inside the entry hall. Its brightness drew me like a lighthouse beacon. As I fumbled to unlock the front door, I glanced over my shoulder to make sure I was still alone. No sign of him.

I pocketed my keys and hurried inside, colliding with another person in the process. I veered back before realizing who it was. Dropping the bag she held, Mrs. Brenner reached out to steady me.

"I'm sorry," I said, mortified as she leaned down to scoop up the scatter of potato peels and marrow bones that had fallen from her sack. I bent down to help her, but the scent of burnt grease sent me reeling, my palm pressed over my mouth. No, not grease. It was a sickly sweet stench, like singed hair, something melted and blackened.

"Are you all right?" Mrs. Brenner asked. "Alter, you're shaking."

"*Ya v poryad*—" The words came out without thinking, strange syllables I couldn't make sense of. I caught myself mid-word, tried again, nauseous with a terror I couldn't name: "Yes. I'm fine. Thank you, but really, I'm fine."

She stepped toward the door.

"Wait!"

She looked back.

"Don't go out there." My face felt hot and feverish. My lips trembled so violently, I could hardly speak. "I think there's someone out there."

Mrs. Brenner furrowed her brow. "Someone?"

"Please, just don't go."

She hesitated. "I suppose I'll throw them out tomorrow morning."

I nodded, relieved. We walked up to the third-floor corridor. I kept my eyes on the floor throughout it all, rubbing my throat. The skin felt bruised and tender.

"Alter, why don't you come in for a cup of tea?" Mrs. Brenner asked once we reached her door.

"Thank you, but I have work tomorrow."

She held the door for me. "I insist." Her tone was firm and no-nonsense.

I couldn't argue when she spoke that way to me. It made me think of my own mother.

Mrs. Brenner's apartment was tiny but fastidiously neat, with the majority of its space devoted to a table that seated six, and a stool for her to perch on when she orchestrated match-making meetings. She kept a photograph of her dead husband on the windowsill, beside the braided horsehair basket that was a gift from her son. Max had gone west to seek his fortune, and upon her blouse collar, Mrs. Brenner bore proof of his success—a tiny nugget of raw gold fashioned into a stickpin.

As I sat at her table, she put the rubbish sack in a covered dish to dissuade the rats and roaches. She cleaned her hands at the washbasin, then ladled some stew from the pot cooling on the potbelly stove.

"I'm afraid I don't have tea," she said. "But I do have cholent."

"You don't have to," I said as she fixed a bowl. "I've already eaten dinner."

"Nonsense. When was the last time you had a good meal?"

Steam wafted from the pot's contents—a thick, hearty stew of barley, beans, and potatoes, studded with chunks of brisket and sausage. The cholent would have cooked all afternoon and evening, until the flavors merged into a rich, savory medley.

She scarcely had time to place the bowl of cholent in front of me before I snatched up my spoon and dug in, seized by a desire I couldn't name. It wasn't hunger, not really, just the primal need to feel my mouth move, to cut the tender meat against my teeth, to have the still-hot grain warm my throat. To be alive.

"Easy now." Mrs. Brenner laughed. "Don't choke."

I finished chewing and swallowed. "It's delicious. It tastes like home."

Strange how that worked. I had tried plenty of cholent since washing up on Maxwell Street, and no matter the difference in taste or ingredients, it always reminded me of Shabbos mornings.

She ladled another helping into my bowl. "Well, eat up. There is plenty more, and it won't keep long."

Eating allowed me to think. So much had happened in the last couple days that my thoughts were scattered. As for these strange episodes, they were the product of grief, the kind that teetered dangerously close to madness. I needed to remind myself, for days after my father had passed, I had often seen him slipping through the inky depths in the ship's wake, still shrouded in the sheets the sailors had wrapped him in.

Mrs. Brenner watched me with a small, thoughtful smile. "Alter, I believe that names have significance, both the ones we are given and the ones we give ourselves. Tell me, do you know my name?"

I paused between bites. "Uh…"

"I mean my first name."

I was too embarrassed to admit I had forgotten, so I drew a name from my head. "Bluma?"

She arched her eyebrows. "Do I look like a Bluma to you?"

I spooned more cholent into my mouth, thinking better than to confess she reminded me of a walking sunflower with her yellow wardrobe.

"It's Alte," she said.

I choked on my food. "Alte?"

"Yes." Her smile thinned. In the glow of the oil lamp, her eyes were as dark as jet, with the same mirrored sheen. "I imagine our births were rather similar, except that on the same night I came into this world, the Angel of Death took my mother from it. Ever since then, I've had a gift."

"A gift," I echoed blankly, then recalled what Raizel had told me in class. "You don't mean… You really read palms?"

"That's only a facet of it. I don't normally read the fortunes of men, but…" She held out her hand, palm up. Her expectation was abundantly clear.

Palm-reading was all superstitious narishkeyt she should have left behind in the old country. And yet… If she did have some kind of gift, what would she see in the lines on my hand?

Thief. Dishonorable son. Shanda.

I laid down my spoon and rose to my feet. "It's very kind of you to offer, but it's nearly midnight and I need to get up early."

As I began to turn away, she seized my wrist. In any other situation, it would have been considered a bold transgression.

"Your lifeline is branched," she whispered.

"I said, I don't want to do this!" I tore my hand away, suddenly nauseated. The stench had returned, muddling my thoughts. Scorched meat. Scorched skin. I thought of the shreds of gray stringy beef floating in the stew, and I wanted to retch.

"Alter," Mrs. Brenner said pleadingly, reaching out to me. "Please, wait. Just listen to me. When I opened the door to you yesterday morning, I saw that a darkness had crept over you. I thought it was grief, but it's different now, Alter. It's spreading."

Oy gevalt, she was utterly meshuge. Before she could say more, I wished her a hasty good-night and fled the room. As I fumbled to unlock my door, I glanced back, half-certain I'd find her lurching down the hall behind me. Thankfully, she wasn't that persistent.

I eased the door shut to avoid waking the others and twisted the lock. When I turned around, Dovid was sitting at the edge of his bed.

"Back rather late, aren't we?" he asked. I couldn't see his face, but I had the uncanny feeling he was grinning at me.

I rested my back against the door, a bit afraid Mrs. Brenner might begin pounding. Her words had shaken me to the core. I took a moment to regain my breath before answering. "I visited a friend after class. What of it?"

He raised an eyebrow. "A friend next door?"

I groaned. The walls really were as thin as I thought. "No, a different one down in the Levee."

"Oh, so *that* kind of friend." Dovid chuckled. "Visiting the brothels now, are we, Alter? You never cease to surprise me."

"Not that kind of friend," I snapped, mortified by his implications.

Across the room, Haskel grumbled in his sleep and buried his face into his pillow. "Will you two be quiet?"

"Not that kind of friend," I repeated, softer now. "And Mrs. Brenner and I were merely talking."

"It didn't sound like a mere talk."

"Just go back to sleep." I yanked off my ribbon tie and slung it over the trunk with my overcoat and waistcoat, too exhausted to bother hanging them up. I stood by the window to make use of the shallow light. By the time I had wrangled myself out of my shirt and tzitzis, I had calmed down enough to at least fold the garments.

"Oy," Dovid muttered as I leaned down to unbutton my shoes.

I swiveled around, angry words already welling on my tongue. "What is it this time?"

"Your back. There's a bad rash."

I reached behind me, tracing my fingers down my spine. The skin felt cool and slightly waxen, numb to the touch as though it wasn't really mine at all. It didn't even hurt.

I twisted around to see myself in the washstand's oval mirror, but all I could make of the rash was a stain a shade darker than the surrounding skin. There was something familiar about the way it crept down my spine, vanishing past my trousers' waistband.

"It's nothing." I didn't want to think about that now. I was tired. So tired. I drove the thoughts from my head and ripped at the shoe buttons with the buttonhook, yanking so savagely that one of the abalone rounds snapped free and rolled under the cot. Lovely.

I collapsed on the bed and stared at the ceiling, because to sleep on my side meant that I would wake with a clear view of Yakov's empty cot. Through the wall, I could hear Mrs.

Brenner moving around in her flat. The floorboards groaned beneath her feet. She could have been doing anything in there.

I sighed, folding my arm over my eyes.

All that about darkness was shtuss. She would have made good company of Motke the Meshugener, who had wandered the streets of Piatra Neamt, harassing travelers he was convinced were possessed by the dybbukim of his loved ones. A survivor of the brutal pogroms that had spread across Russia over a decade ago, Motke had seen the faces of the dead and broken everywhere he looked—his wife, his friends, his neighbors. I remembered him as a strange, shrunken man, his shoulders hunched as though burdened by a terrible weight. Even in Romania, he had been unable to find solace from the ghosts that haunted him.

I could sympathize. More than once since arriving in America, I had followed a man in the crowd, drawn by my father's familiar gait or the wink of sunlight across his gold-rimmed spectacles. But no matter how many times I caught the stranger by his shoulder, the moment he turned around, the illusion was shattered.

Ghosts were fleeting in that manner.

13

THE NEXT MORNING, I left early to avoid running across Mrs. Brenner in the hall. I waited outside until Raizel appeared. She was walking with her mother, a bespectacled woman in a plum-purple dress, whose long, somber face was shadowed by a straw hat adorned with enough silk violets to plant a garden.

"Good morning, Mrs. Ackermann," I said when I came up to them.

"Good morning, Mr. Rosen," her mother said with a brief nod of acknowledgment. "Raizel told me about your roommate. You have my condolences."

She was short like her daughter, but her gaze was cool and confident, and she held her head high, which made her seem taller. When I asked to speak with Raizel for a moment in private, I saw the briefest glimmer of a smile before she caught herself.

"I'm afraid that would be improper," she demurred, before glancing over at Raizel. "But my ankle is rather bothering me, you see, and I would like to rest here a moment. I suppose that if Raizel prefers to walk on ahead, provided she keeps at an appropriate distance…"

"I understand. Have a good day." I suppressed a smile and continued on my way. After a moment, Raizel caught up with me.

"Well?" Her gaze burned with expectation. "Did you learn anything from that acquaintance of yours?"

"He told me that he knows where the Whitechapel Club is, but he insists on taking me there. We plan to go tonight."

"Aaron was my friend, and I owe it to him to find out what happened to him." Her sepia-brown eyes sparked as sharp as thorns. "I'm coming, too."

"What about your parents?" I couldn't exactly imagine Mrs. Ackermann permitting her daughter to crawl out the window in the middle of the night.

"Trust me, they'll never find out."

I hesitated, unsure if I should mention the stranger who had chased me last night. I was beginning to suspect it had all been in my head, a product of stress and exhaustion. "Raizel, something very strange happened yesterday. I think someone was following me on my way home."

"You think?"

"Chasing me, I should say. Just…when you sneak out tonight, be careful, okay?"

Despite its dilapidation and squalor, Maxwell Street had always felt secure and familiar to me. I could read the signs on the walls and speak to everyone I passed. But everything had changed now. I didn't think I would ever feel safe here again.

Work proceeded as usual. I typed up the articles waiting for me on the Linotype's tray, double-checking after each sentence that I had made no mistakes. Once I had affixed the lead letter-blocks into their metal frame, I had Mr. Weiss check my work.

He grunted in satisfaction. "No mistakes this time."

"There won't be any from now on," I assured him.

At lunchtime, I went down to the kosher deli two streets over to buy the newsmen's lunches. The shop was run by a nice Dutch family who had come over a number of years ago. They had two daughters, one my age and the other a couple years younger than my eight-year-old sisters. Hanna, the little one, ran up to me as soon as I entered, tugging at my tzitzis like I was a dog on a leash.

"Hanna, stop that," the eldest daughter, Sarah, called from behind the counter. "It's disrespectful."

"Alter! Did you bring me anything?" Hanna craned her head up at me, brown eyes brimming with excitement.

With her braided hair and inquisitive gaze, Hanna reminded me so much of my sisters that it almost hurt. Every week or so, I had gotten into the tradition of bringing her things I found while emptying the office's rubbish bins. Used paper she could draw on, empty ink jars, worn-down pen nubs she turned into jewelry.

I searched my pockets for something I could give her. No luck. All I found was a piece of lint.

"Nothing today, but I'll try to bring you something next week," I said.

"Aww, all right." Pouting, she sulked off.

"You spoil her too much," Sarah said as I stepped up to the counter. Her smile betrayed her feigned disapproval. "She'll be heartbroken when your sisters arrive."

"But she'll gain two new friends then." I passed her the slip with the lunch orders, along with the money the newsmen had given me. As she prepared the meal, I studied the array of pickled salads and cuts of meat behind glass.

"You must be broiling in that coat," Sarah said as she wrapped up my sandwiches in newspaper.

"I'm just feeling a little chilly."

"I thought you Russians all had ice water for blood."

"I'm from Romania," I reminded her.

"Oh, for a moment I thought that accent..." She chuckled sheepishly.

"It's an easy mistake to make." The dialect of Yiddish spoken in Romania was a lot more similar to other Eastern dialects than it was to the kind spoken in Holland.

"Maybe you're coming down with a flu. You don't look so good."

Her words made me aware of the lingering ache in my muscles and the dull headache that I'd carried with me through the day. I tugged my overcoat a little tighter around myself. "It's because I'm sick of people telling me I don't look so good."

"Forgive me, Alter." With a smile, she cut a slice of babka from the loaf cooling on the counter, wrapped it up, and slipped it in with all the rest. "Consider it on the house. We don't want you wasting away just yet."

14

LONG AFTER DOVID and Haskel had gone to bed that night, I lay awake, listening to the leaden tick of the brass clock. Distant bells rang. I counted the tolls until they struck eleven.

Slipping out of bed, I retrieved my clothes from the steamer trunk. My eyes had long-since adjusted to the darkness, and I needed only the frail moonlight to guide me. For attending Shabbos dinners and banquets hosted by the burial society, I had acquired a secondhand dress coat. Lighter clothes were more expensive and required frequent professional cleaning, so while my everyday trousers and waistcoat looked rather somber in the daylight, they made suitable evening wear. I stuffed my sole necktie into my pocket with my watch. On my way out, I stole Haskel's bowler cap and snatched the antler-handled straight razor from the dish beside the washbasin. Not the best weapon for self-defense, but it would serve in a pinch.

In the corridor, I knotted my necktie and buttoned my shoes. I slipped my watch chain through my waistcoat buttonhole and straightened the fob, a Romanian silver leu whose details were worn to shadows. I checked my father's watch for the time, held it tight for comfort. Time to go.

With the straight razor nestled in my pants pocket, I walked three blocks from the tenement until I reached the chevra kadisha, where Raizel and I had arranged to meet. As I passed the unfinished shul, an eerie orange glow rippled across the building's high windows. Strange. The builders should have gone home by now. Shadows flitted across the walls within, thrashing movement, the silhouettes of flailing limbs—was there a person in there? And that light...

As I leaned into the fence to get a better look, I had the sudden prickly sense that someone stood behind me and swiveled around.

It was a young man engulfed by a fawn-brown Inverness cape that was twenty years out of fashion. His mahogany hair spilled from under his cap, framing dark, intelligent eyes and delicate features.

"Pardon me," I said. "Do you need something?"

"Really?" The boy arched an eyebrow.

I took a closer look at him. "Wait a minute. Raizel?"

"You may call me Rainer," she said triumphantly, giving a tip of her cap.

I turned back to the shul, but the windows were black and unlit. I knew I hadn't imagined the blaze.

"Well, aren't you going to say something?" Raizel asked with a touch of annoyance.

"Did you see a glow in the window just now?" I asked.

"Uh, no."

"It looked like lantern light. And that there was someone in there."

A rumble came overheard. Raizel glanced up, a hint of a smile on her lips. "The reflection of lightning, I imagine. Are you ready to go?"

"This is a terrible idea," I said as we began walking. "And you look like a fourteen-year-old wearing his father's clothes."

"That's because I *am* wearing my father's clothes."

"They'll never let us in."

"Can you be any more pessimistic?"

"I'm being realistic."

"Maybe they won't let you in with your shtetl talk, but when *I* speak English, I sound like a cultured American." She said it with a hint of sarcasm, but it stung like an insult anyway.

"A cultured American?" I lifted my eyebrow. "How very *bourgeois* of you."

She huffed. "You know what I mean."

"Besides, I imagine you sound more like the Kaiser," I said, earning a sour look.

"If we're going with Prussians, I prefer Marx," she declared.

We continued down Maxwell Street. It was three kilometers to the corner of LaSalle and Calhoun, where Frankie and I had arranged to meet, and I planned on walking the entire way. However, only minutes after we left the neighborhood, Raizel chased down a passing hansom cab.

"Wait, it's Shabbos—" I began.

"Consider it pikuach nefesh." Raizel dug through the pockets of her borrowed coat. She handed the driver some coins, and when he tipped his hat at her and called her sir, she turned and gave me a smirk of satisfaction.

We sat side by side in the cramped compartment, close enough that her shoulder brushed mine each time the carriage turned a corner. Our parents would never have permitted us to be alone like this, but it felt natural to me.

I thought there must be something wrong with me. I could appreciate Raizel's beauty, now more so than when she wore a dress. Still, the sight of her didn't fill me with buoyant exhilaration or send my heart galloping the way it had with Frankie, Yakov, and a dozen other boys throughout the years.

"Raizel, were you and Aaron close?" I asked, wondering if she had felt the same way about Aaron as I had felt about Yakov.

"Are," she corrected bluntly. "And yes, we're friends. We've been friends for years now, ever since I moved here."

"I'm surprised Mrs. Brenner hasn't tried matching you with him."

She chuckled. "I can assure you, if she did, we'd demand a divorce within a fortnight. We're not close in that way. We're just… Aaron always takes me so seriously. The newsmen at the *Arbeiter-Zeitung* are pleasant enough, but they call me their little Nellie Bly, and it's like they see me as a novelty. It makes all my hard work feel unimportant. But when I told Aaron I got an article published, you should have seen his face, Alter. He was so happy for me and so impressed. He bought two copies and had me autograph one of them. He's always been that way. When he started talking about Jack the Ripper, I didn't want to crush his hopes. I wish I told him what I really thought about his idea."

When we were a block away from Calhoun Place, a barrage of thunder cracked open the floodgates to the sky. Rain poured down in violent torrents, pummeling the hansom cab's roof and sending the coachman cursing at the sky.

As the carriage slowed to a stop, I began to rise. Because Raizel was seated closest to the door, she stepped out first and held it open to me, rain be damned.

"How gentlemanly of you," I said as we hurried onto the sidewalk.

"Indeed. You ought to curtsy."

"I'm not a 'cultured American' so that's asking too much of me."

"You're never going to let that go, are you?"

I grinned. "I'm afraid not, Marx."

Violent gusts tore at my coat flaps. As I fled across the street, I clutched onto my borrowed hat with both hands, knowing that Haskel would murder me if I destroyed it. By the time we found shelter under a building's eaves, my clothes were soaked through.

Frankie waited at the corner of Calhoun and LaSalle, in deep conversation with a middle-aged man wearing a houndstooth suit that hugged his narrow frame. As we neared, Frankie narrowed his eyes and said something to the man, before striding forward to meet us.

"What's going on here?" Frankie kept his voice low and tame. "You didn't tell me you intended to bring a crowd."

"I'd hardly call one other person a crowd," I said, before Raizel butted in.

"My name is Raizel. I'm with the *Arbeiter-Zeitung*."

A flicker of surprise passed over his face. "Ah, you're a girl. You were smart to wear a disguise. And the *Arbeiter-Zeitung*… If I'm not mistaken, that's a workers' paper."

She perked up in interest. "Do you read it?"

"No, I don't know German. And besides, I don't waste my time reading idealistic bullshit."

I drew in a sharp breath. This was what I had been dreading.

Raizel's mouth flattened into a tight line. Even the darkness couldn't conceal the rage burning in her features. *"Excuse me?"*

"That's what it is, isn't it? Idealistic, meaningless bullshit." Frankie scoffed. "There's always going to be someone kicking you down so they can climb higher. It's just human nature. Why waste your time trying to change the system when you can just game it?"

"Frankie, I think your friend is waiting," I said to keep tempers from boiling over.

With Raizel seething in silence behind me, we joined the man in the houndstooth suit on the sidewalk.

"Mr. Whitby, these are my friends, Alex and, uh, Ryan." Frankie spoke English slowly, with clear deliberation. "Ryan, Alex, meet Mr. Whitby. He is a...business associate."

"A pleasure to meet you." Mr. Whitby tipped his chin in acknowledgment. His blue eyes were genial and closely set, with one magnified by a golden monocle. When he smiled, he resembled a turtle from a children's picture book. "But please, call me Six here. I insist."

"What kind of name is Six?" I whispered to Raizel once Whitby's back was turned.

"It's a number," she said, looking at me as though I was dense.

I rolled my eyes. "I never would have guessed."

Frankie looked back at us and mouthed, *No Yiddish.*

Entering the alley was like diving into a cave. We splashed through shallow puddles, startling flies from their perches atop piles of rotten food. Yellow light emitted from a niche ahead. We stopped in front of the heavy wooden door, whose stained-glass fanlight formed a grinning skull and crossbones.

Whitby held the door for us. "Come in."

At the bottom of the stairs, we found ourselves in a dim entry hall. There were accommodations for plenty of people, but only a few chairs were occupied at this midnight hour. Black wainscoting adorned the burgundy walls. The color scheme conspired with the darkness to make the room seem larger than it truly was, the walls receding into the edges of my vision.

Turned low, the gas jets offered a subdued glow, their flames contained within unusual white fixtures. As I stepped through the door and my eyes adjusted to the gloom, I discerned yellowed teeth, naked sockets fitted with glass orbs that refracted the firelight. My breath caught in my throat.

The lamps were made from human skulls.

Beside me, Raizel paled considerably.

"Those can't possibly be real," she whispered to me.

I swallowed hard. "I think they are."

"I told you, it's not like the Masthead," Frankie said, falling into line beside us. He put his hand on my upper back briefly, as though he meant to pull me close or turn me away from the worst of it. Then his fingers slipped away, and he strode on ahead.

Even greater horrors adorned the walls surrounding us and were fastened by ropes to the ceiling above. Swords, axes, machetes, spears, and crude instruments that resembled primitive torture devices.

Be brave. I stepped deeper into the room. *Fear nothing.*

How was it any different than washing corpses? The dead remained dead, no matter how much we wished they could come back.

As Mr. Whitby led us deeper into the room, he explained that the club was decorated with relics of slaughter. A knife used for murder. Nooses from the execution yard. The lamps were not porcelain or chalkware; they had been made from the skulls of the mad, acquired from Dunning Asylum.

I thought of my father and how he might wash up one day along a beach in England or Greenland or Brooklyn. He must be as thin and pale as these bones now. I wished I would stop thinking about these things. I hated how every time I pushed the thoughts from my head, they rammed back into me like a runaway wagon.

As we passed a mannequin dressed in a frock coat and top

hat, Mr. Whitby stopped to appreciate it. A wicked knife was fixed to the figure's hand.

"Allow me to introduce you three to our club's honorary president, Jack the Ripper." He winked at us. "Or rather, a representative of him. He has yet to honor us with his presence."

"Well, I think we've found our culprit," I whispered to Raizel.

She rolled her eyes. "Speaking of Jack the Ripper, we've heard stories about body parts washing up on Lake Michigan's shoreline. A few weeks ago, a foot was found, still within its shoe. And before that, a skull and torso. Do you think there's a connection?"

"Ah, yes. I heard about that." He chuckled. "The authorities actually believe the parts belong to just one or two people. Both male. Suicides, perhaps. When bodies are in water for long, they begin to rot. The limbs break free at the joints. Because of the shoe's rubberized soles, the feet sometimes float to the surface."

"Oh." Raizel's face dropped.

"But isn't it possible those people were murdered?" I asked.

"Well, I suppose. Nonetheless, those finds hardly fit the Ripper's *modus operandi*. They bear only a slight resemblance to the Thames Torso Murders, and here at the club, we can't even decide if the Ripper was responsible for *those* murders either."

"Well, did someone ever come here asking about those murders?" Raizel asked.

"Not that I recall," he said after mulling it over in silence. "We seldom get guests here."

"I see." Her shoulders slumped in disappointment.

Mr. Whitby led us to the bar at the other end of the room. The gaslight gleamed off the bartender's slicked-back hair and glowed in his eyes like twin moons. Meeting his gaze,

I thought I could see the skull lamp fixtures reflected in his dark irises as well.

"Get me the regular, old friend," Whitby said, slapping his hand on the bar.

"Six, what is the meaning of this?" the bartender asked in English, his voice as smooth and oily as his hair. "These boys don't belong here. This is a members-only club."

"Easy, One," Whitby said. "This place could use some new blood."

"Does he mean that literally?" I asked Raizel as the bartender poured amber liquor into a faceted crystal glass.

"No Yiddish, remember?" she whispered back furiously, before smiling at the bartender and responding to him in English: "We have heard great things about this club."

The man on our left, a mustached fellow with gray eyes, regarded us curiously. Dressed more casually than Whitby, he had his sleeves rolled back to expose a green inked dragon curling up his right forearm, its tail encircling the letters KAT burnt into his flesh. With the dragon's broad horselike face and flattened body, it resembled the sort of zmeu that might adorn a medieval icon or tapestry.

To our right, an emaciated mummy of a man guzzled ruby-red punch out of what eerily resembled a human brainpan. Heavy gold rings glinted on his tobacco-stained fingers. Lowering his cup, he glared at us with cold contempt.

Frankie slid a couple coins across the counter and nodded to Mr. Whitby. "I'll have what he's having."

"We're here for business," I hissed at him.

"And one for my friend, to help him extract the stick from his ass."

"Too bad your drink won't help you develop a brain," I said, but I took the cordial glass he offered me anyway. At the very least, the liquor might thaw the chill the storm had buried in my bones.

"Would you like one?" Frankie asked Raizel.

"Please."

While the bartender poured her drink, I looked back at the entrance. I didn't much care for the lack of windows or the dark walls, not to mention the decor itself. If something happened down here, nobody would know.

"I suppose you three could stay," the bartender said after pocketing Frankie's tip. "On one condition."

I exchanged an uneasy look with Raizel and Frankie.

"What condition?" Raizel asked.

"Each of you have to tell a story."

She chuckled. "Excuse me?"

"It's what we do here," Mr. Whitby explained. "It's the entire purpose of the club. We come here and discuss tales of murder and tragedy."

Ah. That explained the decor.

"But—" Mr. Whitby held up a finger "—the story must be real."

Frankie gave it some thought. "I have one."

"Ah, I knew you'd step up to the challenge, my lad." He took another slug of his drink. "Enlighten us."

"I know a man who can get almost anything you want, provided you can pay the price." Frankie set his glass on the counter. Whenever he told a story, he would gesture for emphasis, and now was no exception. "He barters in stolen goods mainly, but he also has a few respectable clients with more, dare I say, discerning tastes."

I could feel the eyes of the clubs' occupants shifting toward us. The man with the dragon tattoo cocked his head in interest, while the old one tapped his ring-adorned fingers against his cup, which I was now certain was in fact made from a human skull. Skin prickling, I downed the rest of my drink.

"Doctors. Scholars. Professors. They come to him looking for skeletons and jarred organs. Why? I don't know. You'll have to ask him." Frankie nodded toward the skull-lamps adorning the walls. "Quite possibly, he's the same one who found you those. This man, he doesn't just go around digging up graves or rutting through the potter's field over in Dunning. No. He has a particular source, a drugstore owner and hotel man, uh, a—"

"Hotelier?" Mr. Whitby guessed. Frankie cocked a finger at him.

"Yes, that's the word. This *hotelier* brings him these parts. Now, this fence used to be a doctor, and he knows how to identify a skeleton's sex based on, I don't know, measurements." Frankie waved a hand dismissively. "Point is, all the skeletons have been women. Every single one of them."

Frankie trailed off. We waited.

"Well?" Raizel asked after Frankie had taken another sip of liquor.

He arched an eyebrow. "Well, what?"

"Is that all?"

"It's all he told me."

She sighed. "You're a terrible storyteller. I suppose I'll go next. I'm sure you're all familiar with the Homestead Strike, but I doubt you have heard it told this way. Gather close, I will tell you how last year, the fearless anarchist, Alexander Berkman, crept into the office of the oppressor Frick, armed only with a revolver and a makeshift shank, and—"

"Next," Mr. Whitby declared.

"Excuse me? I barely even started."

"Assassination attempts do not count." As Raizel fumed in silence, he turned to me. "I don't suppose you have a story?"

"Um…" I racked my mind for what to say. I had been able to follow along with the conversation up until this point, but I dreaded the thought of having to speak. Maybe it was the club's stuffiness or the sallow glow of the gaslights, but the room seemed to shrink by the moment. I loosened my collar. "There was a bokher, a boy, I mean, who was found…"

As I spoke, the air thickened. I struggled to breathe, yet the words flowed from my mouth, faster now:

"A boy was found in the—" lagoon at the World's Fair, I meant to say, except the words that came out were "—the Pletzl, in an abandoned home, his neck slit. 1889. His name was Daniel. Three others went missing in Paris that summer. There were two boys found in London in 1887, young Jews, just children. They had fallen into the Thames and drowned. There were—"

My voice broke abruptly, as though a pair of hands had grabbed hold of my throat and wrenched the words from me. Seized by a panic I couldn't name, I stumbled back from the bar, nearly knocking shoulders with the tattooed man.

"Excuse me," I choked, pressing my hand over my mouth.

Frankie reached for me, my name forming on his lips.

"I'm fine, I just need some fresh air." I didn't realize I had spoken in Yiddish until the words left me. I twisted away from him and fled for the exit. Even after I reached the stairs and took them two at a time, the gas lamps' glow lingered in my vision like spreading flames.

In the alley outside, I sank against the wall, pressing my cheek to the bricks. As I drew in gulps of cool night air, the crushing pressure on my throat slowly loosened. My panic faded into an absence. I crammed my ribbon tie in my vest pocket and unbuttoned my collar, wiping at the clammy sweat dewed on my neck.

"You dropped this," a voice said from behind me, and I opened my eyes.

The tattooed man held my bowler cap out to me.

"Thank you." I took it back from him and put it on again.

"Interesting story." His English was clipped by a faint accent I couldn't trace. I didn't think it was American, but I couldn't be certain. Southern, perhaps. "How does it continue?"

"I don't know." I must have heard about those murders somewhere. My father must have told me about them when he had first gotten it in his head to come to America, appealing to my mother that the whole of Europe was steeped in Jewish blood.

"Perhaps you will." His gaze focused on something over my shoulder. "Ah. Your friend is coming. Take care."

As the man retreated into the club, Raizel joined me.

"Are you all right, Alter?" she asked.

"I'm fine now. It was just too hot in there." I adjusted my bowler cap. "Where's Frankie?"

"Finishing off his drink." She crossed her arms. "I don't think Aaron would have stayed here long. He doesn't speak English well enough to talk to any of these men."

Several minutes later, Frankie joined us in the alley.

"You ran out of there pretty quickly," he told me. "Don't tell me you can't hold down a single drink?"

I rubbed my eyes. "It wasn't the drink. I'm just... I'm so exhausted. I barely slept last night."

"I can tell. What was that back there? You could hardly call it a story."

"Just something my dad must have talked about once, I think." I sighed. "I don't think anyone here is responsible for Aaron's disappearance."

"Oh, so the murder weapons on the walls aren't suspicious at all?" Raizel asked sarcastically. "Or the skulls for lamps?"

"They're fascinated by murder, but that doesn't make them murderers." Now that I had a chance to think about it, the Whitechapel Club's decorations struck me as ostentatious and overdone as the false medals of a military imposter. "They're playing pretend here."

"I have to agree with Alter," Frankie said, combing a hand through his hair. "The only thing these men are guilty of is their lack of taste. Before you two showed up, I was telling Mr. Whitby about Victor's murder."

"Victor?" Raizel asked.

"An old friend of ours," I explained.

"Mr. Whitby doesn't know anything about it," Frankie continued. "The people here are only interested in the notorious murders. Jack the Ripper. The Servant Girl Annihilator. Boston Borgia. The death of some street kid is nothing in comparison. It happens all the time."

Raizel sighed. "Maybe you're right. In any case, I doubt we're going to gain anything else here tonight. Let's go home."

15

THE NEXT MORNING, I woke with nausea so bad, I had to scramble across the floor for the chamber pot. I retched until my throat burned, an iron band of pain cinched tight around my windpipe. Exhausted, I pressed my cheek against the side of my steamer trunk and pushed the bowl away.

Dovid sat up, pushing back his nest of black hair. "Are you feeling all right?"

"I think it's all the potatoes."

He and Haskel exchanged looks.

"Maybe you should go to a doctor," Haskel ventured. "You're looking a bit pale, and your voice—"

"Don't worry about it." I closed my eyes. "It'll pass…"

Neither of them answered, but on our walk to shul, they kept glancing at me worriedly.

While Haskel and Dovid found a seat in the front, I sat in the back row and took my prayer shawl from my rucksack. At the front of the hall loomed the wooden ark containing the Torah, its velvet curtain adorned with ornate goldwork.

Although my nausea had faded, I still felt cold and stiff.

The chazzan's sonorous chanting soothed me like balm on a burn. All throughout the world, shuls were reciting the same passage from the Torah. It was comforting to know that back in Piatra Neamț, the chazzan had sung these same words just half a day before.

My comfort didn't last. As I went through the standard motions—the rising and sitting, the donning of the prayer shawl, the prayers that came to my lips as naturally as breathing—anxiety stirred in my gut. By the time we began the recital of the Mourner's Kaddish, my anxiety had become dread, and the cramping and dizziness had returned with a vengeance.

I fisted my hands at my sides and stood through it, echoing amen when it was appropriate. My limbs felt frozen stiff, my muscles clenched so tightly that the tendons bulged on the backs of my hands.

From the women's section across the room, I felt Mrs. Brenner's intense dark eyes burning into me. She had tried approaching me before we had taken our seats, but I had pretended not to see her and turned away. I dreaded to imagine what she wanted to tell me.

A darkness had crept over you, she'd said, and maybe she was right. Maybe there was something terribly wrong with me. Something growing inside of me.

I couldn't stop thinking about the clapboard walls, the lack of windows. We would never hear a stranger coming. And the walls would catch fire. And smoke would fill my lungs, hot and smothering, like ashes crammed down my throat—I could taste it now.

I swiveled around, half expected to find flames crawling up the walls. Yet there was only the muted hiss of the gas jets, safely enclosed within their milk glass cradles. No burning. No screams. But it had felt so real only seconds ago.

I trembled, my limbs locked in place. Everyone in the row was staring at me, and I couldn't make a sound.

These thoughts were not my own. But the terror they instilled in me had possession over my body and soul.

For months after my father's death, long after I had arrived in Chicago and found a home in the stained brick and wharfs of the Levee, I had imagined my father still underwater. Sometimes, I'd envisioned him deep below Lake Michigan, scattered in the sand, lost amid the snail shells and algae. Or I'd be walking along the shoreline with the others, and I'd spot him wading up to his waist through the shallows, impossibly thin and pale, as though his time at sea had eroded him.

On one of those walks, I had found a pair of spectacles among the tumbled pebbles. My father had worn spectacles with rolled-gold rims, while these were tortoiseshell. It had seemed like proof nonetheless.

I carried the glasses with me for weeks, until one evening I crushed them underfoot in rage and despair, shattering the glass into splinters, because he wasn't coming back. He never would come back. Somewhere out there in the Atlantic, he was sinking, and sinking, and sinking, forever, and he had left me here alone.

I sensed that these strange new visions came from the same overwhelming grief that had led me to spot my father everywhere during those months. Because seeing my father as he had been in his final moments, over and over again when I least expected it, was better than accepting the fact that I would never see him again.

Back then, as the seasons had changed, I imagined my father less and less, until his face blurred in my mind like a reflection cast on restless waters. It comforted me to know that these visions, too, would go away with time. They had to.

After prayers, I followed the rest of the congregation into the courtyard, where refreshments waited for us, courtesy of generous and well-off members of our community. Rugelach and mandelbrot sat on one table, several jugs of grape juice on another.

I helped myself to some of the treats. As I searched for a place to sit, I spotted another volunteer at the chevra kadisha. Sender watched me warily as I approached, perhaps still a bit sore over the mikveh incident. I certainly wouldn't be forgetting it anytime soon.

I offered him a small smile. "Gut Shabbos."

"Gut Shabbos," he said unenthusiastically.

"There's something I need to know." Glancing around to make sure we were alone, I lowered my voice. "Have there been any bodies that have been found with unusual bruises or wounds? Or bodies that were unable to be washed. Someone my age or younger."

Sender pondered in silence. The victims of violence were buried unwashed in the clothes they had died in, as a cry for vengeance. When a body was found decayed or with devastating injuries, we would dress it in burial shrouds but not wash it.

"There was something," Sender said at last.

"Really?"

"Two weeks ago. There was a worker whose body was found at a kosher slaughterhouse down in the Yards. Lev and Gavril took care of tahara on their own."

"Why?" I asked, baffled. Normally, washing and preparing the body required four volunteers.

"It had to do with the condition of the boy's body. They wouldn't say." He gave it more thought. "I think...something about how there was blood on him, but it was not his own."

"That makes no sense."

"I'm just telling you what I heard."

"If they washed him, that means there weren't any deep wounds. How do you die in a slaughterhouse?"

"Drowning," Sender said.

"Drowning?" I repeated, certain I had misheard him. "That's…"

"Lev said something about drowning or suffocating, and something about blood. That's all I know." Sender frowned, glancing across the courtyard where Lev was engaged in deep conversation with other stiff old men. "Listen, don't tell him I told you this. The parents asked for privacy."

Sender walked away before I could ask him more. I mulled over his answer as I finished my rugelach. Drowning and blood. It seemed impossible, unless the boy had collapsed face-first into a cow's spraying jugular. If I couldn't ask Lev or Gavril for information, there was one other person I knew who might be able to find out more.

Across the courtyard, Raizel stood next to her mother, studying a rugelach as though concerned it might crawl off her plate. I caught her attention and nodded around the side of the building, where the latrine was located. She lifted her eyebrows.

It's important, I mouthed.

Sighing, she nodded and set her plate aside.

The latrine was a simple wooden structure only large enough for one person, with scarcely the room to sit. I closed the door behind me, breathing through my mouth to keep out the stench of raw sewage wafting from the toilet's open hole. Tiny flies swarmed around my face. I waited for a knock before opening the door a crack.

"Is it really necessary for you to hide in the toilet, Alter?" Raizel asked, peeking through the door. "I thought we were past this."

"I don't want anyone to overhear us. Besides, if we're not careful, Mrs. Brenner might arrange another date for us."

"Point taken," she conceded, then gagged as I opened the door a bit wider to let in fresh air. "That smells terrible. Close the door, close the door!"

"Sorry." I eased it shut again.

"So, what is this about?"

"I just spoke with another volunteer at the chevra kadisha. He said that there was a body found at a kosher slaughterhouse two weeks ago. The way he described it, it doesn't sound like it was a regular accident."

"Josef Loew worked at a tannery down in the Stockyards," Raizel said grimly. "With all the strikes that are going on, I was planning to interview him for the *Arbeiter-Zeitung*."

I hadn't known he'd worked there. It seemed like too much to be a mere coincidence.

"You're involved in labor," I said. "You must have friends at the Stockyards."

"Of course I do. I'll see what I can find out."

Gravel crunched under her feet. I waited a moment longer before opening the door. When I returned to the courtyard, Raizel had already taken up her post by her mother. She ignored me completely as I crossed the pavestones.

Already, the other members of the congregation were beginning to disperse. There was nothing else for me here. I snagged another rugelach to save for tomorrow and returned home.

YAKOV'S BED WAS still as he had left it, untouched, the blanket folded back. On his bedside table were loose matches, unused stationery, a penny dreadful left facedown at the page he had stopped reading. After stowing the rugelach in the icebox, I ran my hand over the sheet to smooth out the wrinkles, thinking of the night Yakov had come to live with us.

He arrived in the midst of an uncharacteristic April snowstorm, a sudden downpour of small icy flakes that scratched against the windows like fingernails.

Dovid and Haskel hadn't yet returned from the saloon. When Yakov knocked, I opened the door, thinking it was them.

He stood at the threshold, snow caught in his windblown hair and sooty lashes, his face flushed from the cold. He carried no trunk, only a carpetbag that was fraying apart at the seams.

For a long moment, he merely regarded me thoughtfully. Then the corner of his mouth quirked in a brief smile. "Haskel Lehr?"

I chuckled. "Good guess, but Alter Rosen."

"Alter Rosen," he murmured, as though to commit my name to memory.

"And you are?"

"Yakov. Yakov Kogan. I was told that you have a spare bed."

Before any of us had come to Chicago, a family of six had lived in our garret room. After they had left, the furnishings remained.

"I'm afraid it's not much of a bed," I admitted, stepping aside so that he could enter the room.

He set his bag on the floor and looked around in silence, no longer smiling.

"I hope you weren't expecting something better," I said apologetically, moving my trunk against my bed to make the floor space seem larger.

"No, this is pretty much the way I pictured it." He walked over to the stripped cot, which had been propped on its side and pushed out of the way. "I suppose this one is mine?"

"Here, let me help you."

Together, we wrangled the cot onto its casters. As he smoothed out the lumps in the straw mattress, I sat on my own bed.

"Where are you from?" I asked. His dialect was Eastern, but without the musical cadence I associated with Litvaks like Frankie. Instead, his voice held a low resonating quality, a certain flat and steady intonation I found appealing, like the rumble of distant thunder.

"I grew up near Kiev, but it's been years since I've been back there. I lived with my uncle for some time, and we traveled a lot."

"How did you end up in Chicago?"

His smile returned, but it never reached his eyes. His brilliant blue eyes were as dark as the sea, and carried its same loneliness. "It's a long story."

Sighing, I stripped the blanket and sheet from the bed. Yakov wasn't coming back. He wouldn't sleep here again. Still, it hurt to fold the linen and set it aside, and hurt even more to drag the mattress from the frame so that I could dismantle it. As I rested the mattress against the wall, I noticed a small cardboard box nestled in the ledge between the frame's headboard and side.

I picked up the box. It was surprisingly heavy, filled with contents that rolled against each other. Faded letters were printed on the lid.

"Rim-fire," I read to myself. "Cart...cartridges. Tsvey un draysik—no, thirty-two cal..."

What in the world did *cal.* mean? Calendar?

I opened the box.

Brass cylinders gleamed in the shallow light. I picked one up, rolled it in my palm. Bullets. A slip of paper was wedged into the corner of the box. I unfolded it. It was a handwritten receipt dated April 10, a week after Yakov had arrived in Chicago.

I settled back on my haunches, the box slipping from my hand. My head ached as though I had been struck a blow.

From our first meeting, I had felt a certain solidarity toward Yakov. He wasn't like Frankie, who crackled with excited energy and thundered by like a comet in whose blaze I could only follow. Yakov, in comparison, had been like a mountain lake, its stillness a guise for its cold and vast depth. He had seemed in perfect equilibrium. Not once had I seen him shout for the sheer glee of it or kick over milk crates just to watch them break. Predictable. That was how I had seen Yakov. His rhythm was as steady and reliable as clockwork. He went to work, he disappeared for many hours at a time, he came home, he slept.

He had come here for a reason. He had bought a gun.

I realized now that I had been wrong all along. Yakov hadn't been untouchable; he had been broken to shards inside. Though he had carried himself with a certain chill and proud bearing, his demeanor had been a shield to hide the profound sadness I had only caught a glimpse of that first night.

And he had been hiding something worse than sadness. Rage? Hatred? The potential to kill, certainly. No one bought a gun unless they intended to use it.

17

IN DAYLIGHT, THE Levee was just as gritty as it had been at dusk. Wagons and carriages rumbled down the streets, stirring up clouds of flies from the manure left to broil in the July sun.

On the rooftop to the old hideaway, I found a small huddle of teens playing marbles. Bailey was the first one to notice me as I ascended the fire escape's ladder. Before I even reached solid ground, she had risen to her feet. She scowled at me from under the brim of her mariner's cap. "Not you again!"

The others stopped playing and turned to me. All but one I knew by name and recognized in an instant. There was Andy with his frizz of wooly black hair, and Harry who had lost his right thumb to a sweathouse loom, and Joe, who could slip a ring from your very finger and you wouldn't even feel a thing.

"I can't believe it," Andy whispered, spilling marbles from his hands. "Alex?"

I couldn't help but grin. "It's Alter now. It's been a while, Andy."

"We ought to hurl you from the roof for leaving the way

you did," Harry said, but then he came forward and pulled me into a bear hug.

Around his neck, Harry wore a brass Star of David pendant, a gift from a long-dead sister about whom he'd spoken only briefly. In the past, he'd had the necklace tucked into his shirt, but now it swung freely. I wondered if that meant he was working over Jewish neighborhoods now. Frankie had once mused about sending us into the wealthier Reform shuls over in Kenwood and South Shore, taking an almost perverse satisfaction in the idea of robbing people in prayer.

Once Harry released me, the others surged forward, greeting me with hugs and slaps on the back. I caught Joe with his hand in my waistcoat, and snagged his wrist just as he began to take my pocket watch.

"You've lost your touch, Joe," I teased as he handed my watch back with a sheepish grin.

"If I was really trying, your watch would already be in my pocket."

"Do you know where Frankie is?" I asked, once the boys finished crowding me.

"He's down there." Bailey nodded toward the skylight that led into the attic below.

Some things never changed. Frankie had always spent his Saturday evenings taking the week's earnings to various fences throughout Chicago. In the afternoon, he would prepare the goods, keeping careful tally of what we had found and who had retrieved what.

I descended the ladder into the space below. The ladder groaned beneath my weight but held, and within moments my feet were on worn floorboards.

Dusty fingers of sunlight reached through the skylight and the narrow slates of a gable vent at the opposite end of the room. It was so dim that I could only discern the shapes of things. Cast-iron bedposts, saggy mattresses, the old stove in the corner.

Frankie sat cross-legged across the room, working in the glow of an oil lamp. He had a small jeweler's scale on the floor beside him along with tidy piles of gold and silver. A third pile of leather goods lay not too far away.

He glanced up as I descended, but looked down right away.

"I see that you've now advanced to Fagin," I said.

"Very funny," he said dully, jotting an entry into his journal. "Things have changed since you left. That old fence was giving us pennies on the dollar. Now, I've made new contacts through the Masthead, and when I want to sell stuff, I go in with a list and a number."

"Impressive."

"No one takes advantage of us now," Frankie boasted, jotting another entry into his ledger. "I get a fair value for what I sell, and I take a fair cut. And five percent of everything they bring in, I invest. I don't gamble. I invest. Just like the men at the stock exchange. You know that man from the Whitechapel Club, Mr. Whitby? He's in real estate. He gambles at the Masthead—a 'real high roller,' as the Americans would say—and he told me all about it. Real estate. That's the way to go. More than sixty million dollars' worth of real estate was built here last year, he said, and it's all because of the World's Fair. It's only going to get better once the elevated railroad is expanded. Mr. Whitby says that after the Fair, there'll be such a rush for people to live here, even places like Maxwell Street will be in high demand. It'll just be expanded into another part of Prairie Avenue."

Prairie Avenue sat less than four kilometers from my tenement, on the other side of the Chicago River. Mansions bordered its attractive tree-lined streets. Compared to Maxwell Street, the Prairie Avenue District seemed as though it belonged to a different place and time, untouched by the coal smoke and ruin.

"Not another Prairie Avenue." I groaned. "I can hardly afford rent as it is."

"I can tell. You look like you've been skipping meals. Once I'm done with this, we can grab a bite to eat." He set aside a silver book-chain necklace. "Anyway, I'm guessing you didn't schlep all the way out here just to listen to me talk business. What are you doing here?"

"Well, I was going to start by telling you that Raizel is investigating a lead down in the Stockyards."

"A better one than the Whitechapel Club?"

"I don't know yet. It has to do with a worker who died there."

"That all?"

"No, there's something else." I took the box of ammunition from my coat pocket and passed it over. "I found this hidden under Yakov's mattress. There's a receipt in there, but I can't read the handwriting."

Frankie slid open the box and unfolded the receipt tucked inside. He read it carefully, tracing his finger over the letters. "It's for the bullets and the gun that goes with them. A revolver. I don't recognize the dealer."

"Why would Yakov want a gun?" I asked.

"I'm not the person you should be asking."

"Isn't this your kind of business?"

"Only if he was planning to commit a crime with it." Frankie turned his attention back to the ledger, but by the way he tapped the fountain pen's cap against his palm, I could tell he was mulling the situation over. "You said Yakov had bruises around his throat, right?"

"Yes, as if someone had strangled him."

"There's another possibility," Frankie said.

"Which is?"

He glanced over. "Suicide."

The word jarred me to the bone. Suicide. I recalled how Yakov had looked on the night he died, his features bathed in the garish glow of fireworks. His bright blue eyes. The smoke trailing from his lips, as though he was burning up inside. These last few weeks, he had become tense and reclusive, but that night, he had been at ease. Teasing. His demeanor had radiated an inner calm and resolution, as if he had finally made a decision he would never be able to go back on.

Yakov had bought a gun, but maybe he decided that was too bloody. Maybe he had tried using a rope, only to realize the water could give him a cleaner death, a quieter one.

I searched my memory for a sign, some way I could have prevented it. Instead, I recalled his final words to me.

I'm meeting someone from back home. Besides, I suspect it's not your kind of show.

Someone from back home. Someone from back home. The phrase echoed tauntingly in my head.

"No," I said. "He didn't buy the gun to kill himself."

"Then why?"

"He was hunting someone. The night he died, he told me he was going to the Fair to meet someone. The way he said it, it was strange. He didn't say friend or landsman, just someone…"

Frankie narrowed his eyes. "Who would Yakov be hunting? And why?"

"I don't know." I rubbed my face. "I just don't know. I could tell he was keeping secrets, but so was I. All I know is that he was tense that night. Different. I feel like the answer is right in front of me, and I'm missing it completely!"

Frankie sighed, rising to his feet. "Look, we're getting nowhere by going back and forth, so let's get something to eat."

"The answer isn't in food, Frankie," I said in exasperation.

"Nonsense, food is the answer to everything." A smile eased across his lips. "We can sit and eat like old times, just the two of us, and you can tell me all about your friend Yakov."

18

"I NEED TO think of a boxer name," Frankie said as we walked down the street. It was midday, and pushcart vendors and beggars crammed the sidewalks of the Levee District.

"A boxer name?"

"All the good boxers have names. There's Napoleon, the Belfast Spider, the Fighting Blacksmith, the Trojan Giant, and His Fistic Holiness. The last one's my favorite. I wish I'd thought of it."

I gave it some thought. "How about Samson?"

"With a name like that, I'll end up with my eyes gouged out."

"Oh, wait, how about this? The Slingshot of HaShem!"

"Something a little less biblical, please."

"The Baltic Beast?"

Frankie cocked his head, pondering it over. "That...that's actually not bad."

Another flash of inspiration came to me. "The Villain of Vilne."

He gave me a sour look. "I'm beginning to sense a theme here."

"The Lunatic from Lithuania."

"Now, you're just being deliberate."

I chuckled. "It's not deliberate if it's true."

Frankie shoved me lightly in the shoulder, and I shoved him back. As he strode on ahead, I bit my inner cheek to keep from grinning. A part of me wanted so badly to step into his life again. But we could never go back.

On that autumn night I'd left him, I had made an oath to myself that I would live with integrity. Just because the world was unjust didn't mean that I must debase myself as well. I wanted to become the son my father would have been proud of. By surviving, I would be honoring his memory.

Frankie fell into step beside me. "I almost forgot, after you ran out of the Whitechapel Club, Mr. Whitby invited me to the Sunday evening races. He said that I should bring you along."

"Why me?"

"How should I know? I think he liked your sorry attempt at a story. So, what do you say?"

"I have work until five, but I can meet after then."

Frankie looked at me with pity. "Ah, so they keep you chained to the workbench all day."

"Linotype machine, actually."

"And that is?"

"It's used to arrange typeset for printing. I work at a news-paper."

"Why not come work for me?"

I turned my head, certain I had misheard him. "What did you just say?"

"I mean it. I could use someone like you to work with the fence and keep the ledger. The others are too young and, well, admittedly, not very bright." He ran a hand through his hair. "I know what you're thinking, but we're rising up in the world now, Alter. As I said before, I'm making connections. Just last month, down at the Masthead, I got a meeting with the Bath and—"

"The Bath?"

"Bathhouse John. You know? John Coughlin?"

The name sounded vaguely familiar. "Wasn't he just elected as alderman?"

"Correct, of the First Ward. And like all politicians, he's got his hands in the Levee's workings. He's getting into the protection racket. He's got the police in his pocket now to shake down the brothel lords and bookies, but he said that in the future, he might have need for someone like me, and the crew, too."

"You can't possibly intend to make a life out of this, Frankie," I said incredulously. "Forget about the Baltic Beast, if you keep this up, they'll start calling you Frankie the Felon."

He cocked his head and gave it some thought. "To be fair, that's not a bad boxer name either. Although it will probably end up being more like Frankie the Fugitive."

"I'm serious! What you were talking about back there with the real estate and investments and legitimizing your business, it's a pipe dream. You'll end up dead or in jail before you're twenty, and you'll drag everyone in your crew down with you."

"Excuse me?" He jerked to a halt and stared at me in disbelief. "You waltz into my place as though you own it, ask me for advice, and then you proceed to shit on me? Seriously? Is this how you show appreciation? By insulting me to my face?"

"No. I'm not trying to insult you. I just—" I took a deep breath. Enough hiding. I needed to say this now, or I'd never get it out. "This is wrong, and you know it. What you are doing is theft, Frankie."

"Oh, theft? You don't say?" He leveled his chin, anger rising in his gaze. "And yet when children lose their fingers to looms and grinders, it's called industry. Unlike the bosses, I never take from the most vulnerable. Never from the poor pushcart sellers or ragpickers. I have standards. Don't you dare talk to me as though I'm a common thief!"

"No, instead, you corrupt kids who don't know any better, who have nowhere else to go. You *use* them."

"I *liberate* them," he snarled.

"You use fear to convince them that relying on aid is more dangerous than just outright stealing what they need." I could still remember the stories he had told to frighten the younger boys, vivid tales he invented from thin air about greedy bosses and perverse overseers just dying to sink their claws into innocent workers. True, those things happened, but not the way he described them, as though there were wardens with bad intentions lurking around every corner. If he wasn't such a hustler, he would have made a lovely Marxist. "You tell them that you're protecting them, when really you're—"

"I *am* protecting them, you putz! You realize what this city does to kids on the street, Alter? It devours them. And what life would they have if they ended up in a settlement house, huh? I landed in Castle Garden, I know the way businessmen come through and offer you a job, an American dream of a new life, and next thing you know, you're in a sweatshop working sixteen hours a day, and they call that generosity, they call that a chance at a future."

"And what do you offer them? A life of crime?"

"A fucking choice, that's what! I give them a *choice*!"

Frankie was up in my face now. Before I could stop myself, I shoved his shoulder. He dug his heels into the ground and wouldn't budge, and when I tried again, he seized me by the ribbon tie the way he would a dog on a short leash. We glowered at each other, close enough now I could feel the heat radiating from his body.

"Let go of me," I said tightly.

"You can judge me all you want, Alter," he hissed, leaning in. "You can call me a damn Fagin, but the fact is this—I'd rather be a shanda than someone's little *suka* like you."

"What did you just call me?!"

"I'm just curious, do you lick your boss's boots before or after you clean the presses?"

"Damnit, g-get off." Panting with a sudden shortness of breath, I reached up to pry his fingers off my tie. He refused to let go, instead hauling me closer so he could snarl his next words in my face.

"Fuck you, Alter, and fuck the people who try to convince you that a life as worthless trash is better than rising up."

As the silk ribbon cinched tight, my anger was overwhelmed by debilitating terror. I couldn't breathe. I couldn't *breathe*. Gasping for air, I struggled in his grip. The world swung wildly, darkening around the edges. I fell and landed hard on—

—grass. Slick grass under my palms and knees, the scent of stagnant water flooding my nostrils. The day had tumbled into night in an instant. I reached up with one hand to tear at the fingers that strangled me, but instead of warm flesh, my nails sank into unyielding cord. Rope. No. Leather. Braided leather.

A knee drove between my shoulder blades, pushing me to the ground. I bucked beneath him—*not Frankie, oy gevalt, it's not him anymore*—and tried to shout, but the cord strangled all sound. The taste of blood and dirt welled in my mouth.

I managed to lift my head. Through blurry eyes, I took in the glow of fireworks glistening across the dark water. The reflections of buildings appeared to be on fire. My fingers grew numb, and the numbness spread sluggishly up my limbs, flowing through my bloodstream. Just as I began to black out, the grass gave way beneath me. I plummeted—

—onto wooden slates, tacky with pitch and filth. Panting, I knelt on my hands and knees, too weak to rise. Fingers closed around my shoulder.

I twisted onto my side and cast the hand away. *"Otstan' ot menya!"*

Frankie stared down at me, his brow furrowed. "Alter, did you just…"

"Just stay back." I scooted across the wooden sidewalk until I struck a lamppost. I reached behind me, grasping onto the cast-iron base to anchor myself. If I let go, anything might happen. The ground might give out again. "Please. Don't come any closer. Just give me some space to breathe."

Frankie flinched as though I had struck him. His face contorted in pain and horror. "I'm so sorry. I didn't mean to hurt you. Not you. Never."

"Didn't you see it?" I stammered, looking around us for evidence. The ash of fireworks perhaps, or grass I'd uprooted in my desperate struggles. But the only remnant left was the burning ache in my throat and the stench of spent gunpowder and swampy water muddling in my nostrils.

"I never should have touched you," Frankie continued, raking a hand through his hair. He paced back and forth in front of me. "I'm so sorry. I didn't—I wasn't—I wasn't thinking. I just wanted you to stop and listen. I never meant to—"

"Frankie!"

He stopped and turned.

"Did you see the fireworks or not?"

"Fireworks?" he repeated blankly.

"Yes. And I was being strangled."

He winced. "I just meant to hold your tie. I never meant to apply pressure."

"No, I don't mean you. Someone. With a rope, I think. Or a strap." I swallowed down the heavy lump in the back of my throat, fighting the dismaying urge to cry. "I'm not sure. It was so dark."

"What are you going on about?"

"Something's wrong with me." I pressed my hand over my face. "Ever since Yakov died, strange things have been happening, and I feel like I'm losing control. It's just like what happened back at the Whitechapel Club and then at shul today, only it's gotten worse. So much worse. It's as though there's something terrible growing inside me."

"Alter, if you talk any louder, we'll have an audience," Frankie murmured, squatting down at a safe distance. He glanced over at the pushcart peddler eyeing us suspiciously over her mound of used clothes. "Come. I know just the place to talk in private."

19

THE TEAROOM'S DAMPENED gas lamps and forest green walls gave the establishment a cave-like feel. The spicy musk of tobacco smoke only added to the impression. We found a private table in the back. The dimness soothed me, dulling the hard edges of the day.

"Keemun tea, please," Frankie said as the waiter came by. He looked at me. "Coffee, I suppose?"

He remembered well. But the thought of drinking coffee, bitter as bile and as dark as the grave, made my stomach turn. It would be like choking on dirt.

"Tea is fine," I said.

"With bublitchki and honey cake," Frankie said, and the waiter departed.

I took off my coat and hung it from the hook on the wall. There was mud or worse streaked on my palms, and I wouldn't be able to sit still until I had scrubbed away all traces. "I'll be right back."

"Going to wash your hands?" Frankie smiled. "You really are a good mensch."

No, I'm not, I wanted to tell him, my weak smile straining my lips like they might break.

There was a pitcher and washbasin in the cramped lavatory. I stood for a moment with my back against the door, turning my father's pocket watch around and around in my fingers to ground myself in the moment. Once I had regained my composure, I scrubbed the grime from my palms.

Lifting my hands to my face, I caught the faintest whiff of stagnant water and something else. A tarry odor like hot macadam or turpentine, but with a woodsy edge. What was that? Russian leather? The scent brought me back to my childhood, visiting trade fairs and markets with my father as he pored over bolts of linen, wool, and leather.

I poured clean water over my hands and recited the blessing for eating bread. As I lowered the pitcher, I stared in the mirror above the basin, half wondering if Frankie would find fault in my features, harder than I recalled, or my chestnut hair, well due for a trim. Even my green eyes, which I thought were my best feature, seemed dull and muted.

My throat ached. I untied my string tie, twining the black silk ribbon around my fingers. It had been all I could afford, but I hated it suddenly for how childish it looked compared to the elegant dove-gray ascot Frankie wore, like something you'd tie onto a pet. As I shoved the ribbon into my pocket, I caught sight of my neck.

A faint purplish bruise encircled my throat. I rubbed furiously at the mark, hoping to make it go away. Impossible. There was no way a ribbon could have caused this.

But a leather ligature would, certainly. Wrapped tight enough to cut off all air flow. Tight enough to burst the blood vessels.

I squeezed my eyes shut, grasping onto the sink edge. "Not

real, Alter. It wasn't real. You're letting Yakov's death get to your head."

So, why the bruise? Why the rash upon my back?

It looks rather like a burn, doesn't it?

I curled my fingers against my palm, digging my nails in. The sting should have kept things distant, just the way I needed them to be. Except when I opened my eyes again, the bruise was still there, and it ached even more than the pale crescents my nails had made in my skin.

I retied the ribbon to cinch my collar shut and forced a bright American smile.

First things first. Tea and cakes. That was all I needed to think about right now. Tea and cakes.

Burying my fear deep inside me, I went back to the dining room. In my absence, the waiter had set out a small brass samovar and the fixings of a proper tea—porcelain dishes of fruit preserves and sugar cubes, slender spoons, faceted crystal glasses in brass holders, a kettle containing tea so concentrated that it was as dark as molasses.

Over the samovar's chimney, the waiter had draped a string festooned with bublitchki, small bagel-shaped rolls baked to a glossy sheen. Frankie had ordered honey cake, but the dessert the waiter brought looked nothing like the dense golden-brown slabs of lekach baked for the new year. Served on delicate bone china, the slices of cake towered precariously high. Each square contained layer upon layer of white cream and blintz-thin cake, the top adorned with crumbs and chopped nuts.

"It's medovik," Frankie said, as though sensing my confusion. He pushed my plate closer. "Try it."

Now that we were seated, I was in no rush to spill the trauma of these last few days onto him. I sampled the cake to prolong the silence. The cream's pleasant tang complemented the honeyed taste and spongy texture of the cake layers. It re-minded me of the fried papanasi my mother served with sour cream she made herself.

Frankie poured some tea into his glass, before adding hot water from the samovar. "Do you take it strong or weak?"

"You don't have to serve me," I muttered.

He endeared me with a smile. "Humor me."

"Strong."

After Frankie had fixed the tea to my satisfaction, he passed it over. He added a generous dollop of sour cherry jam to his glass, but I was inclined to drink mine unflavored, with only a cube of sugar to sweeten it. I held the cube between my teeth, so that it dissolved with each sip.

"Since when did you start drinking tea like a Russian?" Frankie asked after I had finished the first cube.

I choked on my tea. "P-pardon me?"

"The sugar. That's how I was taught to drink it, too. I re-member, you used to just mix it into your tea. Two cubes, then a splash of milk, just like a Brit."

"A Brit?"

"My manager does the same."

"How do you even remember that?"

"I don't know. It just stood out to me." He shrugged. "You followed the same pattern with coffee. I notice these things."

"How people drink?"

"Patterns. Like how you would wind your watch first thing each morning, and you'd count the number of times you did it."

The way he said it made me afraid he thought it was pe-culiar. "It's how my father taught me. If I don't wind it con-sistently, it won't keep time as well. And if I overwind it, the mainspring might break."

He shrugged. "You don't have to explain it. I just liked it."

"I never knew you noticed," I murmured, gazing into my cup of tea. My own reflection, unspooled and distorted in the dark liquid, was a stranger to me.

"Those were good times, weren't they?" Frankie asked, adding a dash of milk to his tea. As he put down the small creamer, his hand touched mine. Just for a moment, but long enough to make my heart skip a beat. Had he done that on purpose? I wanted to think he had only added milk to his tea as an excuse to brush up against me.

I put my hand in my lap to avoid tempting fate. If he touched me again, all the feelings I'd kept dammed for so long might come rushing to the forefront. I'd want to kiss him. I'd want to tell him how lovely he'd become in the year since I left... And I knew he'd never feel the same way, that it would repel him, disgust him even.

"Some of them were good," I conceded, reinforcing my mask. "I'm still not going to come back and work for you."

"Yes, you made that abundantly clear," Frankie said dryly.

I took another sip of tea, grimacing at the sting in my throat when I swallowed. The throbbing ache worsened by the second.

"Too strong?" he asked.

I shook my head. "No, the tea's fine."

"Then why the face?"

Somehow, giving voice to my fears scared me even more than leaving them unspoken. But Frankie had always been honest and blunt, even to a fault, and maybe that was what I needed most now.

Before I could lose my nerve, I pulled free my ribbon tie and yanked down my collar. Just touching the bruise made me gasp.

He winced. "Please tell me I didn't do that."

"Not you." I sighed, shoving my tie into my pocket. "I

know you must think I'm deranged, but I'm not. Something is happening to me, Frankie. I thought this was grief, but it isn't grief. It's something more. It's growing inside, and I can't stop it."

Warmth in my palm. Frankie had reached under the table to take my hand, his calloused fingers anchoring my own. He gave my hand a firm, reassuring squeeze. "Start from the beginning."

20

I BEGAN BY telling Frankie about Yakov's death, speaking very quietly to avoid being overheard by the other patrons. He made an obvious effort not to interrupt me, but every other minute, he couldn't help but ask questions.

"Why do you volunteer at a chevra kadisha?" Frankie asked, when I told him about my work at the burial society. "I thought dead bodies made you squeamish, like when we found that old beggar who froze to death."

"They used to, but..." I searched for a way to explain it.

I had fled in terror from the old beggar's body because it had been a reminder of my own mortality. And the first time I had washed a body, I had vomited in the alley behind the tahara house until I was coughing up strings of burning bile. But the second time, it wasn't so bad. And by the fourth or fifth time, I had realized that there was no running from death, when death surrounded us on all sides.

"I was sick of feeling guilty," I said at last, as though that explained it.

"For stealing?" he asked.

"Yes. No. Look, I just wanted to do something right for once."

But it was more than that. I would never be able to give my father a proper burial, but by honoring the dead, I felt like I was rewinding the clock. Making things right again.

When I reached the part about the Linotype machine incident, I expected Frankie to laugh in disbelief. Instead, he just crumbled a bublitchi between his fingers and gazed distantly into his cup of tea. "You look sick, Alter, do you know that?"

"You don't believe me." A sinking feeling formed in the pit of my stomach. "You think it's madness."

"No, that's not what I'm saying at all. I'm just worried about you." He raised a chunk of cake to his mouth, reconsidered, and set his fork down without taking a bite. He leaned across the table, fixing me with those riveting tawny eyes of his. "Tell me, Alter, how familiar are you with dybbukim?"

Magic flowed through the winding streets of Piatra Neamț, if one were to believe the legends. I grew up on stories of holy men parting the river Bistrița, golems shaped from clay, and, of course, those possessive spirits called dybbukim.

"Wait, don't tell me." I laughed, but it came out hollow. "You think I'm possessed by Yakov's dybbuk?"

"Do you have a better explanation?"

"You're mad, Frankie Portnoy." I had wanted someone to talk to, not convince me that I was possessed. In some ways, it was even worse than if he had told me I was mad. "I'm not possessed. This is exhaustion, or it's a sickness. It has to be. I must have caught something from Yakov and—"

"Back there. You said, *Otstan' ot menya.* That's Russian."

"No, I… I told you to let me go."

"In Russian," Frankie said. "Listen to me. I've met someone possessed by a dybbuk."

"Let me guess, he's a boxer, too?" I snarled.

"No. This was back in Vilne."

"You're mad." I shook my head in disgust. "You've been hit in the head too many times."

"Just listen," Frankie said quietly, laying his hand over mine as I began to rise.

I could have pushed out of my seat and left the teahouse. I wanted to. But I didn't move, and a part of it was because the chill had returned to coil in my veins. If this was a dybbuk, it was waking up.

So, I sat back and drank the fresh glass of tea he made for me, without milk or sugar this time, so that the leaves' strong, earthy taste lingered like smoke on my tongue.

"This was back in Vilne, over ten years ago. It was in April, I think, or maybe March. Either way, the first night of Pesach, and it was damn cold. Foggy, too, with a light snow. It was during the Storms in the South, and you know how it can get around that time of year, even in times of peace. You know the fear."

"I do."

From Good Friday to Easter, my parents had kept us inside, with the curtains drawn and the door barred. For as long as I could remember, it had been a yearly ritual. On the Saturday morning after Good Friday, we would walk swiftly to shul, me holding little Rivka and my mother holding Gittel, because the twins had been infants back then, and infants couldn't run. No laughter. No playing. Keep your eyes straight ahead and do not speak. My father, he had carried a heavy walking stick with a brass head. But what good could a cane do against guns, knives, axes, a dozen boots and fists?

When I told Frankie of this, he explained that in the Russian Empire it was even worse. "It's because of what happened to the tsar twelve years ago. The assassination."

"My father told me about that, but he never told me why," I said.

"One of the revolutionaries was Jewish, and you know how much people love to blame us for killing Jesus. Apparently, we all killed the tsar, too." Frankie took another sip of tea. "In Russia during that time, I couldn't drop a book without making my mother plotz. Anyway, we were having a seder. Just my parents, my aunt and uncle, my younger cousins, and me. I could tell the adults were nervous, and it frightened me. I had a good idea even back then why they were afraid... I just didn't know the words for it."

There were so many words. Pogroms. Beatings. Rape. Murder. Infants torn apart by a mob's hateful hands.

"Halfway through the Haggadah, there was a knock on the door, and my father went to answer it. He was a member of our shul's self-defense league—I suppose, it was from him I got my taste for fighting—and there was talk of a body. A Jewish girl found dead in the snow. My father took me with him. I don't know why. Maybe he just wanted to prepare me for violence. By the time we arrived, her family was there, and so was our neighbor's son, who was her betrothed. He must have been our age, and they'd been friends since childhood. I still remember the look on his face. His eyes were dead. There was nothing behind them."

I grasped for a connection. "Was she murdered?"

"I don't know. There must have been a reason for it though, for what happened next, when he fell down beside her. At first, no one knew what happened. He had fainted from the shock of it, they thought. It was to be expected, seeing her like that, lying in the snow. But then he began talking about how cold it was, shivering even though he was sitting right by the fire. It was all he could think about. How snowy it was the night she died. How dark. His voice grew softer and more feminine, while his toes and fingers blistered on their own as if frostbitten."

I shivered, my fingers straying to the tender bruise around my throat.

"We found him outside in the middle of the night, barefoot and weeping, saying that he couldn't find his way home. He just wanted to go home. He had to be chained up after that, to keep from wandering. I remember visiting him with my father, two weeks later, in his family home. By then, he would only answer to her name. In the end? Maybe he choked to death like they said. Maybe they choked him to death, and he died with his father's hands around his throat. Maybe I'm just making this up, bubbeleh, but I guess that doesn't explain what's happening to you. So, why him? Why you? Who knows? Maybe it's just love."

My tea had gone cold. I drank it anyway, in several joyless gulps, hoping for a jolt of energy that never came. When I set the glass down, I was unsurprised to find my left hand trembling. My fingers closed around empty space. Curled. Searching for what? A fountain pen? A knife?

Two weeks. If what Frankie said was true, I just had two weeks left. No. A week and a half before Yakov took over for good.

"I didn't love him." I tightened my hand into a fist, as if that would stop the tremors. It only hid them beneath the skin. "Truly, I didn't. I... How can you even suggest that? It's—"

"Then call it kindness," Frankie said smoothly. "Call it mercy."

Yes, mercy. That would do. I sighed, grasping on to the idea like a life raft. It wasn't love. It was simply reaching out for a drowning boy.

"If this is Yakov's dybbuk, why do you think he possessed you?" Frankie asked.

Because I fell into the mikveh. Because I never got to say goodbye. Because I couldn't save him.

"I don't know." I exhaled slowly. "More important, if you're right, he hasn't taken over yet."

"Then that means there is still time," Frankie said.

"Time for what?" A humorless smile contorted my lips. "To write home, say my farewells?"

"An exorcism."

"Easier said than done. Where am I supposed to find an exorcist?"

"Go to your shul?"

"You know I can't do that."

No matter how well our rabbi thought he could keep secrets, word would permeate through the congregation like the aroma of spice from besamim. The skeptics would call it madness or worse, while the people who believed me might see the possession as a moral failing. I needed to keep this discreet, keep it distant.

"I might know someone," Frankie demurred.

"You?" I laughed, feeling myself teeter on the edge of anger. "Right. I suppose he moonlights as a boxer?"

"He talks like he's been hit in the head one too many times, that's for sure," Frankie said. "But he was a rabbi once, before he was put in herem. People thought him a tzaddik, if you'd believe me."

I highly doubted a Hasidic holy man was hiding in the brick-and-metal heart of Chicago, much less that Frankie, coming from the opposing Misnagdic sect of Judaism, would want anything to do with one.

"Is this some kind of game to you?" I demanded. "Do you intend to drag me across all of Chicago in search of some disgraced rabbi?"

This anger I felt wasn't meant for Frankie, but I wanted to force it upon someone else.

He took my harsh words the same way he had taken my shove—resolutely, unmoving, with a hint of a cold smile.

"I have better uses for my time, bubbeleh," Frankie said, polishing off the rest of his medovik. "Besides, I know exactly where to find him. Whenever the crew comes across anything that looks old or strange or kabbalistic—books, amulets, papers—he takes them off our hands. Pays a damn good price, too."

"So, I'm going to get an exorcism from someone who knowingly buys stolen goods? I'm sure that's going to go perfectly well. Like getting teeth pulled by a grave robber."

"Says the former thief." His smile warmed. "I never said it was a good choice, Alter. But the fact is, you don't have many choices left. And soon you'll have even less. In the end, there's the door. You can walk away. The choice is yours."

21

DARKNESS BLOTTED OUT the sky like a gloved hand, snuffing the factories' smoke trails and bringing a silent calm to the city. I had expected us to root out the exorcist within the shuls and tenements of Maxwell Street, but Frankie surprised me by hailing a carriage that took us to Chicago's outskirts.

The carriage lumbered down the road, jolting each time the wheels snared in potholes. I took out my dad's pocket watch and shifted it from hand to hand. The timepiece's cool weight comforted me, and when the passing streetlamps permitted, I watched the second hand continue its steady revolution around the porcelain dial. It was reassuring to know that the world had not flung out of orbit, that time passed the way it used to, before any of this.

As we left the city behind us for untamed swampland, a strange feeling stirred in my gut. My limbs ached, heavy and leaden, and I had to put my watch away in fear it might slip from my numb fingers. I became so cold, I shivered.

"Are you all right?" Frankie asked, sitting in the seat across from me.

I rubbed my upper arms, hoping to warm them. "I'm just a little chilly. It's fine. I've been cold all day."

"You're cold?" He furrowed his brows. "It's practically a smokebox in here. Any hotter and you'd catch fire."

The reason for my shivers dawned on me.

"He knows." I crossed my arms over my chest and dug my fingers into my shoulders to steady my trembling arms. "Yakov. He knows that something's wrong, and he's afraid."

Now that I recognized Yakov's dybbuk for what it was, I could feel him stirring inside of me like a phantom limb. I couldn't control him or see him, but I sensed he was there.

My dread only deepened as the carriage pulled to a creaking halt. Once we had stopped jostling, Frankie climbed out and offered me a hand. I ignored it as I stepped onto solid ground. I might have been cold, but I was not infirm. And getting possessed hadn't robbed me of my dignity.

Our destination turned out to be an empty stretch of road cut off by a pile of stones and logs heaped in the middle of the path. Lovely. So, if a fallen rabbi who purchased stolen goods wasn't bad enough, we now had to deal with a swamp hermit on top of that.

"He must've paid really well for you to schlep all the way out here whenever you found something nice," I said as we entered the marshy gloom. Frankie had borrowed a lantern from the driver, but the kerosene light was weak.

"He used to live near the waterfront," Frankie said. "But I suppose it got too noisy for him there. I've visited him a couple times since he moved out here, just to check if he's still kicking. He threw me out once he realized I had nothing to sell him."

We continued walking. The darkness soothed me, making it easier to speak. "Frankie, why are you helping me?"

"Because I can."

"I left you. I *abandoned* you."

"Yes, and when you left, I thought you were dead." He paused to step over a log, the lantern casting quivering shadows across the dirt. "I knew how much you hated to steal, and I knew that you were suffering, but I never asked you if you were all right. I felt like I'd killed you myself."

A heavy lump formed in my throat. "I didn't know. I didn't realize how much you cared."

"Why did you go that night?" he asked huskily, the lantern light stoking a fire in his gaze.

"I was scared."

A pained spasm racked his face. "Of me?"

"Of who I had become."

It hadn't been a regular burglary that night, even though Frankie tried to make it sound like one. We worked in teams of two or three, and I knew something was different when Frankie insisted on going into the house alone.

He told me to keep watch, and for the first few minutes I did. Then I crawled through the window after him, because the thought of Frankie being out of sight made me sick to my stomach. Maybe it was just bad nerves. Nobody wanted to be alone on guard duty, especially not on a crisp autumn evening where the air hung as stiff as a curtain and it felt like anything might happen.

Frankie knew our target, had been watching him for long enough to know the inside of his house, the inside of his bedchamber. He had ripped open the feather mattress in search of valuables, littering the floor with mounds of horsehair and goose down.

We were in the middle of raiding the homeowner's silver—candlesticks, besamim, menorah, kiddush cup, the full works—when the door opened. The man froze at the sight of us, his mouth agape. Brown hair brushed neatly to one side, eyes dark like a shark's, a hard wedge of a naked chin, his cheeks cleanly shaven. Frankie pulled his gun before the man could speak.

"Wh-what are you doing here?" the man demanded in English.

I was almost as shocked as the man must have been. It was the first time I had been interrupted during a burglary, and all I could think was that he'd seen my face and he was a Jew.

"Shut your mouth and get on your knees," Frankie said, in a smooth, calm voice that promised violence as efficiently as any gun. How strange it must have been to catch a hint of that yeshivish cadence while staring down the end of a gaping barrel.

The man didn't move. He didn't speak. His eyes shifted back and forth like he meant to memorize us, his face white with rage or terror.

"Would you prefer a bullet in them?" Frankie asked.

Slowly, the man sank to his knees.

I felt sickened. Somehow, this was different than mugging a stranger in a pitch-black alley, than pickpocketing one from behind, or breaking into an empty house and pretending that I'd once lived there as I searched through cupboards and drawers. There was no darkness here to hide me. This man could *see* me. He was staring right at me.

It shouldn't have made a difference, him being a Jew or not. But it did. My face burned with humiliation, and I imagined the old women in my hometown shul, clucking their tongues and shaking their heads. Shanda, they'd say, like judges in their dark veils and headscarves. Shanda. Disgrace. Shame.

"Go get the stuff." Frankie kept his eyes on the man. "Alex? Are you just standing there? Go get it, now."

I couldn't think straight. My thoughts were scattered like broken glass. This was wrong. Everything was wrong. Frankie shouldn't have had his gun.

"You look like a good boy," the man said softly, his Yiddish coming out off-kilter and scratchy, as though it had fallen into disuse. "I can see it in your eyes. You don't want to be here. You don't want to do this."

"Don't talk to him," Frankie barked, kicking the man in the small of his back. It was a restrained blow, dealt with the side of his foot, but the man groaned like something had broken deep inside him.

As I gathered up the rest of the loot with shaky hands, the man's gaze burned into me. My head pulsed with shame and regret, and I couldn't bear to meet his eyes.

"You have it all?" Frankie asked without looking at me. The gun quivered in his hand ever so slightly. I caught a glimpse of his face. With a jolt, I realized he was *afraid*. "Well, do you?"

I swallowed hard. "Everything."

"Good." Then he spoke to the man, and I knew this, because his voice chilled over until it was as hard as ice. "Now, your watch and your ring."

The man took off his ring and pocket watch, freeing the gold chain from his buttonhole. Rather than place the items in Frankie's outstretched hand, he held them out to me instead. Like a peace offering. Like a plea.

"Alter, don't," Frankie said. By then I was already reaching for the ring.

The man's fingers locked around my wrist. He dragged me off balance, twisted me around. I struggled as he linked his arm around my neck, certain he meant to break it.

"Don't shoot!" the man yelled. "If you shoot, I'll—"

A hot smatter of blood fanned across my face as Frankie drove the butt of the revolver into the man's nose. I fell onto my stomach and was beginning to rise when I heard a yelp from behind me, a grunt, the scuffle of boot heels on the floorboards. I turned around to find Frankie on top of the man, punching him.

One fist, then the other, the blows steady and rhythmic. In some way, it was even more brutal than if Frankie had lashed out in an animalistic fury. The gun was by Frankie's feet, and I picked it up before touching his shoulder.

When Frankie looked up at me, his gaze was a thousand kilometers away. There was blood darkening his brown curls. Blood flecked across his lips. And I realized that the boy I'd thought I knew down to the heart, I really hadn't known at all.

That night, I had realized that he wasn't the only stranger. I had become a stranger to myself as well. But it was more than the thievery. I had been frightened by how Frankie made me feel. How I could lose myself for hours watching the way the sunlight teased the contours of his high cheekbones and bronzed his rebellious curls. How just the thought of kissing him set me burning like a firework, the desire so strong I thought it'd tear me to pieces if I had to keep it pent up inside me much longer.

"You could have told me you didn't want to steal anymore," Frankie said as we headed deeper into the marsh. "We could have worked something out. You could have… I don't know. You could have gone to the fence instead of me. You would have probably been good at that, negotiating, keeping it composed, cold. Distant."

"Frankie, I needed to leave. It would never have worked out in the end. It would have been the death of us."

No sooner had the final word left my mouth than Frankie's features darkened. Before I could react, he threw down his lantern and lunged at me as though he meant to kill me.

"Get off me!" I snarled as we grappled blind and grunting in the darkness.

"Get down!" He shoved me back, and like an utter schlemiel, I tripped over a branch and planted my butt in a shallow puddle.

He was just a shadow in a sea of shadows. I glared up at him. "What's wrong with—"

A gunshot shattered the silence of the glade. Heart pounding, I lifted my hands to shield myself, as if that would stop a speeding bullet.

"It's me, Frankie Portnoy!" Frankie shouted, stepping in front of me with his arms raised. "Don't shoot us, old man."

A figure emerged from the tree line. I could only make out his silhouette and the shape of the rifle he held.

"That was a warning shot. If I had wanted to shoot you, you would already be dead." His accent was hauntingly familiar. I would have bet anything that he was from Romania or Bukovina and that he had found his origins in the eastern Carpathians.

"See, Alter, he's almost as rude as you are," Frankie muttered under his breath as he helped me to my feet. "You two will be perfect for each other."

"You could've given me a warning that didn't involve knocking me into a puddle," I growled, swiping strings of mud from the seat of my pants.

Frankie ignored me. "Reb Meir, this is my friend, Alter Rosen. He's—"

"I know what he is," Meir said, keeping his distance. He had lowered the rifle, but only so that its barrel pointed at my legs instead of my head. "I may be old, but I'm not blind, Feivel."

Frankie scowled. "How many times do I have to tell you? I hate that name. It's Frankie now. *Frankie.*"

"Can you help me?" I asked, trying to keep my voice steady. "Yakov's getting stronger, and I don't know what to do."

"So, you know his name," Meir said.

"He was my friend."

Without another word, Meir turned and retreated into the forest. I thought he meant to abandon us here, but Frankie took my wrist and dragged me in pursuit of the man.

AFTER ABOUT FIFTY meters, we reached a small stone cottage that looked as old as the land it grew on, as if it had been here since the beginning of time. Candlelight gleamed through the curtains. It might have been cozy, if not for the animal traps set up in a perimeter around the place, jagged-toothed things trailing chains. Not exactly what I'd call kosher.

Reb Meir waited for us in the glow of the threshold. My heart jolted as we neared. He was tall enough to scrape the door's lintel, his slate-blue eyes set in a long, lean face. There were hints of silver in his beard and sidelocks, but he was hardly the wizened elder I had imagined.

"Come inside," Meir growled impatiently.

"It's okay," Frankie whispered, resting his hand on my lower back. Nervousness made me weak in the knees, and his touch didn't help. "I'll be with you every step of the way."

I swallowed down my unease, stomach twisting, and stepped into the cottage. Books and scrolls crowded every available surface. Sacks and barrels were heaped by the potbelly stove, near a cot with a threadbare blue blanket.

Setting his rifle in a rack on the wall, Meir nodded toward the table. "Sit down."

There was barely enough room to sit, let alone rest my hands. Books crowded the table, their cracked spines gilded with Hebrew.

The recent rainfall filled the cottage with the scent of damp soil. A familiar aroma. A sad one. When my father's business had failed, we had traded our comfortable house in the center of the Jewish quarter for a wattle-and-daub cottage on our neighborhood's outskirts. After heavy rains, I would wake to this same odor, the walls damp with condensation.

I thought of my mother and sisters still there, and it made my chest tighten with longing. Now more than ever, I ached to see them again. Rivka and Gittel must be so big now, old enough to walk alone to market and chase the chickens. I wished I knew what they looked like.

Meir sank into the chair opposite us. If he was a Hasid, he had exchanged his fur shtreimel for a deerstalker cap and traded in his somber frock coat for a green Norfolk jacket.

Even as he took off his hat and rolled a cigarette, he had the cagey demeanor of a domesticated dog gone feral. He refused to take his eyes off me. As for me, I couldn't take my eyes off his cigarette.

"Do you want one?" he asked, after he had lit his.

I cared for tobacco even less than I did for bourbon. Still, I nodded and allowed him to roll me one.

I lit the cigarette with a match and took a drag. The action came naturally, even though I had smoked just once or twice over the last several years. Only when I shook out the match did I realize that I had used my left hand.

"Alter is an omen name." Meir drummed his fingers on the leather cover of a book. "Were you sick as an infant?"

"I was born with a fever. The midwives were certain I would die." Something about smoking calmed me. It was soothing and familiar. I supposed I had Yakov to thank for that.

"I have known quite a few Alters and Altes, and many of them have gone on to lead long and exceptional lives. Unusual lives." His slate-blue eyes pierced through the veil of smoke wreathing his features. "But you can't look toward the future when you're carrying ghosts upon your back."

From a steamer trunk in the corner, Meir extracted a long white robe. It was a kittel, probably the same one he would use on the Day of Atonement. But it was also the kind of garment a groom would wear at his wedding as well as his funeral.

"Will I have to wear tachrichim, too?" I asked, praying he didn't have burial shrouds hidden at the bottom of that trunk.

"Ah, we have a funny one," Meir said with dry sarcasm, although I hadn't been joking. He balled up the kittel and threw it at me. "No. This will suffice. When was the last time you visited a mikveh?"

Normally, I would go to the mikveh every Friday afternoon before Shabbos and also directly after taking part in the tahara ritual. This time, I had forgotten about it entirely.

"Last week before Shabbos," I confessed. "I was so distracted by what happened to Yakov..."

"Nothing that can be done about that." Meir crossed the room. "You'll go into one soon enough. There's a pond behind the house. It will happen there."

While I changed into the kittel, Meir knotted lengths of blue and white cord into the tassels found both on tzitzis and on the corners of a prayer shawl. Like the fringed garment I wore under my shirt, the tassels themselves were also called tzitzis. He counted under his breath, keeping track of the number of knots. Eighteen. Eighteen for chai, for life.

"How long has it been since he died?" Meir asked between knots.

"Only a few days," I said, watching Frankie in the corner of my eye as he leafed through a book on the table. It made me feel safe knowing he was here. He had always been one to protect others.

"Have you been seeing things?"

"Yes." I looked back ahead. "They almost feel like memories, but darker. More dreamlike."

Meir nodded gravely. "Once a dybbuk enters a living body, it grafts itself onto the host's soul. In doing so, it merges with the host's own memories and personality, first distorting them, then slowly replacing them with its own. The visions can be frightening, but they are merely a side effect of that assimilation. You're fortunate to have come here before they worsened. You need to understand, this is not a person. Not anymore."

It disturbed me to hear Meir speak of Yakov that way. The boy who had reached out to me in the mikveh had been afraid. He had clung to me. In that moment, Yakov's fear had been real. Even now I still felt a deep and primal terror coil in my veins, and I knew in my heart that it belonged to him.

"But..."

Meir narrowed his eyes. "But what?"

I hesitated. "He feels afraid."

"Nonsense. You cannot ascribe emotions to a dybbuk."

"I know what fear is."

"When a body is left alone after death, in a state of desecration, the soul becomes corrupted," he said, as though I hadn't even spoken. "It is no longer your friend. It is only a shadow of him, driven by the desires he had in life. The greatest kindness you can give the dybbuk is by helping it pass on, so that it may complete its time in Gehinnom."

Face stinging from Meir's cold rebuttal, I looked down. Against the dark fabric of my slacks, my hands seemed thin and fragile. Easily breakable. Dirt was engrained under the nails from the fall. I thought of how Yakov's hands had looked when I had cleaned them.

Meir finished knotting one tzitzis and moved on to the other. Nausea welled in my stomach at the sight of the braided tassels. I groaned as the heavy ache in my limbs crawled into my spine, seizing my lungs in an icy grip.

"Holding up all right?" Frankie asked.

"Trying," I whispered through clenched teeth, struggling to draw in air. My entire body suddenly felt frigid and immobile, as though my blood had turned to clay. I tried to straighten my fingers, but I could hardly move them now. "My hands. I can't..."

"Hey, Reb, something's the matter," Frankie said, his voice strained as tightly as the cords Meir knotted.

It dawned on me that this was what it was like to be dead. This was what Yakov had been feeling when we had washed him, when he had been buried. Frozen. Trapped. Breathless.

He must have been terrified. He must have felt so alone.

Meir set the finished tzitzis on the table and rose to his feet. He came to me and put his hands on my shoulders. I couldn't see him, couldn't even turn my neck anymore, but just the weight of his palms was reassuring. It reminded me of the way my father used to run his hand through my hair. It meant that I could still feel.

"Take a deep breath, Alter." Meir spoke in a calm baritone. "Breathe in, breathe out. Listen to the beat of your heart. Count it. Remember, you are still *alive*."

As I focused on my breathing, he grasped me by the palm

and elbow, and firmly drew my hand back so that it was per-
pendicular to my wrist. To unfurl my fingers, he first straightened my thumb. It was the same technique we used at the
chevra kadisha, when working on a corpse afflicted by rigor
mortis.

"There we go," Meir said, once he had freed my second
hand. "Good. You're doing excellent, Alter. Just keep breathing. Feivel? Hold his hands for me."

This time, Frankie didn't bother correcting Meir. He cradled my hands against his chest while Meir bound my wrists
together with the braided cords.

Even as the ice melted in my veins and grateful gulps of air
filled my lungs, my unease deepened into dread. I strained
against the cords, overwhelmed by a sense of impending doom.
The ceiling was going to collapse, or a flood was rolling in,
or burning hail would rain down.

"Wait, I can't do this," I stammered as Meir tied off the final
knot. "If we go through with this, it'll kill me. I know it will."

"Don't believe a word he says," Meir told Frankie. "This
is the dybbuk talking."

I wanted to scream in frustration. Why was he talking over
me? Couldn't he tell that this was *me*?

"No, damn you. This is Alter talking." I backed away from
them, striking the table in the process. Books tumbled down,
and loose papers rained on the floor at my feet.

Meir blocked the door. There was no escape.

"Frankie, remember that story you told me," I said quickly,
swinging my head in his direction. "Do you want me to end
up like that boy? Because that's what will happen. This exorcism will kill me. Not Yakov's dybbuk. *This*."

Frankie hesitated. "Maybe Alter is right."

"You mustn't listen to him," Meir stressed as he took a step
toward me. "The dybbuk will say anything to survive. It is a

parasite that will suck every last drop of strength from its host and leave nothing left."

"Damn you, stop calling him that!" I snarled, feinting to the left. "He's more than just a dybbuk. His name is Yakov."

Meir moved to block me, and I darted past him to head straight for the door.

Frankie made a grab for me, catching my sleeve. I shocked myself by twisting around in his grip and driving my knee into his groin. All his boxing skills weren't enough to keep him from crashing to the ground, his hands curled over his wounded parts.

As he cursed at me breathlessly, I shouldered open the unlatched door and tumbled into the night.

"Stop!" Meir shouted. "Alter, don't go!"

My thoughts were so muddled that I didn't know whether it was my life I felt in danger of losing, or if it was Yakov's terror that propelled me forward. It was as though we were two halves of the same animal, sutured together by a bond deeper than flesh.

I blundered through the darkness, crashing through the underbrush. Branches snared my kittel, tearing it down the back.

No matter. Just keep moving.

I made it no more than three meters into the forest before someone tackled me to the ground. Kicking and growling, I struggled against the person's confining hands, twisted around. A hardened face loomed over me, beard like a bear's pelt. Meir.

"Feivel, quit your moaning and help me get him to the pond!" Meir shouted, seizing my bound hands.

Terror engulfed me. If we made it to the pond, it wouldn't purify me. I'd drown just like my father.

"Listen to me, Alter." Meir's grip tightened around my wrists, hard enough to send pain shooting up my arms. "You need to go through with this. The body cannot sustain two souls in equilibrium. It is like a candle with two wicks. No matter what you believe Yakov's intentions are, his dybbuk will first suppress you and then it will consume you. Do you understand me? This possession will eventually kill you."

He was lying. I refused to believe him. If we went through with the exorcism, it would destroy both Yakov and me indiscriminately. I knew it would.

"I said, I'm not doing this!" With a sudden jerk, I broke free of Meir's grip and wormed out from under him. He grabbed onto my legs in an effort to keep me from rising. I tore my ankle away from his hands and kicked him as hard as I could.

He fell onto his side, panting in an effort to reclaim his lost breath. I lurched to my feet.

"Alter, wait," Meir croaked.

I didn't look back. I just ran.

23

THE MOON WAS just a sliver, and after I breached the initial overgrowth, the trees became high enough to block out its meager light. I stumbled through the humid darkness, knocking into trees, blind as a hunted animal. Bullfrogs croaked in a feverish dirge, while larger game, alarmed by my trespass, thrashed through the underbrush, making me feel as though I was being pursued on all sides.

One thought filled my mind: I needed to get home. If I got home, I could lock the door and hide under the covers. Then none of this would be real.

During our hike to Meir's house, Frankie and I couldn't have gone more than two hundred meters from the road. But after five minutes of half running, half stumbling, the forest remained as thick as ever. I slowed to a stop and listened for Frankie's shouts. Nothing. Just silence so deep it felt alive.

You are nothing, the darkness seemed to say, in its overbearing presence, in the humbling vastness of the night sky and the cold, innumerable stars. *You are just a guest here. This was never your home.*

My throat ached as though it had been skinned. I spat into the dirt and stumbled forward, blindly reaching out to feel my way when the closeness of the trees allowed the darkness to circle in on me. I felt cursed like the biblical king Nebuchadnezzar, stripped of power and pride, and driven into the wilderness to live like an animal.

Resting on a fallen tree, I searched the ground for a sharp rock to free my bound hands. I tried rubbing the braided tzitzis against the trunk's rough bark. The only thing I achieved was getting splinters.

A sudden crackling sound startled me, and I lifted my head. Through the trees, a light flickered. The glow of a fire. I froze, trapped between the urge to flee and the unbearable thought of being alone.

Flames crackled, and a wave of heat reached me where I sat. Not a lantern at all. I rose to my feet. During my escape from the cottage, could Frankie or Meir have knocked over a candle? Had I wandered around in a circle?

As I approached the glow, sparks swarmed like fireflies between the trees. The air was laced with the warm, festive scent of pine smoke. I stepped through the tree line, leaving behind the darkness for—

—a sunset so intense, it appeared the sky itself had been set alight. The sun hung low on the horizon, crimson as though engorged with blood.

I swiveled around, but the Illinois wetland had vanished. In its place, a wooden building loomed at my back. Ten meters tall or higher, the structure's entire facade was engulfed in flames. All around it, sunflowers riffled in the breeze, bobbing their heavy heads. The ones nearest to me were burnt into blackened fists.

I stared, stunned and speechless. My heart pounded like a hammer against my ribs.

Faint cries reached my ears. Mouth dry, I took a hesitant step forward. Were there...were there people in there?

The rustling of leaves drew my attention ahead. Beyond the sunflower field, a dark line of trees crested the horizon.

Panic swelled like a blood blister inside me as the forest parted. Now, I heard the snap of branches and groan of falling trunks. A deep, guttural roar shook the trees.

I took a step back, then another, though the flames' heat beat against my back.

Something was.

Something was coming.

Something was coming to devour me.

I turned to flee. I made it two steps before a pair of hands seized me and wheeled me around. The moment my back was turned, the odors of swamp mud and decaying leaves drove out the tang of wood smoke, and darkness flowed in like a thunderclap. A face swam before my vision, barely illuminated by the moonlight—dark intense eyes, unkempt curls spilling over a brow furrowed in worry.

"Get away from me, Frankie!" I tried to pull away from him, but he grasped hold of the tzitzis that bound my wrists. During our struggle, I caught a glimpse of where the burning building had been.

There was nothing there at all.

"Like hell I'll get away." Frankie used his hold on the cords to reel me closer. "You want to get yourself killed out here?"

"I'm not going back there." Tears filled my eyes. My voice caught in my throat like a trapped animal. "You wouldn't listen. You bastard. I told you I didn't want to go through with it, and you wouldn't listen!"

"I know. I'm sorry."

I didn't realize how much I needed him to hug me until he wrapped his arms around my waist and drew me against him.

"I'm sorry," he repeated, stroking his hand through my hair. "I should have listened to you."

I sagged against him, my legs weakening. A miserable sob welled in my throat. "I can't do it. I just can't. It'll be like killing him all over again."

"It's all right. We don't have to go back, if you're not ready. Now, if I let go of your hand, do you promise me you won't run?"

"I promise."

Leaves crackled deeper in the woods. As Meir emerged from the tree line, Frankie stepped in front of me, raising his arm to block Meir from getting close.

"We're going home, Reb," Frankie announced, leveling his chin. "If Alter doesn't want to go through with it, I'm not going to force him."

"You're both making a terrible mistake," Meir croaked breathlessly. Burs clung to his coat and beard. "You must understand, two souls cannot coexist within the same body. The dybbuk must be driven out."

"Would it hurt Yakov, do you think?" I asked. "Would it destroy him?"

Meir didn't answer.

I had heard many theories about what happened to us after death, but even with Yakov's dybbuk shifting inside my veins, I still didn't have an answer. Did we spend some time in Gehinnom and then pass on to a different place? Was it like the kabbalists thought and we returned to earth in another body? Or did we simply cease to be?

I wanted to ask Meir these things, but all I could do was repeat once more: "Tell me, would it destroy him?"

"I don't know," he admitted at last.

"Then I can't. I'll find another way."

As Frankie and I walked across the glade, Meir said my name again. I looked back.

"If you are truly determined to see this through to the end, you should know that there is one other way for a dybbuk to pass on."

"Why didn't you tell us this before, old man?" Frankie complained. "You could have saved me a lot of pain."

"Because the life on this earth takes absolute precedence over the whims of the dead, and for your friend, this method will be even more dangerous than an exorcism." His icy blue eyes pierced into mine. "It is believed that dybbukim possess the living so that they may perform tasks they were unable to complete in life. What were those words he had you write, Alter?"

"You must kill him," I whispered.

Meir nodded grimly. "If what you say is true and Yakov was murdered by the very man he intended to kill, then I fear you will have no choice but to complete the job for him."

FRANKIE AND I found our way back to the roadside and walked along it for a while. The carriage was long gone, but Frankie reasoned that if we reached the city's edge, we'd find another late-night driver to give us a ride.

"I'm sorry I kicked you," I said, after we had made it some distance. From the way he walked, I could tell he was suffering from the effects of my low blow.

"You're lucky I don't plan to have children," Frankie said dully.

He had freed my wrists with a pocketknife after we had made it to the road, but he held my hand as though afraid I would make another break for it. I didn't mind his touch. I welcomed it.

"Don't believe that shtuss about killing a man," Frankie said, curling his fingers through mine. "You're not cut out for that kind of work. We can find another rabbi, a Litvak one this time."

"Okay." My voice sounded very small in the darkness.

"I'll ask around at the yeshivas."

"Right."

"Hey, Alter." He squeezed my hand. "We'll get through this."

I nodded, but I was unable to put into words what I had felt back there. Yakov's fear. His humanity. Oh God, his pain.

I didn't know what to do. Even without a body, in some way or form, Yakov was still here. It was still *him* inside me. If I had an exorcism, I would be killing the boy who had survived the barn fire. And I would be killing the young man who carried water for train boilers. More than once, I had woken from dreams of him, trembling and breathless. By stepping into the mikveh, I would end everything Yakov ever was and could be.

But if I had to hunt down his killer, then wouldn't that be murder as well? I'd be snuffing out a life, no matter how much the man deserved it.

It was like those old Romanian bubbe-meises my mother used to tell me, tales of Faˇt-Frumos venturing out to defeat the fire-breathing zmeu or save the boyar's daughter. In all of them, the hero would receive a warning. Misery waited down one road, and tragedies just as great could be found down the other. There was no higher ground. There was only the descent.

As we continued walking, the darkness soothed me. I wanted to pretend that anything that happened out here would slip away the moment we reached the glow of the city. That was how it was supposed to work; some things just couldn't be talked about in the light.

We made it another few steps before I tugged on Frankie's wrist, stopping him. I needed to say this here, where it was too dark to see his expression and his eyes were just gleams.

"I'm sorry," I said quickly, before I could lose my nerve. "For leaving the way I did, and for all the things I said. I wasn't thinking that night. I just thought I needed to get away, and by the time I started regretting it, I couldn't go back."

"I'm not going to say I'm not mad," Frankie said. "It hurt. It still does."

"I know."

"And for a while there, once I realized you weren't coming back, I hated you even though I thought you were dead. No, *because* of that. And I hated..." He sighed heavily. "I hated that I woke up, and you weren't there resting against the ladder, winding that stupid watch of yours. You were always so quiet around the others, so composed... That made it harder to realize you were gone. Sometimes, when I was with them, I'd look over and expect to see you there beside me, and I'd even get a bit hopeful. But you never were."

My voice clogged in my throat. I blinked back the tears that blurred my vision. "I never knew you cared so much about me. I thought... I remember, you made fun of me when we first met. You said, 'He's so fresh off the boat, I'll bet he still smells like fish.'"

"Because I despised you the moment I saw you."

I felt like Frankie had punched me in the stomach. I stared at him, and he stared back, a patch of darkness lighter than the rest.

"You despised me?" I asked, aghast.

He ran a hand through his hair, averting his gaze. "I'm sorry, that came out wrong. It wasn't *you* personally, it was how you looked. How...how untouched you were by the city. Victor and the others, I met them when they'd been here awhile, when Chicago had already taken away their parents and homes and spat them out on the streets. But you were different. You were pure."

"You're wrong," I mumbled as we stepped back into the moonlight. "Frankie, you think too highly of me."

He looked at me, not comprehending. Why would he? He couldn't see the rottenness inside my soul.

"Alter, are you crying?" he asked softly.

I didn't feel the tears trickling down my cheeks until he mentioned them. With a chuckle of shame and mortification, I wiped them away with my sleeve.

"Frankie, there—" I choked on my words "—there is something terribly wrong with me."

"I know, you're possessed."

"No, that's not what I mean. It's hard to put into words. Let me explain. You see, back in Romania, there was a boy my age who would go from house to house on Saturday mornings to light the ovens during winter. For years, he'd go with his father, but when I was eleven or so, he began coming alone. I got to know him over time, and we somehow became friends. His name was Mircea. He had the most beautiful auburn hair, and his eyes were this remarkable shade of blue. The fact that he was Christian only made him doubly intriguing, like..."

"Tasting the forbidden fruit," Frankie said, and I laughed. My laughter frightened me—it almost sounded like a sob.

"Yes. Yes. I wanted so badly to be acknowledged by him. To be admired by him. Then the summer before I left, we—"

A sudden rumbling stole my next words. Up the road, a swaying lantern cast its glow.

"Hey, hey!" Frankie stepped in the middle of the road, waving his arms wildly. "Stop!"

As the vehicle neared, the lantern light washed over us. It was a wagon hauled by two old dray mares.

"Easy there, nice and slow now," the farmer called to his horses and clucked his tongue. The wagon slowed to a creaking halt before us, all wind-shorn wood and rusty nails, its bed heaped with green squashes and baskets of peaches.

Frankie sighed and lowered his arms. "Thank you. Are you on your way to market?"

"That I am. What are you two doing way out here?" The farmer squinted down at me. "Why's that fellow wearing a nightshirt?"

Frankie brushed off the question with a warm laugh. "My brother sleepwalks," he said. "If I hadn't caught up to him, he'd be halfway to St. Louis by now."

The man chuckled. Frankie was easy to like.

"Well, get on in." The farmer gestured to the back of the wagon. "The mosquitos will eat you two alive if you stay out here much longer."

We climbed into the wagon and settled down among the baskets and sacks. The sweet fragrance of ripe peaches and sun-dried hay settled over us. As the wagon rolled forward, I kept my eyes on the floor, unable to look Frankie in the eye. I could feel his gaze burning into me.

I felt a vague sense of relief, knowing that I hadn't gotten the chance to tell Frankie my secret. He had left religion behind back in Brooklyn, or maybe even before that, back in the old country, but some things were inexcusable. If I told him how deeply I had admired Mircea, his vision of me would be tarnished forever.

We passed the burning building twice more on our long ride. The second time, I cringed in fear and shied away. It was still aflame, only now against a backdrop of Illinois shanties. The third time, the flames had reduced it to a charred carcass amid the smoke-guttering factories and slaughterhouses of the Stockyards. By then, I was too exhausted to feel more than a twinge of trepidation as the hallucination faded into the smog.

I knew it must be the same barn fire that had claimed the lives of Yakov's parents. Trauma had a way of crawling back to you. I supposed even dybbukim weren't spared from remembering.

By the time we reached the inner city, all I felt was exhaustion. I had always thought that if the impossible were to confront me, I would be unbending in my rationality. I should have known that what doesn't bend must eventually break. I could either accept this new reality or retreat from it, and the latter outcome might end up being even worse than the first.

Frankie paid the farmer to take a detour through the wharfs, down a street lined with old but attractive gray-stone houses. Their dark slate roofs and tall hedges gave the buildings an atmosphere of solemn dignity, like matrons sitting shiva. From where the man dropped us off, it was only ten steps or so to the building Frankie called home.

"I rent a room upstairs," he explained, searching his pockets. He pulled out his keys. "It's nice, out of the way. There's an old servant stairwell, so my landlady doesn't have to wonder why I return home so late."

"Ah, so the Levee isn't good enough for you now?" I forced a smile. The humor felt weak even to me.

"I paid too much for these clothes to have them turn into moth food."

"Speaking about clothes, can I borrow some?" I asked as Frankie unlocked the front door.

"Of course. There is a bath downstairs, too. A real one, with plumbing. You'll be able to wash up, get some of that drek off you."

After we had taken off our shoes, he showed me to the bathroom, all porcelain and dark wood, with running water and a toilet operated by a pull chain. The tub was a massive claw-footed affair of enameled copper. I waited for the door to close behind Frankie before twisting on the taps.

There had to be a way to communicate with Yakov. He

was still here, still a person, no matter what Meir had said. I needed to at least try.

As water filled the tub, I stood at the sink and forced myself to confront my reflection.

"Yakov," I murmured, closing my eyes. I pressed my forehead against the mirror's cold surface, poised my fingers over it, feeling as if any moment I'd sink through the pane as though it were a pool of quicksilver. "Yakov, are you here? Can you hear me? Please, show me. Show me how I can make things right. Tell me who did this to you so I can stop them from hurting anyone else."

My body moved on its own, twisting away from the mirror as mechanically as clockwork. I stared at the tub, my heart fluttering against my breastbone. The water became bluer, darker, as the tub filled higher. Like the mikveh. Like a sinkhole opening beneath me.

As the water sloshed against the rim, I regained control of my body. Stepped forward on feet I barely felt. Twisted off the taps.

Yakov wanted me to do this.

I eased into the bath, half expecting the bottom to give way beneath my feet, plummeting into an endless void. No. Solid metal. I sat down, keeping my borrowed kittel on because Yakov had died in his clothes.

Shivering in the frigid water, I focused on its chill the same way I had concentrated on my breathing back at Meir's cottage—not to bring me back but to further distance myself from my body.

Maybe Yakov had been dead when he had slipped into the lagoon's dark water. Maybe his killer had held him under. Was this what he had experienced in his last moments, or did it come after?

"This is not bathing," I whispered as I sank against the side of the tub. My kittel billowed up. I brushed the cloth down to release the air bubbles, waiting for my goose bumps to recede. "This is not bathing."

The tub was filled with clean water that had been gathered in a cistern or pumped from distant pipes. It didn't hold enough water to qualify as a mikveh, nor did it contain the right kind of *living* water. However, it would serve its purpose.

The water stroked my chin, its chill seizing my lungs in a viselike grip. The ceiling was plain plaster, but it would do. All I had to imagine was the tahara house's pulley system, a spiderweb of ropes and iron bolts.

Back. Back. Take me back, Yakov.

Taking a deep breath, I filled my lungs with as much air as they could hold. A faint, acrid odor laced the air. Not sea brine. Harsh and sour, it brought to mind my first year in Chicago. Frankie showing off the old service revolver he'd traded a filched pocket watch for, practicing on milk bottles and tin cans. His eyes aglow with excitement, a beaming smile on his lips. It was the scent of spent gunpowder. Fireworks?

I sank under.

At first, there was only smooth enamel beneath me. I tried holding my breath in, but air bubbles tickled my nostrils, and more escaped my lips. Then a cool night's breeze brushed across my face.

My eyes flew open.

The blackest night. Stars innumerable, cold and white, like the fragments of a shattered sun.

Underneath me, the tub's curved bottom had become damp grass, the musk of dirt and stagnant water in my nostrils.

When I tried to look around me, my body refused to obey. I had a feeling my mouth was open, but I couldn't close it. I couldn't even move my eyes.

There was a sudden explosion, and flames crawled across the sky. Sizzling sparks and smoke trails.

A shadow passed over my vision. The silhouette of a man. He had no face, only a shifting cloud of smoke where his features should have been.

His hand brushed over my face. I thought he meant to close my eyes, but instead, his fingers rested upon my throat and lingered there. Stroked the bruise he had surely made.

"You gave me my true name. My purpose." His voice left him in a low thrum. Vaguely, it dawned on me that he wasn't speaking in Yiddish. "You showed me who I was inside. For that, you have my thanks. I've pierced it into my skin so I'll never forget it."

Tendrils of smoke wafted from his clothes. He was burning inside.

The man nudged me onto my side with his boot. The sky tumbled overhead, unspooling into a reflection of fireworks on water and rising white buildings that appeared as distant and inaccessible as the medieval Neamț Citadel. He gave me another kick, and the weight of my petrified body sent me spilling into the water.

I sank. Deeper. Deeper. He had put stones in my pockets to weigh me down, but they slipped out as I fell. My body caught on a rope submerged across the lagoon floor.

I couldn't move. I couldn't—

—breathe!

Powerful arms encircled me, dragging me from the dark lagoon and onto the cold porcelain floor. I twisted my head to the side and retched up water.

"Damn you, Alter!" Frankie leaned over me, his voice quivering with equal parts anger and relief. "Were you trying to kill yourself?"

"N-no." Coughing, I bent over myself. My throat was on

fire, my eyes and nose watering furiously. Terror filled me as the liquid dripped onto my hand. Not just water. Blood filled the cup of my palm.

"Look at you. Your nose." Frankie swore and pulled the hand towel from its rung. He handed the cloth to me, shaking his head as I pressed it against my bleeding nose.

"It's okay." My shuddering voice didn't sound convincing even to me. "It's from holding my breath. It's happened before when I've gone swimming."

"No, it's not okay. You're not okay, Alter." He raked his hand through his hair, his every gesture sparking with tension. "I was pounding the door and you wouldn't answer. And when I opened the door and saw you underwater, I thought you were dead. You know that? I thought you were *dead*."

The anxiety in his voice made me cast my gaze down in shame. "I'm sorry, but I had to."

"Had to what?" Frankie demanded. "Try drowning yourself?"

"No. I needed to see what Yakov saw before it happened. I had to feel exactly what he felt." I dropped the towel in my lap, shuddering violently. "I saw him, Frankie. Not his face, but—but I know he's a man. Older. In his late thirties or forties."

The stranger hadn't spoken in Yiddish or English, but I had understood him nonetheless. That could only mean he had been talking in a language I knew, either German or Romanian. But what language had it been? Why couldn't I remember?

"Alter, who are you talking about?" Frankie asked.

It dawned on me that I was smiling, and I couldn't stop. The expression tugged at my lips, taut and mirthless. "The man who killed him."

25

AFTER I DRIED myself off and changed into the clean set of clothes Frankie brought me, I joined him in the bedroom. He had traded his elegant evening suit for a breezy white nightshirt, the collar unbuttoned to reveal the smooth muscularity of his chest.

"I'm glad to see the clothes fit." He cocked his head and smiled. "You look rather dashing in them, actually. A true gentleman."

"Flattered," I said dryly, as if that would hide my blush. "Thank you for everything. I won't impose on you any longer."

"Alter, you seriously can't be thinking about searching for that man at this hour?" he exclaimed in disbelief. "You don't even know what he looks like."

"No, I have work in the morning. I need to go home. I'll take a streetcar." As I searched my pocket for loose coins, it took me a moment to remember these clothes weren't mine.

"My keys. My money. My dad's watch." My voice sounded very small to me. "They're still back there with Meir."

"Don't worry about that. I doubt he has much interest in material things."

"No, you don't understand. My dad gave me that watch. I can't just—"

"Alter, calm down." Frankie laid a hand on my shoulder. "I'll take care of it, don't worry. I'll go over to Meir's and get it back, even if it means getting into a boxing match with the old bastard. Just spend the night. I'll sleep on the floor."

"Are you sure?"

"It's no imposition."

I was too exhausted to disagree, much less walk home. "All right. Thank you."

Frankie had always envied the luxurious side of life, and his room was as I had imagined it would be. The walls were all heavy wainscoting and damask wallpaper, while the four-poster bed was fitted with fine linen. Fire flickered within the oil lamp's milk glass shade.

Frankie took the spare coverlet from the closet shelf and spread it on the floor. As he plumped a pillow, he glanced over at me with a smile. "Remember when you first came to live with us back in the Levee, you thought you could catch syphilis from used bedding?"

"Because the beds came from a brothel."

He chuckled. "You were so innocent. I doubt you'd even kissed a girl yet."

"And I suppose you kissed plenty of girls by then?" I snapped, annoyed by the tone of his voice.

"Actually, I hadn't." He glanced back. "Haven't, I should say. At all. Ever."

"But, Frankie, you're so..." I searched for a word. Handsome. Well-dressed. Bright. Intense. "You."

"What about you?" he asked as I sat on the edge of the bed. "Is there a pretty girl at shul you have your eyes on?"

I thought about giving him Raizel's name, but something about the darkness made it easy to speak the truth. "No, there's no one."

"So, you've never kissed a girl?"

"Never," I admitted as Frankie folded the coverlet into a makeshift mattress.

"What about a boy?"

His question struck me like a slap in the face. "What? Did you just ask——"

"It's not anything unusual," he said nonchalantly, still turned away, as though all of society's customs and expectations ceased to exist the moment we lost sight of each other's face. "It happens all the time at yeshivas and boarding schools. Harmless fun, really."

I bit my lower lip, emboldened by the darkness. "Once. Right before we left Romania."

"It was Mircea, wasn't it?" he murmured.

I took a deep breath. "Yes."

Frankie didn't answer. He kept his back to me, his palm flat against the folded coverlet. I thought I must repulse him. The idea left me sick with fear.

"But it was just a foolish dare," I added quickly, before he could respond. "Innocent fun like you said. And Mircea was a wretched kisser. He did it with his eyes closed. On the first try, he missed my mouth completely."

That was a lie. I had been the one to miss.

"How did it make you feel?" Frankie asked, turning to face me.

"It was merely a foolish dare," I repeated, too ashamed to give voice to the joy and desire. I kept my gaze on the floor. "It didn't actually mean anything. As you said, it's just something boys do, and then they grow out of it."

"But how did it make you feel?"

"Alive," I whispered as he came to my side. I rose to my feet to meet him.

Frankie stood with his back to the oil lamp, eclipsing its glow. I couldn't see his face, and I didn't think he could see mine. I could have been anyone. These words could be someone else's, even Yakov's. Except the desire shredding me up inside was so painful, it could only be a part of my heart and soul.

Twenty, thirty, forty years. Fifty even. Fifty years more of ducking my head, nervous glances at other men, the guilt, the fear. If I had to live like this for another half century, no, another year, another day, another minute—it would kill me. Or I would.

"You make me feel alive, Alter. You always have." Frankie placed his hand on my cheek, tracing the curve of my cheekbone.

I leaned into him, my hands finding their perfect place on his lower back.

"Take your time." His voice was husky with desire. "I don't want you to feel rushed. We can just hold hands or hold each other. We could talk about something, anything. I won't kiss you unless you want—"

I pressed my mouth against his, silencing him midsentence. He leaned into my kiss. Through his thin nightshirt, he was all heat and hard muscle. His hot tongue parted my lips, and all I could think about was how he felt inside my mouth, the weight of his hands upon my back, the crisp scent of his cologne.

This was wrong.

So why did it feel so right?

I groaned as he traced his lips down my neck, teasing and sensual in his slowness. He kissed the rapid pulse in the hollow of my throat and paused there for a moment, as though to savor the proof that I was alive. I ought to have stepped away, but my body played rebellion, insolently rubbing against him.

"Wait," I panted. "We shouldn't do this. It's a sin."

"Sins are measured in the pain you cause others."

"But Leviticus."

"But David and Jonathan." Frankie's breath coaxed up the fine down on the nape of my neck as he nuzzled my throat. "If something brings us mutual pleasure and harms no one, it's a virtue."

As his lips found mine again, the tension drained from my muscles. I had wanted this for so long, I wouldn't let fear sully the moment. I needed this.

I FLOATED UP from a dreamless sleep to find myself in a strange room. I couldn't breathe! Lurching up and hacking violently, I curled over myself. I lifted my hands to my throat, expecting to encounter a tight cord. Instead, my fingertips stroked sweaty skin. My pulse fluttered against my thumb.

Panting, I reached across the bed and grasped a fistful of sheet. Alone. I was alone. Yakov didn't wait for me under the blanket, dripping with mud and lagoon water. Once my racing heart calmed, I turned my head to confirm it.

I released a shaky breath, recalling where I was. Of course the room was unfamiliar. I had spent the night at Frankie's.

I looked over the side of the bed. The pile of blankets on the floor was disheveled. Frankie must still toss and turn at night. Some things never changed. Except, in many ways, it felt as though everything had changed. We would never be able to go back from that.

I didn't know if I wanted to. I felt so confused. It was as though he had thrown the world out of orbit all with a single kiss, sent gravity head over heels, and along with it, the rules that I thought governed us.

Sunlight poured through the wide window. My body felt stiff and cold, and my legs ached from running through the woods. The bedside clock was frozen at half past three. It dawned on me that the color of the sunlight was wrong. It was much too late.

A jolt of horror rippled through me. I had work today.

I'd kept my pants and drawers on while I slept. Scrambling out of bed, I searched the floor for the rest of the clothes I'd borrowed. I didn't bother to tuck in my shirttail or find suspenders. I stuffed one of Frankie's silk neckties in my pocket to knot on the way. After fifteen seconds of hunting for socks in the armoire, I decided to forgo them entirely.

After retrieving my shoes from the mudroom, I let myself out through the front door. Halfway down the street, I ran into Frankie, who carried a basket of pastries against his chest. A smile spread across his face.

"How'd you sleep?" he asked.

"Fine, thank you," I said hastily. "Sorry, but I'm late. I need to go to work."

"What about finding an exorcist?"

"I have work." I stepped past him, then hesitated and looked back. "Frankie, last night—it was just, uh, it was the dybbuk."

He didn't answer. His smile was gone now.

I hated this. I hated how afraid I felt, how *terrified*. Not just of our kiss, but the possibility of inevitably taking things a step further. It wasn't just Leviticus—the secondhand clothes I owned were mixed of wool and flax, and if I searched through the verses, I was certain I'd find a dozen other infractions I was guilty of. It was also the hard labor and jail time, punishments that were even more brutal here than back in Romania. It was the shame in my mother's eyes if she ever found out about who I was, and the disgust. I'd never be a part of the family again.

But I wanted to kiss him again so much. No. Just holding his hand, just having him smile at me, would be enough. And yet...

"It wasn't anything serious," I said, wishing desperately I could believe my own words. Saying them was like chewing on broken glass.

"Of course. It was just a kiss." His lips rose again, in a smile as hard and sharp as a sickle. "Harmless fun, like I said."

"Right."

"You should go to work, Alter." He brushed past me.

"I'll see you later." I lifted my hand in a wave, but he didn't look back.

I continued on my way, ignoring the ache in my heart. I wished I'd told him the truth about how I felt.

I decided to cut straight through the Levee on foot until I reached the river's northern bend. At the wharf, workers flashed their tin lunch buckets and grumbled for cigarettes. I pressed a hand over my growling stomach. If only I'd taken one of Frankie's pastries after all. I searched my pockets, praying for a forgotten nickel. Nothing.

After crossing the river, I hopped aboard a streetcar in passing, clinging onto the rear bars for several blocks, until it slowed at a corner.

By the time I reached the newspaper office, I was sick with dread and panic. Without the familiar weight of my father's watch in my pocket, I felt unmoored. I glanced at the clock on my way in and sighed in relief. Just five minutes past schedule. We could work with that.

"You're late," Mr. Weiss growled from his desk as I took my place at the Linotype machine.

"I'm sorry, sir. My bicycle's tire was flat."

He grunted and turned his attention back to his work. The molten lead in the melting pot was nearly exhausted. I hung a fresh ingot from the hook, then sat down and started typing.

"Where's your hat?" Mr. Weiss asked a few minutes later.

"It fell into the river."

He eyed me keenly. "And whose clothes are those?"

"My roommate's."

He didn't look convinced. Even with my shirttails hanging out and the necktie crooked, it was easy to see that the clothes were tailored and finely made. Still, he let it go and got back to work.

By lunchtime, I felt weak and famished. While typing the last article, the lettered keys doubled before my eyes, then blurred into blocky nonsense that I might have mistaken for English if not for the Б and Π and Θ and more strewn among the familiar Latin alphabet. I made so many mistakes that I was forced to melt down the error-filled slugs and retype them with excruciating slowness, digging my teeth into my inner cheek until the letters became Yiddish once more. Mr. Weiss watched me with an eagle eye, and came over when I was finished to check my work.

He stooped over the metal tray containing the letterpress blocks and studied them closely, tapping to make sure that I had wedged each block firmly in place. "Good."

Across the room, I spotted Mr. Lewin with two other newsmen whose names I couldn't place. I caught his eye as I neared and nodded. He smiled back in greeting.

Once the other newsmen had left, I went over.

"I have more news, Mr. Lewin," I said, stopping in front of him. "A boy was found dead at a kosher processing plant down at the Yards. The police also called it an accident, but I don't think it was. I'm having a friend involved in labor look into it."

"A processing plant." He mulled it over. "You'll want to be

careful with that. Men in that industry didn't get where they were by being polite."

"I know."

"Still, I'm glad to see you're continuing to follow leads. I can tell you're putting in hard work. That will take you far in the world."

Something about his words put a bad taste in my mouth.

"I'm not doing this to get ahead," I said. "I'm doing it for Yakov and the boys who disappeared."

"I'm sure you'll do them justice." Mr. Lewin gave me an encouraging pat on the shoulder.

As he walked off, it occurred to me that in the course of a single night, my mission had become extremely more complicated. This wasn't just about giving Yakov a voice anymore or shedding light on the incompetence and indifference that his death had revealed to me. It was about avenging him, which, like preparing the dead, must be accomplished in silence and secret.

I returned from the deli to find Raizel standing at my workstation, studying the Linotype machine.

"I was expecting something a little more outdated," she said when I came over after bringing the newsmen their sandwiches. "There can't be *that* many people interested in challah recipes?"

"You'd be surprised."

After my father had died, I had spent weeks trying to put his death into words. I wrote my mother letter after letter, reading them over and ripping them up unsent, before I finally worked up the courage to tell her. Telling Raizel about the dybbuk felt much like the same. I had rehearsed the confession in my head all morning, only to find that for now silence was the best answer.

"Did you find anything?" I asked as she sat at the machine's chair. Across the room, Mr. Weiss scowled.

"I did," she said with a nod. I expected her to boast, but her expression was grim. "You know the Stockyard bosses? Greedy bastards who make their living on slaughter, who leave their workers standing in filth and guts for hours each day. They mix rotten meat with the fresh and butcher diseased cattle."

"Raizel, I don't need a derasha," I said, earning a humorless look for comparing her enthusiastic explanation to a sermon. She was almost as bad as Frankie. "I already know how workers are treated down in Packingtown. Just tell me what you found."

"Fine," she said curtly. "I'll get to the point."

"Thank you."

"Five years ago, a new boss came to town. His name is Katz. He began by dealing in kosher meat, but he's moved on to the larger market. From what I've heard, he's as cruel and selfish as the rest. That boy you mentioned, the one they found dead, he was found in his factory's waste pit." Her voice was as blunt and hard as the blow of a sledgehammer, and stunned me just the same. "It wasn't blood on him, it was everything else. Guts, shit, urine. He was fourteen. Jewish. An immigrant from Russia. He was found... He was disrobed. The official story is that he fell in and tore his clothes off in a panic, but do you really think someone drowning in liquid filth would spend the time to remove their shirt, their suspenders, their pants, their underwear?"

Shock and horror choked me. I struggled to answer, but I couldn't find what to say. Didn't she know she was breaking all the rules?

In our community, there were things you talked about. There were things you never talked about. There were things you and the people around you pretended not to know, because just to acknowledge that they existed meant they could get into your homes, into your beds, under your skin.

It had always been this way, even back in Romania.

Here was what I had witnessed during my year in the Levee: girls no older than my sisters, weeping in the alleys outside brothels. A child bought for three dollars. A street urchin with filthy dungarees and eyes the wounded blue of fresh bruises, guided by the hand into a public toilet by a much older gentleman.

These things were not spoken about on Maxwell Street. But even things without names existed.

Raizel leveled her chin and regarded me through narrowed eyes. Her look alone dared me to say something, anything. Tell her it couldn't be true. That these things didn't happen to people like us.

"I... I've heard about that," I said at last, self-conscious of how hushed my voice had become. I couldn't raise it above a mutter. I could hardly even bring myself to look at her, as though just talking about something so terrible might cause it to rub off on me and stain. "Not him personally, of course. Happening, I mean. At the chevra kadisha, the volunteers who prepare women... A twelve-year-old girl..."

I couldn't bring myself to say the rest. My eyes burned just at the thought of it.

"On Mondays and Thursdays, Yakov's final stop ended at the Stockyards." I drew in a shaky breath. "The train's water boiler would be refilled there. He'd have to wait."

And maybe when he had been waiting, he had caught Mr. Katz's interest. The man could have invited him to the Fair.

Just the thought that something might have happened to Yakov, that something might have been *done* to him, made me sick to my stomach. No wonder he had possessed me. Such a violation required ruthless justice.

I shivered at the recollection of his killer's fingers stroking my throat.

You gave me my true name. My purpose.

"But Yakov was eighteen," I added quickly. "If someone tried to—to attack him, he'd have been strong enough to fight back. And besides, he was fully clothed."

"Perhaps he heard something he shouldn't have," Raizel said flatly. "Something dangerous enough to have him killed."

"He bought a gun."

She narrowed her eyes. "How do you know this? Why didn't you tell me?"

"While I was cleaning his room yesterday, I found the bullets and the receipt from the shop."

Raizel gave it some thought. "Why buy a gun, if not for vengeance? It checks out."

"But what about Aaron Holtz?"

"Maybe after the Whitechapel Club led nowhere, he decided to search for another lead. He knows more people in meatpacking than I do, so the news could have reached him sooner."

"I know that Josef Loew worked at a tannery in the Stockyards. But Moishe Walden—"

"—works as a courier. If you go around town delivering letters in Yiddish, what are the chances of coming across someone like Katz?"

"It'd only be a matter of time…" I murmured.

She nodded, her sepia-brown eyes burning with intensity. "Alter, I think we need to pay a visit to Mr. Katz."

27

AFTER ASSURING MR. Weiss that I would arrive at six o'clock sharp on Monday morning to finish my tasks and stay even later in the day, he grudgingly permitted me to leave at three thirty instead of five. I met Raizel at the nearby station so we could take a train to the Union Stockyards.

Raizel was dressed in black and Schloss green, her collar secured with a paste brooch meant to resemble amethyst. As we waited for the train to arrive, she caught me staring at her blouse and lifted her eyebrows. "What?"

I averted my gaze, embarrassed by what she must be thinking. Why did it make me so uneasy to look her in the eye, as though she might see the truth about who I was? About what Frankie and I had done.

"You shouldn't wear that shade of green," I said under my breath.

"Oh, so who elected you the Minister of Fashion?"

"It has arsenic in it."

"Did—did you say arsenic?" she sputtered.

"In the dye. My father wouldn't produce clothes in that shade because of it."

She looked back ahead, her face turning rather green itself. "I'm still making payments on it and the skirt that goes with it. I was going to wear them to this year's Yom Kippur Ball."

"This year's *what*?" I choked.

"It's an event put on by Chicago's chapter of the Pioneers of Liberty." She leveled her chin, challenging me with her steadfast gaze. "You're welcome to come along, too, if you'd rather not spend your entire day in shul."

I sputtered for a response. Yom Kippur was our Day of Atonement, spent in fasting and prayer. It was the holiest date of the Jewish calendar, when our fate for the new year was sealed in the Book of Life.

"I don't even..." I shook my head in disbelief. "Why would you have a party on Yom Kippur? Don't you care about tradition?"

"Who does tradition benefit?" Her eyes seared into me. "Tradition would have me up in the women's gallery. It would silence me."

Her words took me aback. Ever since leaving Frankie's crew, I had tried to escape my homesickness and loneliness by becoming a part of Maxwell Street's community. Returning to tradition had been inevitable. Just joining a minyan for evening services or listening to the chazzan's chanting was like stepping back into my childhood home. It didn't matter if it was a mosquito-infested shul broiling in Chicago's muggy summer heat; if I closed my eyes, I was back in Piatra Neamț again.

All this time, I had taken my participation for granted. But for Raizel, it was different. For her, tradition was a shackle.

"I mean, just think about it," she said sharply. "The whole idea of needing to atone is ridiculous when we have done nothing wrong. What exactly do *you* have to atone for, Alter?"

"My father." I spoke without thinking, not even realizing what I said until the words left my mouth. The confession didn't feel like it belonged to me anymore, as though in shouldering this possession, I had exchanged some of Yakov's past for my own.

Raizel fell silent, the anger draining from her face. "But Mrs. Brenner told me he died of typhus…"

"He did." I released a shaky breath. "It crept up slowly, and I didn't notice until it was too late. Not that it would have done any good. There was only one doctor, and he refused to get close to my father. So, I was the one who emptied my father's chamber pot, who brought him his meals, who helped him wash. For how much time I spent in the sick bay, you would think I'd have caught something. Many people got sick on that journey, and at least six others died. But not me."

"Alter, you can't possibly blame yourself for your father's sickness," Raizel exclaimed. "Not that. Not typhus."

"That's not what I blame myself for."

"Then what?"

"I… I began to despise him. My own father. It repulsed me to go in there and see him that way. He was so kind, he'd give a beggar the coat off his back. He treated everyone like mishpachah. But…that man in the sick bay, that *thing*, it barely even looked like him. And all night and all day, he would call to me. Croak and pant like an animal. Demanding. Water. Food. He shat himself, and I had to wipe it off him. I couldn't take it anymore. He stunk. He *disgusted* me. The night it happened, I ignored him. I refused to get up when he called my name, and after a while, I just couldn't be there. I couldn't do it."

A wretched laugh escaped me. I wiped at my eyes, expecting tears. My hand came back dry. When I drew in a breath, I caught a whiff of the ocean breeze.

"I told him things I shouldn't have. Terrible things, so

ugly. I told him I wished he would just die already, how much I hated him, and how could he be so stupid to bring us here? So, so stupid. Couldn't he see it? Couldn't he see that this was what happened to people who go to strange places, places where they have no right being? And he took it all in, silent and docile, like a child. Like a martyr. I left the room. Left him there alone, lying in his own waste, thirsty. I wandered. I don't know where I went. Those hours are gone. I just wandered. When I returned at dawn, they were already wrapping up his body."

"Alter, he was dying. You couldn't have stopped it."

"That's not even the worst part. The worst part is that, my father... When they threw his body into the ocean, I thought I saw the sheet move. And I heard him call to me. I think he was still alive."

"You can't possibly know that," Raizel said, just when I thought she wouldn't respond. I opened my eyes to find her staring at me with the saddest smile.

"But it's possible."

"Is it, Alter? I took a ship, too. I still remember how noisy it was up on deck. Even if he had shouted, I'd doubt you'd have been able to hear him over the wind and the roar of waves."

I wanted to argue, but I couldn't. I felt vaguely stunned, as if she had struck me from a blind spot. Was it possible that I hadn't heard my father at all? Could I have only imagined it?

"Alter, I think anyone could have done what you did," Raizel said softly. "Everyone has a breaking point. And he was sick."

"I just don't understand. Why him? Why *him*?" I looked up at her. "He was such a good man. And he died of sickness, when all those years ago, it should have been me who died of sickness. Don't you understand? The one who got typhus, the one they threw overboard, it should have been *me*."

"Listen to me, Alter." Her sepia-brown eyes searched mine. "There is no reason why your father died, but maybe, just maybe there's a reason you survived."

In time, the Stockyards' gate towered before us, all ivory limestone and rising turrets, as grand as any wall in the White City. I had visited the Stockyards only once before. Back then, the gate had been unadorned but for a stone steer's head. Now, American flags hung from the gate's cornices in honor of the World's Fair. Gilded federal eagles held wooden shields emblazoned in red, white, and blue.

But even the festive display and large welcome sign couldn't distract from the cloying stench of melted hooves and decay. Past the gate, the Yards was a labyrinth of brick walls the color of spoiled meat, smoke-guttering flues, and rickety wooden ramps crammed within two square kilometers. Pens contained thousands of pigs and cattle, and as Raizel and I headed deeper into the complex, the air grew muggy with their earthy animal odors. Even worse smells wafted from the waterway that cradled the Yards' southern edge, a festering stew of blood and guts that bubbled like a cauldron.

It wasn't just slaughterhouses and meatpacking factories that occupied the Yards' four hundred acres. There were fertilizer plants, hide tanners, glue factories, and brush makers. There were dozens of saloons and grub houses, and no doubt more than a few brothels and opium dens nestled among the other buildings like cavities studding rotten teeth. It was a tiny city of its own, nicknamed Packingtown by Chicago's residents.

"Ugh." Raizel scowled in disgust, pressing her handkerchief over her face. "This odor—"

"It's the smell of industry," I said to annoy her.

She cast me a withering look. "More like the stench of capitalism."

At this hour, the Yards swarmed with workers. Men drove swine and cattle, while others hauled massive blocks of ice for cold storage or dragged handcarts loaded with goods. Just as numerous were the vermin, a plague of flies and mosquitos that stirred through the sweltering July air.

Katz's packing plant was located in the northern end of the Stockyards. With its high brick walls and the barbed-wire livestock pens surrounding it, it seemed as impenetrable as any fortress. Smoke wafted from its towering chimneys.

Approaching the wrought-iron gates, we came across the relics of a strike. Broken plywood signs were scattered in the dirt like grave markers, their smeared slogans written in Yiddish, German, and English.

"Does this happen often?" I asked.

Raizel nodded. "This one's been going on and off since Governor Altgeld pardoned the rest of the Haymarket activists back in June. They never should have been convicted in the first place. All these people want is to make enough to take care of their families, and to not have to live with their boss's boot on their back."

As we reached the gates, Raizel's mouth pressed into a tight line. It was common knowledge back in the Levee that the Stockyards meatpackers and the vice district's brothel lords had Chicago's police department and politicians in their pockets. Votes were bought and campaigns were fixed with dirty money. Anyone who threw a wrench into the gears of the city's seedy underbelly was apt to end up at the bottom of Lake Michigan. For someone so active in the labor movement, Raizel surely knew the risk we were taking just by coming here.

She turned to me. "Remember, we're writing an article. About the grand things Mr. Katz is doing here."

"I'm not the one you should be worried about," I said. "I'll give you ten minutes before you douse him with the nearest beverage."

"Don't worry, I'll tell him I was aiming for you."

My smile slipped away the moment she turned ahead. I touched my shirt collar, wincing. The bruise had ached all morning, its color deepening to shades of indigo.

We had rehearsed our questions on the ride over. Raizel thought the important thing was establishing a groundwork, anything that could inadvertently connect Katz to the disappearances and Yakov's murder. I just wanted to get a good look at his face. If he was truly the man behind this, then perhaps the sight of him would awaken the dybbuk inside of me.

Dangerous or not, it was our only lead, and time was running out.

As we walked, Raizel carefully readjusted her sunhat. Billowy lace netting was secured to the brim by two long pins topped with brass spheres. "How do I look?"

"Uh…" She was an attractive girl, I supposed. I liked the absinthe-green shade of her blouse, even though it was toxic. But I knew she wasn't talking about her outfit, and I felt uncomfortable telling her she looked pretty, in case it might be interpreted as something more.

She narrowed her eyes. "Just 'uh'?"

"You look very nice." I cleared my throat. "Very professional."

"No wonder Mrs. Brenner chose you." She turned back ahead, her lips twitching with a smile she fought to conceal. "You're hopeless. We both are."

A guardsman waited at the heavy oak doors of Katz's meatpacking plant. Seeing us approach, he placed his hands on his waist and jutted his chin forward. "What do you want?"

"We're reporters," Raizel said in careful, impeccable English. "We're here for the interview."

"You?" He lifted his eyebrows, bemused.

Her eyebrow twitched. "Yes. Me."

"You're a girl."

"Have you not heard of Nellie Bly or Annie Laurie?" she said incredulously. "Or even Nora Marks down at the *Tribune*? Do you not read?"

He had no answer to that. Hearing the passion in Raizel's voice, I realized that to her, journalism was more than just a job that paid better than working the presses. It was sacred.

"Mr. Katz is expecting us." She took a meaningful glance at her pocket watch. "He arranged for this interview two weeks ago. If you keep us waiting, he will be most displeased."

The man narrowed his eyes. "He said nothing about any reporters."

"Then you may call down his secretary." She snapped her pocket watch shut. "Unless you would rather we interview the bosses over at Armour's."

With a grunt, he stepped aside and allowed us to pass through the open door. He came in after us, a troll-like presence in the dirty light that entered through the glazed windows.

"Follow me," he said gruffly, jangling his key ring.

I exchanged a look with Raizel, before following him down the hall. Abrasive noises echoed from other rooms. The whine of steam. Rumbling machinery. Fleshy, abrupt squelches that turned my stomach and filled my mouth with the taste of char.

The air inside the packing plant was several degrees cooler than outside, on account of the brick walls, but it reeked of the same slaughter. The faint tang of chemicals laced my every breath.

As we ascended the stairs, the air in the passage grew thicker, chillier, so cold that I found myself shivering. Fear coiled in my stomach.

I could feel the air all around me, pressing in like dirt cast into an open grave. Smothering. No windows in the stairwell. Darkness. This overwhelming musk of animal waste and chemicals—almost like the odor of salt water and unwashed bodies.

"P-pardon me." I lurched past them and took the stairs down two at a time. "The air... I have to go outside."

If Raizel answered me, her voice was drowned out by the roar of waves. My feet hit solid ground. As I fled toward the double doors, the floor seemed to roll beneath me.

Not again. Not again.

I threw open the doors and tumbled into the dark—

—silence of the steamship's sick bay, the quiet thrum of the engine rooms vibrating through the floorboards beneath my feet. The room was windowless like the slaughterhouse ramp and tinged with the amniotic scent of the sea. Yet where twin cots should have been, there was now just a long oak desk and tufted leather chairs.

The light had become the putrid green of necrosis, reflected in the bottles of amber tinctures cluttering the shelves. A man stood contemplating the selection. Not the French doctor who had refused to treat my father. A stranger.

"I found them." The man turned to me ever so slightly. The gaslight shone upon the heavy, leonine lines of his features—a mane of sandy-brown hair, eyes the piercing blue of gas flames, a firm mouth shaped around the stem of a briar pipe. "The tickets. Do you intend to hunt him, Yasha?"

"That bastard took everything from me," I heard Yakov say, his baritone turned rough with anger. He felt close enough to touch, as though at any moment I might feel his fingertips trail down my spine or alight upon my hips.

I strained to look behind me, but my body was frozen. I couldn't move a centimeter.

Sunflowers floated in the apothecary bottles, their petals pale and bloated like drowned fingers. Overhead, a chandelier sprouted from the rough plaster, its brass branches leafed with shards of cut crystal. There was only one explanation for this. Yakov's memories and mine were beginning to seep together like blood in water.

Sighing, the man took another draw from his pipe. "True triumph would be to move on and heal."

"You can't heal from something like that, Uncle. You just can't. Never."

Moisture bulged from between the floorboards at my feet. The walls began to drip.

"So, you will have him take your future, too."

"No. I will take his. I found the records. I've traced his footsteps. I know where to find him now."

Like a popped bubble, the walls spilled inward, no longer plaster and wood, but a downpour of salt water. The wave washed over me, pushing me back into—

—glassy midday light, shocking in its intensity, stinging my eyes. I froze in the doorway of the slaughterhouse, gasping for breath. Shudders racked my body. I spat and coughed, desperate to expel the scent of sea brine clogging my lungs.

Moisture dripped down my cheeks. Just sweat, I thought, until a choked sob came from deep inside of me. I bit my knuckle to hone the fear into something real and took deep breaths, steadying myself.

I couldn't allow it to overtake me. Not now. Not here.

Inhale. Exhale. Grind your teeth in.

After another minute or so, I began to feel well enough to go back inside. I found Raizel waiting for me at the bottom of the stairs, her expression torn between concern and annoyance.

"I'm sorry," I said, coming up beside her. I clasped my hands to hide the bite marks dimpling my knuckle. "I don't know what came over me."

She narrowed her eyes. "Is there something you want to tell me, Alter?"

"No. I felt light-headed." I didn't care much for how my voice sounded, and I took another deep breath before continuing. "It's the air in here. The stench of blood. The decay. I'm better now."

"You volunteer at a burial society. I'd think that this wouldn't bother you."

"It's not my fault that I have a working nose," I snapped back. "Besides, this is different."

"In any case, Mr. Katz is waiting for us," she said. "Please try to avoid vomiting on his suit."

I followed her back up the stairs. The chill in my veins didn't return, but halfway up the first flight, I stopped and looked back the way we'd come. A hazy patch of sunlight shone through the open door.

I had the strangest feeling that if I stepped to one side or turned my head just right, that patch of soil outside would suddenly become waxed wood, while the midday sunlight would deepen into the palpitating glow of gaslights.

"Coming?" Raizel asked, looking down at me.

I nodded and kept going.

Mr. Katz's office was located on the third floor. Behind his desk, a bay window overlooked the cattle carcasses swinging down the conveyer system linked to the killing floor above. He stood facing those panes, silhouetted against the sallow electrical lights.

Slowly, he turned to us. My stomach plummeted. Those flat brown eyes. That broad, sharklike face. He had grown a generous mustache in the year since I had last seen him, and there were threads of gray at his temples, but I recognized him in an instant. I would never forget him.

You look like a good boy, he had said, imploring me with his gaze. *You don't want to do this.*

And I had taken the silver from his cupboard. The gold watch chain from his waistcoat. The wedding ring off his finger.

The nose that Frankie had broken had healed crooked, one nostril crushed into a slit. It gave him a strange, off-kilter appearance, like a Parian bust that had slumped during kilning due to some internal imbalance.

Mr. Katz eased into his chair as fluidly as a coiling viper. He steepled his hands on the desk, scanning over us without much interest. "Tom here tells me that you two scheduled an interview."

Raizel looked at me, her smile stiff. There were expectations here that hadn't been in place down below. Now was my turn to speak up, my part to play.

"Yes, that's right," I said, my English coming out stiff and monotonous. "We work for the *Advocate*."

"I see," Katz said. "If you would prefer, we may continue this conversation in Yiddish, although it's been years since I've had to use it."

"That would be appreciated," Raizel said, once we were seated.

"To be entirely honest, I consider it a rather unsophisticated and rural tongue. I wouldn't even call it a dialect. More like a bastardization." A vague smile touched his lips. "Now, English… English is the language of the future. The language of industry. Wouldn't you two agree?"

"I suppose," Raizel conceded, looking as though she was itching to say more. Considering her contributions to the *Ar-*

beiter-Zeitung and the *Freiheit*, she probably considered German to be the language of revolution.

"I suppose," I echoed, then felt foolish for simply repeating her words. Retrieving my fountain pen and journal from my satchel, I pretended to take notes.

Katz's gaze returned to me, and this time stayed. His face remained fixed in an expression of polite indifference, but the finger that had been absently stroking his cheek now edged to his crooked nose. He touched the crumpled nostril, traced the scar that gouged across his cheek.

I felt the blood drain from my face, leaving behind a prickly chill. I tried to smile, but my lips faltered.

"I do hope my scar does not bother you, young man," Mr. Katz said, as though he had only just become aware of my stare. "Or you, miss. I received it nearly a year ago, in some rather nasty business."

"What sort of business?" Raizel asked, giving me a loaded look. She thought this was relevant, didn't she? As though this was the clue that would crack this case wide-open, when I already knew what Mr. Katz was going to say before the words even left his mouth.

"Two street urchins broke into my home and robbed me at gunpoint." His finger trailed lower, following the pale, knotty line to where it hooked under his chin. "My jaw, my nose, my eye socket, broken. They had to wire my jaw shut. The one who did it, I would pay dearly to be put alone in a room with him for just five minutes."

My face felt stiff and numb, as though it had become scar tissue itself. I flinched as Raizel nudged me discreetly. My hand swerved off course, gouging the fountain pen's nib across the paper.

There was only one reason for him to admit something like this. He *recognized* me. I was certain of it.

Mr. Katz smiled. "I do apologize, but we have strayed off topic. Where are my manners? I believe that introductions are in order. I don't recall hearing your names."

"My name is Rokhl," Raizel said. "This is—"

"Asher," I said.

"Rokhl and Asher," Mr. Katz echoed thoughtfully, his gaze on me as he said it. "Good names. Now, what questions do you have for me?"

"Many here in Chicago consider you a self-made man, the kind of immigrant they strive to become." Raizel scanned over her notes. "Why don't you start by telling us a little about your past?"

"I was born in Congress Poland, but I—"

"Where?" I interrupted.

His eyes narrowed. "Varshe, but I moved here over twenty years ago."

"Do you still have family back there?"

"Yes. My parents still live there. I visit them every few years." His smile was dull and flinty. "I am a good son."

My face prickled coldly. Before coming to America, Yakov had lived with his uncle, who had taught at the Imperial University in Varshe. He and Katz could have met there. Something could have happened between them.

After writing something in her notebook, Raizel cleared her throat.

"From what we hear, you're quite the philanthropist. You have donated to a number of admirable causes." Raizel flipped through her notes. "But your career hasn't been without controversy. There have been allegations of abuse toward workers."

"I treat my workers with the respect they deserve," Mr. Katz said, aloof. "A factory cannot run without a firm hand. You cannot show weakness. For a business to operate at its fullest potential, everything must be in top order."

"Overworking them, forcing them to stand for hours without breaks. Restricting access to lavatories." She flipped the page. "In February, a warden poured scalding water on a man's arm—"

"An accident." His voice chilled.

"And what about the incident two weeks ago? The boy they found in the waste pit."

The fingers that had been so lightly caressing the scar tissue now flexed and tightened, his nails digging in. His expression never changed.

"That," he said slowly, like a warning, "was also an accident."

"Of course," Raizel said sagely, before shifting to a more mundane line of questioning. "The World's Fair is, of course, of great interest to our readers. Have you seen an increase in meat sales since the Fair began?"

"Yes. We work closely with the restaurants and various food stands at the Fair and surrounding areas. Daily, we supply the Fair with nearly five thousand pounds of steaks, ground meat, and sausages. Our customers know that when they are buying our meat, it is produced to the highest standards of quality and cleanliness."

He enjoyed talking about himself. About his successes. He had a wife. She was with child.

As they spoke, I jotted down his responses and allowed my gaze to wander restlessly across the room. Cattle carcasses, flayed and butterflied, flitted past the wide observation window. In the corner of my eye, they could almost be mistaken for human corpses.

My throat ached. I paused to massage it, wondering if the pain was a sign of Katz's guilt. The alternative was even worse—that it was proof Yakov was growing more and more powerful, laying down his roots.

"How do you spend your holidays?" I asked a few questions later.

"What do you mean?" Katz asked.

"Fourth of July, for instance. What did you do then?"

His eyes narrowed, and for a long moment he merely regarded me. My skin itched under the onslaught of his gaze, as though if he stared at me long enough, he'd be able to peel back my skin and peer inside me, into all that I was and ever would be—thief, dishonorable son, liar, disgrace.

"I attended a dinner," he said at last. "A rather dull affair, if I must admit. But the company was *delectable*."

The rest of the interview yielded nothing of value, and at the end of it, he escorted us to the entrance himself. On the walk down, his fingertips stroked the small of my back ever so lightly, as though he meant to brush off a fleck of lint. His touch made my skin crawl.

Then Raizel and I stepped outside into the flinty sunlight, the first fireflies emerging to sip from the Stockyards' puddles. As the doors eased shut behind us, she turned to me.

"He was looking at you," she said quietly, her features grim. "All throughout the interview. He couldn't take his eyes off you."

"I know."

ON THE TRAIN back to Maxwell Street, I wrote down what we had learned, compiling the facts into even columns. There were loose connections tying Mr. Katz to Yakov and potentially to the other boys—not to mention Frankie and myself—but it still didn't feel good enough. I needed solid proof, the sort of bloody evidence that would convince a judge to deal out a death sentence. But even then, I wasn't sure if I had it in me to take justice into my own hands.

"You know, I've been thinking," I said. "Raizel, why don't you write the article?"

"Me?" She laughed abruptly.

"I mean it. You said you've gotten your writing published in the *Arbeiter-Zeitung* and the *Freiheit*."

"Well, yes, but neither of those papers would be interested in something like this." She gave it some thought. "If the story were just about Mr. Katz, the *Arbeiter-Zeitung* might publish it, but we'd need more than what we have. We can't just publish an article based on speculation."

"You're right."

"How about this? Let's write it together." She smiled. "It'll be a collaboration."

"Deal." As I scanned over what I had written, the letters blurred into an inky smear. My chin grew heavy. I pinched my inner wrist as I sensed myself beginning to drift off, but it was as though lead ingots had been tied to my chin and eyelids.

A throbbing orange glow appeared in the corners of my vision, casting flickering shadows across the train car. My ears rang with faint noises I couldn't place—crackling and hissing, the groan of wood, indistinct voices that sounded like screaming but were so far away they might as well have been whispers.

Raizel seized my wrist as I began to nod off. "Alter, what are you doing?"

I blinked, jolted wide-awake. "What?"

"Your arm!"

I looked down. My journal had fallen to the floor without me noticing it. I held my fountain pen in my left hand, the nib sunken into the tender flesh of my right forearm. Ink and blood dripped down my skin. I wiped it away frantically, exposing letters scratched into my skin:

KAT

I traced my fingers over the shallow scratches the pen nib had made. Raizel had caught me before I even finished spelling Katz's name, but if she hadn't, what would I have done? Would I have kept writing until I had carved his name from wrist to shoulder, the same way that I had typed *zolst im der-hargenen* into the Linotype machine?

"What were you thinking?" Raizel demanded.

"I don't know." I hastily rolled down my sleeve. "I must have drifted off. I have Katz on my brain."

"You've been acting really strange lately. This isn't normal, Alter."

"I'm fine, Raizel." My voice came out sharper than I intended. I threw my journal and fountain pen back into my satchel. "I'm just tired."

Truly, I was tired. On the walk home, exhaustion pressed down on me. I barely had the motivation to climb to the third floor. I knew what I had to do. I just didn't know if I was strong enough to finish Yakov's last task for him.

A familiar figure was standing outside my door as I entered the third-floor corridor. He turned at the sound of my footsteps.

At the sight of Frankie's sharp, handsome features, I couldn't help but feel a ripple of trepidation. All I could think of was his face on the night I had left him, how slack his mouth had been. The blood flecked across his cheeks and lips. The distant look in his eyes, as though he was peering over his shoulder at something far behind him.

"Took you long enough," he said. "I thought I'd be waiting here all evening."

I took a deep breath, steadying myself as I approached him. "How did you figure out where I live?"

"Same way you figured out where I worked." He ran a hand through his tousled curls, as though self-conscious of having his head uncovered in a place so Jewish that there were mezuzahs on every doorpost. "It wasn't too hard to ask around at the shuls."

I felt like I should say more after the way I'd brushed him off earlier. "Listen, about what I said this morning—"

"Forget about it." He waved his hand as though clearing the air.

"Oh." I couldn't help but feel a sting of disappointment.

"Like I said before, what we did was just harmless fun." Something about the way he said it made my stomach clench. He glanced around the hall, before lowering his voice. "Besides, that thing about Leviticus, it's all shtuss. It's not about them both being men, otherwise the verse would have used 'ish' rather than 'zachar.' Why say 'male' when you could just say 'man'?"

"I don't know," I confessed. I understood Hebrew well enough to read it, but I had always struggled with actually interpreting the passages. I felt as if there was a whole other layer to the Meforshim that I couldn't unlock, no matter how much I read.

"It's about—" Frankie's voice clicked, as though his mouth was dry. He swallowed, his brow creased by a hint of unease. "It's about boys, Alter. About how an adult man shouldn't lie with a boy. Just like the story of Sodom, it's about consent."

Though his analysis nudged my thoughts back to Mr. Katz and the unspeakable crimes he had likely committed, it came as an indescribable relief to hear Frankie say it. He still recalled enough of his former schooling to be able to recite entire blatts of the Talmud from memory alone, a parlor trick he'd shown off to the crew's disbelief and amusement. Somehow, the words felt more legitimate shaped by the rise and fall of his yeshivish cadence.

He cleared his throat and held up the burlap sack he was carrying. "Anyway, enough about that. I brought your clothes and things."

"Did you have to fight Meir to get them back?"

"No, but I had to listen to him kvetch for a solid twenty minutes before he surrendered them. If there's one thing that man knows, it's how to lecture people."

"Thank you," I said as Frankie handed the sack to me. I poked through its contents until I found my father's pocket watch and traced my thumb over the case's familiar dings and scratches. It felt good having the watch back where it belonged.

"How are you holding up?" Frankie asked as I rummaged

for my keys. I didn't want to talk about Mr. Katz out in the hall where Mrs. Brenner could be listening in.

"I'm… I don't know. It's just like what happened with my father." I wiggled the key back and forth in the stubborn lock until I heard a click. "You expect everything to come to a standstill, and in some ways it does, but everything on the outside keeps moving on. I still need to send money over for my mom and sisters, so I still have to work, and I just have to sit there, pretending that nothing has changed."

"That's how life is," Frankie said. "You're breathing, so you have to keep going, even when it doesn't feel like you're still alive. Speaking of which, care to accompany me down to Washington Park?"

"Washington Park," I repeated blankly.

"Remember? Mr. Whitby invited us to the races tonight."

"How well do you even know that man?"

"Well enough to see the value in an invitation." He drew his pocket watch from his waistcoat and glanced at the time. "If we leave now, we should still be able to make it for the last several runs."

"Frankie, in case you've forgotten, I have a dybbuk inside me."

"All the more reason to go," he said, with a smile I would have found appealing if his flippancy wasn't so aggravating. "Since he's a member of the Whitechapel Club, Mr. Whitby might know about deaths that haven't made it into the local papers."

I sighed. He had a point. Besides, my skin crawled at the thought of spending the rest of the night staring at Yakov's empty bed.

Frankie followed me into the room. I could sense that something had changed between us, but I was afraid to give voice to it. It was easier just to pretend that our kiss last night had never happened, or that it had been from exhaustion or the possession.

The only thing I needed to think about now was helping complete Yakov's unfinished business here on earth. But before I could confront Katz, I needed more than just my suspicions. I needed proof.

"There's something I want to talk to you about," I said as Frankie sat on Haskel's cot. "You remember that night I left?"

He pretended to be mesmerized by the scabs on his knuckles, but I caught the way he stiffened. His gaze flicked toward me, cold and wary. "I don't want to talk about that right now."

"We went to that house together and—"

"Alter, I'm not going to repeat myself."

"I want to talk about it," I protested.

"Well, I don't. As the Americans say, 'let sleeping dogs lie.' It's over and done with, and we can't go back to it. Now just get dressed. We're going to be late enough as it is."

I sighed, changing out of my borrowed waistcoat and shirt. For someone who loved to keep a conversation going, Frankie certainly had a talent for ending one. Prodding him more would be like poking an oyster. After enough aggravation, he'd retreat into his shell and harden over, and that would be the end of it.

"You might as well keep my clothes on. They suit you." As I reached for my tzitzis, Frankie chuckled. "Ah, I see. Tuck the tassels in unless you want to get spat on. Oh, don't give me that look. Did Ha'ARI not say that to wear your tzitzis tucked in is to remind yourself of your inner faith and spirituality?"

"I'm just wondering why you eagerly associate with people who spit on Jews."

"Not all of us want to live in a ghetto."

I smoothed out the cotton tunic and unbuttoned my trousers to tuck the tassels in. "Raizel and I went to the Stock-yards today."

"Mmm."

"There was a worker found dead at one of the slaughter-houses. The police called it an accident, but—"

"Uh-huh." He sounded distracted.

"Are you even listening?" As I turned, I was startled to find Frankie staring at me intently.

"If you don't hurry, we're going to be late," he said nonchalantly, taking out his pocket watch to check the time.

"What is it?"

He snapped his watch shut. "What?"

"Why were you looking at me like that?"

"I wasn't."

"You were."

"It's just that you look like you could use a good meal. A nice round of beef or roast goose. I was thinking, once this business is over, I should take you to one of those places down by the lakeside." His gaze flicked down my front. "But I doubt you'll make it past the front doors dressed like that."

I scoffed, buttoning my shirt. "So, my clothes aren't good enough for you now?"

"I'm talking about your tzitzis," he said dryly as I slid on my waistcoat and evening coat. "Most of those places don't serve Jews. You enter the room, and they look at you like you're a mangy mutt. Like, 'oh, dearie me, who let that dreadful thing in?'" He gave a languid wave of his hand. "'Get it out now. It might have fleas.'"

"It sounds like you know from experience," I said, again stealing Haskel's bowler cap from atop his bedpost. I stuffed my necktie into my pocket to knot on the way.

"My manager—that dried-out old Brit who was taking money back at the Masthead—he took me for dinner once to his country club down in Lake Forest. You should have seen the way he calculated the timing perfectly." A bitter smile spread across Frankie's lips. "When the waiter came to take our orders, he said it so smoothly—'oh, but you *do* realize that tenderloin is pork, don't you, Portnoy? I thought your tribe doesn't eat pork?' Like he knew exactly how the waiter's face would change. Like he wanted to put me back in my place. I'll bet all the cooks took turns spitting in my food that night."

I stopped walking, staring at him in disbelief. "Why do you work for someone like that?"

Frankie ushered me forward again. "I'm not working for him. I have an *arrangement* with him. He's not my boss. He's my manager and sponsor. It's different. I'm no one's grunt. You know that."

"Okay, then," I said. "Why not make an arrangement with a manager who actually respects you?"

"You think any of them are any better?" He scoffed. "No. They're all the same, Alter. We'll never be equals in their eyes. They can grit their teeth and tolerate us, but they'll never welcome us into their white cities, because ambition becomes something ugly when it has a Jewish face." He bared his bruised knuckles at me, a startling contrast to the elegant finery of his silver rings. "And no amount of blood, sweat, or fine tailoring will ever change that."

29

THE WASHINGTON PARK racetrack sat on a verdant strip of land along the city's southwestern edge, within walking distance of both the Fair's Midway Plaisance and the University of Chicago. As Frankie and I walked up the cobblestone-lined path leading into the track, I tried to savor the moment. I didn't belong here, but if only for tonight, I would be allowed to enter.

The first thing that struck me about the facility was its cleanliness. The air smelled of pine wax, fresh paint, and cigar smoke, and only when we passed the paddock did I catch the faintest whiff of horseflesh.

Though there were less than two hours of light remaining, the grandstands were filled with spectators. Even more visitors crowded on the lush lawns to watch the horses. Following in the theme of the World's Fair, the racetrack's decorators had ladled on the patriotism with a heavy hand, adorning the balconies and red roofs with American flags and pleated fans in the Stars and Stripes.

Carriages lined the path leading to the mansion that overlooked the tracks. Guests loitered in the two-story veranda that encircled the building, leaning over the railings or lounging against the balconies' pillars. With the building's pitched roof and many windows, I thought it must be a manor of some sort, and told Frankie as much.

Frankie laughed. "And who do you suppose lives there?"

I frowned, rather offended. "Whoever owns the tracks."

"That's the clubhouse for the bigwigs."

"Bigwigs," I repeated. "What's a bigwig?"

"You know. A makher. A boss. The Americans call them the upper crust."

"That sounds like something that would grow on a bowl of porridge left out for too long."

"Won't argue about that. Anyway, forget the names. Point is they don't let just anyone in there. It costs $150 just to become a member."

"Are you a member?"

His laughter caught in his throat, and for a moment, a trace of anger flared in his gaze. He turned away. "You think they have any members named Portnoy in there, Alter? Or Rosen?"

The venom in his voice took me aback. "I just thought… you knew how much it cost, so…"

"You know how I am. I like to collect useless information and parrot it back at people. Besides, I don't have $150 to throw away. Luckily for us, we're guests tonight."

As we approached the doorman, he leveled his chin and regarded us through narrowed eyes.

"You should've worn my clothes," Frankie muttered under his breath, drawing a small manila card from his evening coat's breast pocket. Turning to the man, he switched over to crisp English. "My name is Frankie Porter. I'm a guest of John Whitby."

"Is that so?" The doorman took the card from Frankie and examined it closely. "And who's this?"

"My family's servant," Frankie said. "Don't mind him."

I choked on my words, only managing by sheer willpower to keep from wringing Frankie's neck.

With a grunt of approval, the man stepped aside to allow us to enter.

"Your servant, Sir Porter?" I hissed once we were past the doors. "Is that so?"

"We aren't exactly dressed like brothers. You ought to get a top hat, you know that? Although I suppose a bowler cap is better than that ratty newsie."

"You're not even wearing a hat!"

"I don't wear hats."

"Too afraid they'll cut off the circulation to your brain?"

"Yes. Which I imagine you don't have to worry about, being that you don't have one."

I shot him a sour look, though I knew from the warmth in his voice that he was only teasing. It had been so long since we talked like this. I'd missed it.

The entry hall stretched from one side of the building to the other, an expanse of glittering crystal, plush Turkish rugs, and carved wood. The bronze chandeliers' gas jets produced a softly palpitating glow, casting pools of light across the polished oak floor.

"Billiard room, billiard room," Frankie muttered, glancing into the rooms that branched out from the main hall. The café was deserted at this hour, with the chairs on the tables. In the adjoining room we found Mr. Whitby leaning over a pool table.

He aimed carefully, then thrust the cue forward. The white ball bounced across the sides of the table before coming to a stop without pocketing any points. Sighing, he stepped back to allow his opponent to take a turn.

As we neared, Mr. Whitby brightened at the sight of us. Wearing a dark evening suit and a top hat, he looked all the part of a gentleman.

"Ah, Frankie, I am so glad you could join us. And your friend as well." Whitby turned to me. "Alex, if I'm not mistaken?"

"Yes," I said, taking the hand he extended. "It's a pleasure to see you again."

Whitby's handshake was firm but not forceful, his grip softened by his kidskin gloves. With his periwinkle-blue eyes and broad smile, he presented an air of genuine warmth. His teeth were small and white, like a child's.

The soft *clunk* of pool balls diverted my attention. One by one, several balls vanished into the table's deep pockets. Resting his cue on the table, Whitby's opponent turned to us.

He had a lean, intelligent face with a neatly trimmed brown mustache and eyes as gray as smoke. Though his sleeves were rolled down and fastened by cloisonné cuff links, I recognized him as the tattooed man from the Whitechapel Club.

The man smiled stiffly as Mr. Whitby slapped his shoulder in the friendly American way.

"This, my friends, is my business associate, Gregory," Whitby said. "Unfortunately, he is a far better pool player than myself. Would you two care to join us for a round?"

"Perhaps in a bit," Frankie said, sparing me from having to explain that I had never played pool and would sooner strike my own eye out than hit the ball. "I'm more interested in what's going on in the basement."

Mr. Whitby chuckled. "Ah, you mean the bookmaking. I thought that might interest you. Come, I'll give you the grand tour."

Frankie looked at me. "Are you coming?"

"I'll wait here." I didn't want to venture into that part of Frankie's world any more than I wanted to rejoin his crew. Besides, the less I had to speak English, the better.

As Mr. Whitby showed Frankie out of the room, Gregory gave me a nod of acknowledgment. *"Dobryy vecher."*

"Pardon?"

"Ah, you'll have to excuse me. My Russian is not very good. You are Russian, yes?"

I realized that Frankie must have told Mr. Whitby that he was from Russia, although by imperial law he was considered neither a Russian citizen nor an ethnic Pole or Lithuanian. Mr. Whitby had likely assumed that I was a landsman to him, provided Frankie hadn't told him that outright.

"Er, yes," I said, afraid to say otherwise and risk ruining my cover.

"Alexei then, is it?"

"Call me Alex."

"I visited St. Petersburg several years ago and remember a phrase or two," Gregory said. "May I practice on you?"

Why couldn't Frankie have told Mr. Whitby we were German or Romanian? I cleared my throat, forcing a thin smile. "Of course."

"Now, let's see. Hopefully, it won't be too painful… *Menya zovut Gregory.* Am I saying that correctly?"

"Da," I said, which was the only Russian word I knew other than the curse words that Frankie had delighted in teaching me.

"Rad poznakomitsya?" Gregory cocked his head. "That means 'what is your name,' right?"

I nodded, pretending to be impressed. *"Da,* that's perfect."

"Ah, don't coddle me. I know that my pronunciation is atrocious."

"No. No, it's very good. Almost native."

Gregory's smile remained, but a strange light had entered his gray eyes. Sweat dripped down my neck. I had made a mistake. He knew something was wrong. As he was about to say more, Mr. Whitby returned with Frankie alongside him. Mr. Whitby had a thin brown cigar propped between his lips and was puffing away at it merrily, while Frankie held his own cigar unlit at his side.

"The next race is about to begin, gentlemen," Mr. Whitby guffawed, punctuating the statement with a jab of his cigar, in a flourish as enthusiastic as an orchestra conductor. "My money's on Empire. There's nothing more elegant in the world than a well-bred Thoroughbred, wouldn't you agree? Humans and racehorses are really quite alike in that regard. Pedigree, my boy! Take yourself for instance, Frankie. With your skill for fighting, I suppose you come from a military background. Cossack, perhaps?"

Frankie laughed, but I could sense a strain in his features. If there was a Cossack in his family tree, that particular branch would have been grafted in blood and suffering. "Not nearly as interesting, I'm afraid. Mainly well-diggers and tailors."

"Well, there are always exceptions to the rule, I suppose."

As the two men took the stairs to the second-floor balcony. I stopped Frankie before he could join them.

"Could we find somewhere less crowded? I don't feel good." The heat was getting to me, or the billiard room's confines, or maybe it was the copious amounts of cigar smoke wafting from the gentlemen on either side of us. A dull, throbbing pain radiated through my temples, and my throat felt as though it was collared with barbed wire.

We found a secluded corner on the first-floor veranda, with a clear view of the racetracks below. The sun settled bright as an ember on the horizon.

"Is it the dybbuk?" Frankie asked in Yiddish, after glancing around to confirm we were alone.

"I just need space to breathe." I loosened my collar. "I was burning up in there."

"Not much better out here, with this humidity." He hesitated, looking out across the racetrack. "Back at your tenement, you wanted to talk about the night you left."

"Right." I didn't say more. We had ended things so violently that night, I had a feeling he wanted to discuss this at his own pace, on his own terms.

"Why?"

"It wasn't a normal burglary that night, was it?" I watched him from the corner of my eye. His gaze was planted on the stretch of track, his face unreadable.

"Why does it matter what it was?" he asked.

"You brought your gun."

"I brought it along to all the burglaries. You just didn't see it."

This was something that needed to be taken slowly and ceremoniously, like tending to the dead. I didn't want to push him, so I allowed silence to find its place between us.

"Why do you care all of a sudden about what happened?" he asked after another moment. The way he said it told me it wasn't an invitation to ask more questions. "I thought you just wanted to put the past behind you."

"Raizel and I visited that man today. His name is Mr. Katz. He's a boss down in Packingtown."

Frankie's face showed nothing. "Oh. I see."

"I don't know if he recognized me, but I think he might have something to do with the disappearances of some boys I know, and maybe even Yakov's and Victor's deaths." I selected my words with the utmost care, afraid that if I said something wrong, it would be like opening a doorway. Anything might come out. "I just thought, if you happen to know anything…"

Something dark and primal welled in Frankie's gaze. It was an emotion I didn't quite have a name for, and it chilled me to the bone. All I could think about was a year ago, Frankie bringing his fists down again and again, until Mr. Katz's blood dewed on his face and knuckles. And the pained, bared-tooth grimace on his face when he'd done it, like an animal mauling its own side.

"Alter, he was just some rich bastard," Frankie said curtly. "Bastards like that, they don't get their hands dirty muddling with immigrant boys."

"Frankie, a worker was found dead at Katz's factory. A boy younger than us. He'd been—"

"Listen to me, don't you ever go see that man again, you hear? The last thing you want to do is get on some Stockyard boss's bad side."

The sharpness in his voice jarred me. I swallowed. "I won't."

"You swear?"

"I swear." The promise felt weak even to me.

Frankie sighed, turning back to the track. He felt even further away than before. Untouchable.

"Last month, the American Derby was held here, did you know that?" I could tell from the strain in his voice he was eager to change the subject. He leaned over the railing, tapping his unlit cigar gently against his palm. "Thousands of people came to watch. Guess how much the horse won."

I gave it some thought. "Three hundred."

"Oy gevalt. What do you think this is? A cock fight at your county fair?"

"Five hundred?" That was slightly more than six months' worth of wages for me.

Frankie laughed. "Higher."

"A thousand?" I said, although I found it a little hard to believe that a horse could make in a two-minute race more than what I earned in a year.

"Fifty thousand dollars."

I chuckled. "You mean five thousand, right?"

He said nothing.

"That…" Silently, I did the math. "That's more than I'd make in fifty years. I'd be dead before then."

"Welcome to the land of milk and honey." Frankie turned his attention to the unlit cigar and looked around, presumably for a cutter, before resorting to biting off the tip and spitting it over the railing. So much for playing the part of a gentleman.

"If you intend to become that rich one day, you'll need to learn how to cut a cigar," I said. "Instead of, you know, mauling it."

"Actually, I'm more interested in power than wealth." Drawing a match from his silver vesta case, Frankie lit the cigar. He took a draw and grimaced. "Oy, this is atrocious. It tastes like a filthy ashtray."

"Aren't wealth and power the same thing?"

"They're connected, but not the same. Power makes you untouchable. Wealth doesn't."

I gave it some thought. "But wealth gives you power."

"And yet when there's a pogrom, the rich Jew is butchered alongside the poor one."

"So, what you're saying is that you intend to convert," I said sarcastically.

"I'd sooner kill myself." He sampled the cigar again, this time managing to hold the smoke in for a moment longer before starting to cough. "Ugh, this is worse than opium."

I turned to him, aghast. "You're smoking opium now?"

"Just once. I thought it might help…" He shrugged, looking a bit sheepish. "You know, how I have a hard time sleeping sometimes. I thought it might help with that."

I did. More than once, I had woken to find his cot empty and the skylight window hoisted up. He would spend hours up there on the rooftop, watching the Levee District's inhabitants begin their drunken, violent stumble toward dawn.

"I didn't like how it made me feel, so I haven't tried it since." He held out the cigar. "Here."

I took it from him. It was strangely thrilling knowing that he'd propped the cigar in his lips mere moments before. His own saliva dampened the tip.

The smoke filled my mouth, warm and dry, with a taste like burnt maple. I rolled it over my tongue, savoring it.

"Atrocious, right?" Frankie said.

"Not really. It has a nice flavor."

He arched an eyebrow. "Since when did you become a connoisseur of fine cigars?"

"Not me. Yakov."

A gunshot rang out.

I flinched, lowering the cigar. "Did you hear that?"

"Relax. It's just to show the race is starting."

Down below, the racehorses burst from the gate, like inkblots in the glow of the setting sun. We were too far away to hear their hoofbeats, but as they surged down the track, I thought I could feel the resounding force resonating through my bones.

A mild sense of disquiet passed over me. I took another puff of the cigar, hoping it would calm me the way the cigarette at Meir's had done. On the second drag, the flavor changed subtly, turning bitter. Coughing, I rested the cigar on the ashtray provided for guests.

When I turned back to Frankie, his smile had slipped from

his lips. Confusion darkened his gaze. "Alter, what are you doing?"

Only as he spoke did I become aware of the smooth curve of glass beneath my fingers. I looked down. The ashtray was clutched in my hand. I told myself to let go, and my arm jerked up as though it meant to obey, except my fingers were still clenched tightly around the ashtray's edge. I slammed it against the railing hard enough that I took a chunk out of the wooden trim.

The glass bowl shattered along the circular depression in its middle, leaving me with a jagged sickle of a shard. It wasn't long, scarcely extending past the edge of my hand, but it was sharp. It would serve its purpose.

Nonsensical words swirled through my head: *Dolzhni ubit. Dolzhni ubit. Dolzhni ubit.*

I sensed it meant something a lot like *zolst im derhargenen. You must kill him.*

I stepped toward the door leading into the inner chambers.

"Alter, stop." Frankie seized my wrist. I yanked away, but he grabbed me once more and wheeled me around to face him. "Let go of that now. You're bleeding."

The uproar of hoofbeats filled my ears, deafening, like the crash of waves against a steamship's hull. My fingers felt numb and inflexible, frozen around the shard as though my skin was just a glove for the dybbuk.

My trembling lips shaped around a word; it left my mouth in a stuttering whimper: "Kat-kat-katorz—"

"Katz?" Frankie asked, his features darkening.

This terror that seized my lungs in a stranglehold was the only answer. It had to be him. "Here."

Frankie looked around us. "Is he here?"

"I—I—" Choking on the stench of smoke and soiled saw-dust, I tried to break away from Frankie. He only gripped me tighter, closing his fingers around the hand that held the ash-tray. I wanted to weep, but all that left my lips were the desperate groans of a hunted animal.

He placed his other hand upon my cheek, holding my face steady. "Tell me what you see, Alter."

"It's dark," I heard myself say in a voice that was no longer my own. "It's so dark."

"What do you hear?"

"Hoofbeats. Laughter." I searched over his shoulder for the source of the noises. By now, the horses were completing the final leg of their lap, far enough away that they were just specks. The nearby club members conspired in muted whispers. "Gunfire or fireworks."

Frankie's fingers ground into my knuckles. Slick warmth filled my palm. I couldn't tell whether it was his blood or my own. The throbbing burn in my throat displaced all other pain.

"Alter, instead of the fireworks, I want you to listen to the music," Frankie said. "Don't you hear it? It's coming from the dining room upstairs."

Only when he mentioned it did I become aware of the piano music trickling from the second-floor windows.

My shoulders slowly loosened. I managed to find my voice, weak and trembling, but blissfully my own. "Piano."

"That's right. And look at that sunset. Isn't it stunning?" With his fingers still locked around my hand, he turned to the railing. My body followed.

The sky was a tapestry of gold and crimson, fringed by the deepest indigo to the east. It wasn't dark at all.

"It's beautiful," I whispered.

"Yes. The air is so clean over here, you can see it perfectly. Now, focus on your breathing like Meir told you." Frankie took deep breaths, as though he meant to guide me by example. I tried to follow him, drawing in air when he did, exhaling in turn. We fell into perfect unison. Slowly, the crushing weight on my lungs lifted. If he could breathe steadily, that meant there was no smoke.

"Alter, there are people staring at us, and any minute now, the track guards are going to come over." Lowering his voice to a murmur, Frankie searched my eyes. "And they might be violent. And someone might get hurt. Unless you drop that ashtray now."

"I—I can't."

"You need to."

"I can't."

"Alter, I'm not ready to lose you a second time. Please. Come back to me."

My fingers went slack. The broken ashtray cracked on the floor of the veranda, streaked with blood. Frankie lightly kicked it across the porch. It came to a rest by the group of gentlemen nearby who were watching us with appalled expressions. Even Mr. Whitby and Gregory had joined the crowd. Had they seen the entire thing?

"Good. I knew you could do it." A ghost of a smile passed over Frankie's lips. "Now, let's get you home."

30

BY THE TIME we made it back to Maxwell Street, night had fallen. Twice, I thought I heard footsteps or gunfire, but I knew it was only the dybbuk now. The streets looked unfamiliar in the dark, as though I was seeing the buildings from a different angle for the first time. Grimy brick tenements shifted in the corner of my eye, acquiring decorative statues and rococo stuccowork—the adornments of a European city. Varshe, perhaps, or Paris, or Rome. Yakov had been well traveled.

At first, the changing cityscape frightened me, but after the first several blocks, I looked at the buildings in dazed awe. Yakov must have once admired these places. Had he eaten at this Parisian café once? Had he read a book by this fountain?

Between the chevra kadisha and the unfinished shul, an expanse of sunflowers greeted me. Even at night, the petals were spread like grasping fingers.

A hand closed around my shoulder. "Alter?"

I glanced at Frankie. "Mmm?"

He studied me carefully. "What are you looking at?"

"Oh, it's…" I turned back ahead. In the blink of an eye, the sunflowers had receded into the earth. A raw dirt alley confronted me, heaped with stacks of slates and wooden boards like grave cairns. "It's nothing."

I could tell by his face he was worried. Scared, even.

We parted ways at my tenement. As I opened the door, I heard Frankie's footsteps stop and looked over my shoulder.

He stood on the sidewalk, his back to me. But he must have sensed me hesitate, because he said, "Alter, about that man you were talking about, you say a boy was found at his slaughterhouse?"

"Yes."

"How old was he?"

"Fourteen or fifteen," I said.

"I see." His voice turned cold and flat. "I guess that's what you get for honest work these days."

Frankie walked off. Feeling vaguely queasy, I watched him until he reached the next block, then entered my tenement. I encountered no one on my walk to the third floor. For the first time in a long time, the building was blissfully silent.

While fighting with the stubborn lock, I heard hinges creak behind me. I turned with a sinking heart. Mrs. Brenner stood in her doorway, gripping onto the frame with white-knuckled fingers.

"Oh, Alter." Distress welled in her gaze. "My poor boy. Look at you."

Afraid to hear the rest, I fled into my room and locked the door. She knocked, and I sank against it, sliding to the floor.

"Alter," Mrs. Brenner pleaded from the other side of the door. "Let me in."

Underneath my feet, a grit of black soil spread across the floorboards, creeping from the darkness under the empty cots.

I pinched my arm viciously, but the soil only spread. Bit

my palm. Dug my teeth in. Sunflowers began to sprout between the beds in savage green tangles. Why wouldn't it stop?

"Please, open the door."

"Go away. Just go away." The words left my mouth in a
desperate sob. Mrs. Brenner kept knocking, and I slammed
my palm against the door to drown her out, matching her
rhythm. The downstairs neighbors must have thought us both
deranged.

She stopped, so I did, too.

"It's no longer just smoke that surrounds you, Alter," she
murmured, sounding so close that I wouldn't have been surprised if she'd gotten down on her knees and had her lips mere
centimeters from the panel. "It's fire."

As I listened to her retreat, I allowed my hand to slide to
the floor, my body shaking with ragged breaths. The shallow
cut had reopened on my palm. Blood leeched through the silk
handkerchief Frankie had wrapped my hand in, blotting out
the monogram embroidered in Gothic script. I sank back and
watched the stain spread.

The droplets glistened black in the moonlight, as if I were
charred inside.

That night, I was awoken by the sound of a struggle. Gasps,
the crunch of straw or leaves, a strained groan. Disoriented,
I first mistook the noises as a carryover from my dream. As
I sat up, I discerned a figure leaning over Haskel's bed. The
moonlight glinted off the knife the intruder held. Then the
blade disappeared between them, and when it emerged, dark
liquid streaked its length.

"Dovid, wake up!" I shouted, only to realize as I said it
that his cot was empty. Of all the nights for him to stay out
late, why tonight?

I struggled to free myself from the tangle of sheets. My foot caught in the fabric. I fell onto the floor, nearly sending the bedframe toppling over in the process.

The doorknob scraped back and forth as a person tried to open it from the other side.

"Help!" I shouted. "There's someone in here!"

The man lunged at me. I snatched hold of the chamber pot stowed under the bed and hurled it at him. The heavy porcelain rim caught him in the side of the head, sending his yanked-down cap askew. Though most of the pot's contents splashed across the floor between us, some must have gotten on his face. Liquid glistened in his mustache. He swatted at his eyes and snarled in rage, a guttural sound that was barely human.

The person in the hall had begun throwing their body against the door. It shuddered with each impact.

As the door's cheap lock gave way, the stranger hauled himself through the window. I leaped to my feet and lunged across the room, just in time to catch a glimpse of him descending the fire escape. His hat had fallen off, revealing short, dark hair.

Could it be Katz?

"Alter?" a thin voice croaked.

I swiveled around, recalling Haskel. He was curled on the bed, the sheets streaked with blood. With each ragged breath, more blood coursed between his fingers. I rushed to his side and sank to my knees, barely registering Mrs. Brenner's presence until I heard her say my name.

"Get help," I yelled. "He's been stabbed."

As she ran from the room, I grabbed the sheet and bundled it around my hand to form a compact, pressing it over the wound in Haskel's side in an effort to stop the bleeding. The blade had caught him below the ribs.

Haskel tried to speak, but no words would come, only the heaving gasps of a drowning man. His eyes fluttered shut.

"You're going to be fine," I said, squeezing his hand.

"It hurts so much," he croaked.

"Don't speak. Save your strength."

As he fainted, the clang of police bells filled the air.

31

THE SEVENTH DISTRICT Police Station towered over Maxwell Street's tenements and dusty storefronts. The lobby was ill-lit in spite of the ruby glow of morning spilling through the high windows. It should have made me feel secure to be surrounded by so many officers. Instead, the moment I stepped through the doors, my skin crawled with an anxious foreboding. I had spent several hours resting fitfully in Michael Reese Hospital's lobby, stirred from uncertain dreams by the pealing ambulance bells and the groans of patients. By the time the police summoned me to the station, I had given up on sleep.

Detective Rariden greeted me at the door and steered me into his office, his fingers digging into my shoulder. This time, he was accompanied by a Yiddish-speaking officer who translated him word for word, even the simple questions. It disoriented me to hear the two men speaking, their voices overlapping in a low din.

"What am I doing here?" I asked. "Mrs. Brenner and I gave our statements back at the hospital."

Rariden nodded. "Ah, yes. Your next-door neighbor. She

told us that by the time she managed to get into the room, the man was already gone."

"Yes. The door was locked."

"Strange, that. How was an intruder able to enter a locked room without waking you or Haskel?"

"He came in through the fire escape."

"I see," Rariden said with a smile that would have been disarming, if not for the glint of white teeth when he did it. He showed his teeth the way a dog would. "Would you care to explain your flat's floor plan to us? Draw it out actually. Please."

He turned his notebook to a fresh page and passed it over with a pencil. At his prompting, I sketched out the room, with the door at the top of the page and the window at the bottom. Two beds were arranged against each wall. Mine and Yakov's were nearest to the window, an enviable location during summer but terribly cold and drafty during winter. Haskel's bed sat across the room from mine, nearest to the door.

I laid down the pencil and stared at the drawing. Why would the intruder pass by me and head straight to Haskel's bedside?

Rariden took the notebook from me and turned it around. "Ah. Interesting."

I said nothing.

"Young man, tragedy has a strange way of following you, doesn't it? First your roommate Yakov Kogan is found drowned at the World's Fair, and then your other roommate Haskel Lehr is stabbed in your flat. But don't worry, it was only a flesh wound. It didn't even penetrate the abdominal wall. Once he comes down from the laudanum, I'm sure he'll be able to tell us exactly what happened."

I tugged at my shirt collar. Even though the office rested in the shade and the windows were cranked down, I struggled to draw in air. "I have nothing to do with this."

"Who said you did?" he demurred.

"Whoever broke into our room, he attacked me, too. If Mrs. Brenner hadn't heard us, I don't know what would have happened."

"Yet you ended up without a scratch."

Underneath the table, I grasped my hands tightly to still their trembling. There was so much more I wanted to say, but I didn't know where to begin. If I told the detectives about my suspicions, other truths might rise to the surface like bloated corpses—like Mr. Katz and what Frankie had done to him that autumn night, or what I had growing inside me.

Besides, I had known my fair share of corrupt officials both in the Levee and back in the old country. It was like buying a fish at market. If there was even just a whiff of rot, no matter how fresh the meat looked, it couldn't be trusted.

"Last time I checked, you called Yakov's death an accident," I said icily.

"That was before tonight." When Rariden had taken my previous statement, he had seemed bored and weary. Now, a hint of interest gleamed in his eyes. He had the look of a bloodhound tracking a scent. It occurred to me that perhaps in his mind finding a Jew to blame for the rash of disappearances on Maxwell Street might be better for his department's reputation than simply ignoring them.

"Can you think of anyone who might have a grudge against you or your roommates?" Officer Alperin asked, clearing his throat. He used his Yiddish like a secondhand suit, something worn at the elbows, ill-fitting, and a touch unpleasant. "Perhaps one of you owes money?"

"No." This wasn't a grudge, but it was personal. Katz must

have figured out who I was somehow. He had come to the apartment looking for Frankie and me.

"Are you sure that there is nothing else you can provide us? Did you get a good look at the man?"

"No. It was too dark. He had a mustache and dark hair. That's all I know."

Alperin relayed the information to Rariden.

Rariden's smile returned. His eyes were as cold and flat as slate. "Of course. And he left through the fire escape, the same way he came in. How convenient."

I had no answer to that.

He dipped his pen in the inkwell and wrote out a few more lines. Closed the book and set it aside. Sat there. Watching me.

"You know, these things do not happen at random," Rariden said. "There is always a reason. A history. A wound."

I cleared my throat. "I… I need to go. I have work today."

"Of course," Rariden said.

I hurried from the room. The station seemed even dimmer than before, as if the windows had shrunk since I entered the building. When I reached the bottom of the stairs, I glanced up the way I'd come.

Officer Rariden stood at the top of the stairs. The light streamed through the window behind him, yet his silhouette remained blanketed in darkness.

32

AFTER TELEPHONING THE hospital to check on Haskel, I was too restless to return home. I arrived at work early to finish my tasks from the previous day. The sun was not yet past the horizon by the time I took my seat at the Linotype machine, and I worked in the glow of the single gas jet. Several articles for the Monday paper had been left at the machine overnight. I finished typing them before even the first newsboy arrived, eager to lose myself in the repetition of punching down key after key.

During my lunch break, while waiting for Sarah to prepare the sandwiches for the newsmen, I wrote out a timeline of Yakov's death and described how it fit into the overall chain of disappearances. I omitted the new developments with Katz and Haskel, afraid of condemning myself. There was still enough evidence in the timeline alone to show the police's indifference and incompetence. I showed it to Mr. Lewin when I brought him his sandwich.

He nodded thoughtfully, scanning over the paper. "This is

good. Quite detailed. Why don't you let me hang on to this and reformat it into something more acceptable?"

I was more than happy to oblige.

On my way home from work, I took a detour to the *Arbeiter-Zeitung*'s office, a three-story building clad in tan stone. The printers were already churning out tomorrow's paper, filling the air with the scents of ink and hot metal. The vibrations of the machinery reached all the way to the office space on the second floor.

Through the soles of my shoes, I felt the shuddering with increasing intensity. The noise was so pervasive that I even thought I heard the movements of those giant presses in the walls and the ceiling, as though the building itself were a vast meat grinder.

I searched for Raizel, knowing that she stayed late to walk home with her mother. If Katz had followed us back to the tenement, that meant she was in danger as well. He might not have a grudge against her, but at the very least, she was a loose end in need of tying.

Raizel wasn't in the office space, nor in the printing room below. Her colleagues were of no help, until, on my way out, I came across a newsboy entering the building.

"Raizel Ackermann? She went down to the Stockyards to document the strikes."

"The strikes?" I asked.

He nodded. "Most of Packingtown had walkouts today."

"Thank you." I hurried from the office and caught the tram just as it pulled into the stop across the street. Raizel could have gone to any number of factories and processing plants, but I had a feeling where I'd find her.

Mr. Katz's factory rose before me, all soot-stained brick and dark slate. Rubbish and abandoned placards lay in the dirt. Signs in English, German, and Yiddish. It was nearly supper time, and many of the strikers had gone home or left to partake of the nearby taverns. Only a small crowd remained. I spotted Raizel standing across the yard with a group of women workers in aproned uniforms, their hair tucked under nurse-like caps or white handkerchiefs.

As I neared, she noticed me and broke away from the group. She came up to me, her notebook tucked under her arm. "Alter, what are you doing here?"

"I heard about the strike," I said as she capped her fountain pen. "But it seems like it's over."

"Until the end of dinner, at least. Mr. Katz refuses to concede to the workers' demands, so I suspect the strike will continue through tomorrow. They just brought in one group of strikebreakers, and more are on their way." She furrowed her brow. "Mrs. Brenner told me about your roommate. I heard the police bells last night, but my parents wouldn't let me leave our flat. What happened? Is he going to be okay?"

"He's going to be fine. The doctor said the wound was shallow."

"Are you okay?"

"I'm just glad I didn't wake up to a knife in my gut."

"You think it was Mr. Katz?" she asked, once I told her in more detail what had happened.

"It had to be. He must have found out somehow where we live. After we left the Stockyards, he could have had someone follow us back to Maxwell Street." I turned to the slaughterhouse. "He knows we suspect him."

"But to attack your roommate…" She hesitated. "That feels personal."

"I think he might have mistaken Haskel for me." As I said it, it occurred to me that Katz could have just as easily mistaken him for Frankie. With how dark it had been, Katz would have only been able to see his loose curls.

My jaw, my nose, my eye socket, broken. They had to wire my jaw shut. The one who did it, I would pay dearly to be put alone in a room with him for just five minutes.

Perhaps it had been quite personal after all.

A group of men soon appeared, accompanied by several police officers with their batons drawn. At the sight of the new workers, the remaining strikers began clamoring in protest and grouping forward.

"Stand back," one of the police officers barked. "Make way, unless you want to spend the night in the pen."

As the strikebreakers neared, I turned to Raizel. "This is my chance. If I get inside, I can look around. There might be something in there that can connect him to the other boys."

There had to be something. Anything. Just enough proof so that I could do what I needed to free myself from this possession. I had no doubt now. I would have to take Katz's life with my own hands. For Haskel and Yakov. For the dead.

"Alter, that's a terrible idea. Mr. Katz is still in there."

"Don't worry, I don't plan to confront him." The lie came out smoother than I expected. She didn't look convinced.

Raizel called after me as I merged with the crowd, but her words were lost to the strikers' roars. I passed through a gauntlet of enraged faces and shifting bodies, ducking my head to avoid hurled stones. The doors fell shut behind me with a metallic groan, sealing me in the slaughterhouse's darkness.

33

AS WE WERE herded deeper into the slaughterhouse, I drifted to the back of the crowd. The superintendent took us down a corridor as narrow as the wooden run that bulls were sent through to their slaughter. From there, we passed through a series of rooms crowded with machinery and crates.

The superintendent had to shout to be heard. He spoke in English, and I couldn't make out what he was saying. We climbed to the second floor and then the third. Through the open doorway, I caught a glimpse of line after line of cattle carcasses, butterflied with their ribs exposed like spread fingers. Deeper in, men worked to adeptly remove the large arteries and segment the limbs. Others immersed the carcasses in long vats of salt water murky with the blood and fluids of the cattle that had come before them.

Back in my hometown, slaughter had been something performed in yards or in the fields. For larger animals, our community would employ the help of a shochet, who would kill the goat or cow and prepare it according to our laws. I recalled him as a grizzled old man whose low mariner's cap and dark coat were perpetually stained with blood and grease. He had terrified me at first, but in time I had seen the way he spoke soothingly to the animals we brought him, stroking their fur until they nuzzled against his palm.

This was nothing in comparison. There was no compassion here, only mechanical efficiency. Once the meat was soaked, it would be transported to the lower levels to be ground, canned, pickled, brined, extruded into sausage casings, or cut into chops.

The overseer cleaved five men from the front of the crowd and sent them to work the vats and conveyer system. On my way out, I glanced up at the wide windows of Mr. Katz's office, which overlooked the processing floor. The electrical lights glazed the glass, turning it opaque.

The overseer led us back to the stairs. From there, they would go to the top floor, where the cattle were slaughtered. As the others filed up the steps, I ducked beneath the rickety metal stairwell. I hid there until I was certain the crowd had moved on.

Things descended here. Just as the carcasses were sent down below after slaughter, the blood and offal were probably pumped to the sublevel through a network of chutes and pipes. The same place where a body would be disposed. I imagined that human remains didn't look much different than animal parts after a week in the waste pit or the Stockyards' communal sewer. I needed to go lower.

Before emerging from cover, I made sure my shirttails and tzitzis were tucked in and smoothed down my shirt and waistcoat. It soothed me to take part in this simple routine. I adjusted my tie and reached for my pocket watch, held it tight for comfort.

"You belong here," I whispered to myself. The last two

years, I had told myself this more times than I could count. "You belong."

I stepped down the stairs with my head held high and my back straight. Mr. Katz would likely be in his office if he were still here at all. That was right where I wanted him. He could stay there all evening, until I needed him.

I made it to the second floor without encountering anyone, then continued even lower still. Filtered through the Stockyards haze, the light of the setting sun congealed like rancid lard on the stairs. It would be getting dark soon.

"What are you doing here?" a man barked in English from behind me as I descended the final set of stairs to the ground floor.

I turned around. A man stood at the second-floor landing. Not Katz. Some administrator or superintendent in a starched suit, his flushed face greasy with perspiration.

My plan to pose as an aide shriveled in an instant, along with most of my memorized English.

"I beg your pardon?" I stammered as he came down the stairs.

"You should be up on the killing floor. We need all the men we can get."

The scanty group of strikebreakers—the first of many, I was sure—wouldn't be enough to keep a slaughterhouse of this size in operation. Likely, the guards and administrators were there on the killing floor. Where I should have been.

"I—I can't." I cleared my throat, searching for what to say. Why had I ever thought I could fit in here? "I have a briv, er, a letter for Mr. Katz. His eyes only."

My fingers strayed to my waist, urging to twist up in the tassels of my tzitzis. I held my breath as a flush of irritation crept down the man's neck.

"Well, good luck finding him," the man said savagely,

throwing up his hands. "He should be here, but his office is empty."

"I'll leave it there for him."

"I can't deal with this now. All this nonsense, and the captain has abandoned ship and left a mess to boot." The man disappeared down the corridor at a harried walk. I didn't even think he heard me.

I waited until he was out of sight before turning my attention to the final set of stairs leading to the cellar.

Darkness, the sepulchral silence down below, and the groan of hooves and steam-powered machinery from the levels far above. A cold sweat dewed on my neck as I descended the stairs.

Below, it was a hot, humid labyrinth of shadows, strange vats, and rumbling pipes, not a place of storage but a place of process, the slaughterhouse's digestive tract. My gorge rose at the reek of rotten meat permeating the air. In places, blood had dripped from the drainage pipes and congealed on the floor in puddles of black and burgundy, some blotched with mold.

A shelf along the wall contained a kerosene lantern, spare wicks, matches, and oil. As I lifted the lantern's shade to access the wick, something clattered nearby. I swiveled around, mouth dry.

A rat scuttled from the shadows, dragging a glistening chunk of meat or viscera. It vanished behind a metal barrel, meal and all. I chuckled uneasily and focused on lighting the lantern. My hands shook as the flame flared up. Past the musk of rot, I thought I detected another stench worse than the first. Scorched flesh and scorched hair.

Once the lantern was burning steadily, I rose to my feet and continued deeper into the cellar. From below came the gurgle of running water passing through the Stockyards' sewer system. Even farther in, the silence was broken by a cacophony of strange sounds—the skittering of rats; hissing steam; the hollow, recurring tap of pipes, like the desperate scratching of a premature burial.

There had to be something down here. Bones or scraps of clothes, Aaron Holtz's union fob, Moishe Walden's mailbag, anything to make this all end.

My foot landed with an unexpected clang. I looked down. A metal panel lay flush against the cement. Kneeling on solid ground, I set the lantern down beside me and pulled back the bolt securing the panel in place.

As I lifted the trapdoor, a burst of hot, fetid air billowed from the hole, accompanied by hundreds of black gnats. I reeled back with a groan of disgust, then forced myself to raise the door even higher so I wouldn't have to lean over to look inside.

The hole below was filled with a sludge of soiled water and worse, all the useless and unclean bits discarded during the slaughtering process. A pale form floated half-submerged upon the surface; in the shadows, it took the shape of a drowned man. Heart pounding, I raised the lantern.

No. I exhaled slowly, my shoulders sagging in relief. Not a person. A stained mattress topper, feathers spilling from its torn edge. The bedding had yet to be waterlogged, so it couldn't have been down here long. Perhaps mere hours. When the strikes had reached a fever pitch, Katz must have come down here—to what? Clear out all the evidence in case the strikers seized control of the slaughterhouse?

I lowered the lid and latched it in place, my stomach churning in revulsion. It sickened me to wonder who had brought the cushion here, or who had been brought to it. I hated that I had come here. But this was the proof I had been searching for, as much proof as any. It meant I had no choice now.

I reached for the lantern and began to rise. Movement

shifted in the corner of my vision. As I turned, someone seized me from behind and thrust a damp rag over my nose and mouth. I bucked against his grip, struggling to break free even as the pungent, sickly sweet fumes clouded my thoughts. As the seconds dragged on, my body grew heavier and my movements turned sluggish.

My legs buckled beneath me, and the floor rose up to meet me at a sickening speed. Cold metal beneath my palms and cheek. My ears filled with a hollow ringing.

I grasped hold of the hatch to keep from sliding into the darkness that flooded my vision. Instead of unyielding steel, my fingers sank into loose, warm soil.

Slowly, I lifted my head.

There was no ceiling now, only an endless sky awash with red and gold. I staggered to my feet. All around me, sunflowers swayed in the gentle breeze, nodding their broad brown heads.

I pinched my wrist to rouse myself, but it did no good. I supposed that whatever I had breathed in, its vapors had been strong enough to throw me from the real world into Yakov's.

I didn't want to think about what I had left behind at the Stockyards, or who had seized me, or why the taste of chemicals lingered sweet and strange on my tongue. It all felt rather distant and untouchable, fading to smoke around the edges.

I closed my eyes and craned my head to the sky, finding solace in the honeyed scent of sunflowers and warm soil. I wouldn't mind staying here for a while. After two years engulfed in Chicago's smoggy warrens, it was such a pleasant change to return to the land.

But this was not Romania. Piatra Neamţ was nestled in the shadow of the Carpathian Mountains, with an economy built on logging and cattle raising, not the farming of sunflowers. So, this must be the Pale of Settlement. A small town near Kiev. The scene of a fire.

I opened my mouth to call Yakov's name, but I was afraid that something else might lurk inside the field and be drawn to the sound of my voice. I eased forward, brushing aside the sunflower plants. Some towered over two meters tall, high enough that I couldn't see beyond their petals.

Past my lingering fear, I sensed this was a safe place. Somewhere Yakov might have gone as a child to hide from the world.

Ahead, the plants rustled. Yakov emerged, dressed in the same handsome evening suit and white shirt he had worn the night he died, a bronze watch chain draped across his pinstriped waistcoat.

A smile spread across his lips. "Alter."

I couldn't say his name. I felt like if I tried, my tongue might blister on its own. He stepped closer.

Yakov had come from a town even smaller than Piatra Neamț, but I could never envision him among the pastures and cattle. His enigmatic beauty seemed better suited for dim Gothic chambers and the silence of ruined castles, aristocracy that had cracked around the edges, clothed itself in ivy, and crawled back into the wilderness. With sunflower petals ensnared in his raven-black hair and his eyes violet in the burnished light, he radiated that dark, primal virility now more than ever.

"I should've known you'd be here," he murmured, coming to my side. "You always are."

"Yakov." I choked on his name, fighting back tears. I had never been able to say goodbye, and now that we were reunited, I could hardly even speak.

Gently, he cradled my cheek. His skin was so warm.

I knew Yakov was never coming back to life, but a part of me felt so happy just seeing him here, as he had been. I thought that this must be what it would feel like in the world to come.

He leaned forward. I didn't realize what he intended to do before his lips brushed against my own.

As Yakov kissed me, the sun fled behind the clouds. The darkness blanketed his gaze with filthy shadows and drained the blush of life from his cheeks. Those lips whose warmth still lingered on my skin became blued as if frostbitten and gnawed on by the fish.

With a low cry, I pushed him away and lurched back into the wall of sunflowers.

I half expected the sunflower leaves to dissolve like smoke under my fingertips, but instead, they felt solid and scratchy. I landed in a bed of crushed flowers, breathing heavily.

The moment I looked up again, Yakov was as I remembered—strikingly beautiful and self-possessed, his eyes as bright as lightning.

"Is something wrong?" He cocked his head. "I thought this was what you wanted."

"You're dead," I croaked, staring up at him. Fear prickled my skin, but above all, I felt sadness. For what I could not have. For what he would never be again.

He laughed. "Alter, what are you saying? I'm right here."

"No, you're not, Yakov. You're not here at all."

Yakov Kogan was buried two meters down in a pauper's grave. Two meters down with shattered pottery covering his eyes and his body shrouded in white linen.

I rose to my feet, moistening my dry lips. "You were found in the water."

Yakov's smile faded. Overhead, the golden streaks marbling the clouds tarnished first to bronze, then to indigo. His gaze darkened similarly.

"No," Yakov whispered, taking a step back. His shoes sank into the soil, which had become black and soupy in an instant, the water level rising. "N-no, don't say that."

"You were there all night. Dead—"

Terror burned in his eyes. "No, be quiet."

"Mr. Katz hurt you, didn't he? He *killed* you."

"Shut up. Just shut up." Bowing over himself, Yakov clawed at his cheeks and tore at his hair. "Stop. I don't like this anymore. Why can't I wake up? I want to wake up now!"

I reached out to comfort him, but he tore away from me with a low moan, as if my touch had burnt him.

"Wait," I said, but Yakov had already fled into the foliage. I caught a brief glimpse of his face among the plate-size blossoms, and then the darkness swallowed him.

I ran after him, crashing through the field. Sunflower seeds rained down on my shoulders, their rough stems snapping underfoot and scratching my exposed skin. Overhead, thunderheads formed, dark and swollen as blood blisters. Whips of red lightning crackled through the clouds, thrashing up a bitter wind that filled my lungs with dirt.

"Yakov, wait!"

A horrific idea occurred to me. What if this wasn't a vision at all? What if the same vapors that had brought me here had also choked the breath from my lungs? Or Mr. Katz could have done that himself, with his own two hands. For all I knew, I could be in the waste pit by now.

No. Bile flooded my mouth. No! This was not Gehinnom. I was still *alive*.

As I continued deeper into the field, the water reached my knees. Underneath the cloying fragrance of the decaying flowers, the air was laced with the odors of gunpowder, damp hay, and the dusty musk of horseflesh. Village smells, taunting in their familiarity.

The clouds parted, and the lightning's true source revealed itself—not lightning at all, no, but fireworks bursting in arterial gushes of blue and crimson. The sounds of a struggle filtered through the greenery. Gunshots, far too many to belong to a single firearm. Voices barked words in an unfamiliar, harsh tongue. Choked gasps. Distant cheering and laughter. The grunts and panting of a man in violent labor or perhaps—I thought with a sickening shudder—one seized by ecstatic bloodlust.

I didn't want to be here anymore, but I didn't want to leave either. Desperate to return to the sunset in all its glory, I clawed through the plants, up to the waist now in muck. Darkness ahead, drowned sunflowers circling in, and far in the distance, something broad and white, swaying upon the flooded field. Between the echoing blasts of fireworks, I discerned a flapping sound like the unfurling of membranous wings.

"Someone's coming," Yakov whispered from behind me.

As I swiveled around, the ground liquefied beneath me, drawing me into darkness deeper than the sea. It felt like I was sinking forever.

34

I CAME TO slowly, to the steady drip of water. Coarse rope bound my wrists over my head, the fibers gnawing into the skin. Sour liquid dripped on my closed lips. I tasted it. Harsh and metallic, gritty with dirt or rust. I cracked open my eyes. A network of pipes stretched overhead. My wrists were secured by a rope to one of them.

My arms ached, my fingers were numb, and my head felt as if it were filled with hot pitch. The toes of my shoes slipped over the concrete floor, struggling to gain purchase. As the feeling returned to my body, I managed to find stable footing. It came as an unspeakable relief to see that my clothes were undisturbed, but that respite lasted only as long as it took for my eyes to adjust to the darkness.

Mr. Katz stepped forward from the shadows. Dust stained the knees and sleeves of his linen suit. In the flickering lantern light, the khaki fabric was nearly the same color as his skin, as though his face itself were another garment. His scar might as well have been a wrinkle, and his thin smile a seam.

"I'm glad to see you're awake." Mr. Katz stopped before

me. "You were unconscious for so long, I was a little worried I'd killed you. Chloroform is fickle in that way."

I swung my foot out, aiming for his knee. Instead, my shoe glanced harmlessly off the side of his calf. He stepped back, perhaps to admire his work at a comfortable distance.

"After your little stunt in my office, I knew it was only a matter of time before Feivel showed himself," Mr. Katz said. "However, I didn't exactly have this scenario in mind. I thought you two would come to my house again. I was prepared for that. I have dogs now."

A tremor racked my body. Feivel. How many years had it been since Frankie had used that name? I had always thought that he had left it behind back in Brooklyn.

"Or did you come here alone?" Mr. Katz mused. "Is that it? What exactly did you hope to achieve, following in the strikebreakers as though you were one of them? With those clothes, you stood out like a fly in soup."

Stupid. So stupid. I never should have followed them up to the floor his office overlooked. I had thought the crowd would conceal me, but I should have broken away the moment we had passed through the slaughterhouse's front doors.

Why had I ever thought I could do this?

Katz lingered in my blind spot, so that he was little more than a shadow in the corner of my eye. I kept my gaze ahead and focused on my breathing. Showing fear was the worst thing one could do when confronted by a wild animal.

"We can make this painless. Tell me where Feivel is. Where I can find him. All I want is to have a little chat with him."

"He's dead. He's been dead a year now."

"I don't believe you."

When Mr. Katz came back around to face me, he held a slaughterer's chalaf. My breath escaped in a thin whimper before I could stop myself. Designed to sever a steer's trachea in a single blow, the knife was nearly as long as a man's forearm, with a razor-sharp edge.

"Why are you protecting him?" Mr. Katz asked, resting the flat of the knife against his palm. "What do you have to gain from it? Is it because you are friends?"

"As I said, Frank—Feivel is dead."

"No. That's not it. It's not about friendship at all, is it?" A sly smile spread across his lips. "You *fancy* him, don't you?"

I stared at him, stricken with shock. I felt as though he'd torn me open with his words alone, exposing me to the world in all my ugliness.

"I know that you share this desire. It's in your voice, your mannerisms. On that night you came to my house, I could see the way you looked at him."

"No. No, I'm nothing like you. Damn you. It's not like that—"

"Has the little whore made advances toward you?" His fingers traced the dull edge of the blade. "He can be very cunning, very manipulative. I would know."

My stomach churned in revulsion and horror as his words dawned on me. I thought of the way Frankie had convinced Joe to join his crew, using a disturbing example so vivid it had felt real: *I'm giving you a choice. An alternative. You can go and find honest work slaving away at the looms or assembly lines, but who knows? Maybe somewhere down the line, there'll be a boss or overseer who'll take a fancy to those blue eyes and slim limbs of yours, boychik, and then you won't have a choice.*

Afterward, Frankie had laughed about it, as though it was just a joke. It should have been clear to me all along. Each time he had given those unsettling warnings, he had been airing out his own trauma, distancing himself from it by reducing it to a cautionary tale.

"What did you do to him?!" I snarled.

"I gave him what he was asking for. What I imagine you want from him as well."

Murderous rage scalded me. I writhed against the ropes, consumed by fury that felt so much greater than myself.

"Damn you! I'm nothing like you. My love for him is pure." The words left my mouth before it even dawned on me what I was saying. Yet now that I had started talking, I couldn't stop. I shouted in a desperate attempt to distance myself from Katz's monstrosity. "How dare you even compare us? You hurt people. You *rape* them—"

"I simply give them what they desire, even if they don't realize it. And if they resist, well, you and Feivel are the ones to blame for that." His fingers had strayed absently to his cheek, following the wiry scar that drew a path from his jawline to his crumpled nostril. "My face, it frightens the boys now."

"Yakov Kogan. Aaron Holtz. Josef Loew. Moishe Walden." I snarled the names as though they were curses.

A flicker of recognition dawned in his face. He narrowed his eyes. "How do you know about that?"

Before I could answer, a gunshot resounded through the room. A meter to Katz's right, a pipe shuddered as the bullet ricocheted off it.

Mr. Katz lunged behind me and folded his arm tight enough around my neck that the breath exploded from my lungs in one gasp. He drew me against him and angled the shochet's knife across my throat. Its flat end rested on my cheek, the edge cold as the tip of an icicle and even sharper still.

"Drop the knife, shtik drek." Frankie stepped from the shadows, leveling the same single-action service revolver he'd shattered Katz's nose with nearly a year ago. He must have entered the slaughterhouse with another group of strikebreakers, for he wore the worn denim jeans and collarless shirt of a laborer.

Katz's arm lowered around my chest, only so that he could place the knife directly against the skin under my jawline. I was afraid to even breathe.

"I knew you'd be here," Katz said, his voice tight and hoarse. With anger, I thought, but as he cleared his throat and continued, I detected something like *excitement*. "Rats run in packs."

"Let him go now." Frankie's voice was steady and practiced, but his hands betrayed him. They trembled even after he cocked the Colt's hammer once more. Past the hatred in his gaze, there existed a cold and hollow terror. "If you hurt him, I'll shoot you."

"And if I don't, you'll shoot me anyway."

"Frankie, don't do it," I said. "You'll—"

"Shut your mouth." As Katz shifted, the edge of the blade sliced into my cheek. Not deep, but I gritted my teeth and bit back a hiss of pain. A hot line of blood unraveled down my skin. "Are you familiar with the shechita process? For the meat to be considered kosher, the chalaf must be sharpened to a razor's edge, with no nicks or imperfections. It is sharpened daily here, until it can cut through flesh like butter."

Frankie didn't answer, but the trembling in his hands only worsened. He clenched down on the revolver's handle and steadied his right hand with his left.

"If you don't believe me, it would be my pleasure to give you a demonstration. Perhaps your friend here would like a scar to match the one you gave me?"

"Fuck," Frankie swore venomously, and bent down to place the revolver on the floor. He raised his hands. "No. Please, don't. This is between you and me. This has nothing to do with him. Just let him go."

"Kick the gun away."

"It might go off."

"I said, 'kick it.'"

Frankie lightly kicked the revolver across the room. It skidded to a stop six meters to my right.

"I asked him to come that night," Frankie said. "He didn't know. There's no reason for you to keep him here, when he isn't the one you want."

"Come forward," Katz said. "Slowly."

Frankie stepped closer.

"No. Crawl."

Frankie exhaled a shaky breath and sank to the floor. It sickened me to watch him crawl across the filthy cement on his hands and knees, soiling his palms and trouser legs. All the pride and strength seemed to drain out of him, his shoulders hunched up and his head hanging down in resignation. As he came forward, he projected the appearance of a wounded, pitiful creature.

He stopped before us and met my gaze through his unkempt hair. A spark of hope passed through me. His tawny eyes radiated hatred and fury.

He was planning something. I was certain of it. He would take Mr. Katz off guard when the man least expected it.

"Where is it now?" Mr. Katz murmured. "That insolent pride of yours?"

Frankie didn't answer.

Suddenly, Mr. Katz pushed me out of the way so violently, I spun around. I grasped hold of the rope, toes skidding across the floor before I regained my balance. Behind me, I heard a grunt of pain and the hard *thunk* of a shoe striking flesh.

The noises reassured me. Frankie had been as skilled at street fights as he was at boxing. He would know how to disarm Katz.

I twisted back around.

Frankie curled over, one hand clasped over his head to protect it, the other steadying himself as he tried to rise.

Breathing heavily from exertion or exhilaration, Katz kicked him in the stomach, driving him down again. My gut twisted at the sound of impact. It was almost as terrible as Frankie's breathless gasps.

I strained against the ropes. "Stop, you're going to kill him!"

In the corner of my eye, I spotted a figure moving among the pipes, like a hallucination in her absinthe-green blouse. Raizel had discarded her shoes, hat, and petticoat somewhere back, and had a fistful of her skirt hitched up to keep from dragging as she crept closer. The light glinted off something in her hand.

She made it within two meters before her foot struck a discarded pipe segment. It rolled across the ground with a hollow clang.

Mr. Katz swiveled around, but Raizel was already lunging forward.

She held her two hatpins with their brass orbs nested against her thumb and the twenty-centimeter spikes sticking out. I only caught a glimpse of them as she clapped her hand down.

Mr. Katz screamed in pain and rage, dropping the chalaf to grasp at his upper arm as she danced back. She had thrust the pins up to their shanks. One had caught the meat of his biceps and gone all the way through to the other side, the filigree orb bobbing up and down with his frantic motions.

He tore the pins free. The first prick was merely a flesh wound, but blood gushed from the second hole instantaneously. She had struck an artery.

"Get the gun," I shouted as Frankie threw himself over the knife. "Over here."

Raizel's gaze darted around the room before landing on

the revolver. She made a dash for it, except Mr. Katz already had a one-meter head start.

As Katz raced past me, I seized hold of the rope tethering my wrists to the pipe overhead and swung myself forward, kicking out with both my feet. I caught him in the knee, throwing him off balance. He landed on the floor and scrambled for the revolver, a smatter of blood streaming in his wake. His fingers closed around the handle.

Frankie fell on him from behind and brought his arm up and under Katz's throat.

If Katz made a sound, it was drowned out by the cry that tore from Frankie's lips, as much a frantic sob as a howl of fury.

The knife was as sharp as Katz had promised.

It was over in an instant.

35

WE CROSSED ONE by one through the narrow maintenance passage connecting the cellar to the refrigeration building next door. Damp with condensation, the brick walls appeared to palpitate in the lantern light, thrumming with the resounding force of the steam-powered engines and machinery in the rooms above.

Frankie walked at the front of the line, his hand pressed over his side. I watched him, fisting my hands to keep from reaching out for him. I was afraid to touch him. I was afraid to look away. The shadows were deep here. He might just disappear.

By the time we emerged into the evening gloom to the uproar and bustle of the striking workers, the distance between us had grown even greater. He felt unreachable now.

With the crowd's attention centered on the next group of strikebreakers being herded into the packing plant, our presence went largely unnoticed. There was fresh blood on Frankie's shirt and pants, but blood was as common as water in this city of slaughter.

I pressed my sleeve against my cut cheek until the throbbing pain spread like red-hot pincers, twisting into the flesh and burrowing deeper. In some ways, the sting calmed me. It made it harder to think about anything else.

"Where is the boss?" a man shouted at the policemen keeping the crowd at bay. "Hiding up in his office, unwilling to hear our demands?"

Where was Mr. Katz? He was down in the cellar, among the waste and entrails. I didn't know how long it would take for him to be found or for those remains to be pumped into the river. I thought I should care, but I didn't. Yakov's dybbuk was gone, and I was free. As for Mr. Katz, his blood could shriek from the deep for vengeance. Let it.

"Are you okay?" Raizel asked once we had passed through the Stockyards' limestone gate.

"I'm fine." I looked past her at Frankie's retreating form. From the way he held his side, I could tell he was in pain, but I didn't think I'd be able to convince him to see a doctor. Not now anyway. "How did you get inside? And how'd you know where to find me?"

"One of the canning girls showed me to the back entrance." A wan smile touched her lips. She had recovered her hat with her other garments, but rather than put it on, she picked the straw brim to pieces between her fingers. "I knew you'd be looking for more bodies. I will confess, I didn't expect to help make one."

"What happened back there was self-defense." The sharpness in my voice took me aback. I tried again, in a steadier tone. "It's din rodef. Katz deserved it. He deserved more than it. He should've suffered."

Her dark eyes studied me. "Alter Rosen, you never cease to surprise me."

"Says the girl who impaled a man with her hatpins."

By now, the roads were filled with children swinging their

fathers' meal buckets and workers returning from saloons for the night shift. As Raizel continued in the direction of the railroad station, I approached Frankie with a sinking heart. I wanted so badly to comfort him, but there were no words to express what had happened back there.

He swore at a passing hansom cab. "That's the second one. Can't the shmoyger see I'm trying to flag him?"

Slowly, I released the breath I had been holding. "I think it's the clothes."

"It's always the clothes." Wincing, Frankie pressed his hand against his ribs.

"Do you need to go to a doctor?"

"No, it's only bruised." He glanced over at me, his gaze unreadable. "Do *you* need a doctor?"

"It's just a scratch."

He sighed, turning back ahead to watch for the next cab. "I couldn't get what you said yesterday out of my head. About the worker who died here. How young he was. I knew I had to do something, so I went to Katz's home. I couldn't get inside. His wife was there. His wife. Can you believe it?"

I didn't answer.

"Then I heard about the strikes, and I figured I'd take a note from the anarchist's playbook, go Frick him up, if you catch my drift. I suppose you had the same idea, huh?"

"No, like an utter schlemiel, I just walked in there. I don't know what I was thinking."

A faint smile crept across Frankie's lips. "On second thought, it's probably better if you don't come back to work for me."

I snorted. "Because I'm not smart enough?"

"Because you'll get us both arrested." His smile faded. "I want to go home."

"We can walk," I suggested.

"It's three miles," Frankie said, but after the next coach barreled past, he started walking. "My feet are killing me. I hate these boots. They smell disgusting, and they're too small. I'll have blisters the size of oranges once this is over."

"You can borrow mine," I said, following beside him.

"That'll be even worse. Yours are nearly falling apart."

As we began the long walk to the Levee, I waited for Frankie to continue speaking. Instead, he just looked at his hands, which appeared bare and wounded without his rings. I wanted to ask him if he was all right, but I knew he wasn't.

"Is Yakov still with you?" he asked at last, without lifting his gaze from the pavestones.

"I don't feel him anymore. He's gone." Just saying it gave me immense relief, as though a cord had loosened from around my throat. Wherever Yakov was now, I wanted to believe that I had healed him.

"Good." He sighed. "That's great."

Silence reasserted its place between us. Frankie flexed his fingers, curled them. I took out my pocket watch and watched the second hand continue its steady rotation. At least some things remained unchanged.

We stopped at a public toilet, and I waited outside while Frankie went in. The door was open to promote airflow. I heard each thud he made against the floor or the wall, with his feet or fists, I couldn't tell. Strangled sobs reached through to me. Each noise was like a scalpel to the skin, but I forced myself to stay against the brick wall, scraping my fingernails along the mortar.

About five minutes later, he came out with his hands scrubbed clean, his shirt wet, and his face composed. He knelt at the water pump and drank deeply from the flow.

There was so much more I wanted to ask him, but I knew how invasive questions could be. How unintentionally cruel. I had been asked about my past before—my father, how he

died, where I was when it happened, how it had felt. There
had always been an unspoken presumption that I must lay myself bare for someone else's pity, like some strange organism
that could only be understood by splitting it down the middle
and rooting through its entrails. The fact was this: I was not
entitled to Frankie's suffering.

But he must have wanted to share his pain, because two
blocks later, he began talking.

"I'm sure you have an image in your head of how it happened." His gaze flicked toward me. His eyes revealed nothing. "Of exactly what went down between Mr. Katz and me."

"Frankie, you don't have to—"

"I know. I'm not telling you this because you deserve to
know—you don't. No one does." He turned back ahead, staring at the dusk sky this time. "But you were there the night I
returned to that house. I know you. I know the way you stand
back in silence and observe, and turn things over in your head
like they're a puzzle, until you understand them completely."

My cheeks prickled with heat. I thought about all the small
ways Dovid and Haskel poked fun at me—prude, frigid, prissy,
frum, pious, cold, quiet as a mouse—and I lowered my eyes to
the ground because I was too embarrassed to meet Frankie's
gaze.

"It's something I've always admired about you," Frankie
said, startling me. He smiled absently. "I hate being around
the edges. If I stay out of sight for too long, I feel like I'll disappear. And when you're living in the middle of it all, right in
the moment, it's harder to recognize the bigger picture. Like,
why would a grown man approach a thirteen-year-old boy in
a crowded train station and offer him a job?"

Frankie had told me how he had gotten from Brooklyn to
Chicago, but not what happened after his arrival. His story

always ended as a stowaway at the trainyard and began as a thief in the Levee. I had always thought the time between his Before and After had been unimportant, mundane. Now, I realized it had been everything.

"A *job*." Frankie savored the word, his voice deep with irony and spite. "He offered me a job as an assistant and took me to his home. I was starving, and he fed me. I looked like a good mensch back then... He said it was a mitzvah. He was old enough to be my dad, and I should have known. I should have known. I should have fucking *known*, and that's what I can't get out of my head."

"You were thirteen." I found my voice, but my lips were numb and quivering. "You—you were just a child, Frankie. You couldn't have known."

"I'd had my bar mitzvah. I was supposed to be an adult." His bitter smile slipped from his lips. For a moment, in his face, I caught a glimpse of the boy he had once been, lost and frightened, his gaze hollowed out. "I think it was the drink, or something he put in the drink. Or maybe I just froze up. I don't know. It's as though I left my body. I watched it happen from above, and I couldn't stop it. Oh, why am I telling you this?"

"Frankie, you don't have to. You don't have to tell me anything."

He continued to do just that, maybe because he had carried the memories on his back for so long, he was afraid their weight would crush him. Or maybe because giving voice to something, really claiming it, was the only way to free himself from it.

"After what happened, after what he did to me, I felt stained." Frankie flexed his fingers, regarding his scabbed knuckles, the slaughterhouse grime caught under his neatly trimmed nails. "I felt like everyone could see it, like he'd put a

mark on me. And I couldn't stop thinking about what I could
have done. Maybe I should have fought back more. And if
I hadn't fought back enough, well then, maybe that meant I
wanted it. Or maybe I just deserved it."

"You were thirteen," I repeated, coming to a halt. He stopped
beside me but kept talking. I didn't think he was telling me the
story anymore. He was repeating it to himself.

"The first few months after I came here, they're just a blur
to me. I remember running from that house. I slept anywhere
I could—on the lakeshore, in unlocked cellars, on rooftops. It
was summer, and the mosquitos ate me to pieces. I remember
that. The itching. And it itched even where they didn't bite
me. I thought he'd—he'd given me something, but it was just
my imagination. For a while there, my whole body felt like it
was crawling with filth. The scratching, I think it was just a
way to, you know, scratch out the memory of him. How he
felt. His nails. His stubble. His s-stench."

He gagged on the last word, and I began to reach for him,
only to stop short, afraid my touch would be excruciating. I
returned my hand to my side and curled my fingers against
my palm so I wouldn't be tempted to comfort him, until I
knew that was what he wanted.

Frankie took a deep, wavering breath. His smile returned,
only this time he showed his teeth like a cornered animal.

"I told myself, I'd never let anyone do that to me again.
And I wouldn't rely on anyone, wouldn't put my trust in anyone, couldn't. So, I'd steal if it meant I didn't have to work
under someone else, because I don't know, maybe there'd be
another boss down the line. But then I made friends with
other boys living on the streets, and I allowed myself to get
too comfortable. I began to put down my defenses. And then
you came along, Alter." A bitter laugh left his lips. "You, all

bundled up in your winter clothes, with your tzitzis dangling out from under your coat, and your long hair. When I saw you, it was like I was back in Vilne. You made me feel like I had come home."

36

I EXPECTED FRANKIE to lead me to the two-story gray-stone where he rented a room. Instead, we steered clear of the old residential neighborhoods bordering the Levee and headed deeper into the vice district's underbelly.

The sun sank lower in the sky, filling the world with a luke-warm golden light. Our shadows toppled over the sidewalk's wooden slates, long and black, like soot marks.

I thought I should say something, but there was no proper response for what Frankie had told me. I tried to imagine him at the age of thirteen, and I realized he had probably looked a lot like I had when he found me.

I just know a lamb to slaughter when I see one, he had said. Of course he had.

Anger boiled inside me. I curled my fingers inward, digging my nails into my palms. If Mr. Katz hadn't already been dead, I would have liked to kill him. I wished I had.

As the sun descended below the horizon, we reached the hideaway. Frankie unlocked the door and showed me inside. In the year that had passed, not much had changed, except that the building had fallen into even greater ruin. Roaches scattered at the sound of our approach. Beneath our feet, the floor was a death trap of broken boards and splinter-lined holes. Curls of gray paper hung down the walls like an old man's payos.

"One day when I own this place, we could turn these into offices and rent them out," Frankie said as we passed two doorless chambers. Thin threads of light entered through their boarded windows. In one room, pots and pans were scattered next to a straw-stuffed mattress. In another, heaps of stained cloth, bent nails, and bones had been sorted into even piles. I knew that the items must belong to a ragman, but there was something eerie about the way they were sorted, as though they were pagan offerings.

"Does someone else live here now?" I asked.

"A few people, but the attic is still all ours, of course. The others aren't bad. They keep to themselves and don't say a word."

We climbed the narrow stairwell. Though it was past supper, the attic was deserted. Frankie retrieved the medical kit from amid the scatter of jars and tincture bottles piled on an overturned apple crate in the corner. "Sit down. Let me take a look at that scratch on your face."

As he cleaned the wound and applied disinfectant, I struggled to find the words to dismiss how I felt about him.

"Frankie, what I said back there about love, I—" Oy gevalt, why wouldn't the words come out? "—I meant it like the way you look up to older boys. How brave and strong they are. It's admiration."

He finished bandaging my cheek and tipped my chin up so he could look me in the eye. "Alter, I love you, too."

The words evaporated on my tongue. I swallowed hard. "Wh-what?"

A small smile touched his lips as he sat down beside me. "I mean it, and I don't use that phrase lightly."

"But what you said about our kiss… About how it was just harmless fun…"

"Oy, you can be so dense sometimes." He sighed, running a hand through his hair. "I just wanted you to feel comfortable, like you didn't have to commit or admit to anything. Look, I know we have our differences, but you've always made me feel safe and listened to. No matter what happens next, I hope we could still be friends. And if you're willing, and when you're ready, I'd like to be more than that."

I curled my fingers through his. "I'd like that, too."

Our bodies turned to each other as inevitable as sunflowers following the rising sun. Frankie must have sensed my desire, because his hand slid down my arm. His touch electrified me. When I looked into his eyes, I felt dizzy and exhilarated, as though I was balancing at the edge of a cliff, one step away from falling or flying.

"May I kiss you, Alter?" he murmured.

"Please."

Cradling my cheek in his hand, Frankie brushed his lips against mine. At first, our kisses were sweet and tender, but with each one, an urgency welled inside me. I wanted to distance myself from what had happened back at the slaughterhouse. I needed to feel something more than this. I needed to feel *alive*.

Frankie and I sank onto the bed, the bedsprings groaning beneath our combined weight. Leaning over me, he tipped my chin up and grazed his teeth against my lower lip, his kisses becoming deep and hungry. His mouth's tart sweetness was a dark wine, muddling my senses. A shudder of pleasure rose from deep inside me, rolling slow and languid through my body.

"Am I going too fast?" he panted, breaking our kiss.

"No. More. I want more." I tangled my fingers in his hair and raised my mouth to meet his. The hands that gripped my waist were bruised and calloused, but his lips were soft as velvet, yielding against my own.

Panting, we clung to each other as though gravity itself might yank us apart if we weren't careful. My hands traveled over him, frantic with a desperation I couldn't name. The violent curves of his cheekbones, the coarse linen of his secondhand shirt, then skin over hard muscle and the hot pulse of his heart.

At the sudden creak of footsteps above our heads, we broke away from each other, panting and flushed. I rose to my feet just as Bailey descended the ladder, holding a roll between her teeth. Harry followed close behind her, his Star of David necklace swinging across his chest like a pendulum.

Bailey blinked at the sight of me. After tearing off a chunk of bread, she said, "What are you doing here?"

"Alter's joining the crew again," Frankie said, a bit breathless. He shoved his hair out of his face and picked up his broadcloth jacket from the floor, draping it strategically over his arm.

"I'm not sharing a bed with him," Harry declared. "Give him Joe's bed. Joe is the smallest. No offense, Alter."

"Don't worry, I have no plans to steal your bed. I'm just visiting." I shoved Frankie's elbow to get him to shut up, grateful for the darkness.

"You're no fun," Frankie teased, then turned to Bailey and Harry. "Wipe that schmutz off your face, you two. The four of us are having a night on the town!"

37

AT NIGHT, THE White City was nearly as jaw-dropping as it had been during the day, an endless expanse of electrical lights that shone on the water. As with the gushing fountains and towering ivory walls, the lamps themselves seemed to be the product of a dream.

In the distance, the Ferris wheel towered over it all. Thousands of blinking bulbs lined the wheel's axle and spokes, so that its shape glowed like a beacon across the fairgrounds.

We began our night in the Midway Plaisance. On the train ride over, Frankie had promised Bailey a camel ride. For that reason, our first stop was the Street of Cairo.

As with the teahouse at the Java Village, no expense had been spared to give the Street of Cairo a glamour of authenticity. Bearded men strode by in robes that reminded me of the silk tish bekishes worn by Hasidic men on Shabbos. The buildings were painted in shades of pale limestone and sand, adorned with colorful hieroglyphics and a menagerie of statues depicting gods and creatures.

Yet in its very portrayal, and in the lavish detail paid to its design, there was a certain false glitz, as though the entire exhibit were under a limelight. This place had been created to evoke a reaction, and everything hinted to that. Beyond the crowded storefronts were dark spaces and empty shelves. The Egyptian men and women milled about, some just sitting at their stalls, seeming awfully bored of it all. The only real sense of movement came from the crowds of fairgoers who bustled through the streets, endowing it with the vigor and lively mood I associated with village market days.

As for Frankie, he seemed even more energetic than normal, barreling from building to building as though nothing had happened today. I thought this must be his way of healing.

Along with the stifling crowds, there were jugglers and swordsmen and curio sellers and camels lumbering under the weight of tourists in starched suits and petticoats. There was a theater for performances and a *Sabil-Kuttab*, which Frankie explained was used both as a communal water source and an elementary school similar to our cheders. There was even a mosque, although I doubted that any worship actually occurred behind those walls.

As Frankie and Bailey rushed on ahead, Harry tugged me by the sleeve.

"Is Frankie all right?" he asked. "He seems rather…off tonight."

"Off?"

"You know, excited. More than usual. And tense."

I didn't want to lie to Harry, but it wasn't my place to speak. What had happened today didn't belong to me, not really. It belonged to Frankie. I saw it as no different than tending to the dead. Some things must live in silence.

I tugged my shirt collar. "Frankie's always been tense."

"Not like this." He studied me, a glint of suspicion reflecting in his keen gaze. "What happened between you two?"

I had no answer to that.

While Harry paused to examine the wares in the bazaar, Bailey rushed ahead to squeal in delight at a procession of saddled camels.

"Don't you want to ride the camels?" I asked Harry.

"And end up with a broken neck? I'll pass." He studied a small ceramic figurine of a pharaoh or god. "Do you think these are real artifacts?"

Considering the crate half concealed by the fringed curtain at the back of the store, I highly doubted it.

Frankie took me by the shoulder. "Hey, Alter, I think I see a camel with your name on it."

I looked back at Harry. "You sure you don't want to come?"

He shook his head. "Camels are boring. You know, I heard there's a cowboy show somewhere around here. Now, that'd be worth going to."

"What's with you and cowboys?" Frankie chuckled. "Hate to break it to you, Harry, but it's Buffalo Bill's you're thinking of, and you'll have to leave the fairgrounds just to get inside. Come on, Alter. Bailey's looking like she's going to plotz if we don't get her on a camel this instant."

I followed beside him, feeling a bit dreamy. Despite everything that had happened today, it felt so good to share the secret I had kept buried deep inside me for far too long, and to know that I was not alone.

The camel ride was terrifying. Each time the animal stepped forward, I gritted my teeth and gripped onto the saddle's wooden horn with white-knuckled fists, certain it meant to buck me off.

"Camels don't buck," Frankie said, always eager to share his knowledge. "At least, I don't think they do."

Once the ride ended, Bailey wanted to do it again. Frankie walked along beside her while I retraced my steps back to the bazaar. The crowd had died down to a few stragglers. Harry was nowhere to be found.

Several dark alleys twisted off from the main street, leading to deserted storefronts. I peeked down them to see if he was relieving his bladder. The fabric awnings rippled in the breeze, producing a sound like the flapping of many wings. No sign of him.

I returned to the end of the camel ride in time to watch Frankie offer Bailey his hand as she dismounted the camel. A small smile touched my lips. Why hadn't I seen it before? He had always prided himself as a protector.

"I think Harry ran off," I said as they came over.

"Sounds like him," Frankie said, rolling his eyes. "Let's go to the Ferris wheel next."

"Shouldn't we wait for him?" Bailey asked.

Frankie snorted. "He's sixteen. He can take care of himself."

We followed the midway east toward the White City's dazzling courts. Now that I had an opportunity to admire the Fair's layout, I realized that there was an intentional structure to the midway. The closer to the viaduct and the women's building, which were the threshold to the White City's grand expanse, the more Westernized the exhibits became. It disturbed me to realize how the builders had treated the other locations. If their placement had been designed to symbolize a separation from the Court of Honor's technological advances, then what messages were their actual content meant to send? What was being said here, and by whom?

The Ferris wheel was even more overwhelming up close than at a distance. It loomed over us as precariously as the Tower of Babel, a marvel of glass and steel. We waited in line until we were ushered into one of the glass-enclosed cabins, each wide enough to hold sixty people. Elegant chairs of wire filigree sat on rotating platforms. As the low thrum of steam-powered engines resonated through the metal beneath my feet, I shifted uneasily.

"Are you certain this is safe?" I asked as the wheel began to turn. I gripped onto the edge of my seat, curling my fingers into the gaps between the wires. Was it just my imagination, or was the carriage swaying?

"Of course it's safe," Frankie said. "What, you expect it to roll off?"

"Yes, exactly!"

"I have to agree with Alter," Bailey said, looking rather ill. As the carriage hoisted in the air, the room darkened. The only light came from the electrical bulbs attached to the wheel's spokes.

The Ferris wheel's speed increased. Frankie reached between the seats and squeezed my hand. "Just keep your eyes on the window."

The darkness emboldened me. I linked my finger through his as we rose higher, higher. The fairgrounds stretched below, a wealth of glittering lamps flanked by the endless black expanse of Lake Michigan. I leaned forward in breathless awe, thrilled by our dizzying height. I had never been so close to the sky. I had never seen so many lights.

It was so beautiful. I wished Yakov could have seen this, that we could have gone here together when he was still alive. He must have had regrets and parts of himself he was afraid to acknowledge or share. I swore to myself that I wouldn't live in fear or silence anymore. I would live the future he had been deprived of, and I wouldn't look back.

38

THE NEXT MORNING, I was roused by the sound of Haskel's groaning. He had been discharged last night, and Dovid had brought him home. For a wound like his, which hadn't damaged any organs or blood vessels, the risk of infection in the hospital's crowded poor ward was more dangerous than remaining in bedrest at home.

"Are you okay?" I asked, shifting out from under the sheets.

Dovid was still asleep under his covers. He could sleep through anything.

"The laudanum's wearing off," Haskel muttered through clenched teeth.

I measured out a spoonful and brought him a glass of water when he downed the drug with a grimace. Once he had settled down some, I checked his wound. The sutures were neat and tidy. No pus or swelling.

"Will you be all right on your own today?" I asked as I cleaned the wound.

"I doubt Mrs. Brenner has any intention of leaving me alone."

"Probably not," I agreed with a small smile. When I finished dressing the gash in clean gauze, I looked up and was startled to find tears beading in his lashes.

"I just don't understand," Haskel muttered, closing his eyes. "I can't stop thinking about it. Why is this happening to us?"

"It's over now. Whoever that was who stabbed you, he's not coming back."

"You say that, but you can't know it."

"I do."

At work, it came as bittersweet to sit down at the Linotype machine and copy articles. Now that Mr. Katz was dead and Yakov was avenged, everything would return to as it had been. My article, of course, would have to be buried. The risk of implicating ourselves in Katz's death was too great. Still, at least justice had been served. That felt like enough.

I finished an article about a Torah dedication and began another about a play at the Maxwell Street theater. My eyes ached from the strain of typing. I started on the third article. My fingers froze halfway through the headline:

DROWNING OR MURDER? JEWISH IMMIGRANT, 18, FOUND AT FAIR.

Stunned, I lowered the paper from the tray and read it. Then, not trusting my own eyes, I read it over again. And a third time.

Although it was written in Mr. Lewin's words, my notes formed the article's heart. By focusing solely on Yakov's death yet hinting at the disappearances of other boys, he had left the article open-ended like a penny dreadful. He transformed Yakov's death into cheap, pulpy entertainment with his lurid descriptions. He never once touched on the fact that Yakov had been an actual person, someone with history and dreams. It was a good thing I hadn't had a chance to tell Lewin about Haskel or Mr. Katz.

"Alter, where are you going?" Mr. Weiss asked as I rose to my feet.

I drew the papers against my chest, my hands trembling. I felt as though I was burning up inside. "I'll be right back, sir. I need to talk to Mr. Lewin. There's a page missing from his article."

Mr. Lewin sat at his desk on the third floor, crouched over his typewriter like a vulture dining on carrion. When he saw me coming, he gestured to the cabinet in the corner. "Fetch me another ream of paper, will you, Alter?"

"Are you going to tell me what this is?" I held up the leaflet.

"That, my boy, is the front-page article for tomorrow's paper. Or at least it will be if I can butter up the head editor."

"No, it's not." I shook my head, hurling the papers onto his desk. "You stole my story!"

He lifted his eyebrows. "Excuse me?"

"I told you that I was going to write this article. You told me it was a good idea, encouraged me to take notes on it, and then you *stole* it! You didn't even care about Yakov at all. This was all about making money for you!"

He cocked his head, tapping his lower lip as though he found the concept absolutely befuddling. "If I recall, I told you to research it for me. In the role of an editorial assistant."

"He was my friend, you bastard."

"And that's why you're the last person who should be attempting to write this article."

"You call this an article? You've turned his death into a source of entertainment, into a sideshow!"

Mr. Lewin gave a laborious sigh, gathering his papers into a pile. "I read your notes. They were incoherent, inarticulate. Absolutely unsophisticated. Your writing might be considered adequate in a backwater shtetl in Russia—"

"—I'm from Romania," I snapped.

"—but it won't do here in the big city. I'm telling you this for your own good. Stick to being a press boy and fetching sandwiches." He clucked his tongue. "At least, that's a job you're good at."

"I'm not typing up this drek," I said as he thrust the article back into my hand.

He smiled pleasantly. "Then I suppose I'll have a talk with the head editor."

"Go ahead, and give your stolen article to him, too. Or better yet, jam it up your ass." Before I could think better of it, I tore the article down the middle, cast the pieces to the ground, and stomped on them. It felt quite liberating. The only thing that would have felt better was if I'd done the same to Mr. Lewin's face.

As I was about to say more, from behind me came the harsh rap of a cane striking the floor.

"Alter Rosen," a cold voice said.

I turned slowly.

The head editor, Mr. Stieglitz, stood in the doorway, his gloved hand curled around the silver head of his cane. "May I have a word with you in my office?"

I nodded mutely and followed him into the hall, sick with dread.

Mr. Stieglitz sat down at his desk, his face as cold and expressionless as a memorial bust. He rested his cane against the wall with excruciating slowness and steepled his hands. My breath caught in my throat. I knew what that pose meant.

My lower lip trembled uncontrollably, and I bit my inner cheek to steady myself, to bring me back into the moment.

"Mr. Le-Lewin..." I cleared my throat and tried again. "Mr. Lewin stole my—"

"Alter, when you first came to work here, I sensed a certain hint of, dare I say, truculence," Mr. Stieglitz said blandly.

"I don't know what that means, sir."

"Defiance. Disdain." He raised his eyebrows. "Perhaps you think you are deserving of a better position? Perhaps you think this role is beneath you?"

"No, sir. No. I've always done my job quietly, without complaint. It's just, Mr. Lewin, sir. I wanted to write an article to bring attention to my roommate Yakov's death, and he stole my idea!"

Stieglitz sighed wearily, and all I could think was that he looked like a man readying himself to put down a mad dog. "I am afraid that I have entrusted you with too much responsibility for someone of your age."

My heart sank. "No."

"You must understand, this is a business. It's like a machine. It can only run efficiently if all the cogs are in order. I need someone who can be reliable."

"Mr. Stieglitz, sir. I am reliable. I'll do better, I promise." I ran a hand through my hair, looking everywhere but at him. If I stared at him straight on, I'd burn up. "Please. Please. Don't do this."

He took a thin fold of bills from the top drawer of his desk, licked his finger, and peeled several off. After some consideration, he added in several silver dollars. "This week's pay."

"You can't do this. Please. You can keep this week's pay, just let me keep my job. I need it. My family needs it. They'll starve without me. I'm sorry." I took a deep breath. "Tonight, I'll stay two—no, three hours after. I'll clean all the presses. I'll do anything."

"This isn't personal." His voice was calm and evenly punctuated, like the tap of Linotype keys. "And it isn't just about these last several days. This has been something I've thought about for a while now. In retrospect, you were never suitable for this position in the first place."

"You bastard, I did everything you asked of me."

My words rolled over him without impact. Only when I lifted my head and stared him straight in the eyes did he flinch. A hint of unease passed over his features. That spasm of emotion thrilled me almost as much as it frightened me. It meant that I had gotten through to him.

He rose to his feet as though aware that remaining seated made him vulnerable. "Will I need to have you escorted out?"

"No." I picked up the money, wishing I had the courage to slap him across the face with it. "I won't make a scene."

"Good."

I strode through the door, slamming it behind me.

39

LIFE DID NOT wait for the living. I spent the next several hours going from business to business on Maxwell Street, inquiring about work. After the fifth door closed in my face, it dawned on me that come tomorrow, I might finally find out whether Frankie's description of the textile mills had been true.

I sat on a tenement stoop and pressed my hands over my face. My eyes stung with the salt of my sweat. I needed only forty more dollars to pay for my family's passage, minus what Mr. Stieglitz had just given me, but even that felt impossible. I'd never get my mother and sisters here.

I picked up a chunk of broken brick and squeezed it in my hand until a throbbing ache radiated through my palm. Anger flared like an oil spill inside my veins. I threw the brick down, cracking it in two on the cobblestones. Leaped to my feet and searched the blue sky for proof of God's presence.

"Is this what you want, HaShem?" I snarled at the sun, which shone on in indifference. "Damn you. Tell me what you want. Tell me why you're doing this!"

There was only silence. Of course there was, because when had He ever answered my prayers?

I blotted the tears from my eyes and laughed.

A year of staying on my best behavior, and what had it gotten me? Endless nights holding my breath, too afraid to tell Yakov how I truly felt. Tedious days at a job that I never found satisfaction in. Tending to corpse after corpse, just so I could pretend that hiding myself among the dead would inoculate me. As if that would ever keep the Angel of Death from finding me, when over and over, *he always did.*

I was done walking around with my head down and my eyes on the ground. My eyes were wide-open; I finally understood it now. Frankie had been right: this world did not protect the kind or the weak. It devoured them.

With nowhere else to turn, I went to the tahara house. I made sure to switch out my flat worker's cap for my yarmulke before I passed through the solid oak doors.

At this hour, only a few members of the burial society remained in the building to take care of administrative duties and funeral arrangements. I found Lev in the storage room, overseeing a delivery of linen tachrichim with the same stern solemnity he displayed when tending to corpses. I stood to the side, not wanting to disrupt Lev's business. He stiffened at the sight of me.

"These will do, thank you," Lev said to the deliveryman, and dismissed him with a brief wave.

Once we were alone, Lev came up to me. I forced a smile. "Good afternoon."

"Alter, what are you doing here?"

I moistened my lips nervously, tracing the lines in the tile floor so I wouldn't have to meet his eye. "My boss let me go."

I sneaked a glance at his face. His features were as unyielding as a mask, showing only enough sympathy to be considered adequate.

"I see," he said. "That's unfortunate. I'm afraid I don't have time to talk right now. There are two funerals today, and I have Kuna watching over a woman in the other room when he should be digging graves."

"I'm not here to talk. I was actually wondering if there were some paid jobs I could do around here until I find work?"

Although the chevra kadisha was run by volunteers, the mortuary itself was privately owned, in affiliation with the cemetery. I cringed at the thought of becoming a gravedigger, but it was better than searching for work at Chicago's sweatshops and slaughterhouses. Since most of the work took place in early morning, I could supplement my income with a nighttime job, such as lighting lampposts.

"We could use a shomer for the woman Kuna is watching," Lev said. "Just until Mrs. Ephron and the others can prepare her."

Shemira, the act of guarding our dead, was one of our oldest burial traditions, dating back to the days when desecration and vermin were true threats. Unfortunately, not much had changed since then, if the Whitechapel Club was any indicator. Unlike washing the dead, payment could be received for shemira, since it was for the benefit of the living.

"That's fine. I can do that." It wouldn't pay much, but I preferred it to begging. Besides, maybe by the time the women volunteers arrived, Lev would have thought of another job I could do.

Lev grunted in approval. "Good. Follow me."

I walked with him back to the entry hall. When we passed the door that led to the washing room, I thought I heard the soft sound of waves lapping against a shoreline. Impossible, but it made me stop anyway.

Lev looked back. "Is something wrong?"

I pinched my inner wrist to ground myself. "No."

Following him into the corridor, I tucked in my tzitzis. It was improper to wear the tassels hanging out when in the presence of the dead.

We entered the room at the end of the hall, a windowless chamber lit by gaslights. A covered body lay on the table.

Stooped over in the chair in the corner, Kuna, the gravedigger, flipped listlessly through a well-creased book. Dressed in drab black, with his mariner cap pulled low and his dark hair framing his lean face, he resembled a bedraggled crow. He rose as we entered, gave me a solemn nod, and then left the room to continue his duties.

As Lev followed him out, I sat in the chair and picked up the book Kuna had left. Tehillim. It was tradition to recite psalms when watching over the dead. I turned to one of my favorite passages and read aloud, "'The Lord is my shepherd; I shall not want. He maketh me to lie down in green pastures: He leadeth me beside the still waters. He restoreth my soul.'"

I stopped, frightened by the sound of my own voice. It was lower than I recalled, a dark, smoky timbre.

I cleared my throat and tried again. "'Yea, though I walk through the valley of the shadow of death, I will fear no evil: for Thou art with me; Thy rod and Thy staff they comfort me. Thou preparest a table before me in the presence of mine enemies: Thou anointest my head with oil...'"

Clearing my throat hadn't helped. I realized it wasn't just my voice that had changed, but my pronunciation of the words themselves, the vowels marked by a clear Russianized dialect.

Cold sweat beaded on my neck. I closed the book without finishing the verse, afraid that if I kept reading, my voice would truly become Yakov's. And he might tell me things. Things I didn't want to hear, such as what it was like underground. Like how it felt to decay. Like what exactly Mr. Katz had done to him.

Yakov's killer was dead, so why was he staying behind? What did he have to gain from this?

I shivered.

Except for another chance at life. A warm body instead of a rotting one.

As I set the book on the floor, a burst of harried voices rose from deeper in the building. I got to my feet and peeked into the hall.

Two police officers carried a shrouded corpse bound to a wooden stretcher.

"Last door," Lev said, guiding them down the corridor.

It wasn't terribly uncommon for the police to deliver. After all, some people we washed died on the streets. Still, I couldn't help but feel a twinge of dread. What if it was Mr. Katz?

As the policemen passed, the corpse's hand slid from the shroud's bindings and dangled limply, already too stiff to sway freely. The arm was slim and sparsely haired, without wrinkles or kidney spots. My mouth went dry. It could only have belonged to a youth.

The officers brought the boy to the room at the end of the hall. As they came back down the corridor, I leaned out the door.

"Excuse me," I said, "but who was that you just brought in there?"

"Just some street kid," one of the policemen said. "He's been in and out of our station since he was twelve, the poor brat. Looks like he finally got what was coming to him and pickpocketed the wrong man."

"Where..." I moistened my lips nervously. "Where was he found?"

"Down by Hyde Park."

My breath caught in my throat. By the Fair.

As the men left, they held the door for Mrs. Ephron, the head volunteer for women. She and several other volunteers filed down the hall. I stepped out of the room so that they could take the woman I was watching, and waited until they passed before going to the door at the end of the hall.

In the other room, Lev leaned over the table, lighting a candle he had placed at the head of the shrouded body.

"Should I prepare tachrichim?" I asked.

"No, he will be buried in his clothes," Lev said, which told me all that I needed to know. The only time a body was buried in its clothes was in the case of murder, to evoke God's vengeance.

As Lev stepped aside, I reached out to tuck the arm back into the shroud and froze. The hand had only four fingers. Its right thumb was gone.

"Is something the matter?" Lev asked me keenly, and I realized that I had my hand still raised, and that it had been raised like that for the last several seconds.

"N-no." I lifted the limp arm onto the wooden board and covered it with the shroud. The skin felt fragile and greasy, like waxed paper that had curled in an oven's heat.

When I looked back at Lev, he was studying me with a puzzled frown. What did he see in my face?

"Do we know his name?" I asked, choosing my words carefully. It was a perfectly innocent question. During the washing process and burial, we would refer to the dead by their Hebrew names, and their Yiddish names if we didn't know the former.

"Herschel Ehrenreich. Apparently, he's been well-known to the police for a while." Lev sighed. "Boys these days. What have we become?"

My head swam with nausea. Feeling on the verge of retch-ing, I grasped hold of the table to steady myself, drawing in uneven breaths.

I waited until Lev left the room before approaching the table, my legs slow and uncooperative. It was a violation to uncover a body in this setting, but I didn't care. I needed to see for myself.

"Herschel, I ask mechilah from you for any disrespect this might cause you," I whispered. Slowly, I pulled back the shroud, exposing him to the unforgiving gaslight.

Tears filled my eyes. Mud and worse stained Harry's clothes. Dry blood caked the brass Star of David pendant he wore around his neck. His shirt was torn down the middle, as was what lay beneath the shirt. The wound was profane.

Stumbling back from the table, I clasped my hands over my mouth in a struggle to contain the wave of bile that surged up my throat. I fled from the room, tumbling into—

—a sunflower field, dead and flooded. The rotting flower petals sloughed off in my fingers as I wheeled forward, sunken to the knees in the muddy water. I caught myself before I could fall.

Weeping echoed from between the rows. The sky overhead was as filmy white as a corpse's eyes, no sun, just a tepid glow from beyond the horizon.

I stared up at the sky, feeling as though I'd been dealt a dizzying blow. God, no. Why was I back here again? Why wouldn't this nightmare just end?

I swiveled around, but there was only the charred building I had glimpsed during my vision at Meir's. I turned back ahead.

There was nowhere left to flee. I knew if I ran, the sobbing would pursue me, and the water would thicken into quicksand. I needed to confront this head-on.

I waded toward the source of the crying. Brushing aside the sagging brown stalks, I entered the next row. Yakov knelt in the water, cowering with his hands over his eyes and his face centimeters from the glistening surface.

I thought how easy it would be to come up behind him and push him under, hold him down and fill his mouth with mud, the way he must have died. Maybe it would be a mercy.

"Yakov."

He flinched at the sound of my voice and turned around. His bright blue eyes confronted me, as wide and feral as an animal's. Mud slicked his dark hair, encrusted his cheeks.

"Why are you still here?" My voice broke. "Mr. Katz is dead. We killed him. We avenged you. So, why aren't you leaving?"

Yakov's features contorted with such rage that my heart stammered in my chest. He bared his teeth at me, eyes flashing.

"Do you understand me? He's gone, Yakov."

"Dolzhni ubit," he snarled, rising to his feet. His entire front was slick with muck, as though the flood's headwaters had flowed from the still chambers of his heart.

My breath caught in my throat. It couldn't be. Was Mr. Katz not the killer? And if not, then could Harry's death have been more than just an awful coincidence, the result of a foolish choice to pickpocket the wrong man? Harry had been wearing his Star of David necklace after all.

Tears sliced through the filth on Yakov's cheeks. *"Dolzhni ubit!"*

"Yes, but who?" I cried as he strode toward me. "Who do you want me to kill? Just show him to me!"

His hands curled around my throat before I could say more. I expected his skin to feel clammy and slick, but it was dry. Gasping for breath, I seized hold of his fingers as his grip tightened. Not fingers anymore, not even living flesh. A braided cord of black leather wound around my throat. It was a whip. I lifted my head.

Black smoke engulfed the figure standing before me. I struggled in his grip. His chest split down the middle, exposing the flame-filled hollow within him. As the fire spread, his coat sleeves burned away, and his arms began to scale from the heat.

My knees buckled beneath me. I plummeted through the ground, and landed in the real world. Pain jolted through my tailbone as I slammed into the cold tile floor of the chevra kadisha's corridor. I tried to rise and fell down again, my hands slippery with sweat.

Panting, I scooted against the wall, seeking comfort in the unyielding plaster. I reached for my fallen yarmulke, then froze as several red droplets landed on the floor. Hot liquid streamed down my face. I wiped under my nose with the back of my hand. Blood.

I closed my eyes and leaned against the wall, nauseated with fear and too weak to stand. My throat burned as though scalded.

Meir's words echoed in my head: *The body cannot sustain two souls. It is like a candle with two wicks.*

I was running out of time. I didn't know how much longer I had left. But if I went through with the exorcism, I would be severing my only lead to finding Yakov's true killer. And whoever the man was, he was escalating. Two boys dead within days of each other, and these were just the ones I knew about. I needed to do this, before he killed anyone else important to me.

40

RETURNING TO THE room, I covered Harry with the sheet. I sat with him while Kuna dug his grave, reading from Tehillim. My voice continued to change, until I felt as though Yakov stood in the room with me, lingering just out of sight. I didn't care. This was mercy and kindness. This was what it meant to be human. It was the last thing that I could give Harry.

The sun had begun its descent by the time I returned home. When I reached the third-floor corridor, I was startled to find Raizel and Frankie standing next to my door. They turned as I neared. Frankie smiled, but a dark cloud hung over Raizel's features.

My mouth trembled. What could I tell him? How could I even put into words the horror of it all?

I cleared my throat, and began tentatively, "Frankie, something happened—"

"I know about the dybbuk, Alter," Raizel said before I could finish.

"Why did you tell her that?" I demanded.

He lifted his hands. "Don't be upset. It just slipped out. She has that effect on people."

"What else did you tell her?"

"Mostly, I regaled her about my charming personality and impeccable taste."

"He's lucky we weren't drinking tea," Raizel said. "Otherwise, it would have ended up on him."

I exhaled slowly. So, she knew. That was one less thing I needed to get out of the way.

"They haven't found Mr. Katz yet." A weak smile touched Raizel's lips. "From what I heard through my friends at the Stockyards and the SLP, the police think he left town. With everything that's going on, if he is found, it'll probably be spun as a political assassination. I imagine the police will be visiting the *Arbeiter-Zeitung* in good time."

"Better that than the alternative," Frankie said.

There must have been something in my face, because Frankie's smile slipped from his lips as I stopped in front of him.

"Alter, what's wrong?" he asked quietly, placing his hands on my shoulders. He reeled back with a grimace of shock. "Your skin. It's so cold."

"Yakov's still inside me." My voice left me in a cracking gasp. "And it's worse, Frankie. It's so much worse. I was at the chevra kadisha. Harry is dead."

"Who's Harry?" Raizel asked.

Frankie stared at me, his face blank. Then he chuckled. "What is this? Some kind of joke?"

"I was there when the police dropped him off."

"That's impossible. You must be mistaken." A desperate smile tugged at the corners of his mouth. "Alter, we saw him last night."

Raizel retreated to Mrs. Brenner's door to give us some privacy. She pretended to be mesmerized by the squashed cockroach lying on the floor.

"He's dead, Frankie!" I said.

"No! He isn't." Frankie raked his hand through his hair, still smiling. "You're confused. That's all right. It's the dybbuk. It's understandable."

"No—"

"Don't worry. I went down to several shuls on Maxwell Street this morning. I think I've found the right rabbi. He's a Litvak like me. He'll be able to help you. He'll get this nonsense out of your head."

"I'm telling you the truth."

His smile shattered. "I... I don't understand. Mr. Katz is dead."

"I'm so sorry."

"Mr. Katz is dead," he repeated.

"He was a monster, but he wasn't the one who killed Yakov."

He looked from me to Raizel, then back again. A small choking sound came from deep inside of him; he ground his teeth together and stifled the noise. Twisting away from me, he punched the wall, once, twice. I flinched at the grisly crack of plaster.

"I made sure Harry was treated with respect," I said quietly. "I stayed with him until the end. I did everything by the book."

He struck the wall one more time, only this time with an open palm.

"He was never alone."

Frankie took a deep breath, stepping away from the wall. The scabs had reopened on his knuckles and his fingers were trembling.

"Thank you," he muttered, holding his hand against his shirt to staunch the blood.

Raizel rejoined us. "There has to be something we're missing. Something we've overlooked."

"I might be able to help," a voice said from behind us.

I turned around.

Mrs. Brenner stood by her door. As she stepped into the hall, it dawned on me that all this time, she had been ready to lend a hand. Each time she had offered her help, I had turned away. Why?

Because of my barricades. Because getting close to someone was dangerous, right?

I was such a putz.

Raizel swallowed, clearly taken aback. "Mrs. Brenner, we were just practicing our roles for the theater. One of the aid groups is putting on a performance of—"

"Miss Ackermann, I am appalled by your audacity to lie to me," Mrs. Brenner said, then clicked her tongue at Frankie. "As for you, young man, I do hope you'll refrain from knocking another hole in that wall. This building has enough holes as it is."

Frankie turned to me, wiping his eyes. "You nearly bit my head off because I told Raizel about the dybbuk, but it certainly sounds like you've been hollering it to the entire tenement."

"She figured it out on her own."

Mrs. Brenner gestured to her door. "Please, come in."

I sighed, filing in with the others. Once we were seated and Mrs. Brenner had put a kettle of tea on the small potbelly stove in the corner, she turned to me. "Alter, do you remember the day you arrived here on Maxwell Street?"

"It was October. Chilly. Right?" I remembered being cold,

although I had a feeling some of the chill had been a residue of the night before.

"Yes, a crisp October morning. It was sunny out, and that's the strangest thing. Because when you knocked on my door by mistake, you were soaked to the bone."

I frowned, puzzled. "No. That's…"

"It was just a glimpse. Just for a moment. But I could see it in you. And when you came close, that smell. I knew that smell. It was salt water." A faint smile remained on her lips, but her dark, intense eyes seemed to pierce right through me. "I call them glimmers. Ever since I was a little girl, I've seen them."

I recalled how cold she had been to Yakov. Every time they had passed in the hall, she had tensed visibly, wrinkling her nose as though he'd carried a terrible stench with him.

"What about Yakov?"

Her mouth tightened into a firm line. "He was burning. Constantly. Sometimes just smoke and sparks, sometimes engulfed in flames. The way you are now."

I stiffened. Underneath the table, Frankie took my hand in his.

"Tell me everything," Mrs. Brenner said.

So I did, omitting only the parts that would condemn us— my feelings for Yakov that lingered like a stone in my throat even now, my love for Frankie and our shared history, and the blood that stained our hands.

"You two should have brought me in sooner," Raizel said, once I had finished. "You've been going about it the wrong way this entire time."

Frankie bristled. "How so?"

"You're stumbling about like a pair of headless chickens, when you have a witness to Yakov's death sitting right here."

"Oh, of course." Frankie turned to me. "Yakov, would

you be so kind as to tell us who killed you? Give us his name, height, and birth date, please, just so we can be sure."

"Enough, you three," Mrs. Brenner said sternly, putting an end to all bickering. "Alter, you say that he's shared visions with you. Correct?"

"They're more like fragments of memories, and he doesn't share them. They're just overflowing from him."

"That's good. From what you've told me, it's clear that Yakov was searching for someone from his past, so if we methodically go through every memory, there might be a clue. Now, let's start with the first vision you saw."

"A burning barn."

"And you didn't think that this was worth telling me until now?" Frankie said in exasperation.

"Yakov told me that his family died in an accident. That a cow knocked over a lantern while a neighbor was drunk. I just thought…"

"A cow knocked over a lantern," Frankie repeated, then chuckled in disbelief. "Alter, this farm wouldn't happen to have belonged to a Mrs. O'Leary, would it?"

"Excuse me?"

"That's how the Great Chicago Fire was supposed to have started," Raizel explained.

"But that's what he said."

"Clearly, he blurted out the first lie he could think of." Frankie sighed, rubbing the bridge of his nose. "Are you sure that it was a barn?"

"Uh, I think. It was made of wood."

"Most shuls in the Pale are made of wood, too, because of restrictions on using stone. And if this happened in his childhood, it could have been during the pogroms."

My stomach churned. Perhaps the reason Yakov had possessed me was because he had been chasing after the same atonement I had yearned for all along. For surviving when the people close to him had perished. "But why wouldn't he have told me that? We were close. I thought we were friends. I... I told him about my father."

"If you came to a city intending to kill someone, do you really think that you would tell another person of your intentions?"

I had no answer to that. Sinking back in my chair, I thought of all the signs. Details emerged in my mind like bones dredged from deep water. During my vision of Yakov's body being dumped into the water, his killer had spoken a language I could understand. I had thought it was German or Romanian, but only now did it occur to me that it could have just as easily been a language that Yakov had known.

"Yakov told me once that he had studied Russian until he could speak it fluently without an accent," I said, thinking of the bitter pride in Yakov's voice when he had told me that. He had emphasized the last part. No accent, so no one would know he was Jewish. "I remember, it seemed...off to me. His uncle taught in Varshe, so you'd think he'd have wanted to learn Polish."

There was only one reason for Yakov to learn that language. All along, he had been preparing for this, if not on American soil, then back in the old country.

"Russian," I whispered. "The man we're looking for is Russian."

"A Russian pogromist in Chicago," Raizel said sardonically. "That won't be hard to find at all."

"Did Yakov ever show you what this man looks like?" Mrs. Brenner asked.

"No. It was dark, and his face... I suppose it's like what you see when you look at me. Smoke and fire." I rubbed my face. My eyes were dry and burning. "There has to be a way to communicate with Yakov."

"Perhaps there is," Mrs. Brenner said, rising to her feet. She rummaged through the drawers of her cabinet and returned with a handful of stationery, an inkwell, and a dip pen.

Underneath the table, Frankie placed his hand on my knee. It comforted me to know he was here with me. I reached down and laid my palm over his, just for a moment, before picking up the pen and dipping it in ink.

Mrs. Brenner clucked her tongue. "Left hand, dear."

I switched the pen to my left hand. I expected it to feel strange, but it was as though I had always held it this way.

"Yakov, who killed you?" Mrs. Brenner said, after taking her seat.

I waited for him to take control. A minute passed. Then another.

"Russian," Raizel said. "Does anyone know how to say it in Russian?"

Frankie sighed. *"Yakov, kto tebya ubil?"*

Nothing happened.

"Perhaps if you try writing the question out?" Raizel ventured.

I tried. After I had finished jotting down the letters in Yiddish, my left hand kept moving, but it was only to repeat the question in Russian. Frustrated, I threw the pen down.

"This isn't work—" Red droplets spilled across the paper, as though the ink had turned to blood. I leaned forward, mesmerized. What was going to happen? Would letters magically form from the stains?

"Alter," Frankie said breathlessly, his fingers digging into my knee.

Warmth dripped down my chin. I pressed my hand to my nose and mouth. My palm came back glistening with blood.

So much blood. I began to rise, but my knees buckled beneath me and I landed hard on the floor.

Tremors shook my body with such violence I was unable to rise off my stomach. The toes of my shoes scraped against the floorboards. In the corner of my eye, the walls rippled, first becoming awash with cracking flames, then receding into the churning black waters of the Atlantic. I dug my nails into the gaps between the boards, terrified that the floor might give out beneath me at any moment.

Hands seized my shoulders. Whimpering, I tried to shake them away, but then a thick cord coiled around my throat. I writhed in a blind panic as the leather strap tightened, cutting off all airflow.

Frantic with terror, I struggled in the killer's grip. As I grasped hold of the cord, my fingers closed around warm flesh. My vision swam back into focus.

I had Frankie up against the cupboards, crouched atop him with my hands around his throat. His fingers ground into my wrist bones as he struggled to pry my fingers off him.

"Get…off…me," he panted through gritted teeth.

Appalled, I released him and settled back on my knees. Then I backed away even farther, afraid to get close to him. "I didn't mean to…"

He rubbed his throat. "I don't think Yakov likes me very much."

"It wasn't you, Frankie," I insisted as Mrs. Brenner came to my side. I took the damp dishcloth she offered me and wiped at my nose and mouth. "I wasn't seeing *you*."

"I know." He didn't even look angry, just weary.

"We know it's not your fault, Alter," Mrs. Brenner said, righting the fallen chairs.

"Why won't he just tell us?" I wiped my hands and laughed

in despair, the taste of blood welling with the words. "I don't understand."

"We can't expect him to write or talk the way he did when he was alive," Raizel said. "We don't even know if he is able to think like us anymore."

She had a point. Maybe when you were dead, there was no such thing as the past or present, only fragments. Maybe, instead of dreaming about burning shuls and burning people, Yakov was trapped on a ship in the Atlantic, watching body after shrouded body—an endless chain of them, really, because wasn't that how it always worked in nightmares?—get consumed by the waves below.

"You look like you could use a rest, Alter," Mrs. Brenner said with a small smile, taking the bloodied cloth back from me. "Why don't you go back to your room? We'll discuss this more in the morning."

It wasn't even dark yet, but I was in no state to argue. I allowed Frankie and Raizel to walk me to my room, hating their glances of concern.

Raizel hesitated at the door. "My parents are probably wondering where I am."

"It's all right," I said. "You can go."

She reached into the hidden pocket sewn into the side of her skirt and took out a book bound in brown paper. "I know this isn't a good time, Alter, but when you have a chance, read it. I borrowed it from a friend at the *Arbeiter-Zeitung*."

My breath caught in my throat as I read the title. *Forschungen über das Rätsel der mannmännlichen Liebe*. Research into the Riddle of Man–Male Love.

"You know," I whispered.

She gave a rueful smile. "I had my suspicions."

"Since when?"

"Since Mrs. Brenner's matchmaking dinner. I remember

how you wouldn't stop talking about Yakov. Read it. I don't agree with all of it, but the author does bring up some interesting points. Perhaps once you're done, we can discuss it."

As she walked off, Frankie and I entered my room. Haskel was sprawled out on his cot in a deep sleep. Sitting on my bed, I flipped absently through the book. It was all in German, and my head ached too much now to attempt reading it.

Frankie glanced over my shoulder and smiled knowingly. "Interesting."

"I thought you couldn't read German."

"Ah, yes, because what in the world could '*mannmännlichen*' possibly—"

I slapped his arm to get him to be quiet and stowed the book under my mattress for safekeeping. It felt like a stick of dynamite. The title would be easy to suss out for any Yiddish speaker with a half-decent grasp of the Latin alphabet. Later, I'd have to find a better hiding place.

My hands began to tremble the moment I had nothing to hold on to. Looking down at them, I had the unsettling impression they belonged to someone else. I flexed my fingers just to reassure myself that they were still my own.

"I don't think I have until tomorrow," I said quietly to avoid waking Haskel. "There has to be something we could do."

"An exorcism," Frankie said blandly.

"No. Not that." I rubbed my face. Think. Think. "If Yakov can't tell me who killed him, maybe he can show me. Remember how I went into the bathtub? In that vision, I saw him being dumped into the water. If I can re-create his death, maybe I can go back even further."

"No, that's not going to happen," Frankie said, raking a hand through his hair. "It's too risky. The last time you tried that, you nearly drowned."

"It's the only lead we have left. And we're running out of time."

"Alter, you don't know what effect triggering these visions will have on your body. Just look at what happened back there. This isn't right. This isn't safe. For all you know, it might just give him the means to take over!"

I looked Frankie in the eye. "Do you trust me?"

"Of course, but—"

"This is my choice." I took a deep breath, preparing myself for what I was going to say next. "We need to go back to the Fair and do it exactly as it happened. I need you to choke me."

His eyes flared in disbelief. "What? Are you mad!"

Haskel grumbled, stirring on his cot. Frankie glanced his way before turning back to me. I rose to my feet and followed him from the room to give us some privacy.

"I'm not going to choke you," he hissed, once we were alone at the top of the stairwell. "If I hurt you—"

I squeezed his hand. "You won't."

He hesitated, searching my eyes. "Alter, if I make a mistake, you could die."

"I know."

"Then why risk it?" Frankie demanded. "Why go to such lengths for a boy who's already dead?"

"His murderer will kill other boys if I don't stop—"

"Just tell me the damned truth."

"I think... I really cared for him." My voice dropped to a whisper.

"Just call it what it is, Alter," Frankie said, looking at me with such sympathy, my sinuses burned. "We both know. There's no reason to hide it anymore."

"Love." As I said it, something seemed to give way inside me. For so long, I had kept up my barriers. I felt them crash down one by one. "I loved Yakov, and I never told him. I couldn't tell him. It's too late for that now. I know I can never bring him back, but I want to do right by him. I need to see this through to the end."

Frankie sighed. "If it's for love, I suppose I have no choice. But I'll only agree if we do it on my own terms. We need to take precautions. I'm not doing it while you're standing up, since you might fall, and I won't use a rope or cord, even if that was how Yakov was killed. And the moment your eyes close, I'll stop. Fair?"

I nodded. "Thank you."

"Now, let's go back to the White City and get this over with once and for all."

41

FRANKIE WANTED TO hail a hansom cab, but instead, I forced the two of us to walk to the nearest tram stop, the way Yakov would have done. Tram stop to tram stop, we sat at separate ends of the car, not talking. Even when we reached the train station, all he did was slip a silver dollar into my hand on his way out the door.

His careless generosity left my face prickling with heat. As I followed Frankie up to the elevated platform, I promised myself that I would pay him back someday. Somehow. For everything.

Sitting by myself on the train, I tried to imagine that I was Yakov.

"I'm meeting someone from home," I whispered aloud, leaning back in my seat. I wished I had a cigarette. Pretending to be him, I took my vesta case from my pocket, clunky and unfashionable compared to the slim brass one Yakov had worn suspended from his watch chain. I flipped the match safe's lid up and down, but stopped once the nearby passengers began glancing suspiciously in my direction.

The Fair's concourse was packed with tourists dressed in their Sunday best, bright satin and chiffon and silk. I lost sight of Frankie in the crowd, but I didn't pause to look for him. We would find each other.

I passed through the gate, paid my way. I retraced the path I had taken several days before. The gilded Statue of the Republic rose before me, set alight by the setting sun until it glowed as brightly as the angel Dumah's flaming sword.

I hated this place. I hated all that it had taken from me. I hated myself for believing that I ever belonged here.

I rested against the railing overlooking the basin and waited until I spotted Frankie before continuing on my way. As I walked, I counted the people I passed, clearing my head of everything else.

At first, I felt hopelessly alone. Yet as I headed deeper into the White City, I detected the faintest trace of burnt gunpowder on the breeze. Pressure cinched around my throat when I swallowed. I was getting closer, if not to where Yakov had been killed, then where they had found him.

Soon, I found myself at a secluded area north of the Court of Honor, a wooded island carved from the lakeside, lush with gardens, dense foliage, and manmade streams. Fairy lamps and paper lanterns were strung along the pathways. This was no wilderness, but manicured groves of red-fringed switchgrass, buckthorn, elm, and black cherry, carefully tended to give the illusion of a wild space.

I strayed from the path and retreated into the shadow of the wooded canopy, as I sensed Yakov had done. I knew it in my heart—he had been *pursuing* someone. A residue of his anticipation coiled in my gut.

I stepped up to the brink where the solid ground plummeted to the water, bent down, and ran my fingers through the exposed dirt. Chunks of turf were dug up as though by frantic hands.

It had happened here, in this shadowy grove. Away from the eyes of fairgoers. I circled my fingers around my own throat; my palm felt cold and coarse, not living skin anymore, but braided leather.

I lifted my gaze to the sky. Blossoms of red and blue fire spread silently through the low clouds, marbled gold and pink by the setting sun. Fireworks.

A twig snapped behind me. I turned around, as Yakov had done—I knew it, I *felt* it—but Frankie was the only person to emerge from the underbrush. Of course.

"What were you looking at?" Frankie asked, coming up to me.

"The fireworks."

He glanced up with a frown. "Alter, there's nothing there."

I closed my eyes for a moment, feeling rather dizzy. The stench of gunpowder mingled with other stranger odors. Wet dirt, filled chamber pots, birch tar used to treat expensive Russian leather, scorched hair, sea brine.

Two souls cannot coexist within the same body, Meir had told me, and maybe he was right. I wasn't sure anymore where Yakov's memories began and mine ended. Time was running out.

"Let's just get this over with," I whispered.

Frankie nodded gravely. "Lie down."

I settled onto the damp grass. The thicket hid us from curious eyes. In the mounting twilight, it was unlikely we would be spotted from the pathway, unless someone were to approach.

Staring at the maroon sky, I tried to summon the memory of the flooded field from my vision at the slaughterhouse, or rather, those brief sensations that I had glimpsed there—the stench of soiled sawdust and manure, the distant voices and laughter, the shuddering of oilcloth in the wind like the flapping of vast membranous wings.

This wooded bower was where Yakov had died, but not where his night had begun. He had followed someone here.

Frankie climbed on top of me. He swung his leg over my side, his calves firmly straddling my hips. His closeness would have been thrilling, if not for the fear that wreaked havoc on my nerves and twisted my stomach into knots.

Frankie rested his hands upon my throat. Like someone searching in the dark, he gently guided his fingers down my skin. He set his fingertip upon my thrumming pulse, and I knew he must feel the same blood that roared in my ears.

"Are you ready?" he asked.

"Yes."

He curled his hands around my throat. "Now, you're going to struggle."

"I know. Don't stop when I do."

"It's going to hurt."

I smiled faintly. "It needs to."

No sooner had the words left my mouth than his fingers cinched tight, severing my breath.

42

I HAD RESOLVED myself to go under without resistance, but my body moved on its own. I writhed beneath Frankie in a blind panic, trying to pry his hands from around my neck. He rode out my struggles with ease, the pressure of his thighs grounding me.

Excruciating pain radiated through my throat. Within seconds, the sunlight blurred, filling my vision with a throbbing crimson glow. The ground suddenly dissolved beneath me. I plummeted past clumps of dirt and torn grass, through the soil, into the light, the—

—sunlight spilled through high windows, filling the room with a warm glow. White porcelain tiles beneath my palms and knees. The walls of the long room were painted a rosy peach. White accordioned curtains. White wrought-iron beds.

Heavily disoriented, I staggered to my feet, grasping onto a bedpost to keep from falling. The room spun in dizzying circles around me. Through the open windows came trilling birdsong and the silvery laughter of children at play.

The room was as silent as a tomb; it took in the outdoor

noises and sealed them inside itself. Most of the beds were shielded off by curtains. As I stepped deeper into the room, unpleasant smells flooded the air. Stale vomit, lye soap, ammonia, herbal ointments. The stench of a ship's sick bay.

"Yakov?" I called out.

I moved from one bed to the next, peeking through the gaps between the curtains. Human forms swaddled in burial shrouds rather than bandages, dirt dusting their skin, their eyes and mouths covered with chunks of shattered pottery.

Just like the sunflower field, this was not a genuine memory but the distortion of one. The shrouded corpses and the pulley system stretching across the ceiling were my own contributions.

I reached the opposite end of the room where linen curtains diffused sunlight around the final bed. I stepped past the partition.

Instead of a cot, there was an elevated wooden table. The sort used for washing corpses. A young boy lay on his stomach, the sheet drawn up to his waist, so that he appeared to be cut in two. Bandages cocooned his torso.

The boy was a stranger to me, but something about his dark hair and the shape of his features tugged at my memory. Even before he opened his eyes, a name formed on my tongue.

"Yakov."

As I reached his side, he stirred and looked at me. His eyes were as dull and gray as cinders, burnt out. He didn't try to sit up. Just lifting his head must have been excruciatingly painful.

"You know me, don't you?" I rested my hand over his. His hand felt so small and fragile, as though it was blown from glass. I feared the lightest touch might shatter him.

"He's coming," the boy whispered.

"Who, Yakov? Who's coming?" Still holding his hand, I

twisted toward the door. I couldn't see much beyond the partition, only a sliver of peach-pink wall and white porcelain.

"Tugarin."

"Tugarin? Was Tugarin the one who killed—"

My voice died in my throat as a noise came from the other side of the partition. The heavy flapping of the curtains being whipped in the wind, or perhaps the rustling of many wings.

Slowly, I let go of his hand. As the flapping grew louder, the sun's golden glow tarnished into the frail sheen of moonlight. The room darkened until all I could make out of Yakov's face was the terrified gleam of his eyes.

Holding my breath, I stepped past the curtain. A ravaged dirt lot confronted me, encircled on all sides by electrical arc lamps as bright as full moons. The acrid stench of scorched flesh overpowered everything else.

I swiveled around, but Yakov was gone. The hospital ward had dissipated like smoke into that desolate stretch of earth, surrounded by shadowed structures. The darkness disguised the rising structures' true form, but I could tell they were slotted and made of wood. Not walls. Stairways perhaps or the scaffolding of gallows. Another fragment from Yakov's memories.

As I turned ahead, a massive form emerged from the darkness, intruding into the electrical lights' harsh gleam. Grasping limbs. Bared jaws, gnashing teeth. Haunches made from burnt arms and offal, a serpentine tail ridged with human vertebrae. Not any single person, but a multitude of them, some charred to the bone, some with faces I thought I recognized. Crawling over each other, fused—*melted*—to each other in the shape of a beast. Upon the creature's back were wings made from soiled white tarpaulin or hospital curtains, melted onto the flesh and veined with throbbing arteries.

I staggered back in terror, only to strike a hard, unmov-

ing body. I sensed Yakov standing behind me, but I couldn't
turn. His palms pressed against the sides of my head, keeping
me looking forward, confronting the monstrosity. In the corner of my eye, I could only see a hint of him—eyes as incan-
descently blue as the heart of fire, a briar of dark hair dewed
with lagoon water.

"They called it an accident." His breath brushed against the
side of my neck, tickling my skin. "A fallen candle perhaps,
or a spark from the eternal flame. It was Shabbos. There were
twenty of us in the shul at the time. No one around to warn
us until it was too late. And once it was over, no one would
believe the words of an injured child, that Tugarin Zmeyevich had burned down the shul. It took me so long to remember what really happened. I buried my memories down deep,
like the dead... But like the dead, they cling to you, Alter.
They cling, and they *always* come back."

"Tell me who he is," I said frantically. "Show me what he
looks like. Show me so I can find him."

"Alter, you've already seen his face."

The beast lumbered toward us, panting and snarling, fiery
sparks seething from its many mouths. Its arms reached out
for me, smoke flowing from beneath its skin. I turned to run
and made it two steps before its—

—lips crushed against my mouth, blowing smoke into my
body. I flung my hands out in a panic. I didn't recognize the
form looming over me until my palms slammed into Frankie's
chest. He tumbled back and planted his rear in the dirt.

"Baruch HaShem, you're awake," he said breathlessly, one
of the few times I had heard him ever thank God. His warm
complexion had blanched to an ashy pallor, beads of sweat
gleaming on his brow and cheeks. "I thought... I thought I
killed you. You stopped breathing."

My mouth trembled too violently for me to speak. I couldn't

escape from the image of the monster. It had felt so real. A part of me feared that the beast had followed me into the waking world and was lurking somewhere nearby, under the water or in the twisted branches, watching with eyes like liquid fire and sparks seething from its soot-blackened teeth. I looked around to make sure we were alone.

Frankie studied me intensely. "Alter, are you all right?"

I nodded mutely.

He retrieved a silver flask from his pocket. After taking two deep gulps, he passed it over. "Here. This will help."

The flask was filled with syrupy bourbon that scalded my throat on the way down and warmed me from the inside out. The metal rim chattered against my lower teeth. I spilled droplets on my sleeve and my lap, and only managed to get down a mouthful. Each time I swallowed, it felt like someone was crushing my windpipe. I took several sips before the shuddering in my limbs subsided.

"Better?" A small smile touched Frankie's lips as I handed the flask to him.

"Tugarin." My voice came out in a shuddery croak.

He furrowed his brow. "What did you say?"

"Yakov told me the name of the man who killed him. It's Tugarin Zmeyevich."

Frankie sighed, looking tired and baffled. "I can't believe it…"

Excitement sparked inside me. "Do you recognize it?"

His jaw worked silently. He looked down at his hands, then shook his head in disgust and rose to his feet. "Alter, that isn't a human name."

"What do you mean?" I was taken aback by the frustration in his voice.

"I mean that your friend wants us to chase fairy tales!" Pacing between the bushes, Frankie took another swig from his flask. Then in a sudden flare of anger, he hurled the container to the ground, spilling bourbon everywhere. "This was all useless. I almost killed you, and what did he give you? The name of a dragon in a damned folktale! We're getting nowhere, and that's what he wants, isn't it? He's wasting our time until he weakens you enough to take control, and you're just going to let him, because for some reason you think he ever gave a damn about you!"

"You're wrong, Frankie." I stood, grasping onto a tree until the vertigo passed. "It isn't like that at all."

"It isn't?" His features burned with anger, but his eyes were filled with unshed tears. It dawned on me just how badly I had scared him. "Then tell me, why is your face so white? Why are you trembling?"

"That's—"

"And the worst part is, you're not even fighting it. You're just letting him consume you, and you're forcing me to be witness to it."

"I never asked you to get involved!" I snapped, his anger spurring me into irritation of my own. All my nerves felt raw now, as though the dream had flayed me. "You're the one who told me I have a dybbuk inside me. You're the one who brought me to Meir. I didn't ask for any of this."

"Well, I'm sick of it. I'm done." He ran his hands through his hair and turned away from me. "I'm not going to watch as you slowly kill yourself with your good fucking intentions!"

"Fine," I snapped as he strode off. "I don't need your help. I'll find Tugarin on my own."

"Be my guest." Snatching up his flask from where he'd dropped it, he glanced back with a mirthless smile. "Have fun chasing fairy tales. Maybe you'll come across Baba Yaga while you're at it."

As he stepped past the trees, a sudden realization struck me like a lightning bolt.

A dragon. With a shudder of shock, I recalled Mr. Whitby's companion. His slate-gray eyes and narrow face, the well-groomed mustache. The inked dragon curled around his right forearm, its tail encircling the letters KAT branded into his skin. He had spoken to me in Russian as though he had known the language, not tentatively, but with purpose and a hint of mockery.

You've already seen his face, Yakov had whispered.

I should have known the moment I had scratched those letters into my arm with the pen nib. Not KAT for Katz. I hadn't written those letters in the Latin alphabet. It had been Cyrillic, the script that Russian and Ukrainian were written in.

My breath seized in my throat. I had stood within a mere meter of Tugarin. He had looked at me, and I had looked at him. And neither of us had recognized what each other harbored under the skin—deep inside him, the scaled shadow of a dragon; inside me, two souls entwined.

Heart pounding, I raced onto the pathway. "Frankie, wait."

"Leave me alone, Alter." He kept walking even as I caught up to him. "I'm going home."

"I know who Tugarin is."

Frankie froze and turned. "Excuse me?"

"I know who he is," I repeated breathlessly. "The man who was with Mr. Whitby. Gregory. He called himself Gregory. He had a dragon tattoo on him."

"It's a coincidence."

"I was so certain it was Katz, it didn't even occur to me until now." I rolled up my sleeve, baring the letters I had scratched into my forearm. "KAT for KAT, not Katz."

Frankie furrowed his brow. "I don't follow."

"The tattoo surrounded a brand."

His expression darkened. "KAT stands for *katorzhnik*. Hard labor convict. It's used to mark criminals who are sent to Siberia. But if he was Russian, I'd have known. I'd have heard it in his voice."

"How many times have you heard a Russian speak English?" Even now, I couldn't discern a Yiddish accent in spoken English, when the accent was my own.

Frankie didn't answer.

"Have you ever heard Gregory speak Russian?"

"No. He showed up at the Masthead a few weeks ago with Mr. Whitby. I only met him once before the Whitechapel Club, and we only exchanged a handful of words in English. He seemed a bit cold actually."

"Why didn't you tell me this when we were at the Whitechapel Club?"

"I thought Mr. Whitby had invited him there, being his business associate and all."

"How exactly are they business associates?"

"Real estate, I imagine." Frankie raked a hand through his hair, his voice rising in agitation. "How should I know? I doubt Gregory's even his actual name. More like Grigori."

"It all makes sense now. He must have followed us back to Maxwell Street after the horse race. That's how he knew where I lived." I gave it more thought. "Mr. Whitby might know more about where we can find him. He might even be in danger."

"Damnit, you're right." Frankie swore under his breath. "We need to warn him."

"Should we go to the Whitechapel Club?"

"No, I have an even better idea. We're going to make a house call."

43

MR. WHITBY LIVED in Kenwood, an idyllic stretch of town houses and Queen Anne–style mansions sprawled along the shoreline. Located just five kilometers from the fairgrounds, it took us only thirty minutes to reach it by cab.

By then, the sky had darkened to the rich, honeyed depth of Baltic amber. I glanced at my pocket watch as the carriage rolled off. Six thirty.

"Do you think he'll be home?" I asked.

"Probably. It's too early to go to the clubs, and weekdays are slow for the races."

Even though a pleasant breeze rolled off the lake, the heat and humidity were relentless. I unbuttoned my waistcoat and the first two buttons of my shirt to provide some relief. Dressed in shabby pants, with sweat already leaching through the armpits of my white cotton shirt, I felt out of place amid the neighborhood's neatly manicured lawns and lavish estates. A wispy cloud bank stretched low across the horizon, like wool pulled thin by a spinner's hands.

Mr. Whitby lived in a handsome brick house overlooking

Lake Michigan's dark waters. As the last house on its street, it was set back from the surrounding properties and shielded by a grove.

"Are you sure this is it?" I asked, studying the home. With its rising towers, limestone columns, and jutting gables, it resembled a small fortress, as inaccessible as it was foreboding.

"I'm positive," Frankie said as we walked up the pavestone drive. "When I went to a dinner party here, he wouldn't stop boasting about how that limestone was Italian."

The windows were dark. Frankie slammed the heavy brass knocker twice against the pane, then stepped back to wait.

"No gaslights on," he said, peering through one of the decorative glass panels on either side of the door. "It doesn't smell like anyone's been cooking dinner either. He should be home now."

"Does he have any servants?"

"Not any live-in ones." Frankie squinted. "I don't like this. It looks like someone knocked a hole in the wall in there. There's a broken vase on the floor. I want to take a look around."

I followed him along the side of the house. We went to the eastern end, where trees provided cover. When Frankie came to one of the cellar's window wells, he climbed into the brick-lined hole.

"Frankie, what are you—"

He drew his penknife from his pocket and inserted the blade between the glass and the wood mullion of the pane nearest to the wall. With a smooth twist and jerk of the knife, he pried the glass from its frame and caught it in the palm of his left hand.

"Frankie!" I exclaimed as he carefully set the glass down. "When you said a house call, I didn't know you meant a break-in."

"Don't plotz. I'll pay him for the repairs." He knelt down and reached through the empty pane to flip the inner lock.

"I don't think this is a good idea."

"Do you have an alternative, Alter? Do you want to wait for Mr. Whitby all night, if he's just lying dead in there?"

He had a point.

The window frame groaned as Frankie lifted it outward, its hinges ungreased and neglected. He crawled feetfirst through the opening and disappeared from sight.

I followed after him, landing two meters below on a packed dirt floor.

It was too dark to see much more than the shapes of things. I lit a match. It flickered and died within moments, as though the air was waterlogged. The second match lasted long enough for me to gain my bearings. On a nearby shelf, I spotted a small stockpile of candles. When I lit one, the flame sputtered only once, like a newborn's first breath, before burning steadily.

The candle cast its glow. Brick walls, wooden bracing and support posts, shelves filled with dusty contents.

"A bit strange not to have live-in servants, don't you think?" I asked. "For a house of this size, I mean."

"He told me he liked his privacy. Now, be quiet."

We climbed the stairs, and I held the candle as we proceeded down the ground-floor corridor. In the foyer, there was an overturned side table and a broken vase as Frankie had said. Grimly, he poked the toe of his shoe through the shards. My breath seized in my throat. The fragments were speckled with dry blood.

"Frankie, that's—"

"Shh." He lifted his finger to his lips and reached into his coat to access the shoulder holster snug against his left side. My stomach twisted at the sight of the gun, recalling the waste pit and how Mr. Katz had looked at the end, with blood guttering from the crevice of his throat.

We continued deeper into the house. Kitchen, pantry, library, den, study. It staggered me how many rooms there were. It had been a while since I had stepped foot in an actual house, and the wood and whitewashed cottages back home were nothing like this.

In the smoking room, my gaze was drawn to the top hat dangling from the brass coatrack. I realized now why Haskel had been targeted instead of me. That hat. That damn bowler cap. I had worn it both to the Whitechapel Club and the races, and when I had returned, I hung it from Haskel's bedpost. To Gregory, it must have been like a beacon.

"I'll take the upstairs," Frankie whispered as we reached the staircase. "Go back to the study. If Gregory and Mr. Whitby are business partners, there might be records in there. At the very least, letters or telegrams. Anything that might tell who he truly is and where we can find him."

I returned to the study. There was not a single smudge of ink on the marble desktop, and the floor was so pristine, I could have believed it had been waxed yesterday. I set the candle on the desk and yanked open drawers, rifling through the contents.

Photographs of streets and houses, folded copies of blueprints, letters, deeds, contracts, and more. What Frankie had said about the real estate was true. Mr. Whitby owned property all throughout Chicago. He had even reached out to tenement owners on Maxwell Street.

After scanning over a handful of documents, I rubbed my eyes. My head ached from the strain of reading English.

The floorboards creaked behind me. I sighed. Perhaps Frankie could make some sense of this.

I lowered the papers. "Hey, think you…"

I heard the hard, heavy click of a revolver being cocked.

"Hands in the air," Whitby said, his voice as soft as the hiss of an adder. I turned, stunned to find him standing a mere meter away, his gun aimed at my head.

I had never watched a person be shot before, but I had seen the result. Once, I had helped prepare the body of a man who had suffered a gunshot wound to the head. The family had called it an accident, but we all knew the truth. The wound had been grotesque.

"Hands in the air," Whitby repeated. His eyes were wide and owlish, his lips working like pale grubs. A fresh bruise marbled his cheek.

My heart slammed against my rib cage and saliva pooled in my mouth. If I tried to rise, he'd shoot me in the back. I'd bleed out on his polished mahogany floor.

Although every instinct screamed at me to flee, I lifted my hands in the air. I felt very distant, as though I was watching myself do it from afar.

"This isn't what it looks like." My voice clicked in my throat. "The broken vase. The blood—"

"You think you can creep in my house like this? Like a rat?" He moistened his lips. "I can shoot you."

With the gaslights unlit, the room was banked in shadows. Of his face, I couldn't see much more than the boring holes of his irises, which appeared as dark and empty as his gun's muzzle.

"Please, you must believe me." My voice sounded small to me. I swallowed down the buildup of saliva, but it came back in an instant, harsh with the taste of stomach acid. "We were worried about you."

"Stealing. Conniving. Sabotaging me."

"No."

"I can shoot you," Mr. Whitby repeated, shaking his head

in evident disgust. "Now I know that Portnoy bastard came to me for a reason. I know that one of your tribe must have sent him to the Masthead, sent him to interfere with my plans, just like they sent the other one."

"Other one?" I whispered, stricken.

Could he mean Yakov?

"The kike at the Whitechapel Club. The one who came around asking questions back in May." Whitby's lips peeled back in a smile, revealing small white teeth. "He's at the bottom of Lake Michigan now."

No, not Yakov. My stomach dropped. Aaron Holtz.

"So, who is it?" Mr. Whitby asked. "Who are you working for? The Rothschilds?"

"I don't understand. Meyn English. I speak not no English—I mean, I can't speak good English." I tried to say more, but then he cocked the revolver's hammer, and my voice shriveled in my throat.

"You'll pay for this."

As he spoke, Frankie eased silently though the doorway. Mr. Whitby began to turn, only to freeze in his steps as Frankie pushed something against the back of his head.

"I'd advise you to drop your weapon," Frankie said crisply. "Now."

Whitby's revolver clattered against the floorboards. He lifted his hands. "Wait—"

Frankie brought down the butt of the revolver against Whitby's skull before he could finish. His eyes rolled back in his head, and he collapsed to the ground.

Frankie leaned down to press a hand against the man's throat, then picked up the gun and rose. He looked almost pained. "Are you all right?"

"I—I'm…" I swallowed hard, steadying my voice. "I'm fine."

He pressed Whitby's gun into my hand. "You'd better hold on to this."

I didn't know how to use it. Didn't want to. I tried to give it back to Frankie. When he wouldn't take it, I stuck it in my pocket.

Sliding his gun into the holster nestled under his coat, Frankie rolled Whitby onto his side and freed the man's silk ascot tie. With a couple swift movements, he bound Whitby's hands.

Whitby stirred and cracked open his eyes. He tried to sit up, but Frankie stepped on his chest and pushed him down against the floorboards.

"Not so fast." When Frankie spoke English, the change in his voice was striking. Gone was the musical cadence I had grown to admire; his words were all ice and tempered steel, his voice as frigid as the Baltic north he hailed from. "You're not going anywhere."

"Rot in hell, kike," Whitby hissed.

Frankie drew in a sharp breath, as though he had been struck.

"That's right, I know what you are." Whitby said it almost gleefully, like a nasty child. "Kike, kike, ki—"

Before Mr. Whitby could let loose more crudities, Frankie abruptly jammed the toe of his boot against Whitby's mouth.

"Such a filthy mouth," Frankie said, and though he kept his voice tame and cold, anger flared in his gaze. "I'd have no qualms with breaking it. Understand, bigot?"

Whitby didn't answer, on account of having his tongue pinned by Italian leather. When Frankie returned his foot to Whitby's chest, the man glowered at him with petulant rage, his monocle dangling down his bruised cheek.

"Who broke the vase?" Frankie asked. "Was it the same person who gave you that bruise?"

"Just someone who I had a little disagreement with," Mr. Whitby muttered.

"Tugarin?" Frankie scoffed at Whitby's bewildered expression. "Your business partner, Gregory. Perhaps he calls himself Grigori or Grisha? Was he the one?"

"Enough about us," Mr. Whitby said, leveling his chin. "Let's talk about you. I spoke with your manager. You're no Russian. You're a Jew named Feivel Portnoy."

"Good job, you found out the same name that's on my immigration records."

"I know where to find you and your family."

"You know the name of a boy who, in all respects, died nearly five years ago. As for my family, your 'business associate' has already killed two members of it, and I'm not going to let him kill a third." Hatred shone in Frankie's gaze. "But while we're on that topic, do *you* have parents? You have people you love? Maybe you deserve to feel what it's like to lose someone important to you!"

I grabbed Frankie's wrist. He looked back at me.

"Frankie, enough," I said, reverting to Yiddish. "Threatening him is just going to make him stop talking."

"No, kicking his teeth in would do that."

I lowered his arm so that the gun was pointing at his feet. "Let me try."

Frankie sighed. "Be my guest."

"We're looking for your business partner," I said to Whitby, the English awkward and unwieldy on my tongue. "Who is he?"

"I'd expect you to be acquainted with Grigori." He said the name the Russian way: *Gree-goar-eey.* "Or his work at least."

"You'd better start talking, shtik drek," Frankie snarled. "I'm losing my patience. Tell us who he is now!"

"Someone who is doing what this country should have done

years ago." He gathered enough saliva to spit at Frankie, but most of the drool ended up oozing down the side of his face instead. "Tell me, why is it that your race is driven from every country whose shores you land on? Why can you never find a place that will take you?"

"Because of people like you," I said flatly.

"No, I'll tell you why. It's visceral, the disgust your presence evokes in ordinary people. It's primal. Your hooked noses, your beady eyes, your nappy hair. Just looking at you two makes me so ill, I could retch. It's like looking at a maggot. A goddamned maggot."

Frankie looked at me. "Do you want me to break his jaw?"

"No, then he won't be able to talk," I said, although it was a rather tempting offer.

"I have long admired the resourcefulness of the common people who must deal with the Jew. I said as much when I met Grigori for the first time. I was the one who brought him to the Whitechapel Club, who listened to his stories of grandeur. We are kindred spirits, you see. His kinsmen have been neutered and domesticated by the interests of powerful Jews, just as America has fallen under the tyrannous control of the Rothschilds and their banks. Back in Russia, he wanted to change that, and the Jews punished him for it. They branded him as a criminal and sent him to the Siberian waste, all for doing what must be done."

I couldn't understand all of what he was saying, but the words I did understand made my blood boil. There was never a way to escape it. If you were a poor Jew, then you were a parasite, living in a hut with a dirt floor or the filth and squalor of a tenement you could hardly afford. If you were a wealthy Jew, you were a vampire, a conniving evil sucking the blood of the common people. The proof was right there—no matter how high we climbed, there would always be someone a step higher, to stomp down on our faces.

"Still, for all Grigori's virtues, he is impulsive. He would rather target street kids than think higher. He lacks restraint and true vision." Whitby gave a tedious sigh. "I hoped to nurture that in him, but even now, he refuses to listen to reason. I told him as much earlier. As you can see by the state of my foyer, he didn't take it very kindly."

"You mean you're the one who told him to kill?" I demanded.

"No." He chuckled. "He was already doing that when I found him. In London at the American Exhibition, and in Paris at the Exposition Universelle. Rome, Bologna, Berlin. Wherever the show goes, he goes, too, to root out the infestation in your hovels and your ghettos. Culling, he calls it."

I thought back to what I had said at the Whitechapel Club, the words that had flown from my mouth in such a flurry, I had hardly even comprehended what I was saying:

A boy was found in the Pletzl, in an abandoned home, his neck slit. 1889. His name was Daniel. Three others went missing in Paris that summer. There were two boys found in London in 1887, young Jews, just children. They had fallen into the Thames and drowned.

Yakov must have tracked Grigori down somehow, followed the path of destruction he had carved through Europe, until it brought him to the shores of this goldene medina. He could have sent letters to the heads of the Jewish communities in those cities. Perhaps all those stories about traveling Europe with his uncle had been built on lies, and he'd actually gone to those cities alone, burning through his inheritance until he washed up in Chicago with hardly more than the clothes on his back.

"Was it Grigori who killed Aaron?" I asked, then clenched my jaw as Mr. Whitby stared at me in confusion. Of course he wouldn't know Aaron's name. I doubted it had occurred to him that Aaron even *had* a name. "Aaron Holtz. The boy who showed up at the Whitechapel Club before us, the one asking questions. Was it Grigori who killed him?"

Mr. Whitby sneered. "What do you think?"

My hands curled into fists. I wouldn't have minded if Frankie decided to kick his teeth in. I wished that I had the will to do it myself.

Before I could do something that I'd regret, Frankie stepped forward. "Tell us where we can find Grigori."

"Why would I do that?"

"Because we are godly people," Frankie said quietly, leaning down to stare him in the face. Whitby laughed, but there was nothing funny about the look in Frankie's eyes. "We believe in justice. Biblical justice. The kind that comes at the end of a sword. Now, you tried to hurt my friend. You would have killed him, if you could have. Therefore, according to our laws, I have full jurisdiction to jam this gun—you see this, yes?—up your ass."

Whitby's laughter died in his throat. He licked his lips, his eyes flicking to the gun in Frankie's hand. I couldn't even tell what Frankie was planning, and that unsettled me. I rested my palm on his arm, but he shook my hand away and cocked the revolver's hammer.

"I can shoot you in the gut," Frankie said when Whitby didn't answer. "It will be slow. Painful. If you don't bleed out on the floor, your insides will rot from whatever you catch in the hospital, if they're not rotten through already."

"You wouldn't." But the bravado had evaporated from Whitby's voice.

"I've killed a man before," Frankie said.

Whitby gulped, his Adam's apple bobbing. He opened his

mouth, then closed it again, before beginning tentatively, "If I tell you, you'll let me go?"

"Yes," Frankie said.

"He'll kill you both, so it doesn't matter whether I tell you or not."

"He can try."

Whitby moistened his lips once more. "Go to Buffalo Bill's Wild West Show. You'll find him there."

44

SEVERAL BLOCKS AWAY from Mr. Whitby's place, we hailed a hansom cab. It was nearly twenty till eight, but the coachman assured us that he could get us to the Wild West Show only a few minutes late of the eight o'clock showing.

As the coach barreled down the street, Frankie held his pocket watch to the radiance of the lantern on his side of the coach. He watched the seconds tick by.

"Thank you, for what you did back there," I said. "I don't know what would have happened…"

"I wish I shot him." He shook his head. "Ever since you told me about Harry, I feel like I've been burning up inside, Alter. I wanted to kill Mr. Whitby. I wanted to kill him so much. I wanted to shoot him in the face for what happened to Harry. I wanted—I wanted—I didn't. I didn't because you were there."

He drew in a deep breath. Exhaled. Closing his eyes, he pinched the bridge of his nose. Moisture gleamed in his thick lashes.

"It's all right," I whispered, placing my hand on his knee. "You can cry."

He wiped his eyes with the back of his hand, his jaw trembling. "I just can't believe Harry's actually gone. I mean, he was there last night. He was right there."

"I know. I'm sorry. I'll show you where his grave is so you can put a stone on it." I wanted to cry, too, but the tears wouldn't come. Just in the last year, I had tended to so many of the dead and comforted so many mourning families. Some of those people I had known. In many ways, this felt no different. It was simply what it meant to be human.

"Do you still have that gun?" Frankie asked a few minutes later, without looking at me.

I reached down and found its heavy weight at my side. Through my coat, it could have been anything. "Yes."

"Do you know how to use it?"

"No," I admitted, grimacing as the coach careened around a corner so sharply, I expected us to crash.

"Give it to me."

I did as Frankie asked. From the perch above, the coachman wouldn't be able to see us through the cab's solid ceiling. Still, I felt nervous and exposed just holding the revolver, my stomach churning with anxiety. I couldn't imagine actually pulling the trigger.

In the glow of the coach's lantern, Frankie opened the cylinder. All six chambers were loaded. He took the bullets out, bits of brass and lead that winked in his palm, then had me put them back in.

After he had finished instructing me on how to shoot the weapon, I took it from him. It wasn't a sword to slay a dragon, but it would serve its purpose. He curled his hand over mine, stopping me.

"Before you pull that trigger, you need to remember what

you have at stake," he said. "What you have to lose. Killing
Grigori won't bring the dead back to life."

"I know."

"And for anyone who sees it, you will be the aggressor."

"I need to do this." I slid his fingers off my hand. "For
Yakov and Victor and Harry. For all those who died alone."

The Buffalo Bill's Wild West Show was housed in a massive open arena across the street from the World's Fair, a dirt
lot lit on all sides by electrical arc lamps that emitted a radi-
ant purplish-white glow. Now that I knew what I was looking at, I recognized it as the vast expanse I had witnessed in
my vision at the fairground. What I had originally thought
were walls of gallows were actually elevated wooden benches.

Popcorn and wads of paper crackled beneath our feet as we
proceeded through the rows of seats. We had arrived almost
twenty minutes late, and the benches were packed to capacity.
It took nearly five minutes before we found seats. We sat side
by side on a rickety bench that quivered under our weight,
under the bright, buzzing glare of the spotlights. The air was
hot and humid, pungent with the odors of sweaty wool, sawdust, and animal dung.

We had arrived in the middle of a sharpshooting act. The
woman held a long-arm nearly as tall as she was, shooting
hollow glass orbs and targets effortlessly. Each time her partner threw a glass ball in the air and it exploded into a corona
of glistening dust without fail, the ringmaster crowed, "Another one for the Peerless Lady Wing-Shot, folks!" or "My
god, Oakley's done it again!"

Any other day, I would have been enthralled by the experience. Now, anxiety stirred in my gut each time a gunshot
echoed through the stadium. When she shot a cigar from her
partner's lips, I had to grit my teeth to hold back the low cry

that threatened to break free, thinking of how the man would look if she missed, how Harry had looked on the washing table, how I might look if we failed.

After she cleared from the arena, the ringmaster stepped forward and lifted his hands, quelling the audience's deafening applause. He waited for silence to descend over the stands before speaking up again.

"And now, from the steppes of Russia, get ready for the brave Cossacks of the Caucasus!"

"I can't believe it..." Frankie muttered under his breath.

Six horsemen in white coats flooded the arena. They called out to each other in a flowing, sibilant tongue. I shifted in my seat, the wooden board hard and cold against my rear.

"Tugarin Zmeyevich," Frankie said distantly. "In the stories, he looks enough like a human that he can ride horses and wield weapons. He has paper wings."

"That sounds like our dragon in Romania, the *zmeu*, except for the paper wings."

"In Russian, it is *zmey*. So, Zmeyevich means 'son of dragon.'" He crossed his arms, watching the horsemen with his jaw held tightly. "It's a metaphor, of course, like everything else. Replace Tugarin with a Tatar or a Jew, and it becomes a tale of how the hero Alyosha Popovich—literally, 'son of priest'—drives back the heathens from pure, unsullied Eastern Orthodox Kiev."

"A child wouldn't have known that," I said quietly. At that age, fairy tales were dark, simple things, their hidden metaphors worn down so that they fit comfortably in a child's grasping hands. Violence for violence's sake, cruelty for cruelty's sake. There needn't be a meaning to it.

At seven years old, Yakov wouldn't have understood the reason for the pogroms or the full magnitude of the destruction. So, when he had escaped those flames, perhaps in those final moments of consciousness, he had seen a man on a horse. A man much like these men, with his white coattails billowing behind him like a pair of paper wings. And Yakov would have known then that Tugarin was real.

As we watched the men ride around the arena, Frankie explained that Cossacks formed the military might of the Russian Empire, where they were required to serve for twenty years. I already knew about the Cossack Uprisings back in the 1600s and 1700s, as well as the brutal pogroms that they had committed during those times. While nothing had happened on a similar scale since the Koliyivshchyna rebellion in the 1760s, beatings and extortion weren't uncommon. Hatred of Jews was entrenched in all levels of the tsarist government, and though Jews also served in the military, promotion was dependent upon conversion.

The Cossacks lined up in the center of the arena, dismounted, and hitched up their horses. Forming a circle, the men began clapping their hands. The steady beat of palms vaguely reminded me of dancing the hora at my cousin's wedding, where, after accidentally stepping on the foot of a neighborhood boy I admired, I had retreated to the sidelines and clapped in rhythm with the other guests. I felt a little like I did back then, my face hot and itchy, my palms moist with sweat, and my heart knocking against my ribs in a nervous, jolting tempo.

"Do you see him?" Frankie asked tightly. "Do you see the bastard?"

Two of the Cossacks broke free of the circle and ran to the center, drawing their swords. I flinched as steel came in contact with steel, the sharp metallic *twang* accompanied by a flash of sparks. The two leaped and twirled around each other in fervent circles, every so often drawing close to exchange blows, like two hawks locked in a fatal spiral of courtship.

The younger of the pair, a teen whose lambskin hat shielded eyes as dark and riveting as jet, was clearly the more talented swordsman. But his smooth, graceful parries were met with fierce tenacity from his partner—the other man, at least six centimeters taller, put all his strength behind his blows, as though this weren't a performance at all. As though he wanted to make the boy bleed.

As I caught sight of the man's face, my throat tightened. A tall hat of fetal lamb balanced like a wasp's nest on Grigori's head, shadowing eyes as hard and gray as mica, with the same shallow gleam.

"That's him," I whispered. "He's right there."

A low groaning overhead. I lifted my head, holding my breath. The oilcloth awning over the seats shuddered as a hard wind slammed into it. Was it my imagination or was the structure swaying? Any minute now, it might come crashing down on our heads, smothering us in the endless red, the air moist and burning with terror sweat and frantic gasps, screams in my ears, colliding bodies.

Gagging, I lurched to my feet and pushed past Frankie. I couldn't stay here. Couldn't keep watching this.

Once I had made it some distance from the arena, I paused to catch my breath. Sweat drenched my back, and my limbs trembled uncontrollably. After a few minutes, I heard Frankie come up behind me. His hand rested gently on my back.

"Are you all right?" he murmured, stepping around to face me.

"I'm fine. I just… I need to breathe."

Frankie's gaze focused on something over my shoulder. I turned, my gaze landing on three Cossack riders trotting past, relieved of their duties.

Hatred seared Frankie's features. He snarled something at

them in Russian. I didn't understand what he said, but I recognized the insult in his voice.

The roar of horse hooves. One of the Cossacks rode up to us.

At the sight of his face, my blood went cold.

"Ubiytsa Khrista." Grigori's eyes burned with hatred and recognition. To make his message clear, he spat at me and repeated his insult in English. "Christ-killer. You never should have come here."

Before I could respond, Grigori's whip leaped forward like a meadow adder. A searing pain curled over my shoulder and my heart seized with an icy shock. It took me a moment to understand what had happened. I thought sweat was dripping down my chest until I looked to see pinpricks of red leaking through my shirt.

The air crackled with tension, charged with the crowd's confusion and excitement. Dozens of eyes on me. What were they hoping for? A fight? A pogrom?

"Bastard," Frankie snarled, and lunged for Grigori. As the whip came down again, my right hand flashed forward out of reflex and seized the whip midswing. It must have stung smartly, but I didn't feel a thing. I dug my fingers into the braided leather and yanked Grigori from his mount.

As he landed on the ground, a surge of intense rage rushed over me, murderous wrath that felt like a fire had been stoked beneath my skin. I switched the whip to my left hand without meaning to, without even realizing it at first, took hold of its worn handle, lifted it.

"Eto dlya moyey mamy."

And I brought it down on his shoulders.

"Eto dlya moyevo otts."

And I struck his face, splitting open his cheek from lip to earlobe like a rotten orange.

"Eto dlya vsekh lyudey, kotorykh vy ubili!"

The words must have meant something to me—*to Yakov*—because suddenly hot tears coursed down my cheeks. I drew back the whip to bring it down once more, but several pairs of hands seized me midswing, took the whip, wrenched me back.

I bucked against the crowd's grasping fingers, growling and kicking like an animal. I tried to reach for the revolver in my pocket, but their hands restrained me. I didn't know what I would do. I would rip his eyes out. I would bite his nose off. Crush his skull, his face in.

"Tugarin!" The name tore from my lips in a savage howl, as sharp and biting as a curse. Yakov's dybbuk writhed within me, clawing my insides into a hot, burning frenzy. His enraged shrieks echoed through my blood and bones like earthquake tremors, threatening to tear me in two: *Dolzhni ubit! Dolzhni ubit!* Kill, kill, kill him.

"Alter, get ahold of yourself," Frankie shouted, grabbing my shoulder. I tried to elbow him, but someone else had my wrist. "Calm down!"

"Damn you, Frankie, let go of me!" Rage flared through me. I needed to get to that man. I'd kill anyone who got in my way. "It's him. It's him. It's him."

Frankie released me, but other hands took his place. Slowly, Grigori rose to one knee, panting for breath. Blood and dust mingled on his chin and beaded in his mustache. As we locked eyes, he reached for the curved shashka on his belt.

Suddenly, the clomp of hoofbeats filled the air. The crowd parted to make way for the young swordsman who had partnered against Grigori in the performance. He jumped down from his horse and stepped between us, his back to me.

"Prekrati!" the boy shouted at Grigori, lifting his hands to pacify him. *"Chto s toboy?"*

His interference did little to quell the rage burning in my

veins. I struggled to free myself from the strangers' grips, snarling words I didn't know, in a language I had never learned. Grigori stared at me, his eyes the gray of ashes.

Hands wheeled me around, pushed me down. Cries of alarm and excitement filled my ears. They were real this time.

Someone kicked me in the side, and I bowed over in the dirt, cupping my hands over my head to protect it. Everyone was pushing and shoving, the air hot and feverish with their frantic breaths. What were they trying to escape from?

Through my tented fingers, the white flare of arc lamps dulled into a sullen crimson glow. Hands seized me by the shoulders and hoisted me up, off the raw dirt floor and—

—my feet touched down on a solid floor of age-silvered oak. In a moment, the arena lot had become an enclosed smoke-filled space. Log walls led up to a vaulted ceiling painted blue to resemble the night sky; the stars blistered and peeled away as flames crept across them.

"The door won't open!" someone howled, and others cried out in despair.

"Yasha, don't you dare let go of my hand," a man said, gripping me tightly. He towered over me like a Goliath. The smoke was so thick, I couldn't catch more than a glimpse of him—bright blue eyes, black hair, a weathered face imprinted with fear and the deepest sorrow, as though he already knew our fate.

Flames crackled overhead like demonic voices. The air scorched my lungs, reducing my breath to frantic wheezing. As Yakov's father dragged me to the front of the chamber, I searched for an exit. Maybe a Chicago sewer grate where there should have been a window, or a ship's steam stack in place of the carved Torah ark. No. Nothing. Just toxic clouds of black smoke and human-shaped shadows pounding at the walls.

Three meters up, there was a window shaped like a porthole. In the heat of the flames, the glass had exploded, rimming the sill with jagged teeth. He let me down so that he could push one of the pews against the wall.

"Climb onto my shoulders," the man croaked, squatting down atop the bench. I did as he asked, grasping onto the wall to steady myself. The wood was so hot, it blistered my palms.

I crawled through the window, the glass sliced into me. An even more agonizing pain spread down my back. The smell of burning skin and hair filled my nostrils. I didn't realize until I hit the ground outside that the stench was my own.

Gasping for breath, I rolled in the dirt in a desperate attempt to put myself out. As the flames diminished, I sank onto my stomach, too weak to even scream.

Sunflowers bobbed gently in the breeze, gilded in the light of the setting sun. Through the encroaching darkness, I saw a rider approach on horseback. The torch he held set him alight. His skin cracked and split open, but there was only more fire beneath, his coattails rippling behind him like a pair of wings.

A name welled on my tongue: "Tugarin."

As he stopped before me—

—the arena's electrical lamps flooded my vision. Overhead, the night sky loomed black and starless.

"Are you all right?" Frankie asked, helping me to my feet. "I lost sight of you for a moment. I thought you were going to get trampled."

People jostled us, the air filled with their shouts of alarm and excitement. I could almost believe I was still in the fire, except the air I breathed was cool and untainted. Wincing, I pressed my palm over my wounded shoulder.

"What's going on?" I had to shout to be heard above the crowd.

"Police!" a voice bellowed, followed by the unmistakable

whack of a club striking flesh. "Police! Break it up! I'm telling you, break it up now!"

Everyone in Chicago knew the last thing you wanted was to get caught in a riot when the police came in. The cops were eager to put their taxpayer-funded billy clubs to good use. Even with the World's Fair just across the street, I doubted they were apt to discriminate between tourists and trouble-makers in the heat of the moment.

"Break it up! Break it up!"

"Come on!" Frankie hooked his fingers around my elbow and pulled me through the crowd, shoving past the people who got in our way.

As we stumbled through the fray, I glanced back the way we'd come, not sure what I expected to see. A burning shul, maybe. Or a boy on fire.

Nothing, except for the uproarious crowd and swarms of cops like black hornets. No sign of Grigori.

Frankie didn't release my elbow until we had found safe refuge in an alley several blocks from the entrance to the Wild West Show.

"Why didn't you shoot him, Frankie?" I demanded, once we had stopped. "Damnit! You have a gun. Why didn't you just shoot him?"

"Alter, calm down," Frankie said, and I realized I was breathing so rapidly, I couldn't even catch my breath. The stench of smoke still filled my nostrils. My throat ached so fiercely, I was sure it must be scorched.

I felt electrified at the thought of confronting Grigori, hurt-ing him, killing him. I wanted to kill him. This wasn't me. These feelings belonged to Yakov.

"We need to go back there," I said, but as I reached for the revolver in my pocket, Frankie seized me.

"No," he said forcefully. "No. We're leaving."

"But—"

"If you go back there, what will you do? Are you going to shoot him in front of half of Chicago's police department? Well, Alter?" Frankie shook his head, his eyes burning wildly through his unkempt curls. "You want to get your head bashed in by some overexcited cop? No. We're going. Now."

"We can't just let him get away with this!" I spoke so sharply that my voice cracked. "What about Victor? What about Harry?"

"We'll avenge them," Frankie said, searching my eyes. "Trust me. We will. I promise you that. But we're not going to make any stupid mistakes either, you hear? I'm not just going to let you get hurt again, damnit! What happens next, we're going to do it together."

45

BACK AT FRANKIE'S place, I sat on his bed while he laid out salve and gauze on the nightstand. At his instruction, I took off my waistcoat and shirt, flinching when my fingers brushed against the welt. The scratch was shallow, but the area surrounding the abrasion was as red and swollen as a chain of kielbasa sausage.

Frankie dabbed at the welt with a clean rag soaked in soapy water. I winced each time he touched me. After wiping away the blood, he wrung out the cloth into a bowl. With a stray bit of gauze, he applied a waxy yellow ointment to the wound, then loosely bandaged it.

"Frankie, what are we going to do?" I asked once he had finished.

"We'll go to the police in the morning," he said, shocking me with his levelheadedness. I had expected him to have concocted some plan by now to get Grigori alone and take him down for good.

"You know as well as I do that the police won't listen," I protested. "We need to stop this ourselves, Frankie."

"You have a family, Alter. You have sisters, a mother. Do you really want to sacrifice everything? For what? So, you can pull the trigger yourself?"

His blunt questions took me aback. I didn't know how to answer.

"Trust me, Alter," Frankie murmured, sitting down beside me. He placed his hand over mine. "This isn't you. You're not a killer."

"But what about the dybbuk?" I asked. "If I don't kill Grigori—"

"I imagine the end result is more important to Yakov than how it happens. A noose works just as well as a gun."

I sighed, relenting. He was right. This desire, this murderous *need* that sent my fingers curling inward, my nails cutting into my palms—it was everything ugly inside of Yakov, left to grow inside me like a thornbush. If I succumbed to it, the hatred's roots would choke me; its thorns would embed in my soul, until it truly became mine.

"We'll go to the police first," he said when I didn't answer. "The least we can do is hear what they have to say."

"All right…"

"Good. Now, let me get something for that shoulder of yours." His lips brushed against mine in the lightest of kisses before he rose to his feet and left the room.

Raindrops struck the roof above. Sitting on the bed, I watched the uneasy flicker of streetlamps dance across the window. Voices echoed from down below. Frankie's landlady had returned. I could hear him talking to her in English, but I couldn't discern what they were saying.

Frankie returned, holding a bottle tucked in the crook of his arm and a tumbler in either hand, each filled a quarter way with golden liquid. He sat down on the mattress beside me and handed me a glass. "This will help."

"Really?" I took a whiff of the liquid, catching a hint of its light honeyed aroma. "You shouldn't drink so much."

"There's been a lot to drink about these last few days." He nodded toward the tumbler. "Now, bottoms up. Doctor's orders."

I lifted my drink in a toast. "L'chaim."

"L'chaim," he echoed, tapping glasses with me.

L'chaim. To life. After the last few days, the toast felt like a sick joke.

I sipped the liquor. Just as I thought. Sweet as syrup and so potent that it made my eyes water. "What is this?"

"*Krupnikas*, made with honey. It's supposed to be good for you."

I drank the rest. The liquor stoked a soothing warmth in my chest. By the second glass Frankie poured for me, the pain in my shoulder had mellowed to a subdued throbbing. As I lifted my glass to my lips, I noticed that his remained full.

"You're not drinking," I said.

"Ah, so it's a race now?" Frankie polished off his glass. "Satisfied?"

"Very." A small smile touched my lips.

He restlessly tapped his fingers against the cut crystal. "Let's talk."

"About what we're going to do to Grigori?"

"How about your family? Still saving up money to get them over here?"

"I have a hundred dollars saved up. I just need forty more."

"I could lend you some money," Frankie said, pausing to splash another finger of liqueur into his glass. "Twenty dollars every few weeks. You could pay it back slowly, no interest."

His offer shook me so much I choked on my *krupnikas*. I stared at him, breathless. Twenty dollars was more than what had been my weekly paycheck.

He turned to me. "They'd be here in time for Rosh Ha-shanah."

"I can't accept that. I'll find another job."

"It's just twenty dollars. It's not that much. Besides, what am I going to spend it on?" He cupped his bloodstone watch fob in his palm. "Another fob? Some cuff links or a nice watch? I spoil myself too much as it is. You'd be doing me a favor by taking it off my hands."

My face burning with shame, I took in the sight of Frankie. His polished boots, the thick gold watch chain cinched across his waistcoat, the handsome fob.

"Thank you, but I can't accept your money," I said firmly, despising myself for my pride.

"Give it some thought." He took another sip of his drink. "Maybe you'll wake up tomorrow and realize this is just the dybbuk talking."

"You know what?" My voice came out soft and a bit slurred. I supposed I was drunk after all. "Deep down, you're a good mensch, Frankie."

"Oh ho, so you've seen through my disguise." He took out his pocket watch to check the time. I blinked heavily. In the hissing gaslights, the watch's golden case glowed like a beacon.

We drank. We sat in soothing silence, listening to the leaden tick of the hallway clock and the barking of a nearby dog. To-morrow, we would finish this. For good.

I lifted the glass to polish off the final drops of *krupnikas*. My fingertips brushed my lips; my hand was empty. Befuddled, I looked down. The glass lay on the floor in pieces.

"Sorry," I said, reaching for it.

"No, it's okay." Frankie had risen to his feet without me realizing it. "Don't worry about it."

I bent down to pick up the pieces anyway. My eyesight suddenly blurred, and I felt myself swoon. I had to stop and lean back, afraid I might fall.

What was happening to me? This wasn't another vision coming on.

"Frankie." My tongue barely cooperated. "Something... Something's wrong."

His features clouded together like smoke. "Just rest, Alter."

"F-Frankie." I tried to stand and toppled over instead. I struggled to hoist myself from the mattress. It felt as though my body weighed a thousand kilograms. "You—what did you do?"

"I'm sorry, Alter. I'm not a good mensch." Resting his hand upon my chest, Frankie eased me down again. Darkness flooded my vision. "I never was one. That's the difference between you and me."

46

WHEN I WOKE, my head felt as though it had been stuffed full of cotton, and my mouth tasted of rancid honey.

I swung myself up and immediately regretted it. The room wobbled in frantic circles. Groaning, I lay down again and waited for the nausea to pass.

Frankie was gone. Of course he was. The bastard.

Judging by the quality of light, it was already eight or nine in the morning. Whatever he had slipped into my drink had been strong enough to knock me out for hours.

It wouldn't have taken him more than an hour to return to the Wild West Show. Plenty of time to take care of business. Unless...

No! I wouldn't even think about it.

I struggled to my feet and searched for my shirt. He had left it folded on the dresser and laid my keys and pocket watch atop it, like an apology.

By the time I buttoned my clothes and tucked in my tzitzis, I felt a bit more in control. Whitby's revolver was in my coat pocket. After some struggle, I managed to open the cylinder. The bullets were all there.

Downstairs, I was greeted by the scent of freshly brewed coffee, a smell as disarming as it was disorienting. After ten months on Maxwell Street and over twelve months in an attic before that, I expected mornings to smell like dust and mildew.

Voices echoed down the hall.

"As I told you, there is no one here by the name of Alter Rosen," a woman said, her voice strained by annoyance. "And I am certainly not going to give you a twenty-cent tip, no matter what Frankie said."

"But he told me—" a young boy said.

"I don't care what he told you. Now, leave."

"Wait," I said as I barreled into the foyer. A fair-haired woman stood at the door, draped in the polished jet and black lace of a mourner. She turned at the sound of my voice.

I swallowed hard. By the moment, the air in the hallway seemed to grow thinner. Something was terribly wrong.

"I suppose you are Alter Rosen?" She said it almost wearily.

"Yes."

"This is the first time he's brought home a guest. Did you stay up there all night?"

"Drunk. We were…" I tried again. "We were drinking in the Levee. I didn't want to walk home."

"I do hope you will not make a habit of it, or Frankie will have to find alternative housing. I will not abide by strangers in my home."

"It won't happen again." I went to the door to see who she had been talking to.

A message boy stood on the front steps. He was no older than twelve, and his scraped knees, tattered shoes, and windblown hair spoke of a life spent dodging wagons.

He offered me a smile, the relief clear in his face. "Alter Rosen?"

"Yes."

"Frankie Portnoy paid me fifty cents to tell you there's been an incident."

"An incident." My voice echoed in my ears. It sounded so much like Yakov now, I barely even recognized it. "Is he...?"

"He's at Michael Reese Hospital. He was found this morning down by the fairgrounds. Somebody shot him."

The carriage ride to the hospital was an hour-long free fall. Even with my coat on, I felt frozen and feverish, my body all nausea and cramped muscles. My hands were so stiff, I could hardly move them; death loomed closer here.

Paralyzed with dread, I sat through the ride imagining going to the tahara house. It would be cold, as it always was, and Frankie would be waiting in the washing room like a wax doll, gray and shrunken.

I never wanted to see him that way. I didn't even want to think about it.

Death was not kind or glorious; it was not the Lord's kiss that claimed Aaron and Moses. Like a greedy child gorging on clusters of grapes, the Angel of Death tore all of the beauty and dignity from a person and left behind a terrible, dripping mess. What was the end? The end was blood and piss and shit, and trying to move frozen limbs without resorting to dislocating them. The end was typhus.

Why had I ever thought I could change that?

By the time the carriage pulled up in front of the hospital, I was certain I was too late. I jumped onto solid ground before the carriage had stopped moving, stumbled forward, regained my balance, kept moving. The revolver in my coat pocket slapped against my thigh with each step; I reached inside and held it, afraid of accidentally shooting myself in the leg.

The hospital was a Goliath of brown brick and gleaming glass, looming over a green lawn as bright as bread mold.

"Frankie Portnoy," I said breathlessly to the first nurse I came across. "He was brought here. Is he all right? Where is he?"

She balked at my questions. "I'm sorry, I don't know who that is."

"He might be going by the name Feivel Portnoy or Frankie Porter."

"Give me a moment, please. Let me ask around."

After inquiring with several other nurses and two doctors, she was able to find where they had placed Frankie. She showed me to a recovery ward at the far end of the building. In the hall, I passed an orderly pushing a shrouded gurney, a lump of a body.

Not him. I stared straight ahead, refusing to look back. It couldn't be him.

We entered the same room the gurney had been wheeled from. Choked with dread, I expected the nurse to lead me to an empty bed, her hands folded and her face shaped in careful sympathy.

I'm so sorry, she would say. *You good mensch, you were too late. The dragon ate him.*

No. There in the corner, I spotted a familiar head of tousled brown curls and released my held breath.

They had given Frankie a cot by the window, shielded from the other beds by a linen divider. He was tucked in like a child, the white sheet folded at waist level, his arms resting on either side of him. Bandages encased his bare chest.

"Frankie." My voice came out in a whisper, my mouth so dry that my throat clicked when I swallowed. I sat down by his bedside and put my hand over his. He didn't respond to my voice or touch. His warm complexion had blanched to an ashen gray, his thick eyelashes cast over the bruised crescents of his lower lids.

I struggled to swallow the choking lump in my throat. "Frankie, it's me, Alter."

No response. Could he feel my presence? Did he know that I was here?

"He probably can't hear you," the nurse said, stripping an empty cot of its sheets.

My breath caught in my throat. "What?"

"He was given laudanum." The nurse emptied another patient's bedpan into a tin bucket. The stench of waste soiled my nostrils. There were other odors under the first. Rot. Decay. Burnt flesh.

"When will he wake up?" I asked, but she was already moving on. Clearing out the final bedpan, she left the room.

I turned back to Frankie once she was gone and held his hand even tighter, as if that could convince him to open his eyes.

"Please, just come back to me," I whispered.

His fingers pressed against my palm like slivers of ice. Just hours ago, his grip had been warm and strong. The change was gut-wrenching. If I didn't know any better now, I could have been gripping the hand of a corpse.

"Alter," he mumbled, so softly that I almost thought I imagined it.

"Frankie!" My vision fogged up with tears of relief as he cracked open his eyes.

"You got my message." He sighed deeply. "I was afraid… you wouldn't be there. I'm sorry for what I did. I'm so sorry."

"No. No. Don't apologize."

"Listen. I heard them." He spoke laboriously, his slurred

voice trailing in and out. "Mr. Whitby and Grigori... They were talking...about starting a fire."

An involuntary shiver racked my body as I recalled the burning shul, the smoke scorching my lungs. I leaned forward in my seat. "A fire? Where?"

"It's all cloudy." His eyes fluttered shut, his breathing slowing down. "I'm so tired."

"Hey. Hey." I squeezed his hand. "Don't fall asleep yet. Try to remember."

"The fairgrounds. This afternoon."

"The Wild West Show?"

"No. Cold. Cold..." His fingers loosened in mine. He rested his cheek against the pillow and slipped into sleep. I sat there for a moment longer, counting his breaths, just to be sure.

I lifted his hand to my lips and kissed the battered knuckles, kissed the clammy fingers. I drew up the covers to warm him. "I'll be back."

He didn't answer.

Before I left his room, I emptied out all the pitchers and water basins, the way you were supposed to do after a person had died. What the nurses had probably forgotten to do. The Angel of Death washed his knife in the water, soiled it, poisoned it.

If I hadn't met Frankie at the World's Fair, the Angel of Death wouldn't have marked him. That was how it felt, at least. That greater forces were at work here than just Grigori and me, and more blood would be spilled. In giving me my name, my parents had deprived the Angel of Death of his rightful due. Now, after seventeen years, he was finally coming to collect.

47

THE ELEVATED TRAIN lurched forward, belching smoke from its flued chimneys. I kept my eyes planted on the floor, counting the specks of mud and lint. By the time the train reached the last stop, it was crowded with tourists.

I paused on the platform and took in gulps of cool air. Stepping aside to let other passengers pass, I checked my pocket watch. Two o'clock. The next show wouldn't begin until three, which gave me plenty of time to scout out the area and see where the Cossacks were rooming.

I didn't know how I would kill Grigori now that he knew what I looked like, only that I had to try. I didn't have a choice. With each passing hour, my body felt less and less like my own. As I descended the stairs to street level, I had the persistent and disturbing sensation of floating above myself.

The crowd diverged at the bottom of the stairs, most heading to the World's Fair, some going in the direction of the Wild West Show. I merged with the latter group and followed them across the street.

The afternoon crowd was mild in comparison to the masses

that had confronted Frankie and me the night before. My calm didn't last. As I entered the lot in the group's wake, I felt exposed and vulnerable, nauseous with fear. My wounded shoulder throbbed in agony.

After I bought a ticket, I broke away from the crowd and retreated into the shadow of the bleachers. There was something comforting and homey in the scent of damp wood and livestock. Breathing in the warm, musky fragrance, I remembered Piatra Neamt, the taste of cheese blintzes, and the crowing of roosters in the morning. The past felt so close, I could reach out and touch it.

But the past was not a place to which I could return. It was a frozen memory, a dybbuk. All that mattered now was the future. I needed to keep moving.

You belong here, I told myself firmly as I walked between the small tents at the Wild West Show. *You're American. You belong.*

Still, when I came across a pair of workers sharing a cigarette between them, it took all my confidence to meet their eyes and nod. Neither man smiled, but they didn't frown either, which I took as a good sign. I kept on walking, passing paddocks filled with horses, cows, and shaggy-furred cattle that I realized must be buffalos.

At a hitch near one of the pens, a Cossack performer tended to his horse. I caught a glimpse of his face as he retrieved a brush from the bucket at his feet, and quickly retreated into the shadow of a tent. It was the young swordsman who had intervened during the fight, standing between Grigori and me.

The boy glanced my way, but I didn't think he saw me. I retreated before he could take a closer look and continued deeper into the grounds.

Soon, I came to an area occupied by white tents. I situated myself in the shadows and waited.

I drew out my pocket watch and counted the minutes as

they ticked by. Twenty minutes until the show began. If the other men hadn't already left their tents, they would soon enough.

A sudden gust swept through the showground, rattling the tents and sending a cowboy chasing after his hat. The flapping of the oilcloth resembled the rustling of vast wings. A realization struck me in an instant. In the vision I had experienced after Mr. Katz had chloroformed me, the object I had seen swaying atop the flooded sunflower field had been a canvas tent.

There was only one explanation. On the night of his death, Yakov had been here. He had been watching. Waiting. He must have followed Grigori from the Wild West Show to the White City, or perhaps he had been lured there without even realizing it, like a bloodhound led to a pitfall.

After several more minutes, a group of Cossack performers appeared from one of the tents. I couldn't make out the men's features from where I stood, but I knew that Grigori must be among them.

I lingered out of sight, afraid to come out of hiding. When no one else appeared and the men were out of sight, I took a step from the shadows.

"I guess it's time to go," I said, waiting for a voice to tell me otherwise, or invisible arms to tug me back. No such thing, just a mooring warmth that spread between my fingers. The soothing pressure of a hand holding my own.

"He never gave you a chance to live, did he?" I murmured.

Silence. But the memory of the burning shul was the only answer I needed.

Before I could change my mind, I hurried to the tent. I drew open the flaps and ducked inside, entering the cool shade.

Cots, trunks, and rickety shelving occupied the space. There were six beds total, two against each wall, steamer trunks at their feet. If I could find Grigori's trunk, perhaps there would be a clue to where he intended to start the fire. At the very least, I could find evidence connecting him to Mr. Whitby or proof of his crimes.

I searched through the first trunk, rummaging through clothes and keepsakes. Nothing of interest.

The owner's name was written on the lid in greasepaint. Владислав Петровић. It might as well have been Chinese or Arabic. The second time I looked at the letters, they began to look a little more like Yiddish, and by the third glance, they resolved into an alphabet I could understand. Vladislav Petrovich.

I moved on. I couldn't explain it, but I sensed that when I found the right trunk, I would just *know.*

As I plowed through the second trunk, I strained to hear the sound of approaching footsteps. My body was a knot of raw nerves and nausea, my lungs crushed against my rib cage like a prisoner in an iron maiden.

By the third trunk, I was ready to give up. My frantic search uncovered a plethora of random objects—clothing, shoe brushes, buttonhooks, photographs of wives and sweethearts, tins of wax and pastes—things that seemed so ordinary, so *human.*

I didn't know what I expected to find. I needed to remind myself that this man, whoever he was, was not a monster. Not on the outside, at least.

The fifth trunk belonged to someone named Grigori Antonovich and yielded more of the same ordinary trappings. Near the bottom, I found a dusty box painted with Russian lacquer-work. I opened the box's lid, shedding light on a scatter of trinkets—a tarnished silver chain, braided bits of human hair, a flour-sack doll rubbed raw by a child's hands. At the bottom of the container, there was a small pile of cotton squares, some stiff and brown, others merely dappled. An involuntary shiver racked me, and I dropped the stack of swatches back in the box.

During tahara, it wasn't uncommon for a person to continue bleeding after death. When that happened, we would collect the blood, the dam nefesh, on cloth swabs that would be buried with the body.

I had assisted in enough washings to know what I was looking at.

Grigori hadn't kept these remnants to inter them with the dead. These were keepsakes. These were trophies.

I picked up the doll. Its hair was black yarn, and its eyes were shoe buttons. It barely weighed anything at all, the sort of toy a little girl could carry everywhere. Tears prickled my eyes. This was not the proof I had been searching for, but it was proof, nonetheless. Of what exactly? I didn't even want to think about it.

Behind me, there was the soft, dry whisper of the tent fold being parted. I turned, box in hand, as the young swordsman stepped inside.

I dropped the doll and drew the revolver from my pocket. "Don't move!"

He stopped, his dark analytical eyes flickering from the gun in my hand to the doll that lay in the dust, then back again.

"You're not a thief," he stated plainly.

His frank statement jarred me. It wasn't until the final word left his mouth that I realized he hadn't been speaking in Yiddish, even though the words had sounded like Yiddish when they passed through my head. I had Yakov to thank for that, I supposed.

"I'm not," I said at last.

"There's no need for the gun."

A familiar shame crept over me, the shame of slipping past

a stranger in the street and relieving him of his wallet without him even knowing it. I had made an oath to myself that I would never steal again. This wasn't stealing, but it felt like it.

The boy took a step toward me, and it took all my self-control not to raise the revolver and track his movements. He was not my enemy.

"Yuri Ilyitch," he said.

"Excuse me?"

"That's my name."

"I'm not giving you my name."

"I don't expect you to." He leaned down and picked up the flour-sack doll. When he lifted his gaze, sorrow welled in his eyes. "Did you find this in his trunk?"

"And the rest." I set the box on the cot and stepped away so that he could examine it closer. As he sorted through the box's contents, I explained to him about how Yakov had been found at the fairgrounds.

"I believe you," Yuri said, after a long moment. "Two weeks ago, he returned in the middle of the night, his clothes covered in blood. He told me...he told me that he had butchered a swine running loose. He threatened to kill me if I told anyone."

"Why are you helping me?"

"I have no animosity toward your people. I think we're more similar than you realize."

I laughed before I could stop myself, then felt a twinge of remorse. Holding Yuri responsible for the actions of his predecessors was no different than being called Christ-killer. He was innocent of any wrongdoing. There was no blood on his hands.

"I mean it," Yuri said. "My ancestors came from the Danubian Sich. In the 1700s, we were exiled from Russia and settled in parts of the Ottoman Empire. For my family, it was Bucharest and Brailov."

Bucharest and Brailov? A jolt of shock rippled through me. Those cities were in Romania.

"I passed through Bucharest on my way to America," I said. "But I've never been to Braˇila, what you call Brailov."

"Neither have I. This was my great-grandfather's time. Seventy years ago, we returned to Russia and were welcomed back by the tsar. My family has lived there ever since, but..." Yuri sighed. "But I long for more. I want to travel. I want to see the world."

"As do I." I parted the flaps at the rear of the tent. "But there's something I need to do first."

"Grigori Antonovich," Yuri said.

I looked back.

"He was supposed to perform today, but I saw him leave about fifteen minutes ago. He said he was going to the Fair."

"Thank you."

Yuri hesitated. "I can come with you. Help you find him. You don't need to do this alone."

I smiled thinly. "I am not alone."

48

AS I RETRACED my steps through the showgrounds, gun-shots echoed in my ears. Long after I had left the Wild West Show behind me, I could still feel the vibrations of those explosions, a thrum as steady as a second heartbeat.

I entered the World's Fair through the side entrance across the street from the Wild West Show. The cashier took my last half dollar without remark and gave me a ticket.

The first several times I had gone to the White City, I had been awed and overwhelmed by its beauty. Now, all that confronted me were its shadows—the swarming crowds of people, the trash littering the walkways, the hollow spaces.

If Grigori had come here in a suit and top hat, he would blend in as effortlessly as any American. Finding him wouldn't be easy.

As I hurried down the verdant walkways and pastoral gardens of the midway, I saw it through his eyes. Here was the Congo, here was Japan, here was Albania, here was Cairo—snippets of the world replicated and sterilized, confined behind walls and fences like animal exhibits.

In Grigori's perfect world, there would be no shtetl, only the depiction of one. A family sitting around a pair of Shabbos candles, surrounded by a barrier that observers could peek and prod through. No. Nothing so ordinary, so domestic, so *blameless*. More like a moneylender with a hooked nose and corkscrew payos, one gnarled hand clutching a sack of money close to his heart and the other hand outstretched for more. Frozen like that. Forever.

For people like Grigori and Mr. Whitby, it needed to be that way. There needed to be a memory of us, even if it was a false one. Because once we were gone, who would they blame next?

I tore through crowds, searching for Grigori. The midway yielded nothing. The Court of Honor, nothing. The Grand Basin—an empty reflection.

I wanted to yell in aggravation. The White City was a labyrinth of lagoons and tended gardens, and spread throughout it all, towering buildings crammed from floor to ceiling with exhibits. Animals from foreign lands, preserved in formaldehyde or embalmed and stuffed with sawdust. Paper goods, linen that would go up in smoke, toxic paints and chemicals. He could have been anywhere.

As I followed the Grand Basin along, something snagged at the back of my mind like a splinter. Something was wrong about this entire situation. Why would Grigori come here to set a fire, even if it had been at Mr. Whitby's bidding?

The White City was a symbol of America's grandeur. It was not a shul. It was multicultural, but only as a way of demonstrating America's superiority over all. So why a fire? Why here?

I stepped up to the map plastered onto the wall of the bandstand. So many places. If the purpose of the fire was to send a message, it would be set at the Court of Honor, no doubt.

Except the Court of Honor showcased the most expensive exhibits, so it would also be swarming with Columbian Guards.

At the corner of the map, a building name caught my eye. Cold Storage.

Cold, Frankie had whispered from his laudanum daze. He hadn't been asking me to tuck him under the blanket. He had been *warning* me. That had to be it!

I twisted around and rushed back toward the western entrance. As I neared, the rumble of trains filled my ears. The Cold Storage building was located by the railroad tracks, out of sight and overlooked. A perfect place to start a fire and make a hasty escape.

I slipped though a crowd of tourists strolling along the walkway, narrowly avoiding being impaled by the metal tip of a lady's parasol as she bobbed it merrily about. A part of me resented the group's laughter and ease. I wanted to seize those gentlemen by their starched collars, shake them, and shout, couldn't they see what was happening here? What *would* happen?

My anger frightened me.

As the crowd passed, I spotted a tall figure whose cheek bulged with a thick pad of bandages. I skidded to a stop and tugged down the brim of my cap to conceal my face. Grigori's gaze scrolled over me in disinterest, and why wouldn't it? Wearing my tzitzis tucked into my pants and a newsboy cap instead of a yarmulke, I was indistinguishable from those in the crowd.

That was the awful irony of it all. He targeted us because he could see us, but the moment I took away identifying clothing, I became invisible.

But you can't hide what you are, I thought, falling into step behind him. *Not anymore.*

Everything that was rotten inside him, I would drag into

the light. Although it might be the death of me, I couldn't turn away from this. I was done doing that. I would never turn away from anything again.

My father's death had been meaningless, and the violence in this world was meaningless, too. But that did not make my life meaningless. I refused to believe that my fate was already written for me, even before the Day of Atonement.

Life was not some never-ending tragedy. Just as for every bitter herb there was sweet charoset, hope and joy persisted alongside suffering. And even someone like me had the ability to change things.

Grigori vanished into a fray of tourists, and I followed after him. Elbows and shoulders butted and shoved me. I raised one arm in front of me to ward them off and put the other in my pocket to make sure the gun was still there. My fingertips stroked the handle. Six bullets.

I could've tried taking Grigori down from afar, but I was afraid of hurting innocent bystanders. Besides, I needed to be absolutely sure. I needed him to look me in the face and tell me, *Yes, it was me all along.* Because once there was an admission of guilt, a murder became an execution.

I broke through a tangle of bodies and searched for Grigori. Farther down the path, he walked at a leisurely pace, as self-assured and confident as a wolf prowling its territory. And wasn't that what this place was—a hunting ground? A *haunting* ground?

Ahead, he turned off the path and entered through the double doors of a massive building whose four corners were adorned with decorative cupolas. One great tower rose from the center of the roof, crested with an American flag that billowed in the wind.

The sign near the entrance read Cold Storage. Cold Storage, like somewhere a corpse would be put to keep it from rotting.

As I reached the doors, a figure rushed from the darkness within the building. I reached for the gun in reflex, nearly drawing it before it occurred to me that Grigori was not one meter tall. The little girl ran past giggling, followed by a boy of similar age. I watched them disappear down the path, my hand resting on the butt of the revolver, my mouth dry. A little girl in a yellow dress, oh God, I had nearly shot a little girl who couldn't be any older than my sisters back home.

I took a deep breath and pinched the back of my hand, twisting the skin until my eyes watered.

Focus. I dug my nails in, wishing to bruise myself. *Just focus.*

Gradually, my heartbeat slowed. After my breath returned to a steadier rhythm, I stepped inside.

The first floor consisted of one vast room. True to its name, this building exhibited ice machines and refrigerators, machines I had only read about until now. Hulking things of metal, enamel, and glass, the steam-powered machinery filled the room with a rhythmic hum, like the stomach processing its food.

The Cold Storage building wasn't nearly as alluring as the Court of Honor or the midway. As I walked up and down the rows of machines, I didn't pass a soul.

In the larger refrigerated chambers, hooks impaled butterflied swine and cattle rimed with frost, their pale ribs gleaming in the shallow light. Looking at them indirectly, I could almost mistake their forms as human.

I withdrew the revolver from my pocket once I was certain I was alone. Fully loaded, it was heavier than I expected it to be. I didn't want to hold the trigger, afraid I might pull it in sudden reflex, so I rested my finger on the trigger guard.

Up and down the aisles. Over the hum of machinery, I could hardly hear my own footsteps. If someone was creeping up behind me, I would never know it.

I glanced over my shoulder just to be sure. No sign of him.

At the other end of the hall, I reached a staircase. Pausing on the first step, I looked back down the hall, as empty as it had been when I first entered. I had no choice but to go up.

I edged up the stairs one at a time, holding my breath as if the sound might drown out his footsteps. My hands were trembling, but I didn't try to pinch myself this time. It would only make more bruises.

Chasya. Silently, I tested my mother's name on my tongue, tried to commit its shape and sound to memory. Then I took another step and whispered my sisters' names. Gittel. Rivka.

The more I sounded out their names, the more they sounded like prayers. Maybe it wouldn't be saying Kaddish for the dead that protected me from the Angel of Death but reciting the names of the living.

At last, I made it to the landing. As with the level below, the second story was all one room. The sunken floor was in- laid with massive slabs of ice that had been smoothed into a seamless surface. Ghostly, curving tracks swept over the rink like the flights of birds.

I recognized those tracks from the many winters in Pia- tra Neamt, where I had stumbled out onto the frozen pond with a neighbor friend, dull blades tied to the bottoms of our shoes. The last time we had done it together was when I was eleven, and the year after that, he went out on the ice alone. That was the year all our parents' warnings about thin ice and frigid water became true.

Although the ice rink was surely too shallow to drown any- body, as I proceeded deeper into the room, I felt as though I was centimeters away from crashing through the floor. I kept to the solid walkway that stretched along the rink, separated by narrow pillars.

Across the room, tables had been set up for comfortable seating. A man in dark clothes sat at the table nearest to me.

Grigori?

I advanced forward cautiously, concealing the pistol under my coat. After several paces, I stopped.

A dark puddle spread beneath the security guard. Blood dripped, dripped, thin hairlike strands that trickled to the floor. There was a second smile under his chin, fresh and oozing.

49

BEHIND ME, THE door banged shut. The latch fell into place with an audible click. I turned.

Grigori shed his dark overcoat. Underneath, he wore common clothes—a buttoned shirt, a cravat, and a waistcoat draped with a silver chain and fob—and uncommon adornments. On his belt hung a neatly wound whip and a niello sheath for the dagger in his hand.

"I thought it would be better this way," Grigori said, striding forward. He sheathed the knife, took the whip from his belt. His fingers flexed around the leather grip, probably itching to give me a cut to match the one I'd dealt across his face. "For us to talk alone."

As Grigori took several more steps, my finger shifted to the trigger.

"Did they find him yet? That boy you were with?" In the frigid air, his breath hung suspended like dragon's smoke. "He came back to the show last night, after it had closed. He tried to find me. What he didn't expect was that there would be two of us."

I waited until he had made it another three meters, close enough for me to get a clear shot at him, before I leveled the revolver hidden in my coat.

"Don't move!" The command came from my mouth as abrupt and jarring as shattered glass. It was my voice this time, but the words still felt like they belonged to Yakov. I had spoken in Russian, not Yiddish. "Don't come any closer."

His eyes narrowed and his feet locked in place. "Ah. I see. So, that's what you were hiding."

"All those boys. My friends. You killed them. You killed all of them."

"Is that why you have come here? To avenge them?"

"Why did you do it?" All of a sudden, I needed to hear it. I needed for him to explain the meaning behind it all, the pogroms, the massacres, the burnings that pursued us through the centuries like a dybbuk we'd never be able to tear ourselves free from. "Why do you hate us so much? What have we ever done to you?"

"You are impious and transgressing." He was six meters away now. "You are the murderers of God."

His words scalded me, left my cheeks burning hot. I had a dismaying feeling of being eight again, eight and lost in the wrong part of town, harried by farmers' sons. My rage and indignation were the same now as they had been then: how could I refute my role in a crime that had happened nearly 1900 years before I was born, if it had even happened at all?

"How—how could you…" I choked on what to say. "How could you possibly believe that? We're people. We're just like you."

Four meters.

"No," he said. "You are an infestation."

His words caught me in a stranglehold. I felt thrown under a limelight, reduced to a role I had never wanted but that I had been born to play. Half a myth and half a human being. In his eyes, that was all I was, a stage actor, a cutout, Shylock and Fagin and Judas all rolled into one.

"You're wrong," I growled.

I might have been his perfect enemy, but I would not be his perfect victim.

"Back in Kiev, the others outcast me for what I did," Grigori said, prowling closer. "They had grown fat and comfortable in their dachas, behind their gates and closed doors. Their eyes were blind. They couldn't see that the true power comes when you're on horseback, in the rat dens, and can do *anything* to the Jews. And why not? You muddy the blood of the proud Russian people. You invade our towns like vermin, and that is what you are. No, you are not people. You are roaches."

My eyes stung. He said it like it was so simple, like this was the natural way of things. Like we deserved it.

And all those people he had killed, he had never even known them.

"The only way to get rid of an infestation is to prevent it from spreading. Burn it out. The Jewesses can be impregnated with proper Slavic offspring and will be purified after the first few generations, but the males are disease carriers. Worthless. Their only purpose is to die."

"You bastard. You don't know anything." I wanted to laugh. I wanted to weep. The joke was on him. If my father had been Christian, it would have made no difference.

Three meters away and edging closer.

Everything that had happened before this—the ship, the chevra kadisha, the grief and anger—it all felt like preparation for this single moment. Like this was the reason I had survived so long, the reason my parents had given me my name. So I could kill him.

My fingers tightened around the revolver's grip. This was how it must be. There was no other option. I pulled the trigger.

Silence.

The blood drained from my face. Impossible.

I tried again. Nothing happened, not even when I gave a third pull of the trigger.

Grigori smiled.

"Ah." He took another step closer, flexing the whip in his hand. Testing it. He was close enough to make a lunge for me if he wanted to. "You haven't been keeping track of your bullets."

The whip leaped forward. I jumped back, felt it cut the air above my head. The light glinted off a piece of metal embedded in the leather tip, a shard to slash and disfigure.

Barely had I caught my balance before he bolted forward, the whip raised once again. I swiveled around and fled across the ice, toward the door at the other side. *Please, let it be a second exit.*

I yanked open the door. Not locked, thank God. It led to a staircase, but one that winded upward to the level above. No time to waste. I raced up the stairs two at a time, praying that there would be a door above, a solid one that I could lock tight and hunker down behind. Or a weapon to bash his skull in.

I reached the top of the stairs, which led into an open loft. No windows or doorways. Ahead, a sea of darkness broken by vague geometrical shapes. A labyrinth of crates and barrels.

I proceeded blindly through the crowded space, patting the space around me, grasping at edges. Anything might lie ahead. A dead end. A trapdoor that would send me crashing to ground level thirty meters below.

After about nine meters, I reached a wall of boxes filled with wood wool. Nothing useful inside. Too small to hide in.

The stairs groaned as he ascended them. I wished I had

something huge and heavy I could hurl down at him. I pressed my body against the crates and tried to make scenery of myself, fumbling with the revolver. There had to be a way to get it to work.

"My older brother served in the tsar's personal guard." Grigori stepped into the room. "Twelve years ago, on a cold March morning, a bomb went off when he was escorting the tsar to the Winter Palace. My brother was crippled. His leg was gone. Turned into mincemeat. All because you reprehensible Jews got it in your mind to kill the tsar."

In March of 1881, I had been back in Romania. I had been just a child. That was the year that pogroms had spread across the Russian Empire, the year my father and mother had realized our time in Europe was limited.

"He didn't live long, but he was in pain the rest of his life," Grigori said as I freed the revolver's cylinder. "He died because of your lust for power and control."

He was not talking about me. He was talking about his idea of me: the radical Jew, the conniving Jew, the greedy and ambitious Jew who would kill a king for a taste of power. Yakov had given Grigori the name of a dragon, but he was not the monster in this tale. I was.

"Something needed to be done. So, I went out hunting. I came across some Jews on the road and had my fun with them, but I soon grew bored of petty beatings. A few broken bones and missing teeth were nothing like what my brother experienced in his final days. It was sunset by the time I arrived in the village. There was one of your temples there, an eyesore of rotten wood, stacked haphazardly, without taste or culture."

A trace of sulfur filled my nostrils as he lit a match. He was close.

"There must have been an evening service. Have you ever

seen a living person set alight? The hair goes up like a torch
and the skin bubbles. The eyes melt."

Though Grigori's voice was receding, the glow of his match
grew brighter. The scent of sulfur became acrid and choking. Smoke.

"There was a boy. He couldn't have been older than six.
He escaped from the blaze and collapsed in the dirt, wounded
but alive. I rode up to him, thinking I should put him out of
his misery. And that was when he spoke to me. He told me
what I truly was inside. The dragon."

He paused, and something crashed to the floor nearby. The
echo of splintering wood made me flinch and nearly drop the
revolver.

"And that was when it came to me like a beautiful revela-
tion. It was an epiphany. At that moment, looking into his
eyes, I knew my purpose in life. My destiny. To rid the world
of you. To become God's flaming sword."

I pressed on the cartridges just to be certain they were
secure, making sure that the hole nearest to the barrel was
loaded. As I shifted the cylinder back into place, another light
appeared on the other side of the room. For a terrifying moment, I expected a second figure to emerge from the darkness—Yakov striding forward, cloaked in the same flames that
had scarred him. Then the wave of heat hit me, and I realized
what Grigori was doing.

He was starting fires.

50

FLAMES CRAWLED UP the walls, casting off billowing black smoke and crackling whips of sparks. My eyes stung from the heat. Choking for breath, I pressed my shirt over my mouth and nose and eased away from the second glow. I crouched low, knowing that if I rose to my full height, Grigori would see me.

A hollow thud came to my right. I swiveled around and lifted the revolver. The gun quivered in my hand, following the dark, shifting patterns of the smoke. Not him, just the crash of a burning crate. I had to take my finger off the trigger to avoid firing off a shot, afraid the flash of the muzzle would alert Grigori to my location.

As I retreated back the way I had come, the floor's heat radiated through my shoes. The floorboards had been treated with varnish or paint, which bubbled in the fire's heat and turned as sticky as flypaper. Any hotter, and my shoes' gutta-percha soles might melt to the floor.

The smoke filled my head, muddled my thoughts. I couldn't conceal my coughing, could hardly even breathe. Forget about staying hidden. If I stayed here any longer, I'd die. Gagging on the vapors, I threw myself forward blindly, batting away the sparks that landed on my skin.

Ahead, I could barely discern a square of light through the shifting smoke. It had to be the door! Several steps from the landing, the whip caught me around the ankle and dragged me off balance. I landed on my hands and knees, hard enough to bruise. The revolver flew from my hands and skittered across the floorboards.

I rolled over and reached for the whip. Just as my fingers closed around the braided leather cord, Grigori landed atop me. He slammed me back into the floor, all ninety kilos of him boring down on me.

I grappled against his gouging fingers, his hot breath fanning against my cheeks. My injured shoulder screamed in pain. He reeked of mildew and horse sweat. Savage growls erupted from deep inside his throat.

He had one of my arms trapped beneath his knee, but with the other, I reached out, desperately searching for the dropped revolver. It suddenly occurred to me why it hadn't worked. I hadn't cocked back the hammer like Frankie had shown me.

My fingertips stroked metal. I tried to pick up the gun, but instead only managed to push it farther out of reach.

Before I could try again, Grigori's hands closed around my throat. His grip was clammy but mercilessly tight, cutting off all airflow.

I bucked beneath him, gasping for breaths that wouldn't come. As I struggled to draw in air, my head pulsed in sickening waves.

Looming above me, Grigori didn't speak. The firelight gleamed in his eyes, or maybe it was his eyes that gave the fire its light. His body shook with urgent panting, like a bloodhound on a short lead. He was *enjoying* this.

Seconds passed in unbearable slowness as darkness sank in. A cold draft buffeted against my chest, and the shadows resolved into the silhouettes of many wings.

I trembled in the grips of terror even greater than what had engulfed me the moment Grigori's hands closed around my throat. I struggled to speak, to plead for mercy, but I couldn't breathe.

I was sinking into—

—the scent of sea brine flooded my nostrils on a wave of cold Atlantic mist. Slowly, I opened my eyes. Through a skein of fog, the sun gleamed as hard and silver as a freshly minted leu.

My feet were on solid ground now. Ahead, the ship's prow jutted into the fogbank. A small crowd had gathered near the low railing, surrounding a swathed form.

My heart jolted. This couldn't be happening.

"Wake up," I whispered, stepping toward the crowd. I barely felt my legs beneath me. The watchers loomed like phantoms, silent and shadowed, their faces just blurs.

I couldn't speak. I stood there, petrified with shock and horror, as the sailors gave my father's body to the sea. I stood there, and stood there, and—

Overhead, the indifferent sky. A small crowd stood at the low railing, surrounding a swathed form.

"Stop!" I fought my way to the front of the crowd, straining against hands that felt like wings. The people held me back as the body tipped over the railing and vanished into the sea—

"Not again! Please, not again!"

As the sailors lifted the shrouded body for the third time, it trembled. Weak fingers dimpled the sheet. And then it tipped—

"Stop! He's still alive!"

And then, a fourth time, a fifth time, the body slid over the railing—

Sobbing violently, I struggled in the grip of the crowd as the shrouded body was lifted for a sixth time. There were ten hands. There were a hundred hands. A thousand, crushing me beneath them.

What was this?

This was death.

This was Gehinnom, the realm through which all souls passed.

The shrouded body—

Ten times, I watched the body be lifted. Twenty. Innumerable.

Slowly, I sank to my knees on the frosty wooden deck and allowed the crowd to block me. I wasn't going to fight it. This was not punishment, just what must be done. The abrasive Atlantic winds and the salt of the sea would eventually cleanse my soul.

"Alter," Yakov murmured softly, and I lifted my head. He stood in front of me, dressed as he had been on the night he died. No mud on his face this time. His eyes brimmed with such pity and sadness, I sobbed and crumpled over myself, ashamed at how close I had come, so very close, just to fail. The way I always did.

"Don't look at me," I cried, hiding my face with my hands. "I don't want you to see me this way!"

I knew how the light could turn cruel at certain angles, exposing me for how I must be now—eyes sightless and weeping blood from burst vessels, features swollen blue and grotesque, the bruises of fingertips around my throat.

Sinking to his knees before me, Yakov parted my hands and tilted up my chin. His eyes were as dark and deep as the sea; I could lose myself in them forever.

"You can't stay here," he said, holding my hands in his. "You need to survive."

"I—I can't." Sobs racked me. "It's too late for everything."

"No, it isn't. Not for you." Gently, Yakov helped me to my feet. "You need to fight."

The crowd's hands tightened around me.

"Fight!" Yakov shouted.

I struggled against the weight of their bodies, until it was no longer hands that held me, but wings of blood-gummed feathers studded with a thousand eyes and writhing tongues.

Yakov joined me in my struggle, wrestling against the creature as though he were channeling his namesake. I broke free of the Angel's embrace and raced toward my father as the two sailors lifted him. I shoved them aside. My fingers curled around my father's trembling fingers. I held tight as the—

—darkness shrank back to the confines of my closed lids in an instant. Past the roar of blood in my ears, I discerned a faint crackling. My cheeks prickled as a sudden wave of heat washed over me.

I opened my eyes.

Flames crawled up the walls and ceiling, casting off billowing black smoke and the whip of sparks. My eyes stung from the blaze. Choking for breath, I snatched up the revolver, cocked its hammer, and staggered to my feet. No use. The crimson glow revealed an empty room. Grigori was already gone.

The smoke disoriented me. My legs collapsed beneath me after several steps, and I sucked in the breathable air near the floorboards. Hauled myself forward, toward the stairs, gagging and nearly unconscious. The floor was so hot now, my palms burned. When I touched the edge of the landing, I laboriously sat up and levered myself down the stairs one at a time, too weak to walk.

Ten steps down, the air was cleaner, and I was able to breathe. I grasped hold of the bannister and pulled myself to my feet. My legs shuddered beneath me but held. As I fled down the stairs, the clang of fire bells filled my ears.

Down below, the rink's surface glistened with water, but not enough to make a difference in dampening the flames. The staircase to the second floor had been long, but the one leading to ground level was longer still. It seemed to stretch much farther than I'd initially thought. As I stumbled down the stairs, I had the disconcerting impression that I was entering the bowels of the earth.

At last, I reached the first floor. The machines continued to rumble even as smoke filled the room. I threw open the double doors and tumbled into the cool, breezy afternoon.

A crowd had gathered near the entrance to the Cold Storage building. They clustered around me, the air filled with their excited voices. Sharp splintery syllables, words I couldn't understand.

My legs buckled beneath me after several steps. A man reached out to steady me and helped me to a bench some distance from the building.

"Are you all right, son?" he asked in English, squeezing my shoulders. "Do you need a doctor?"

Tears blurred my vision, turned everything into a haze of color. I wiped them away with the back of my hand and stifled a sob. "Neyn. No. No doctor."

He stepped back to give me room to breathe. I held on to the edge of the bench, not trusting myself to stand just yet.

The crowd grew by the minute. I searched for Grigori among the shocked faces. At the edge of the group, a man stood with his face craned upward and his lips parted in wonder. He held a pair of tortoiseshell lorgnette glasses to his eyes, to get a better look at the flames climbing the building's walls.

My breath caught in my throat.

That face. I knew that face.

Mr. Whitby.

51

THE CROWD PARTED to make way for a group of fire-fighters, their bronze helmets glinting like the regalia of knights. Mr. Whitby didn't stir as I stepped behind him, his gaze locked on the inferno.

I put my arm around his shoulder and tugged him close. He turned with a scowl of distaste and began to pull away, only to freeze as he caught sight of me.

"I have a gun." I spoke quietly and slowly, taking great care to get the message across. "If you run or shout…"

He swallowed hard, his gaze shifting to where my hand was tucked under my coat. "How… You…you should be dead."

"Come. Walk." I nodded toward a dark sprawling building farther down the path, its walls glistening with arch after arch of segmented windows. My eyes burned from the smoke, and each time the crowd gasped, I felt as though my stomach was being wrung between cruel hands. I couldn't stand staying here another moment. It was hideous.

Mr. Whitby looked back at the fire. When I prodded him

with the gun through my coat, he got the message and stepped forward.

"You won't do it, boy," he said as we walked down the path. I held on to his coattail to keep him from running. "Do you know how I know this? Because of your commandments. Thou shall not kill."

I didn't respond. I needed to think about what I'd say next, carefully lining up my words like rows of even masonry, so that there could be no misunderstandings.

Everyone we passed had their eyes on the blaze. Once we reached the building, I tugged him to the side, away from the gateway with its concentric arches and ornate repoussé facade. Unlike the grand ivory buildings in the Fair's Court of Honor, these walls were painted in garish shades of red and bronze as though colored by a premonition of fire. I stopped as we reached an isolated alcove at the far side of the building, well away from the crowd that had gathered to watch the smoke rising. I drew the gun from under my coat.

"Why are you doing this?" I croaked, keeping my hand close against my chest to shield the view from outsiders. "Why here? Why a fire?"

He didn't answer.

"Damn you, tell me why! Tell me the truth. What is the purpose?"

"I am a gambler." Mr. Whitby's gaze remained on the revolver. "The greatest thrill comes from games where the stakes are the highest."

"The stakes?"

"The real estate prices in this city will rise exponentially in the aftermath of the World's Fair. That much is a given. Chicago will be known as the treasure of the heartland. Everyone will come to marvel at it. However, one thing holds this city back. The eyesore that is Maxwell Street." His mouth twisted in a smile. "Your filthy ghetto is a stain on our city. Maxwell Street should just burn, and if it takes Little Italy and Pilsen with it, all the better. Once the ashes settle, that land will be dirt cheap and up for the grabbing. In my hands, that entire area will become another Prairie Avenue."

"No," I whispered. It couldn't be. This fire had only been a distraction, a controlled burn to keep the fire department busy. "You're mad. You'll burn down the entire city. You'll kill thousands."

"I am a gambler!" He made a lunge for the revolver.

I pulled the trigger.

The gunshot was drowned out by the cacophony of fire bells. As Mr. Whitby collapsed to the ground, I lowered the revolver. My hands were shaking so badly, I was afraid I might squeeze off another shot by mistake. I slipped the gun in my pocket to be safe.

Against my better judgment, I squatted down and turned Mr. Whitby over onto his back. Blood welled through his white shirt, muddying the fabric. It should have sickened me, but I had seen corpses so many times, I took in the sight of gore like a distant memory.

His fading gaze focused on me.

"Tell me…" My voice caught like phlegm in my throat. I tried again. "Tell me where Grigori is going to set the next fire."

Mr. Whitby smiled. Bloody saliva welled from between his teeth, inky in the dimness of the alcove, as though he was rotten from the inside out. He grasped onto the front of my shirt and pulled me closer, his hot breath reeking of flyblown meat.

"You'll try to find it, and you'll be too late." His hand slackened and fell from my shirt. The shadow of reeling wings passed over his eyes. "May it all burn."

52

OUTSIDE THE FAIRGROUNDS, I hailed a hansom cab. I had no money, but I unclipped the Romanian leu from the end of my watch chain and passed it through the trapdoor in the ceiling.

"It's silver," I reassured the driver as he turned the coin over in his hand.

"Doesn't look like any silver I know." He tapped the coin against the lantern's copper shade, listened to it ring. Sniffed it. "All right then. Where we off to?"

"Maxwell Street. Please hurry."

As the man shut the trapdoor, I sank against the seat, giving myself a chance to breathe. The carriage rolled forward. I flinched at the crack of the coachman's whip, my swollen throat tightening uncontrollably. If I closed my eyes, I knew I'd see it—the inky black expanse of the Atlantic and the swarm of bloodstained feathers. A thousand bulging eyes and writhing tongues.

I held my face in my hands and pretended I was back home.

I whispered a few lines of a childhood song I remembered my mother singing:

"'Girl, girl, I want to ask of you, what can grow, grow without rain? What can burn and never end? What can yearn, cry without tears?'" Moisture welled in my eyes. I swatted the tears away, furious at myself. The next few lines of "Tumbalalaika" returned to me like a cool palm upon a fevered brow. "'Foolish lad, why do you have to ask? A stone can grow, grow without rain. Love can burn and never end. A heart can yearn, cry without tears.'"

Slowly, my pounding heartbeat returned to a calmer rhythm and the nausea receded. I kept my hands raised for a moment longer, breathing steadily and rubbing the bruises around my throat.

The minutes passed in excruciating slowness. After we had crossed over the river's northern bend, the carriage stopped. Ahead, a snarl of pushcarts and wagons clogged the road. I swore under my breath and rapped on the trapdoor until the coachman lifted it.

"Is there a way around it?" I asked.

He looked over his shoulder. "We're boxed in from behind. The horses won't tolerate me backing up like this, and it's too tight to turn around. We'll have to wait for it to clear."

"How far are we from Maxwell Street?"

"Another mile or two, I reckon."

I jumped out of the hansom cab and darted between the pushcarts, shoes skidding over slime-encrusted pavestones. As I ran, faces passed through my head. Mrs. Brenner. Raizel and stately, bespectacled Mrs. Ackermann. Haskel. Dovid. Lev. Sender. Some would surely make it out alive, but others would perish in their own homes and businesses as the flames spread. And the sky tonight would be alive with the rustling of the Angel of Death's wings.

I needed to warn people. I seized the wrist of the first man I came across, gripping on like a drowning sailor as he scowled in disgust and shook my hand away.

"There's going to be a fire," I said quickly. "You need to get out of here."

"The kid is drunk," he muttered to his wife and kept on walking, shooting back a sour glance after making it a safe distance.

I realized that if I kept doing this, people wouldn't just think I was drunk. They would summon the police, who would unceremoniously dump me in Dunning Asylum. I could go to the authorities myself, but what then? Officer Rariden was already suspicious of me. If I told him the truth, I would risk implicating myself in Mr. Whitby's shooting.

As I continued down the street, it dawned on me that I was only blocks from the *Arbeiter-Zeitung*'s office. It had been a mistake not to rely on Yuri's help when he had offered it, just as it had been a mistake not to listen to Mrs. Brenner in the first place. I couldn't go to the police without incriminating myself, but that didn't mean I needed to do this alone.

At the *Arbeiter-Zeitung*'s office, I was greeted by a flurry of grinding presses and typewriting. On my way through the doors, I nearly collided with a newsboy carting a stack of newspapers practically as tall as he was.

"Today's papers, fresh from the presses!" he announced in German, thrusting a paper at me expectantly. "Strikes continue at the Stockyard!"

"I don't want a newspaper," I snapped, and his face fell. "Do you know where Raizel Ackermann is?"

"Alter, don't harass the newsboys."

I turned to find Raizel scowling at me from the other end of the lobby.

"I wasn't—" I swore under my breath as the boy pushed

his cart over my foot and stepped back to give the brat some room to get through the doors.

Raizel came to my side. "What are you doing here?"

"You have to come with me. There's going to be a fire on Maxwell Street."

Her eyes flared in alarm. "A fire?"

I pushed through the doors. "I don't know where, but if we don't stop it, it'll end up destroying the whole neighborhood."

"Wait, are you telling me you found Yakov's killer?" Raizel demanded. "How? Who is he?"

"A Cossack."

"A Cossack?" She furrowed her brow. "What is a Cossack doing in Chicago?"

"I'll tell you on the way. Let's just go!"

As we hurried down the road, I explained to her how Frankie and I had rushed to Mr. Whitby's place after triggering the vision at the World's Fair. When I relayed what Mr. Whitby had said about the Jewish boy at the Whitechapel Club, she froze.

"Aaron?" she whispered, moisture welling in her eyes.

"I think so. I'm so sorry, Raizel."

She pinched the bridge of her nose tightly. I could see her struggling with the urge to cry. When she lowered her hand, her eyes flared with fury and grief. "They'll pay for this!"

"Mr. Whitby already has." Nauseated by the memory of his final moments, I explained my role in his death and described the fire at the fairgrounds. Once I got her up-to-date about Grigori and the rest, I turned to keep going. I took no more than two steps before she grabbed my wrist, pulling me to a halt.

"If we keep running around like this, we're going to get nowhere," Raizel said. "Think. If you were Grigori, where would you light a fire?"

A sinking dread grew in my heart. By now, the fairgrounds would be swarming with firefighters struggling to put out the blaze. All of Chicago's attention would be on the fire at the Cold Storage building.

Think! I needed to think!

Mr. Whitby had surely been driven by numb, mechanical logic when he had chosen the Cold Storage building as the place to set the first fire. Grigori was different. I doubted even he could name the needs that burned inside him.

I pinched the bridge of my nose and concentrated until my sinuses burned. If I were him, where would I start a fire? It wouldn't be just anywhere. There would be significance to it. Ceremony.

Grigori's words passed through my head: *An eyesore of rotten wood, stacked haphazardly, without taste or culture.*

"A shul," I whispered. "It's going to be at a shul."

In Piatra Neamț and the surrounding towns, many of the shuls had been built with age-darkened wood from the firs and beeches that populated the Carpathians. I knew that to Grigori, what had resembled a blight had probably been a modest building from the outside, so as to avoid making a target of itself. The inside would have been a wealth of carvings, soaring domes, and paintings.

The shuls of Maxwell Street were all brick and clapboard, some with plaster walls painted to resemble stone. There were no shuls with walls of exposed wood here, except for one. The unfinished shul by the chevra kadisha.

53

TWO STORIES HIGH, the unfinished shul stood level with the brick buildings surrounding it. Backlit by the glow of the sun, it appeared prematurely burnt.

As we entered the building, Raizel retrieved a hammer from the scatter of tools lying in the corner. The scents of pine oil, tar, and sawdust hung in the air.

Stepping deeper into the sanctuary, my foot skidded in a slick patch. I looked down. A trail of clear liquid snaked across the floor.

Raizel bent down, traced a finger through the mess, and raised it to her nose. She took a sniff and turned to me. "Turpentine," she whispered.

Grigori was here, and he had been coming here all along, hadn't he? Perhaps the lantern light I had glimpsed in these windows the night Raizel and I met to go to the Whitechapel Club hadn't just been a product of the dybbuk. The stranger who had pursued me down Maxwell Street in the dead of night, after emerging from this very building, had certainly been real.

I drew my revolver from the pocket where I had stashed it. This time, I made sure to cock the hammer as Frankie had shown me. I needed to end this. Now.

"Get the police," I whispered to Raizel.

"No!" Her eyes flared. "I'm not leaving you."

"If he kills us both, this place will—"

A floorboard creaked deeper in the sanctuary. I held my breath and eased forward. Reaching the cover of some stacked crates, I readied myself. Raizel found refuge behind a pile of boards.

I could do this. I had already shot one man. I squeezed my fingers tighter around the revolver's ivory handle.

Stop trembling, I ordered myself sternly. *You are strong.*

This was not murder. It was an execution. Din rodef.

As Grigori emerged from the side chamber, I opened fire.

He reacted in an instant, pivoting even before the second gunshot rang out. He dived back through the open door. I barreled after him, already cocking the hammer a third time, praying I had landed a hit.

This liquid roar in my ears, this taste of char on my tongue—this was terror and the overwhelming will to live and the potential to kill. My hands had stopped shaking after the second pull of the trigger, and I held the gun steady. Three bullets left.

Blood splattered the floor of the stairwell that led to the women's gallery above. I caught a glimpse of him at the top of the stairs and fired once more as he darted through the opening. I couldn't tell if I hit. Too late to turn back now. I took the stairs two at a time, aware that if I hadn't wounded him fatally, he would be waiting for us above. I must be ready.

Two bullets left.

As I reached the second-floor landing, a flash of steel glinted in the corner of my eye. Grigori's knife slashed through the air centimeters from my face, close enough that I felt it *whish*. I stumbled back. I began to aim the revolver, but he was already lunging forward. I had no time to shoot.

I ducked underneath his raised arm, thrust the gun in his direction, and fired blindly. A scalding pain spread through my shoulder as his dagger cut into my skin. We tore away from each other. Blood coursed down his side. My bullet had merely grazed him.

Just one more bullet.

"How are you still alive?" he hissed, slashing his knife at me. "I know that I killed you. How can you survive that and the fire?"

"I am the Jew you can't kill!"

"You're a cockroach, an infestation!"

The women's gallery was a treacherous expanse of crisscrossed beams, only partially floored. Sections of railing lay against one wall. The balcony led to a four-meter drop. Ropes stretched across the ceiling, attached to a makeshift pulley. Even more wires and cords dangled down from the metal scaffolding that stretched to the roof.

In these close quarters, I was unable to back up without the risk of ensnaring myself in the ropes or breaking my ankle in one of the gaps between the floorboards. As Grigori came toward me, Raizel rushed at him from behind.

"This is for Aaron!" she shouted as her hammer caught him square across the shoulders.

Grigori howled in rage and swung out at her. They were so close to each other, I was afraid to shoot in case I hit her instead. She ducked underneath his knife, but he snagged her by the hair with his other hand and slammed her into the wall. Her head met the plaster with a sickening thud, and she collapsed to the floor.

"Raizel!"

Immediately, Grigori swiveled around and came at me, giving me no time to react. His whip had appeared in his hand like magic, pulled from his belt in the heat of the moment. He gave a fluid snap of his wrist, and the leather coil lashed forward with a fearsome *crack*, catching me across the back of the hand. The metal shard embedded in the whip's tip cut me nearly to the bone. The shock of the blow was so great, I didn't even realize I had dropped the gun until I heard it clatter. My entire arm felt as though it was on fire.

"Now, I'll make sure you stay dead," he growled, advancing on me. I backed toward the balcony's brink, reaching behind me to grope desperately for a weapon.

Behind him, Raizel rose to her knees.

Grigori took another step forward.

As I reached the balcony's edge, my foot caught on a piece of wood. I toppled over a pile of beams, grasping onto the edge of the pulley in an effort to regain my balance. The motion shifted the wooden platform that the pulley was attached to, which in turn caused the ropes to move. I misgauged my distance and fell anyway.

On my way down, I caught hold of the edge at the last moment. Gasping in exertion, I dug my fingers into the unvarnished wood. My feet kicked the empty air as I struggled to hoist myself back onto the balcony.

The pulley swayed wildly, as did the ropes. One rope ensnared Grigori around the chest as he lunged for me, yanking him back. He reached behind himself, hacking blindly at the cord, but only succeeded in becoming more entangled, both in the rope and the oilcloth that had been draped from the scaffolding above.

Raizel rushed to my side to help me back onto solid footing. Overhead, the pulley groaned.

Grigori swore and struggled, his face contorted in rage. The knife slipped from his hand, yet his arm remained twisted behind him, wrapped in the oilcloth.

"Christ-killer! This time, I won't leave you for the flames." He spat out the words with such hatred, saliva flew from his mouth like poison. "I'll crush your head in. I'll tear out your heart. I'll—"

His foot glanced against the beams stacked on the lift, sending them cascading down. Raizel and I scooted out of the way to avoid being brained by one. The difference in weight was enough to jerk him up, hoisting his body from the floor and cinching the rope even tighter around his throat.

Something cracked inside of him. His body shuddered convulsively, and his feet kicked out once more, before going slack.

I sat there for a moment longer, terrified that the minute we turned our backs on him, he would descend from his snare of ropes as nimbly as a spider. Yet in the darkness he hung there, and in the darkness he remained. His body swayed gently, the white oilcloth crumpled around his midsection like a pair of paper wings.

The tension slowly drained from my body. "It's over."

Raizel staggered from the floor, pressing a hand to the bump on her head. She spat on the ground at his feet. "May his name be erased!"

"No." I rubbed my bruised throat, recalling the rustling of many wings and the low roar of the Atlantic. "May he suffer and remember."

54

AS GRIGORI'S SWAYING body stilled, I tried to rise. My legs failed to obey me.

"Alter?" Raizel looked back.

"I... I can't stand." I could feel my legs beneath me, and my ankle still throbbed where it had slammed against the stack of timber, but even when I cinched my fingers around my calf, the limb refused to obey.

As I was about to say more, a wave of pain struck me with the force of a runaway wagon. It felt as though my skin was being flayed from underneath, the sensation so excruciating my throat constricted around my scream and let out only a thin whinnying moan. I curled on my stomach, heaving until I retched up a thin clear bile marbled with blood.

"Alter!" Raizel sank to her knees before me.

"Yakov is trying—" I groaned, closing my eyes to block out the pain. "He's trying to leave."

When Yakov's dybbuk had cleaved unto me, our souls had fused pelvis-to-pelvis and breastbone-to-breastbone, conjoined like twins in utero. That bond could not be gently dissolved. It must be ripped down the middle.

She placed her hand on my back. "What should I do?"

I thought I might vomit again if I tried to speak. Gritting my teeth and squeezing my eyes shut even tighter still, I pressed my cheek against the cool wood. Hot liquid streamed from my ears and nostrils.

"Oy gevalt, that's blood." Raizel lurched to her feet. "We need to get you to a doctor."

"No. Chev—" I gagged on the word, but only dry-heaved this time. Once I caught my breath, I forced out the rest. "Chevra kadisha."

"You want me to take you to the chevra kadisha?"

I nodded breathlessly.

She helped me to my feet, one hand supporting my back and the other holding my left arm crooked over her shoulder. Grasping onto each other, we stumbled across the balcony like a wounded chimera. My legs nearly gave out as we reached the stairs, but we took them one at a time, with excruciating slowness.

Outside, the afternoon was a riot of noise, movement, and color, smeared to shades of red and gray. I could barely tell if we were still walking or how much time had passed. It felt like hours.

Voices filtered down to me.

"...he okay?"

"Tahara..." That was Raizel.

"A hospital..."

"No. No... Tahara house."

The world dissolved away for a while. The creak of a door being opened. Soothing dimness. My legs gave out beneath me and I collapsed against the entry hall's marble floor. The stone was cool against my cheek.

"What happened? Did he fall?" Lev's voice echoed in my ears. I'd never heard him sound so frantic.

"Dybbuk," I croaked out. It was not my voice anymore. I couldn't recall what mine had once sounded like.

"What's he saying?"

"Mikveh." I closed my eyes to save my energy. Their voices faded in and out of focus, dissolving into a din like the roar of the ocean. Raizel was shouting, and then Lev began raising his voice, too. I wished they'd be quiet. After an uncertain amount of time, Gavril and Sender joined in on the argument. All I could say was, "Mikveh. Please, I need tahara," over and over, until blood filled my mouth and the room dimmed.

Were these my words, or were they Yakov's?

"It's okay," Raizel murmured in my ear. "They're going to do it."

I felt several sets of hands lift and carry me. Through the haze, I discerned the volunteers' faces. By the time they laid me on the washing table, I could no longer feel my limbs.

Lev and the others showed me the same reserved respect they held while tending to the dead, averting their eyes whenever possible, their faces solemn even as fear and confusion darkened their gazes. They did not speak to me.

Gavril cut my clothes from my body, pulling them away in fragments, a sleeve here, the leg there. I closed my eyes to spare us both the embarrassment, then opened them again, terrified of the darkness. When the shears' dull edge brushed against my skin, there was no chill, only pressure.

As Gavril worked, Sender wiped the blood from my face and ears. His hand trembled, and worry welled in his brown eyes. The damp cloth felt blissfully cool against my skin. I wanted to weep with gratitude.

The pain started to ebb. Somehow, that was even more terrifying than the burning itself. I could still feel where

Yakov and I were fused, as though my consciousness was being stretched taut to the point of splitting. His agony and anguish rippled through my muscles and bones; for him, this division was surely just as excruciating.

After I was fully undressed, they laid me on the slotted board attached to the pulley and conveyed it to the mikveh. The ropes creaked and shuddered. Lev stabilized the board as it descended, lower, lower.

Water lapped against my sides. Sender gave another tug of the rope, sending me under. The water—

—squelched beneath my feet. I looked down to find myself ankle-deep in muck afloat with the shriveled heads of dead sunflowers. Ahead, Yakov regarded the shul's charred carcass.

"It's called the *rasputitsa*," Yakov said as I waded over to him. His gaze remained fixed on the blackened ruins. "It happens every autumn and spring, but that year, there was also terrible flooding. After my back had healed, I remember coming back here with my uncle. There was nothing left in my house. It had been stripped to the bones by the peasants. And this place…this filthy place was the only proof that my mother and father hadn't just gone off on some exquisite journey to a faraway land. They were truly dead."

Tears filled my eyes. "I'm so sorry, Yakov. For everything."

"I know." He turned to me. "I swore to myself that day I would do whatever it took to hunt down that monster. My uncle thought I was a traumatized child. In the early days, I spoke of dragons. Over time, the real memories emerged."

"How did you find him?" I asked. "How did you know he was here?"

"My uncle knew tsarist officials back in Kiev. In the last months of the sickness that claimed him, he reached out to them. I suppose curiosity got the better of him. I had told him what Tugarin Zmeyevich had told me as I lay wounded in the dirt—'This is for my brother, who your people butchered in St. Petersburg'—and from that, my uncle was able to find Tugarin. Or a trace of him. His real name. His age. The host he had descended from. He had left the empire after completing his prison sentence for another murder, the butchering of a rabbi's son in Odessa. He joined the Wild West Show, and while they were entertaining kaisers and queens, he brought death and suffering wherever they went. After my uncle died, I used the inheritance he left me to begin my hunt. I wish I'd been able to finish it."

"You did. Grigori is dead now. He's never going to hurt anyone ever again."

"I never wanted to get you involved. I hope one day you'll be able to forgive me for what I put you through."

When I had reached out to Yakov in the mikveh, I hadn't realized how exactly he wanted me to help him, or what sacrifices it would entail. Yet, I knew that in that moment I would have done anything to bring him back to life.

"I made my choice," I said firmly.

He nodded, his gaze welling with sorrow. "I suppose this is goodbye then."

I looked around us. "This place..."

"Is my Gehinnom. I suspect I'll be here for a few months yet, but it's time for you to leave."

"Yakov, wait," I cried as he strode toward the ruined shul. As I stumbled after him, the mud grew even deeper still. "Yakov, I love you!"

"I love you, too." He looked back at me and smiled so sadly. "That's why I have to let you go."

I opened my mouth to answer as I sank under. Instead of mud, I drew in a mouthful of water. Lurching up and coughing, I seized onto the side of the wooden board to keep from toppling into the mikveh.

Gavril smiled weakly, extending his hand to me. "Welcome back to the world of the living."

55

WHAT HAPPENED AT the chevra kadisha was not spoken about again. Tending to the dead was an act of ultimate kindness, and such things were meant to be performed in silence, for an audience who would never acknowledge it. The volunteers considered their intervention no different.

The builders found Grigori the next morning. From Raizel, I learned that it had been dismissed as a tragic accident. If Lev and the others suspected the truth, they did not say a word. People trespassed in unfinished buildings all the time, after all. He never should have gone where he didn't belong.

The same indifferent system that had allowed Grigori to kill with impunity had made it so he died anonymously. He had been buried without funeral or rite in the Cook County Cemetery at Dunning, amid the mad and the unknown dead.

As for Mr. Katz, his body was dredged from Bubbly Creek a week later. In the overflow, police also recovered Moishe Walden's clothes and mailbag. Suspecting Moishe had connections to anarchist groups in Chicago and had helped assassinate Mr. Katz, despite only being sixteen, the police put out a manhunt for him. He was never found.

Like many things in Chicago, Katz's death slipped from public memory, and everything returned to as it had been.

Within days, Raizel found me a temporary job working the presses at the *Arbeiter-Zeitung*. It was slow and boring but familiar, which was what I needed. I could lose myself for hours arranging typeset, inking and oiling the presses.

I visited Frankie every day after work to help him out to the garden. Raizel and Mrs. Brenner came often as well. The first week, Frankie had looked terrible, but just like Haskel, he was quickly growing stronger.

On one of my evening visits, as Frankie and I were sitting under a mature oak and eating the chocolate babka Mrs. Brenner had lavished him with, he shocked me by saying, "I've decided to quit stealing."

I turned my head, certain that I had misheard him. "What did you just say?"

He leaned against the tree, a corner of his mouth quirked in a thoughtful smile. "Knowing how hard you're working to get your family back gave me an idea. There are so many people here who lose touch with their loved ones. Men who run off to escape their responsibilities and leave their families to starve, or children who flee abusive homes and get wrapped up in even worse business. And it's not just that, but tips about races and matches are gold in the Levee, and there are plenty of new immigrants who need advice on adjusting into American society. I want to start dealing in information."

"What does your crew think of this?" I knew they had come to visit. More than once during the last couple weeks, I had walked in to find Bailey or Joe playing cards and chess with Frankie.

"Joe swears he'll go off on his own, but I think I'll be able to turn him around. The others like the idea. Ever since what happened to Harry, I think we've all been hoping for a new start."

Fireflies darted through the sultry orchid twilight. The humid breeze carried the honeyed fragrance of late-blooming alyssum, an aroma that muddled my senses almost as much as Frankie's herbal cologne.

"I think it's a wonderful idea," I said.

He rested his hand on my thigh. "The thing is, I need someone a bit more clean-cut at the front of the business. Someone who can sit down with families and comfort and reassure them. If I do it, they'll think I'm there to break their kneecaps."

I couldn't help but smile. "In other words, you need a good mensch."

"A good mensch indeed." He walked his fingers up my leg. Each light touch sent a spark racing up my spine. "What do you say?"

I took his hand and pulled it down, holding it out of sight between us. "If it's clean work, it would be my pleasure."

He looked around to make sure that no one was watching, then leaned over and brushed his lips against my mouth in the gentlest kiss. "Then let us begin."

EPILOGUE

FLURRIES OF SNOW raced across the shipyard, carried on fickle winds that blew the gritty flakes against my face one moment, then against my back the next. Stretching to the horizon, Lake Michigan was the color of slate and frothy with whitecaps. The drifting steamboats resembled primordial creatures that the winter chill had lured to the surface.

Frankie and I huddled on the docks, smothered in layers of wool and fur, as we watched passengers stream down the gangway of the SS *Christopher Columbus*.

My stomach fluttered with nervous excitement. I had waited so long for this day. I couldn't count how many nights I had lain awake, imagining our exact moment of meeting. It was hard to believe it was finally happening.

Shrill boat whistles echoed in my ears as I searched the crowded platform, my fingers numb from clutching my placard so tightly. Painted across the board were the words Welcome to Chicago, Chasya, Gittel, and Rivka Rosen!

Departing passengers fanned around me, their careless elbows brushing against my body. Several hundred breaths steamed the air.

"What if they don't recognize me?" I asked, shifting the sign to my other hand to give my right one a rest. "It's been nearly three years. Gittel and Rivka must be so big now."

"They'll recognize you," Frankie said.

"Maybe they're on a different ferry," I said as the last trickle of people walked down the gangway. Everyone was beginning to disperse. Blinking the snow from my eyes, I scanned the faces of those who lingered, searching for two children among the diminishing crowd.

"Alter?" a soft, tentative voice said.

I turned at the sound of my name. A sob welled up in my throat at the sight of a tall auburn-haired woman gripping the hands of two little girls. Silver threaded the coils of hair escaping from my mother's headscarf, and her face was more gaunt than I remembered it, but I recognized her in an instant.

All three, all still alive, baruch HaShem. I dropped the placard as Gittel and Rivka lunged at me, both crying out my name. I hugged them tightly, unashamed by the tears stinging my eyes.

"You look so much older," I said, once they loosened their grips enough to let me breathe. I blinked the moisture from my eyes and studied their faces. Their pouty lips, doe-brown eyes, and snub noses were so alike, the twins were practically mirror images of each other.

"Gittel?" I guessed, turning to the one on the right.

Her brow furrowed. "It's me, Rivka."

I sighed.

"No, I'm Rivka," said the other one, nudging her sister in the side.

"Don't tease your brother," my mom said as the twins broke

into giggles. She patted the head of the girl on the right. "This one's Rivka. And the little troublemaker is Gittel."

The twins giggled and clung to each other, delighting in their joke. I smiled to hide my embarrassment. Of course the one on the right had been Rivka. She had that scar on her cheek to prove it, where she had run into a branch one summer.

"This is my friend, Frankie Portnoy," I said, turning to him.

"Oh, I think we're a bit more than just friends." His mouth twitched with laughter that he struggled to contain.

"Is that so?"

"We're business partners, too," I explained, leaving the rest unsaid.

"Business partners?" My mother lifted her eyebrows, looking impressed. "It's a pleasure to meet you, Frankie. A friend of Alter's is a friend of mine."

Something about the hint of a smile she gave me afterward made me think that she had known all along who I was. The thought comforted me.

"Alter, I should be heading off to work," Frankie said. "I'll see you tomorrow, all right?"

"Thank you for coming with me," I said.

He smiled. "My pleasure."

While Frankie set off for the Levee, I waited with my family as the luggage was unloaded. After securing their two trunks, we took the elevated train home. As we passed the White City, a bitter taste filled my mouth. It had been several months since the Fair had ended. There was talk of turning the site into a landmark, a vision of America's exceptionalism and status that would endure for years to come.

"What's that?" Gittel asked, tugging at my sleeve. She pressed her face against the window, staring enthralled at the sprawl of ivory buildings.

"Last year, there was a fair there," I said. "People came from all over the country to visit it."

"Is it still open? Can we go there?"

"No, I don't think so. It's over now."

"It looks like a kingdom in a fairy tale," Gittel murmured, mesmerized.

"It isn't," I said, wishing to hold her close and warn her: *don't be deceived, those walls aren't polished marble, they're particleboard, sawdust, and plaster, colored white with lead.* The canals had been dredged from swampland; the picturesque waterfront hacked out of the lakeside by the shovelful. No one had ever lived in those buildings, and no one ever would.

I realized it now. I understood it completely. The White City had never been a city. It was simply the hallucination of one.

★ ★ ★ ★ ★

A NOTE FROM THE AUTHOR

As a teen in the early to mid-2010s, I could name only two or three YA books with Jewish main characters, all of which focused on the Holocaust. That representation never settled right with me, but it wasn't until the aftermath of the Charlottesville riots and the Tree of Life synagogue shooting that I realized it was in my power to change it.

I will admit that this book was inspired by anger and indignation—at the anti-Semitism I have faced in my own life, at the perpetual cycle of violence, at the fact that I cannot go into a synagogue or Jewish community center without first thinking of where a shooter might enter. I wanted to write a book where the Jewish characters weren't just passive victims, but where they fought back and rose above the people who wished to do them harm.

The idea for this plot was sparked in part by an article I had read about the serial killer H. H. Holmes, who was active in Chicago at the same time as the 1893 World's Fair. He namely targeted women and was believed to have killed up to two hundred victims. His case got me thinking about life in Chicago during the 1890s, and the World's Fair in general, and what message exactly the fair was trying to send. I thought about how interesting it would be to write a book with a Jewish protagonist set during the Fair, in a time when thousands of Jewish refugees were escaping the rising anti-Semitism in Europe. The murder mystery plot came later.

In Romania during the 1890s, Jews like Alter were not considered naturalized citizens. They were forbidden from holding certain careers, and many were derided as vagrants and expelled from the same country they were born in. Jewish immigration from Romania was dwarfed by an even greater wave of immigration from the Pale of Settlement, an imperial Russian territory encompassing much of modern-day Poland, Ukraine, Belarus, Moldova, and Lithuania, along with parts of Latvia and western Russia.

Because Ukraine and Lithuania were a part of the Russian Empire during that time, I made a conscious decision in the book to refer to Frankie and Yakov as Russian immigrants. However, at the time, and well into the twentieth century, Jews in imperial Russia and the Soviet Union were not considered ethnic Lithuanians, Ukrainians, Russians, etc., but were instead identified ethnically as Jews on their official documents.

Up until the 1880s, the majority of Ashkenazi Jewish immigrants came to America from German-speaking countries. By the 1890s, the German Jewish immigrant community was assimilated in American society, so they had various feelings about the new immigrants from Eastern Europe, who spoke mainly Yiddish and were more religiously observant.

Although Jews fled to America to escape anti-Semitism, anti-Semitism was not dead here. Nativists called for restrictions on Jewish immigration; eventually, their wishes would be granted with the Johnson-Reed Act of 1924, which contributed to Jewish refugees fleeing the Holocaust being sent back to their slaughter. In the late 1800s and well into the 1900s, Jews in America faced exclusion from some schools and universities, businesses, career fields, and towns. Still, unlike in Europe, the discrimination was not state sponsored and did not accumulate into massacres, only isolated acts of violence.

In Chicago at the time, Jewish immigrants mainly settled in tenements along the West Side, in the area known as Maxwell Street. In many ways, it was its own self-contained community, with a market and various stores, kosher butchers, synagogues, and even a Yiddish theater. The living conditions there were poor and overcrowded, and primary sources illustrate the struggles and perseverance of the community.

Along with inhumane living conditions, Jewish immigrants were also exposed to unsafe working conditions. Many of them were employed in sweatshops, where they were forced to work for long hours. This led to the establishment of Jewish trade unions and socialist organizations. Like Raizel, some Jewish immigrants even followed American society's growing interest in anarchy, leading to the founding of organizations such as the Pioneers of Liberty.

While working on *The City Beautiful*, I wanted to explore not just the social conditions of 1893, but also the politics. Anarchy in particular intrigued me, especially in how the political movement was woven into Chicago society at the time. Until researching this novel, I hadn't thought of anarchy as a particularly historical movement, so it was interesting to read about the way it differed from my modern perception. The *Arbeiter-Zeitung* was an actual anarchist newspaper active in Chicago during that time, and the references to the Haymarket Affair and the assassination attempt on Henry Clay Frick are real as well.

I think one of the things I most enjoy about writing historical fantasy is trying to work in historical details and fit the story into the overarching timeline. While I was drafting this story, there came a perfect moment when I realized that I wanted it to be set between the Fourth of July and the Cold Storage Fire. That served as the initial frame for the plot. As I continued to research, I was able to add in even more details, like the Whitechapel Club and the Brave Cossacks of the Caucasus exhibit at the Wild West Show (which, unbeknownst to audience members at the time, featured Georgian trick riders instead of actual Cossacks).

Like many things at the 1893 World's Fair, the reality was less important than the perception. The glitz and glamor of the World's Fair was only a stone's throw from overcrowded tenements and a river polluted with slaughterhouse filth; while in the fairground itself, entire countries were reduced to caricatures meant to bolster America's reputation as superior. In writing this book, I wanted to shed a bit of light on both the good and the ugly, of what I love about our country and what shames and troubles me.

GLOSSARY

besamim: Spices used in the Havdalah ceremony, which marks the end of Shabbos.

bisl: A bit, a little.

bokher: Boy or young man.

boychik: A term of endearment for a young boy or a young man.

bubbeleh: A term of endearment.

bubbe-meise: A Jewish grandmother's version of an old wives' tale.

chalaf: A sharp, smooth knife used in the slaughtering of mammals and birds for food in accordance with the Jewish dietary laws of kashrut.

chazzan: A person who leads prayers in a shul; also known as a cantor.

cheder: An elementary school focusing on Jewish learning and Hebrew.

chevra kadisha: Literally meaning "Holy Society," it is a Jewish burial society, tasked with caring for bodies of the deceased and preparing them for burial.

dam nefesh: A term used in burial societies to refer to the blood that continues to flow from a wound or orifice after death, which must be buried with the body.

daven: To recite Jewish prayers.

derasha: A sermon, generally preached by a rabbi in a shul.

din rodef: A traditional Jewish law that permits killing someone if that person is trying to kill another; also known as "law of the pursuer."

drek: Manure or excrement; inferior merchandise or work; insincere talk or excessive flattery.

dybbuk: In Jewish folklore, a malevolent wandering spirit that enters and possesses the body of a living person until exorcized.

frum: Religious, pious.

Gehinnom: Literally translated as "Valley of Hinnom," this is a purgatory where souls are said to stay for up to eleven months (or, in rare cases, twelve or more) as their souls are judged.

goldene medina: The Golden Land.

Haggadah: The text recited at the Passover seder.

HaShem: Literally translated as "the name," this is the Hebrew term used to refer to God.

Hasid: A member of Hasidism, an ultra-Orthodox sect of Judaism that originated in Ukraine during the 1700s.

herem: An excommunication or a ban.

Kabbalah: Jewish mysticism.

Kaddish: A Jewish prayer recited in the daily ritual at the shul and by mourners at public services after the death of a close relative.

kashrut: Jewish dietary laws.

kiddush: A ceremony of prayer and blessing over wine on Shabbos or a holy day.

kittel: A white robe worn by Jewish men and women during certain holidays; also a customary burial shroud for religious Jews.

kosher: Foods that conform to the Jewish dietary laws of kashrut.

kvetch: To complain.

landsman: A fellow countryman.

Litvak: Jewish person from an area once known as the Grand Duchy of Lithuania, or, more simply, a Lithuanian Jew.

makher: An influential person, a big shot.

mechilah: Forgiveness.

Meforshim: A category of rabbinic literature that serves as a commentary on a specific book or text.

mensch: A person of integrity and honor.

meshuge: Crazy, foolish.

mezuzah: Literally meaning "doorpost," this is a small case hung in the doorways of Jewish homes, which contains a scroll written with words from the Shema.

mikveh: A bath or water source used for ritual immersion and purification in the Jewish religion.

mishpachah: Family.

Misnagdic: A sect of Judaism that traditionally opposed Hasidism.

mitzvah: A commandment of God, a good deed.

narishkeyt: Nonsense, foolishness.

nu: An interjection that is commonly used to prompt a response, akin to "well?"

oy gevalt: An expression of horror, shock, or awe.

payos: Sidelocks or sideburns.

Pesach: The Jewish holiday, also known as Passover, meant to celebrate the Exodus of the Jewish people from ancient Egypt.

Pesukei DeZimra: A group of daily prayers recited during the Jewish morning services.

pikuach nefesh: The principle in Jewish law that declares the preservation of human life is more important than any other law or religious obligation.

plotz: To be overcome with strong emotion.

pogrom: A riot or massacre, in particular one against Jewish people in Russia or Eastern Europe.

rasputitsa: Russian word that refers to the biannual mud season.

reb: Jewish form of address, akin to "mister"; it can also be used as an abbreviated form of "rebbe."

rebbe: A spiritual leader in the Hasidic movement of Judaism.

schlemiel: An inept or clumsy person.

schlep: To carry or drag.

schmaltz: Rendered poultry fat.

schmo: A jerk or obnoxious person.

schmutz: Dirt or grime.

seder: A ritual feast eaten on the first night or the first two nights of Pesach that mark the beginning of the Jewish holiday.

Shabbos: Also known as Shabbat or the Sabbath, this is the Jewish day of rest beginning on Friday at sundown and lasting until Saturday at sundown.

Shacharis: The morning prayer of Judaism; one of three daily prayers.

shadchante: A professional matchmaker, typically female.

shanda: Something scandalously shameful.

shashka: A sharp, single-edged curved sword; in 1834 it became the official sword of the imperial Russian army.

shechita: The slaughtering of certain mammals and birds for food in accordance with the Jewish dietary laws of kashrut.

Shema: A Jewish prayer recited daily, at both morning and evening services.

shemira: The act of guarding the dead.

shiva: A seven-day mourning period following the death of an immediate family member, commonly used in reference to "sitting shiva."

shmoyger: A worthless person or someone who is a good-for-nothing.

shochet: A person officially certified to perform animal slaughter, in reference to the shechita process.

shomer: Someone who watches over the dead.

shtetl: A small Jewish town or village historically found in Eastern Europe.

shtik drek: Slang for piece of shit.

shtreimel: The fur hat worn by married Hasidic men on Shabbos and other Jewish holidays.

shtuss: Nonsense.

shul: A Jewish synagogue or temple.

tachrichim: Traditional simple white burial shrouds, usually made from linen.

tahara: One of the most important elements of a proper Jewish burial, this is the ritual purification ceremony for the dead performed by members of the chevra kadisha.

tallis: A fringed garment with tzitzis on each of its four corners, traditionally worn as a prayer shawl by religious Jews.

Talmud: A comprehensive collection of texts and subsequent commentaries that is the primary source of Jewish religious law and Jewish theology; originates from the second century CE.

tefillin: Small leather boxes worn on the head and arms by religious Jews during morning prayers.

Tehillim: The Hebrew name for the book of Psalms, which is the third section of the Hebrew Bible.

teshuvah: Literally translated as "return," it means repentance and atonement.

tichel: A headscarf.

tzaddik: A holy or righteous man.

tzitzis: Refers to the knotted fringes on Jewish religious garments. Colloquially, tzitzis can also refer to the tallit katan, the fringed garment that some religious Jews wear under their shirts.

vey iz mir: An abbreviation of the Yiddish expression "oy ve iz mir," meaning "woe is me."

yarmulke: A skullcap; also known as a kippah.

yeshiva: A seminary or school where Jews study religious texts.

ACKNOWLEDGMENTS

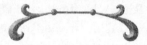

So much work goes on behind the scenes to create a novel. It is a group effort and requires time and devotion from multiple people. Without the help and support of the people listed below, this book would likely still be a four-hundred-page paperweight in a drawer somewhere.

First of all, I want to thank my agent, Thao Le. I am so grateful to have the opportunity to work with her. Thao has supported me every step of the way, and her faith in me as an author has made me approach my writing with even more confidence and drive.

Next, I want to thank my editor, Rebecca Kuss, whose invaluable insight helped me find and draw out the heart of this story. Under her guidance, *The City Beautiful* has become so much stronger. I can't begin to express how thrilled I am to have been able to work on this novel with Rebecca, and I look forward to working with her on more projects to come.

Additionally, I want to thank everyone at Inkyard Press who helped make this novel a reality, including the art department and the publicity and marketing teams.

I would also like to express my gratitude to Will Cordeiro at Northern Arizona University, who read the manuscript in its earliest form as part of my honors independent study. Will's feedback and advice gave me the motivation to complete this novel and encouraged me to really examine the story I was trying to tell.

I am grateful to have such a wonderful writing circle. A special thanks goes out to my critique partners: Brenda Marie Smith, Laura Creedle, Cassandra Farrin, Alexandra Gill, Sonya Doernberg, Jessica Russak-Hoffman, and Diamond Wortham. I would also like to thank my friend Paxton Gyves for talking me down from my moments of writer's block and imposter syndrome and for raving with me about Victorian aesthetics.

Thank you for reading
The City Beautiful!

Turn the page for a sneak peek at
Aden Polydoros' next immersive novel,
Bone Weaver!

1

AS THE AUTUMN wind pawed at the boarded windows like a wolf trying to break in, I arranged my medical supplies next to the teacup containing the severed finger. Needles and water, handspun thread, and clean rags.

"This is the second time this week, Galechka!" I exclaimed, picking up the finger. The first knuckle twitched when I touched it, then curled inward, prodding tentatively against my palm.

"I fell down again," Galina mumbled, extending her arm across the table. She was in better condition than the other upyri in my family and still had most of her hair and flesh.

"Be more careful. Keep losing fingers, and someday you won't have any left." I took her left hand, examining the damage. Her skin was discolored and withered, buffed with a sheen of lavender oil to keep from tearing. Mine was a reminder of what hers had once been—smooth and still warm, a sandy beige against her waxen complexion.

"Can you make a pretty one this time?" she asked. "Like one of your rushnyky?"

"Okay, but promise me you'll try not to lose anything else."
I gently tapped a finger against her forehead. "You don't want
me to reattach your head, do you?"

Galina giggled. "No."

She didn't wince when the needle pricked her. I used a geometrical stitch, embroidering her skin in a delicate red lattice
of interlocking lines and diamonds. No blood welled up. The
liquid had long since evaporated from her veins.

It made me proud being able to do this small deed for her.
So much had fallen apart in my life, it was satisfying to know
that I had the ability to sew things back together again. At
least in this way, I could make a difference.

"This will protect you," I said, tying off the final knot. My
birth mother had taught me that the embroidery was a talisman against ill luck and the Unclean Force, a corrupting energy that sickened the body and soul. Over the years, I had
decorated the walls of our house with rushnyky I had made
using found linen. Some good must have come from the tapestries and their lucky embroidery, because the wilderness
had yet to claim me.

After snipping the tail of thread, I cleaned her hand then
bandaged it. Later, I'd probably find the strips of velvet scattered across the floor, forgotten as she admired my embroidery.

When Galina flexed her reattached finger and laughed, I
smiled. Just that raspy sound made all my effort worth it.

"Thank you, Toma." She curled her fingers to test them.
"Will you come exploring?"

"I can't. It's too wet for me out there."

"We can search for treasures."

"Don't you have enough of those?" I teased, gesturing at
the array of objects lining the shelves along the wall. Jars filled
with ceramic pipe stems and tarnished coins sat alongside bottles dredged from the mud, the glass so old that it had acquired

an iridescent gleam. She had found brass artillery shells, which I engraved and turned into vases, until each windowsill overflowed with cotton stems and wildflowers.

"Please." Galina scrounged through her dress pockets and came out with a handful of faceted barrel-shaped beads. "Look what I found in one of the houses."

"Is that how you lost your finger? You shouldn't be digging around in those kinds of places." I took the beads from her, rolling them around in my palm so they caught the firelight. "These are beautiful, Galechka. They're so blue, they look just like sapphires."

She smiled in excitement, revealing teeth like river pearls. "You think they're sapphires?"

"They could be," I said, although I doubted sapphires would be so heavily chipped.

"I didn't know they were blue."

I felt a twinge of sadness. Did Galina even remember what the color blue looked like? She admired things for their shape and feel, but she'd never know the ring of embroidery around her finger was as crimson as the berries of a guelder rose.

"I want to see if I can find the rest of the necklace, but I don't want to go alone." Galina pocketed the beads when I handed them back to her. "It's scary in there."

I sighed. I wasn't looking forward to caving my skull in with a fallen beam, but how could I refuse her? "It's going to get dark soon. If it stops raining, we can go tomorrow, all right?"

"Oh, fine." Galina rose to her feet. A draft intruded through the door as she opened it, rustling the bundles of herbs and wild garlic nailed to the rafters. She looked so fragile standing there, framed by the bruised sky and dark tree line, as though the world might swallow her whole. There wasn't much of her left to give—year by year, more hair fell out in chunks, and just in the last summer, she had started carrying her lost milk-teeth in a sachet I'd sewn myself. It frightened me. Someone as small and delicate as her seemed prone to disappearing.

"Don't lose anything else!" I called after Galina as she closed the door. If she answered, a resounding thunder blast stole her words.

To fight off the chill, I busied myself by cleaning my supplies in the water basin. Once everything was put away, I added another log to the massive masonry stove that occupied nearly a third of the room. Every night, I cleared the ashes and made sure there was enough wood and tinder. I needed to be careful to keep the fire going. It wasn't as though I could conjure flames with magic.

Magic was a gift reserved for bogatyri and witches, not someone like me. Thinking back to my childhood among the living, I could recall only a handful of magically endowed individuals, all high-ranking soldiers or nobility. While the heroic bogatyri in Galina's storybooks were occasionally peasants, in reality the Three Sisters never bestowed their gift on commoners. It was always the duchesses, the earls, the captains, and the commanders who wore the deep-purple epaulettes and sashes of the bogatyri. And in the tales, it was them who hunted creatures like my family for their kingdom's honor.

Witches, or kolduny, were a different story. Their powers came from the Unclean Force, and they infiltrated all levels of society. With a single glance, a koldun—or his female counterpart, the koldunia—could spoil a person, cursing them with disease and misfortune. Just a few words uttered from a koldun's mouth could be fatal, or so the stories told. I'd never met one myself, and unlike creatures like upyri or rusalki, I wasn't even sure if kolduny existed in the world. Perhaps they had died out years ago.

After closing the stove door, I sat down to work on my newest rushnyk. The tapestry was my most ambitious one yet—it was so long it billowed down to my feet, the folds of white linen covered in a wealth of geometrical embroidery. I'd dyed the thread myself, hand spinning it from flax and steeping it in madder. I couldn't wait to see how the rushnyk would look once I finished.

Just as I was done embroidering one corner, Galina burst through the door.

Smiling, I lowered my needle. "Too wet for you?"

"There's someone out there," she cried, her voice breaking on the last word.

"Someone?" I asked, baffled.

"Like you, Toma. Someone like you. I think he's still alive!"

I barely had enough time to grab my hunting satchel from the shelf and tug on my gloves and embroidered buckskin coat before Galina herded me into the downpour.

Windblown trees, craggy outcroppings, a couple of decaying houses, so much rain. So cold. The storm's chill worked its way into my bones.

Galina raced across the ground with coltish ease, a tiny figure held together by rags and leather belts. I hurried after her, swatting away the rain that stung my exposed cheeks.

Someone alive. Someone like me. How long had it been since I'd last seen a living person? More than a year, certainly. Two or three, at least. The moment the hunter had spotted me, he'd dropped his snared rabbits and rushed off, leaving me with a nice dinner but a sinking heart. I had spent the entire day afterward searching my dark eyes for any sign of blood or fading and pawing at my hair in terror that the black strands might break away in ash-tinged fistfuls, until I was reassured that I hadn't transformed into an upyr as well.

At the thought of encountering another living person, my breath seized in nervous excitement. One of my favorite pastimes was watching airships pass overhead and fantasizing about the distant lands they were traveling to. But it was a different thing altogether to look into another human's eyes.

Galina led me down to the river. As we approached the bridge, a pale figure flitted through the wind-torn shallows. I caught a glimpse of long hair and shining eyes before the rusalka retreated into deeper waters.

The river spirits ignored us as we crossed the bridge. I had never been attacked by rusalki, but I had once seen them swarm a caribou, all thrashing limbs and burgundy hair, until the water ran red with blood. It wasn't uncommon to find gnawed bones and scraps of hide littering the banks.

My feet touched down on solid ground. I lifted my gaze to the horizon and gasped. A trail of smoke rose in the distance, black against the downpour.

"Come on, come on," Galina urged, tugging at my sleeve.

The wind changed directions, blowing the smoke toward us. Each breath I took was sullied by its acrid odor. Pressing my coat collar over my nose and mouth, I broke into a run, heading toward the fire's source.

Galina and I took a natural trail formed by decades of deer migration. When the underbrush thickened and obscured our path, we wove our way between red currant brambles and clumps of spurge laurel overladen with berries as black as ink drops. I curtained her with the flap of my buckskin coat when we strayed too close to a thornbush, wary of what its barbed branches might do to her skin and hair.

Before long, the forest thinned. Hornbeams and young oaks replaced the towering spruce and beech trees, permitting in sallow radiance. A pall of smoke caught the sunlight and trapped it in hazy columns.

Ahead, I spotted the deflated remains of an airship ensnared in the trees. Not one of those minnow-shaped vessels that occasionally passed overhead, but a smaller machine whose rowboat-like wicker compartment was open to the elements. Loose ropes and mounds of soot-blackened canvas hung from the branches. A man lay face-down beside the ruined basket, his blond hair streaked with mud.

Stepping carefully over the rubble, I made my way to his side. Here and there, broken machinery bristled from the soil. The barrel of a gun or cannon, and a scatter of brass shells each no longer than my finger. This vessel had been built for war.

I would know—to the south, the wilderness was scarred with overgrown craters and trenches on the verge of collapse, and whenever I hunted in that area, I had to proceed warily. Unexploded ordnance studded the land there, and though the black powder had gone impotent with age or decay, barbed wire and broken glass lined the ground like teeth.

Galina hid behind me, her twig-like fingers grasping at my coat. Her eyes had long since wasted away, but I knew that in her own way, she could see. And while she was incapable of producing tears, I could tell when she cried because her sorrow twisted like a dagger deep inside me.

"Is he dead?" Galina whispered.

"I don't know." I sank to my knees beside the wheat-haired man. If he was dead or dying, I didn't want her to see it. Didn't want her to be reminded of her own last moments. "Go find Mama and Papa. Hurry."

Galina rushed into the forest. I waited until she was out of sight before turning back to the man.

"Hey, are you okay?" I lightly shook his shoulder. "Can you hear me?"

Groaning, he struggled into a sitting position and lifted his arms to ward me off. Weak veins of fire pulsed across his skin, sizzling in the rain.

I froze.

A bogatyr.

"You need…you need to help him." His voice was scarcely louder than a whisper as the flames throbbed, fizzled, and then receded. He sank against the basket, his eyes clouding over like silty puddles. "He needs a doctor."

"Who does?" I whispered.

Before he could answer, a pole clattered across the ground. I turned, suspecting it had only been the wind, but then a scrap of canvas bulged as something stirred beneath it. Crawling over, I pulled back the flap.

There was another young man beneath the wreckage. He wore a gray wool coat and broadcloth trousers. His face was almost as pale as the ashes caught in his dark-brown hair, his full lips chapped and blued from the cold. Even in unconsciousness, there was a cruel edge to his features, something hard about the cast of his mouth and his sunken cheeks.

"Is he alive?" the bogatyr mumbled, knitting his hands over his stomach as though to hold part of himself in. Blood darkened the crisp white linen of his uniform shirt. Though he was a bogatyr, there was no trace of indigo on him, not even a ribbon pinned to his collar or piping down his sleeves.

I took off my glove and pressed a palm against the dark-haired boy's cheek. The heat of his skin shocked me. When he drew in a shallow breath, I found myself holding my own breath in turn, feeling as though I was witnessing something precious.

My shoulders slumped in relief. "He's still breathing."

"Praise the Three," the bogatyr said with a sigh.

The dark-haired boy stirred and cracked open his eyes. They were the palest gray, as though they were simply reflections of the sky above. He flinched when he saw me, but he was too weak to shy away.

"My name's Toma." I returned my hand to my side, worried my touch might be hurting him. "Don't be afraid, I'm a friend."

"Mikhail." His voice was scarcely louder than a whisper.

"You're safe, Mikhail. Just hold on. My parents are on the way."

"They're coming."

A flash of alarm rippled through me. "Who's coming?"

"They'll kill me." His eyes fluttered shut, his breath slowing. "Run, or they'll kill you, too…"

I said his name once more and repeated my question. He muttered something unintelligible before slipping back into unconsciousness.

I turned to the bogatyr. "Who's he talking about? Who's coming?"

"The Fraktsiya," the bogatyr said grimly, his gaze planted on the horizon. "They're here."

I followed his line of sight. In the distance, a dark blotch surfaced behind the clouds like a bloodstain. Rising to my feet, I squinted against the rainfall. Slowly, the form took shape, materializing into a small dirigible much like the one scattered across the ground at my feet.

An explosive rattle shook the air, as loud as hail on an izba's roof. In an instant, holes appeared in the ground at my feet. A bush shuddered to my right, its boughs splintering as the projectiles struck it.

Heart hammering against my rib cage, I threw myself to the ground and scrambled toward the cover of the deflated balloon. The canvas would provide no protection from gunfire, but at least it would hide me.

As another volley of bullets pierced the glade around us, the bogatyr raised his bloodied hands toward the sky as though to beg the goddesses for intervention.

"Long live the Tsar." Blood bubbled from the bogatyr's

mouth and slid down his chin, diluted pink from the rainwater. Curls of smoke wafted off his palms and forearms. "Glory unto him. May the Three Sisters lead him to victory!"

Crackling flames raced up his arms and leapt from his spread palms in a blazing gout, setting his gaze afire with reflected light. Raindrops evaporated in an instant, forming a scalding cloud of steam as the blaze arched toward the balloon. The two pilots jumped out of the basket seconds before the craft exploded into flames. Bags of fabric spread out above their heads, slowing their fall to a smooth, slow descent.

Carried away by the wind, the pilots disappeared from sight. Smoke billowed from their balloon as it crashed in the depths of the forest.

"You got them!" I turned to the bogatyr.

My smile dropped from my lips as I saw that he had crumpled onto his side. His eyes confronted me, their pupils fixed on a distant point.

I couldn't stand his sightless gaze. Crawling over, I gently pressed my hand over his eyes and closed his lids. I waited for a moment after lowering my hand, hoping halfheartedly that the bogatyr would open them again. His eyes remained closed.

Only a small percentage of people came back, and even the magic-endowed bogatyri burned or dismembered their fallen to prevent resurrection. Still, after spending so much time among the dead, I had come to expect it.

Rising to my feet, I returned to Mikhail's side. He hadn't regained consciousness, but at least he was still breathing. I tried to wrestle him onto my back and nearly collapsed under his weight. Not good. I'd never make it back to the house this way.

I racked my brain for a solution. If I couldn't carry him, maybe I could drag him.

Drawing my hunting knife, I cut a square of canvas from

the deflated balloon. I laid the sheet over Mikhail to shield him from the rain and retrieved rope and more rubberized cotton from among the wreckage.

Once I had gathered my supplies, I rolled the tarp over him, and bound it tightly. The layers of oilcloth enclosed his body, protecting him from the elements.

I looped the remaining rope through two of the holes riveted in the tarp, fashioning a rudimentary lead. Afraid that my sloppy invention would fall apart, I tugged carefully on the rope. The waterproofed canvas slid effortlessly across the mud.

Dragging Mikhail forward, I cast a worried glance behind me. The smoke from the boys' dirigible was as good as any beacon, and the downpour did little to conceal it. It would only be a matter of time before those two men—*the Fraktsiya*—made their way to the glade, and I intended for us to be long gone by then.

We headed deeper into the forest. As the minutes passed, the ache in my hands turned into a steady throbbing, and my legs wobbled from exhaustion. At last, I spotted a dark gash through the trees and sighed in relief. The river. Just a little farther.

Rusalki swam through the shallows, exposing a hand here, a webbed foot there. Their skin was even paler than Mikhail's ashen complexion, their limbs disproportionately long compared to their gill-split torsos. One lifted her head above the water as we neared, her burgundy hair curtaining her face. I couldn't see much more than her flared nostrils and the curve of her full lips—slick and crimson, like a gaping wound—but even that brief glimpse was enough to send a shiver down my spine.

I had never seen a rusalka lift her head above the water before. Maybe she could smell Mikhail. Smell his blood.

I swallowed the lump in my throat and stepped onto the rope-festooned bridge. The rusalki swam back and forth beneath us but didn't attempt to climb up. I avoided looking at them directly, instead focusing on the path ahead.

One step after another. The slick wood creaked, and the bridge swayed in the grasp of the storm. One step after another. Why couldn't I have been born a bogatyr? I would have killed to be able to levitate Mikhail right now.

No sooner had I reached the other side than two figures appeared ahead. Recognizing my parents' lurching gait, I sighed in relief. Galina followed behind them.

"We need to help him," I said as Mama pressed her hands against my face, my hair, my ears—all the parts of her that had withered.

"You're not hurt, are you?" Her voice crackled like frost underfoot; it grew softer each year, until I was afraid that one day it would fade away for good.

"I'm fine, but Mikhail isn't. I think he's dying, Mama." I swallowed hard. "And the other boy, the bogatyr, he's dead. They killed him."

"Toma, Galina, return home," Papa said, his words muffled by the wooden mask covering his face. His entire body was restrained in leather belts and scraps of hide and oilcloth, leaving no amount of withered flesh exposed. His garments were the only things keeping him together, with the rusty splints providing additional support for where his joints failed him.

"But, Papa, Mikhail—"

His mask turned to me, a careful construct of the face he had lost, carved by his own hands. No eye holes, just the bulbous shapes of eyes, uplifted like those on a saintly icon. "Return. We will take him back."

I wanted to argue, but I knew better. While my legs could

fail me halfway up the next slope, Mama and Papa could go on until time tore them apart.

"All right." I took a step back. "Come, Galina. Let's go."

I hurried in the direction of home, only glancing back when Galina and I climbed a low hill. My adoptive parents held the makeshift sled's rope, soldiering on with grim determination. I hoped that the strain wouldn't lead to torn muscles or severed limbs, the unfortunate consequences of pushing their bodies past the breaking point.

Once Galina and I reached the homestead, I immediately filled a pot with well water and placed it on the stove in preparation to make herbal tea.

"Toma, what can I do?" Galina asked, tugging at my sleeve to catch my attention. She had followed me to the well and back like a ghost, always a step behind me. "Please, I want to help him."

Normally, the sleeping nook atop the masonry stove would've been the best place for an injured person to rest and recuperate. I knew from experience that the warmth radiating from the masonry could soothe even the worst fever chills. But considering how much trouble I'd had with just dragging him here, I doubted we'd be able to lift Mikhail onto the shelf.

"Can you get extra blankets from the chest?" I asked. "He's been out in the cold for so long, we need to make sure he's warm."

"Warm," Galina repeated softly, as though it were a spell or a blessing, and then she hurried upstairs. As I listened to the steps creaking beneath her feet, my heart swelled with nervous excitement.

I could count the number of living people I'd seen over the years on the fingers of one hand. Usually, after taking one glance at my family, they ran off screaming. If Mikhail survived, maybe we could become friends. And if he died, perhaps the same strange force that had resurrected my new family would also allow his sentience to remain after his body failed him.

Just as the pot of water started to boil, the door opened, and Mama and Papa dragged Mikhail inside.

I hurried over. "I've prepared my bedroom."

As I followed them into the room, Galina's fingers plucked anxiously at my skirt. I hadn't heard her approach, but she could be so silent sometimes, easing across the floorboards like a shadow.

Stopping next to my bed, I untied the ropes from around Mikhail's body and peeled back the oilcloth. My heart dropped. Against the fabric, he was white and deathly still. As I reached out to see if he was still breathing, he stirred briefly. His sharp face contorted in pain, shadows carving out the hollows in his cheeks as a low groan escaped his lips.

Mama and Papa hauled him onto the mattress. I leaned over the bed and drew back the flaps of Mikhail's coat. Bloody gemstones spilled from the saturated fabric and scattered on the straw-stuffed mattress.

Stunned, I picked up a couple of the faceted jewels. They were cold and sticky against my palm. Rubies and diamonds, as if his blood itself had hardened into stone. I spotted the source sticking out of his coat's ripped lining—a pocket of fabric lighter than the rest, torn open and contents scattered.

Placing the gems on the nightstand, I unbuttoned his shirt. My stomach lurched at the devastation beneath—blood coursed from a hole in Mikhail's shoulder, slickening his entire left side.

Papa examined the wound.

"He's been shot." Papa's voice was low and gravelly through

his wooden mask. As he spoke, he twisted the lead ring on his finger around and around, a memento forged from the bullet that had taken him.

My gaze drew to the flintlock musket above the fireplace. If the people in the other dirigible survived, and if they came searching for Mikhail, would I be able to protect us? How could an old musket compare to rapid gunfire, let alone the powers of bogatyri?

No. I hardened my heart to the fear that seized me. Mikhail was my responsibility now. The moment I had touched him, I had known in my heart that his life was something to safeguard and cherish.

Everything that was alive out here, I had to kill for my own survival, from the plants I farmed and foraged to the animals I hunted. But this was different. I *must* be the one to save him.

"How can I help?" I asked, my voice firming with resolution. "There must be something."

"We need to stop the bleeding," Mama said. "Galechka, fetch some samogon from the cellar. Toma, bring me your sewing kit, clean bandages, and a lit candle."

After finding the supplies, I returned to my bedroom and laid everything out on the bedside table. Already, Mama had started cleaning the skin surrounding Mikhail's wound with a samogon-soaked rag. As I leaned over him, the alcohol's pungent fumes stung my nostrils.

At Mama's instruction, I heated a sewing needle in the candle's flame. By the time the needle cooled enough for me to touch it with my bare hands, the rag that Mama held against Mikhail's shoulder was already dyed red. The blood had soaked through to her own hand-wrappings, staining the layers of deteriorated dowry lace and buckskin.

In the flickering candlelight, shadows settled under Mikhail's closed eyes. He was fading fast.

I threaded the needle and slid it beneath his skin. My fingers ached and blisters had risen on my palms from holding onto the rope lead, but I forced myself to steady my hands as I sutured his wound.

Blood welled from between the stitches the moment I knotted the thread and snipped its tail.

"It's not working…" The words came out choked and breathless, my voice tight with dismay. "I—the bleeding. I can't stop the bleeding."

Mama sighed deeply, resting her hand on my shoulder. "Toma, I'm afraid there's nothing else you can do for him. It's as I feared. He's lost too much—"

"Your rushnyk," Galina said suddenly. "Use your stitching like you did with me."

Drawing in a deep, shuddery breath, I turned to her. "Galina, that's not going to work."

"It works," she insisted, wiggling her reattached finger as though it was proof. "I promise. It really does. Please, just try it."

I hesitated, looking back at Mikhail. He had lost so much blood already that it was only a matter of time before he succumbed to his wounds.

My gaze drew to the rushnyk hanging above my bed. Unlike the other tapestries in my room, the embroidery was not of my own hand but my birth mother's. It was the only thing I had from the *before*, an inheritance I had carried from my village, past the border of the Kosa interior, and into the wilderness. I remembered now, my mother had wanted me to carry it, to wear it, because…

"If they come after you, this will protect you, Tomochka," my mother had said, and wound the rushnyk around my shoulders the way she had once draped it from the shelf in our altar corner. I remembered being cold and afraid, but I couldn't remember who she had been talking about. She'd squeezed my shoulders and stared at me, pale and drawn, with snow caught in her ebony hair. "Please, always keep it with you. No matter what happens."

Now, I looked to Mama, unrelated to me by blood but more substantial than the woman from my memories. She wore the mask Papa had carved for her—not her own face, but a visage modeled after the brass icon of the goddess Voyna that hung in the corner. Carved of curly birch and buffed to a sheen, the mask gleamed with a silken glow when the candlelight rippled over the wood's natural whorls. The sadness emanating from her was at odds with Voyna's proud, chiseled features and furrowed brow.

"He's going to die, Toma," Mama murmured.

"Not if I can save him," I said, and exchanged the black thread I had used to suture the bullet hole for thick floss dyed red with madder root. The moment I strung the needle, a calm settled over me. Once more, I looked at my birth mother's rushnyk, its embroidery so ornate that I had never been able to replicate the designs exactly. Something about this felt so right, so *familiar.*

I got to work. Interlaced chevrons, wheels, lines reminiscent of sown fields. With each stitch, I felt an intoxicating confidence swell inside of me. I could do this. I had to.

Between stitches, I blotted up the blood that swelled through the seam. Mikhail groaned, his muscles tensing. The design became just as elaborate as the rushnyk hanging over my bed, radiating out from his sutured wound like the sun's corona.

Once it was over, I snipped the remaining thread and washed away the blood. Mikhail's skin was almost as white as the linen he lay on, but his wounds had already clotted over. His chest rose and fell in deep, even breaths.

I sighed, my shoulders sagging as the last residual tension drained from my limbs. Somehow, I had managed to keep him on this side of our world, at least for tonight.